# THE QUEEN'S SCRIBE

## AMY MARONEY

Artelan Press

ebook ISBN: 978-1-955973-08-3

Paperback ISBN: 978-1-955973-09-0

Cover design by Patrick Knowles.

Map by Tracey Porter.

Find more books by the author at www.amymaroney.com

❀ Created with Vellum

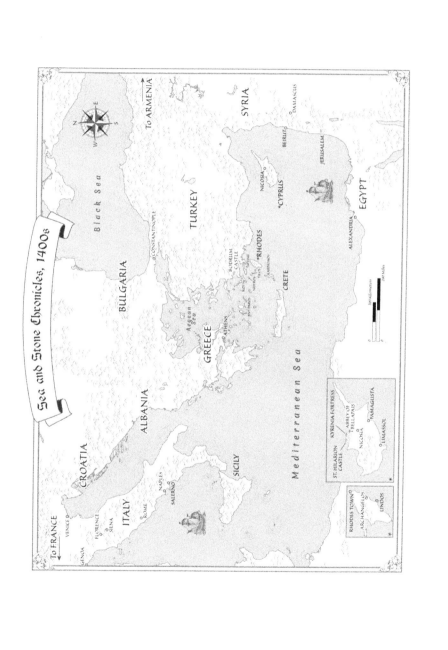

Sea and Stone Chronicles, 1400s

To FRANCE

CROATIA

ITALY

GENOA
VENICE
FLORENCE
SIENA
ROME
NAPLES
SALERNO

SICILY

ALBANIA

BULGARIA

Black Sea

N
W      E
S

To ARMENIA

CONSTANTINOPLE

TURKEY

SYRIA

DAMASCUS

BEIRUT

JERUSALEM

GREECE

Aegean
Sea

ATHENS

BUDRUM
CASTLE

RHODES
*RHODES

CRETE

NICOSIA

*CYPRUS

ALEXANDRIA

EGYPT

Mediterranean Sea

RHODES TOWN

ARCHANGELOS

LINDOS

ST. HILARION
CASTLE

KYRENIA FORTRESS

ABBEY OF
† BELLAPAIS

NICOSIA

FAMAGUSTA

LIMASSOL

100 Kilometers

100 Miles

# CHAPTER 1

Summer 1457
Off the Coast of Cyprus

THE MERCHANT GALLEY teetered on a cresting wave and pitched forward with a sickening lurch. Estelle's heart battered her ribs like a leashed falcon desperate to take flight. She drew in a breath, then regretted it. The air in this cramped cabin smelled of sweat and seawater, and her chest felt weighted by stones.

Each time she opened her eyes, there was nothing but blackness, thick and cloying as syrup. Signora Rosso snored lightly beside her, oblivious to Estelle's suffering. Surely, a night had never passed so slowly. When would dawn come? When could she wake her chaperone and escape the galley's hold?

The anxious thoughts came faster and faster, goading her pulse into a wild rhythm. She pressed her hands over her heart, willing it to slow.

*Calm yourself. Find the thread of a memory and pull.*

She hurtled back in time a dozen years, imagining the oak-studded hills of Auvergne, land of her birth. In her mind's eye, she saw a young girl picking daisies in a lush meadow.

*There I am. But where's Étienne?*

She conjured up her brother's figure emerging from the shadow of an oak tree, racing through the waist-high grasses.

"Come! The mare's had her foal!"

Estelle smiled in the dark, remembering the joyous exuberance of his shout. She made a circle of her hands, weaving together imaginary daisies. On that long-ago day, had she placed the crown of flowers upon Étienne's head? Kept it for herself? Abandoned it in her excitement to see the newborn foal? Sleepiness crept into her mind like mist, stealthy and silent, ready to claim her.

Then the wavering blare of a horn tore the memory into shreds. She dragged her eyelids open, anticipating the second trumpet blast, the signal that dawn had arrived.

When it came, she said a silent prayer.

*A day's voyage left to Cyprus, the captain said last night. Santa Maria, I beg you, protect us on these seas today.*

"Signora Rosso," she said. "It's dawn. The trumpeter gave the signal. We can go above decks."

The widow groaned. "Do you ever sleep, child?"

"Not trapped in a ship's cabin, as I've told you each day since we left Rhodes."

Estelle stood, smoothed her wrinkled skirts, straightened her cloak. She longed for a bath.

"Please, signora. You say yourself it's better up there. You can breathe. You can think. The saints hear your prayers—"

"Give me a moment." Signora Rosso's voice was roughened by sleep. "You may be able to spring out of bed light as a feather, girl, but not all of us are seventeen anymore."

Estelle bounced on her toes while the widow hauled herself out of bed, checked the placement of the rosary beads around her neck, and adjusted the folds of her long black cloak.

"I think I've finally got my sea legs. My head's stopped spinning for the first time since we boarded this galley, God be praised." Signora

Rosso shuffled to the door and unlatched it. "Carry my cushion, will you?"

"It's already under my arm." Estelle fought an urge to push past her chaperone and take the steps two at a time.

Above decks, the wind had died down to a soft breeze. The ship rolled gently in barely perceptible swells. Crewmen gathered in the bow, receiving orders from their commander for the morning's tasks. The oil lamps lashed to the masts still burned, for fog blurred the horizon in every direction. Soon, though, the sun's rays would warm Estelle's skin, chase away the last tight bands of dread constricting her chest.

She offered her free arm to Signora Rosso. They made their way to the stern, to their usual spot under a waxed canvas shelter. Estelle plopped the cushion on the low box that served as Signora Rosso's seat. Then she sank down on the well-scrubbed oak planks between a neatly coiled flax rope and an unarmed crossbow mounted to the gunwale.

While Signora Rosso closed her eyes and said her prayers, Estelle tipped her head back and took greedy gulps of salt air. A sensation of calm seeped through her body, banishing the agitation she'd been plagued by all night.

The stifling cabin below decks was nothing more than a prison cell. The terror that descended upon her there consumed every fiber of her being—set her heart racing, her limbs trembling, her mind on fire.

"Did you pray to Santa Maria yet?" the widow asked abruptly, her eyes fixed upon Estelle in an accusing stare.

"I was likely the first person aboard to pray to her. Before the crew was up, even."

Signora Rosso snorted. "I doubt that. The holy lady is never far from a sailor's mind."

"Anyone on the sea is at her mercy," Estelle pointed out.

"Especially those who suffer from seasickness, like you and me."

Estelle did not respond. Though she'd never admitted it to Signora Rosso, her problem was not seasickness. But the truth was complicated, and she was a private person.

"What sign were you born under?" Signora Rosso rubbed one of her rosary beads between her forefinger and thumb. It was carved in the shape of a human skull.

"Virgo, with Leo rising."

"Virgos are reasonable people. They tend to be honorable. I don't know you well enough to say for sure, but you're quiet like a Virgo. Leos always seek a battle, yet I see no spark of fire in you." The widow tapped a finger against her lips. "The problem is Virgo's not a water sign, nor is Leo. Once you're off this despicable sea, your health will be restored."

"I hope so," Estelle said.

The widow had not let Estelle out of her sight since they'd left Rhodes last week. Until today, she'd spoken mostly to herself, moaning about her poor health, her hatred of sea voyages, and her husband's relatives in Venice who had never shown kindness until she returned there to oversee the dispensations of his will. This was the first time she'd seemed interested in conversation. But as the morning progressed, Estelle became convinced the woman simply required a pair of ears to absorb her superstitious prattle.

An officer shouted a command in Genoese from the bow deck, and a cabin boy scurried up the mainsail mast. In a moment, his response floated down to the stern.

"They've lost sight of the other ships in our fleet because of the mist," Estelle reported. "They're going to. . ." She cocked her head, straining to hear his message. "Signal the vessels with trumpet blasts and keep the sails lashed until visibility improves," she finished.

The widow gave her an approving nod. "Well done. I still don't understand how a French girl knows Italian so well, especially if you only learned it these past few years."

"My tutor in Rhodes was quite skilled."

The galley shuddered, buffeted by a wave. Estelle grasped the long arm of the crossbow's wooden tiller to steady herself. It shifted under her touch, swinging to point toward the bow deck.

"But you told me a girl taught you." Signora Rosso's eyes narrowed. "Not a tutor."

"I had a girl tutor. Her father is Venetian, and her mother is Greek."

"Telling lies is a grave sin, you know."

Estelle bit back a saucy retort, as she had so many times growing up with a sharp-tongued mother. After a long, steadying breath, it was safe to open her mouth again.

"Girl tutors exist. That's why I'm joining King Jean's court in Cyprus, after all. To be a French tutor."

"So your parents told you." The widow snorted. "But the truth is you're going to Cyprus to find a husband. Why else would a girl your age be sent to a foreign court? Your mother spoke of nothing else when we met."

A flicker of anger ignited in Estelle's belly. She tamped it down, her thoughts straying to those last weeks in Rhodes Town. When the invitation had come for her from King Jean to join the Cypriot court as tutor to his daughter, Princess Charlotte, Maman had been enthusiastic—but she'd never said a word about marriage. Neither had Papa. Both her parents had seen the king's invitation as a great honor. For her part, Estelle had agreed to the plan with both trepidation and excitement. Though she dreaded leaving her family, the thought of being companion to a princess and earning a salary from the royal court of Cyprus made her pride swell.

The trumpets blared a complicated pattern, signaling their location to the rest of the fleet. An answering blast of sounds echoed thinly across the water. Were there three other ships in the fleet? Four? Estelle could not recall.

"Perhaps you'll play at tutoring," Signora Rosso went on, "but in the end you're there to make a match. Is your father a nobleman?"

"Yes, but what does that—"

"King Jean wants French-born nobles in his court," the widow asserted. "That's why you've been summoned. That's your value to the king. You'll see when you get to Nicosia. The capital is full of folk with French names who can't speak their own language."

Wind snaked over the gunwales, carrying a cool tendril of mist that penetrated Estelle's cloak. The lashed sails and riggings thumped and rattled in response to the wind's caress. From the corner of her eye, she saw the ship's cat, an orange tabby with a nicked left ear, trot toward the hold.

"Your best chance of marrying a man who's both noble and rich is in Cyprus, not Rhodes." The widow's voice was softer now, cajoling. "If you marry well, your whole family benefits. You seem intelligent enough. Think it over. In time, you'll agree with me."

Estelle's mind flew to Papa's strange farewell on the dock in Rhodes Town. He'd been oddly nervous in those last moments, tongue-tied, unwilling to meet her gaze. But that had been due to his sorrow at their impending separation, not because he was hiding something from her.

Hadn't it?

Her shoulders stiffened. Could Signora Rosso be right?

"You've got quite a pretty face." The widow leaned closer. "I imagine you'll have a bevy of suitors. If you're lucky, the king will give you to one of his favorites."

Estelle scrambled to her feet and moved away. The unsettling thought struck her that the woman could be mad. She spouted her strange words with conviction, as if they were carved in stone.

*Ignore her. Signora Rosso makes as much sense as a crow jabbering in a tree.*

Gripping the gunwale with both hands, Estelle expelled the air in her lungs with a great whoosh. She leaned on her elbows, distracted by a movement in the waves. Then a sudden coldness gripped her chest. Directly below her, a man scrambled up a rope dangling from an iron hook embedded in the ship's hull. Two other figures emerged from the mist, swimming with quiet, powerful strokes toward the galley.

She took a step back, a scream stuck in her throat. In the next instant, the man launched himself over the gunwale.

"God protect us!" Signora Rosso shrieked. "Pirates!"

The man advanced on Estelle, a blade flashing in his hand. In a panic, she grabbed the crossbow's tiller and swung it hard against him. He staggered back, his bare feet tangling in the coiled rope. The dagger clattered to the deck.

"Holy Virgin!" Signora Rosso wailed. "Merciful God! Santa Maria, have pity!"

Estelle snatched up the blade while the man struggled to regain his footing. He steadied himself, then sprang at her.

The terror that had muted her a moment ago was eclipsed by a sudden swell of fury.

"No!"

Thrusting downward with the blade as she shouted the word, she sliced his arm. With a roar of outrage, he lunged for her again.

Footsteps pounded the decks. The air filled with male voices raised in alarm. Two men pounced on the intruder and pinned him facedown, an arm's length from Signora Rosso. The widow scrabbled her feet away, almost falling off her little box.

Estelle leaped aside as the sailors dragged their captive toward the bow of the ship and other crewmen dispatched his advancing comrades with swords and pikes. The trumpeters issued a series of frantic horn blasts. From afar, other ships in the fleet returned the trumpet calls.

The mist began to lift, revealing a sleek single-masted vessel bobbing nearby. Men swarmed its deck, wielding bows, curved swords, and iron hooks attached to lengths of rope. The dagger trembled in Estelle's clammy palm as a sailor dumped a box of arrows near the crossbow. Had her heart ever pounded this ferociously? She struggled to breathe.

"Pirates!" the sailor bellowed. "Infidels!" He turned to her, snatching the blade from her hand. "Go below, in the name of God!"

Signora Rosso seized Estelle's shoulder. "Move, girl! They'll take us captive otherwise!"

Linking arms with the widow, Estelle pushed through the crush of seamen to the hold. In the cabin, Signora Rosso sank to her knees, babbling a prayer that rose and fell like an endless wave.

Estelle fumbled with the door latch. She pushed her trunk against the door, then flung open the lid. Under her clothes were two items her father had entrusted to her on the dock at Rhodes harbor. One, a book, she cast aside. Then her fingers struck the hard leather of a dagger's sheath.

She drew out the blade.

"What is that?" Signora Rosso asked between sobs, wiping her eyes with the edge of her cloak.

Estelle gripped the polished bone handle. "A gift from my father. I pray I won't have to use it."

When the widow spoke again, her voice was tinged with wonder. "There is fire in you after all, child. I should have known. The stars are never wrong."

# CHAPTER 2

Summer 1457
Nicosia, Cyprus

THE GALLEY ENTERED the calm waters of Famagusta's harbor, passing a tall stone tower on one side and a massive seawall on the other. Estelle stood on deck in the glaring sun with Signora Rosso and the widow's two servants.

Shading her eyes, she watched each vessel of the convoy glide into the harbor. The pirate ship was among them, now captained by officers of the merchant fleet. Its surviving crewmen were locked in the hold. Their muffled groans sent shivers over her skin.

An anchor splashed into the water nearby from one of the vessels. The Scottish captain of the galley appeared on the deck, shouting orders to his crew. Impulsively, Estelle stuck an arm in the air and waved at him. He raised his hand in return. A stab of homesickness struck her. Master Fordun was a friend of her father's and the last connection she had to her family in this foreign place.

She looked away before tears started to fall, studying her surroundings. Many of the structures crowding the waterfront were sinking into ruin. The docks were strewn with refuse. This harbor was larger than the one at Rhodes, with more buildings along its perimeter. But the polished veneer of order and prosperity at Rhodes harbor was missing here.

Once on land, Estelle followed Signora Rosso and her servants along the crowded dock, struggling to find her balance. It seemed as if she were still afloat, untethered to the earth, at risk of vanishing into the cloudless blue sky.

When the luggage had been loaded into a handcart by Signora Rosso's servants, they all made their way to a small structure whose door was flanked by a pair of Genoese guards in red leather armor.

Signora Rosso took Estelle by the elbow and pulled her inside, where a man sat behind a table, his quill poised over a leather-bound book.

"What brings you to Famagusta, signora?" he asked, squinting against the sunlight streaming through the open door.

"That's my business," Signora Rosso snapped. "Let's get this tariff paid, signor. I can't bear the stench of rotting fish much longer."

Estelle glanced at her chaperone sidelong. The widow had traveled from Cyprus to Venice, where her husband's funeral mass had been held. During her return voyage, on a stopover in Rhodes, Estelle's parents had hired Signora Rosso as chaperone for the journey to the Cypriot court in Nicosia. Why this had to be concealed was a mystery.

The man made a whiffling noise with his mouth. "You're Venetian; it's obvious from your accent. The only place you Venetians care about in Cyprus is Nicosia."

The widow glared at him. "Now that you've ferreted out our destination, are there any other travelers in the harbor on their way to the capital? I'd like to get on the road today."

"Two royal servants were on the fleet that just arrived from Alexandria. They hired a mule cart. You may be able to ride with them." He peered over their shoulders, studying the luggage in the cart outside the door. "What goods to declare, signora?"

"None."

He studied her for a moment, expressionless. "We'll have to inspect your things to be sure. Or you can double the normal tariff and we can avoid any inconvenience."

She scowled and rummaged for two golden coins, then thrust them at him with a curt nod.

"Excellent. Sign here." He handed her the quill and pointed at the open book. "And sign for the rest of your party, too."

"I can sign my own name." Estelle straightened her shoulders. "Please."

Signora Rosso did not respond, but when she'd finished writing, she passed Estelle the quill.

Estelle scratched out her signature with a steady hand.

The man raised an eyebrow. "Where did you learn to write like a scribe?"

"That's my business, signor."

When she turned away, she saw Signora Rosso holding back a smile.

"Typical," the widow muttered as they threaded their way toward a large covered mule cart. "One ducat for Famagusta, one for him. Put the Genoese in charge of anything and corruption flourishes."

Estelle's body slowly adjusted to the solid ground beneath her feet. Two women passed them lugging a basket of silvery fish between them, arguing in a language that sounded like Greek, Italian, Arabic, and French all tangled together. Estelle listened hard, trying to unspool the blend of familiar and strange sounds.

When they reached the cart, one of the interior benches was occupied by two bearded men garbed in silk tunics and soft leather shoes.

Signora Rosso gave a start of recognition. "Signor Derian, is that you?"

"It is indeed, Signora Rosso." The man extended a hand to help her. "Please, join us. My condolences on the loss of your husband. He was a respectable citizen and a fine merchant. Nicosia will not be the same without him."

The widow clambered into the cart and settled herself. "Your words are a solace, signor." She glanced at his companion. "Your friend is a notary as well, I take it?"

The man's tongue flicked out to wet his thin lips. "No. I'm a scribe."

Signora Rosso tapped Estelle's arm. "Like you, mademoiselle." Without waiting for a response, she turned back to the men. "Any trouble with pirates on the journey from Alexandria?"

"Not this time, praise God," said Signor Derian. "I heard the Genoese fleet from Rhodes was not so fortunate."

"It was horrible. Their scout nearly slit my throat." Signora Rosso's gaze slid to Estelle. "This brave girl saved me from certain death."

Estelle blinked, taken aback by the praise.

Signor Derian studied her with curiosity. "That's a story I'd like to hear."

His companion smirked. "It should be quite entertaining."

There was something in the second man's gaze that made Estelle's muscles tense.

She averted her eyes and fidgeted on the hard bench as the servants crammed into a separate seating area concealed by a wooden panel. The driver cracked his whip, and the wheels creaked into motion. Soon the heavy clop of hooves against the dusty road drowned out the bustle of the harbor.

"So is this brave girl a relative of yours, signora?" Signor Derian asked once they'd passed through the city gates.

The widow shook her head. "Newcomer to the court of King Jean."

"I'm to serve as French tutor in the household of Princess Charlotte and her husband, Prince João," Estelle said, annoyed at being discussed as if she weren't there.

Signor Derian cleared his throat, exchanging a glance with his companion. "You've not heard, then. Prince João, God rest his soul, is dead. Such a sad business. He'd not even been in Cyprus a year. His family in Portugal will be devastated to hear the news."

"The poor princess, only fifteen and already a widow!" Signora Rosso's fingers flew to her rosary beads. She raised her gaze to the heavens, her mouth moving in silent prayer.

Estelle struggled to find her voice. "But how could that be?"

"An illness that came on like lightning. We heard the news in the harbor. His funeral was held at Santa Sophia cathedral in Nicosia yesterday." Signor Derian dropped his voice. "More than one source told me he was murdered by the queen's chamberlain."

Estelle recoiled. "Waterfront gossips can't be trusted," she managed to say after a moment. "That's a terrible accusation to make."

"The queen hated that young man," Signora Rosso announced, as if she had consulted an oracle. "It's common knowledge."

Estelle tried to swallow. A lump as big as a quail egg had formed in her throat. She had not given the queen much thought until that moment. Now she could think of nothing else.

*The princess will still need me,* she reminded herself. *Perhaps now more than ever.*

"I'm going to the palace myself," Signor Derian said. "I have a delivery that must get to the king before I rest."

He smiled, his teeth glowing white against his beard, and she was slightly reassured. His warm, low voice reminded her of Papa's.

Signora Rosso stuffed a cushion between her head and the cart wall. "That makes two of us."

It was nearly dark when the cart entered the gates of the royal palace in Nicosia. In the courtyard, two footmen removed their luggage. Signor Derian and Signora Rosso climbed down from the cart, and Estelle followed in their wake. Torches illuminated the ironwork of the portcullis, casting sinuous shadows on the cobblestones.

Once inside, Signora Rosso demanded to see the steward, who greeted them in Greek and confirmed the court was expecting Estelle.

"I've a few letters from Alexandria for His Majesty," Signor Derian said to the steward. "The king's chamberlain expects me."

"I'll accompany you to the chamberlain's study in a moment," the steward replied, signaling to a young servant woman. "A bedchamber is ready for you, mademoiselle," he added to Estelle. "Antonia will show you the way."

Signora Rosso clutched Estelle's arm, her bony fingers like iron pinchers.

"I have one piece of advice, mademoiselle. Trust no one. Pay me a

call in the Venetian quarter when you get settled. Mine's the house
with the dolphin door knocker."

"Thank you, signora."

*I'd rather pay a call to a pirate's den*, Estelle thought tartly as the widow
retreated.

"There are some kind people in this court, mademoiselle," Signor
Derian said. "You'll see. Signora Rosso's grief has turned her mind to
dark thoughts, I'm afraid. For my part, I always find keeping busy the
antidote to loneliness. If you're truly talented with a quill, there are
always manuscripts and records to copy in the palace library."

"Thank you, Signor Derian, but tutoring will occupy much of my
time."

"As you say." He leaned closer, his voice soft in Estelle's ear. "When
you meet the queen, speak Greek. It will make your life here easier."

Antonia led her through hushed corridors, two manservants
trailing them with Estelle's trunk. Candles burned on circular iron
candelabras suspended from the high ceilings. Heavy wooden chests
and tables gleamed in the soft light.

Estelle stepped gingerly on the polished marble floors, wishing her
shoes weren't so stained by seawater. She'd been wearing the same
clothes for more than a week. Surely, she looked and smelled as disrep-
utable as she felt.

There was no sign of grief anywhere. No banners of black crêpe, no
wreaths or garlands. No one they encountered wore mourning clothes.

Finally, they arrived at an open doorway. Antonia waved her
through. The two men deposited the trunk by the far wall.

"It's a small chamber, but you're lucky to be just off the courtyard
garden." Antonia smiled. "Your sleep will be scented by flowers."

Estelle glanced around, grateful for the bed in its carved wooden
frame, the window facing the courtyard. She stifled a yawn.

"All you can think of is bed, I'll warrant." Antonia flapped a hand
toward a copper tub half-hidden behind a screen. "First, your bath.
Cool, to give you a respite from the heat, and scented with rose water."
She turned down the bedcovers and used a candle to light an oil lamp.
"You'll be presented to the royal family tomorrow, so you'll need a good
night's rest."

Estelle's chest tightened.

*Come now,* she chided herself. *You survived a pirate attack at sea. You can manage an audience with the King and Queen of Cyprus.*

"Why is there no sign of mourning?" she asked the maid. "The palace gates, the doors, the windows—no black banners anywhere."

"Banners went up the day the prince died on the king's orders, but the queen's guards tore them down."

Estelle stared at her in disbelief, sure she had somehow misunderstood Antonia's Cypriot accent.

"Poor thing." Antonia patted her arm. "Let me help you undress and bathe, then you'll have a good rest."

"No, thank you." All Estelle wanted was solitude. "You may leave me now."

*Breathe.*

Estelle barred the door behind Antonia, then unlocked her trunk and found the book. She rocked back on her heels, turning the pages in the golden lamplight. This book, with its recipes and secrets of falconry, had been conjured up by Papa, but every word was in Estelle's hand. She studied the inscription on the first page.

*For my friend Michel Pelestrine, with gratitude. May God protect you.*

Tomorrow, she would find Monsieur Pelestrine, master falconer to the king, and deliver the gift to him.

In a haze of exhaustion, she undressed, bathed, and stumbled into bed. The dagger in its leather sheath sat on the table beside her.

She fell asleep staring at the weapon.

# CHAPTER 3

Summer 1457
Nicosia, Cyprus

ESTELLE FLUNG open the shutters at dawn. Sunlight flooded her chamber from the courtyard. A breeze carried the buzz of insects and the scent of jasmine inside. She smiled at the sight of two parakeets in a pomegranate tree outside her window, chittering to one another.

"Telling secrets, are you?" she asked softly.

She watched them until the clanging of bells drowned out their song. From the sound of it, Nicosia had as many churches as Rhodes Town.

Soon Antonia rapped at the door, calling a cheery *"Kalimera."* When Estelle admitted her, she bustled in carrying a pitcher of water and several towels. "Did you rest well?"

Estelle shrugged. Her few hours of sleep had been punctuated by dreams of stormy seas and pirates. "Well enough."

Antonia plucked a small sack from her belt and withdrew two fresh figs from it. "Here. These will satisfy you until it's time for a proper meal."

Estelle nodded her thanks, then set about getting ready.

"I have no mourning clothes," she said after washing her face and hands. "Will that displease the king?"

"It's not him you should worry about displeasing." Antonia eyed the wine-red skirt, matching square-necked bodice, and black-and-white satin sleeves Estelle had laid out on the bed. "Is this all you have to wear? The queen doesn't care for French styles. She wants her court to be Greek."

Estelle took that in, perplexed. "But the king is French. All the kings of Cyprus have been French, haven't they?"

Instead of answering, Antonia picked up a white silk runner from a table near the window and draped it around Estelle's shoulders. "We'll make do with what we've got. My mother used to say, 'In a drought, even hail is useful.'"

Estelle followed Antonia to the reception hall. A group of courtiers milled about outside the doors, waiting to be announced. Antonia left her standing near several bejeweled women who wore high-necked gowns and long headpieces that flowed nearly to the floor. As at the harbor, these women spoke oddly accented Greek peppered with words and phrases from other languages.

Estelle tried to ignore their curious glances as courtiers disappeared through the doors to the reception hall, each entrance heralded by a gong. She was relieved to note many of the names announced by the steward were French.

When the steward announced her, the murmurs and stares of the others in the antechamber faded away. The doors shut behind her with a soft thump.

On a dais, the black-clad King Jean lolled in a massive gilt-encrusted throne, his slippered feet resting on a leopard-skin rug. Queen Eleni reclined on a fur-draped settee, clad in a gown of brilliant violet silk. Her nose protruded sharply from her thin face, and her full-lipped mouth was unsmiling.

On the other side of the king sat a young, delicately built woman dressed in black. Enormous kohl-rimmed eyes dominated her features.

*Princess Charlotte,* Estelle realized. *How sad she looks.*

Ranged along the wall were the courtiers who had already been announced, talking amongst themselves.

Two men dressed in black velvet doublets approached the king, whispering in his ear. One of them gestured at Estelle.

"Approach!" he ordered. "The king wishes to speak with you."

"Our new French jewel has arrived." The king's voice was so thin and languid Estelle had a hard time hearing it, and his French was oddly accented. "Welcome to our court."

His face was puffy and red-cheeked, his eyes hooded by heavy brows.

Estelle sank so low into her curtsy that she struggled to rise again. "Your Grace." She turned to the queen and curtsied again, more smoothly this time. "Your Grace," she repeated. Then she did it one more time in the princess's direction.

After another whispered consultation with his advisors, the king sat up a little straighter.

"Soon you shall teach my daughter proper French," he said. "Our court has strayed far from its roots in recent years, I'm sorry to say. But we must never forget the Lusignan dynasty has flourished thanks to our French blood."

"Yes, Your Grace." She still did not understand why, with a French king for a father, the princess would need instruction in the language.

*Be patient. You'll learn the answer soon enough.*

"Greet the princess in your pretty French," he commanded. "Show her how it's meant to be spoken."

"I am happy to meet you, Princess Charlotte."

The young woman's gaze settled on Estelle. She did not respond.

"Princess *Charlotta* has neither the desire nor inclination to speak that language," the queen said in rapid Greek, training a sharp look at Estelle. "We shall have to find another use for you, though if you can't speak Greek, you'll be of little value here."

"Perhaps I *do* want to learn French, Mamá." The princess's voice was high and childlike. But then, she was barely fifteen.

Before the queen could reply, one of the king's advisors addressed Estelle in stilted, nearly incomprehensible French.

"How was your voyage from Rhodes, mademoiselle?"

"Aside from a pirate attack, it was uneventful, my lord," Estelle said in Greek, remembering Signor Derian's counsel to use the language during her audience with the queen. Sweat trickled down her back.

The queen laughed, studying Estelle with new interest.

"Your Greek is quite good for a Latin girl. If you can learn our Cypriot dialect, too, you might prove yourself useful here after all."

The king clucked his tongue, doggedly reverting to French. "There's not much to recommend the common tongue. It's a strange soup of languages."

"The fact that all Cypriots speak it is reason enough to recommend it," his wife retorted.

The next courtier was announced, diverting the royal family's attention. Estelle backed away from the dais, finding a place along the wall next to a young woman dressed in the Cypriot style. Her thudding heart slowed.

"You did well." The woman spoke in Greek, fiddling with her gown's high neckline. Estelle spied the bulge of a jewel under the thin fabric.

"It's kind of you to say, but I could not be sure, myself."

The woman's smile seemed genuine. "I was new here once, too. It will get easier, I promise you. I'm Louise de Cappelle. One of the princess's ladies-in-waiting."

Estelle returned the smile, the tension in her muscles easing.

Courtiers continued to enter. Several knights wearing the familiar black tunics of the Order of St. John were waved forward for questioning about their sugar plantation on Cyprus. A group of men dressed in the Muslim style, with ornate turbans and sashes at their waists, were ushered to the dais to meet the royal couple. Only a few of the women wore Latin-style clothing, like Estelle. When Signor Derian entered, she could not help smiling, relieved to see a familiar face.

"You know that notary?" Louise asked.

"I met him yesterday," Estelle admitted. "On the journey from Famagusta." A thought struck her. "Will the king's falconers be presented today?"

Louise stared at her in bafflement for a moment, then burst out laughing. "Oh, my dear, how amusing you are. Most of the falconers are in the mountains, at St. Hilarion castle."

Heat flared in Estelle's cheeks. How would she be able to give Monsieur Pelestrine his book? She'd assumed he would be nearby, always in the vicinity of the king.

Half listening to her companion's observations, Estelle studied the royal family. The king looked dangerously close to nodding off, while the queen raked her gaze over the crowd. Princess Charlotte—*Charlotta,* Estelle reminded herself—sat stiffly in her chair, seemingly oblivious to the crush of people.

A reed-thin man hovered at the edge of the dais near the queen, occasionally creeping to her side and consulting with her in whispered tones.

"Who is that man?" Estelle couldn't help asking.

"The queen's chamberlain," her companion replied. "They were raised together by his mother. The queen calls him her foster-brother."

Estelle observed him carefully. On the wagon ride from Famagusta, Signor Derian had said the queen's chamberlain was responsible for Prince João's death. Was this man truly a murderer?

A male voice boomed from the corridor. The queen flinched, a pained expression on her face. Princess Charlotta leaned forward, her eyes alight.

The doors flew open, and a tall, bearded young man strode in. He was dressed in long white robes edged in gold thread. Rings glittered on his fingers, and a golden cross studded with rubies hung from his neck. His handsome face was split wide in a grin.

"Papa!" He ascended the dais with outstretched arms.

"The king's son," Louise said. "His father made him an archbishop three years ago, when he was just thirteen. He has a palace of his own, and gold—so much gold."

"I didn't know the princess had a brother." Estelle's brow furrowed. "How can he be an archbishop at his age?"

Louise's voice softened to a whisper. "His mother is the king's mistress."

King Jean's eyes lit up. "Jacques, my boy!"

The young man grasped his hand, kissing it with affection before enfolding his father in a long embrace.

"That is unseemly behavior, boy," the queen hissed. "You'll damage the king's throne."

The young man casually disentangled himself from his father.

"Your Majesty." He bowed with exaggerated deference to the queen, then glanced at the princess. "Sister, I've a gift for you, something that's sure to lift your mood—a falcon. I shall bring it to the courtyard one day soon and have my falconer demonstrate its skills."

Estelle's heart leaped. Could the falconer be Michel Pelestrine, her father's friend?

Princess Charlotta smiled.

The queen hardened her gaze. "She won't accept it."

At her words, the animation drained from the princess's face.

The young man's back was to Estelle, but the tense set of his shoulders made clear his displeasure.

"Those ridiculous robes." The queen flung an angry look at her husband. "Tell him to give back his cross of gold, his rings, the revenues from the Latin churches he supposedly oversees. Give the archbishop's palace to a true man of the cloth."

A ripple of murmurs coursed around the room.

Estelle waited for a fierce reaction from the king. But instead, he shrank back in his throne, wide-eyed.

*Does the king fear his wife?*

She dismissed the idea as soon as it surfaced in her mind. He must be controlling his temper; he would wait to vent his fury in private.

"Jacco is charming, you'll see." Louise's voice was calm and assured in her ear. "He can't help who his mother is."

"Jacco? I thought his name was Jacques," said Estelle, confused.

Louise shook her head. "Only the king calls him that. His mother calls him Jacco, and so does everyone else."

"Who is his mother?"

"She's called Cropnose, for the queen bit off her nose when she found the woman in bed with her husband."

All the air escaped from Estelle's lungs.

*Dear God, what is this place? Am I safe within these walls?*

"There are others more deserving of punishment in this chamber than my brother, Mamá." The princess's voice, hard with rage, interrupted Estelle's thoughts. "My dear husband would be sitting next to me if the court of Cyprus weren't a nest of treacherous vipers."

A curious thing happened to the queen's face then. The anger visible there a moment ago vanished, and in its place appeared a look of barely concealed satisfaction. A tiny smile played around her lips.

"I tire of this," the king complained, standing. "Bring my wife her chair so she can return to her apartments."

He trundled from the chamber, his courtiers dropping into low bows and curtsies as he passed.

A half-dozen male servants trotted in carrying a litter with a seat upholstered in cloth of gold. Several ladies-in-waiting helped the queen from her settee into the litter. Her chamberlain took up a position at the front of the entourage, admonishing the crowd to make way.

"Is the queen injured?" Estelle asked.

"She is poorly," Louise replied. "I've never seen her walk."

After the queen's retinue filed out, Jacco climbed the dais again and held out an arm to the princess. She rose and laid her fingertips on his sleeve. Together, they descended the steps.

His gaze roved across the crowd as they moved toward the doors. When his eyes met Estelle's, he raised one brow, his full lips twisting in an intimate smile.

Estelle regarded him uneasily.

*He's smiling as if he knows me—as if we share a secret.*

Should she return his smile? Would it anger the princess? Oh, what should she—

Louise gripped her by the elbow.

"Curtsy," she hissed.

# CHAPTER 4

Summer 1457
St. Hilarion Castle, Cyprus

GABRIEL BAYOUMI RAN the mare as hard as he dared until the black pines grew so dense he feared she would collide with a tree. Slowing her to a trot, he studied the terrain ahead. Though dusk was falling, the deer's tracks were visible in the soft layers of pine needles carpeting the forest floor. The leopard had been hard on her trail, and he could just pick out the imprints of the cat's paws. He grimaced. The ravine was a stone's throw away. Had both animals plunged to their deaths?

The mare nickered, uneasy.

"You're safe with me, *aggeloc*."

The Coptic word for *angel* had been his mother's favorite term of endearment when he was a boy. It was a comfort to him still.

He stroked the mare's neck. "By all the saints, nothing good can come of this."

Her ears flicked back each time she heard his voice. Somewhere in the forest canopy, a bird let out a long, piercing whistle.

There was not much light left. It would have to be enough.

A path descended into the ravine a short distance to the north, if he recalled correctly. Giving his mount an encouraging pat, he pointed her nose in that direction.

If it weren't for the leopard, he'd turn and make for the castle. But he had no choice. None of them did.

The hunting and hawking party had been in the mountains for nearly a fortnight, training peregrine falcons from the North Sea and leopards from Africa. The expedition had gone well until this afternoon. The falcons had performed admirably. All those hours spent taming them, calming them, feeding them, curing their maladies—as the master falconer, Michel Pelestrine, often told him, it was work that required much patience.

For several years now, Gabriel had managed to pass himself off as a patient man. Perhaps he was becoming so. Upon accepting the position of royal under-falconer, he'd quickly learned the raptors sensed his emotions. Harboring anger or frustration never paid off. The birds beat the air with their wings, lunging against their leashes when they were disturbed. The less time wasted calming them, the better. So he had learned to calm himself.

A trumpet sounded. When the mishap occurred this afternoon, the men had fanned out in search of the leopard and her quarry. Hunters to the west, hawkers to the east. Gabriel was a good tracker. Finding the animals' trail had been an easy task for him. Now, though, he would have to carry the job through to its end.

No matter what awaited him at the bottom of the ravine.

When his horse picked her way down the steep, crumbling path, foreboding tingled at the back of his neck. He felt trapped down here. If the leopard was still alive, she likely did, too. The air was still, the light muted. A branch snapped, and he stiffened in the saddle, twisting around to glance behind him. Nothing was there.

A few moments later, he found the leopard. She lay on her side in the shadow of a boulder, her ribs rising and falling rapidly, blood leaking from a wound over one eye. When he dismounted and moved toward her, speaking softly, she did not flinch. Making a quick examination of her body, he shook his head. One of her back legs was bent at an unnatural angle. Who knew how many other bones were broken beneath that silky pelt?

The deer lay dead not far away. It was curled in on itself, its spindly legs tangled together.

"Holy Virgin." Gabriel passed a hand over his face. "What a mess."

He glanced at his horse. She was used to carrying extra burdens. But she could not tolerate the weight of both a deer and a leopard, in addition to him. He'd have to walk through the night, leading her—if he could even get both creatures loaded on her flanks.

No. The deer would stay. It would become supper for other forest dwellers. The king was obsessed with his leopards, and when they died, he had their pelts turned into rugs and throws. This was a young animal, intended as a gift for the king's spoiled son, Jacco. Behind King Jean's back, everyone called the young man the Bastard. Not Gabriel, though. He knew only too well how it felt to be the target of that insult.

Gabriel wiped sweat from his brow with a sleeve, thanking God the leopard had not yet been gifted to Jacco. When the fellow was displeased, anything could happen. And none of it good.

He studied the leopard in the murky light. Her eyes were glassy. He could see the pain in them.

Sliding his dagger from its sheath, he crouched at her side. "Forgive me."

"Gabriel!" Michel ushered him into the castle's stables, relief in his voice. "Praise the saints. I was beginning to wonder—"

"She's dead," Gabriel interrupted the older man, sliding down from the saddle. He turned to untie the ropes holding the leopard on the horse's flanks. "She sprang on a deer's back just as it reached the ravine's edge. The fall did most of the work. I finished it."

"The king will be sad to lose her, but he'll be happy for the pelt."

Michel helped him lay the dead animal on the ground. The horse dropped her head, blowing hard from the climb up the hill to the castle.

Gabriel scratched the mare's nose. "She deserves some extra hay. And all the water she wants."

Michel signaled to a stable boy, who led the horse away.

"I'll see that the pelt is removed and cured properly." Gabriel swayed a little on his feet, suddenly aware he hadn't eaten since morning.

"One of the others can do it. You're due a meal, a bath, and some rest, for you've a journey ahead of you tomorrow. We got word that a shipment of falcons has arrived in Famagusta from Rhodes. My friend Cédric de Montavon arranged them as a gift from the Grand Master of the Knights Hospitaller for the king. The galley that transported them belongs to a Scottish privateer. It'll be anchored in the harbor there all week. While you're there, you'll have to inquire about fetching another leopard from Alexandria for the king." Michel fumbled in the purse at his waist. "And—I almost forgot—a letter came for you."

He thrust it at Gabriel.

Nodding his thanks, Gabriel pushed the folded square of linen paper into his own purse and headed for the kitchens.

Famagusta. His worst memories—and his best—were rooted in that city. The thought of returning to his birthplace always inspired a nauseating blend of anticipation and dread in his gut. But this time, he'd ignore the past and take advantage of the diversions near the harbor. Meals in his favorite tavern, cards at a gaming table, and perhaps a visit to a courtesan.

In the kitchens, he sat near the hearth, shoveling in a bowl of roasted goat and a hunk of dry bread, washed down by ale. When he was sated, he broke the letter's seal and read it by candlelight. As he studied the words, the exhaustion that shrouded him like a heavy cloak lifted, replaced by a flood of anger.

It had been more than a year since he last got word from his father. And with each passing day of silence, his relief had deepened. Now his father's words swam before his eyes. As usual, the letter was short.

*I will soon conclude my business in Barcelona and return to Famagusta. I am eager to see you, Gabriel. We have much to discuss. I will send you a message when I arrive.*

No words of farewell. Just the letters of his name inked heavily at the bottom of the page.

*I am eager to see you.*

Written by another man, that could mean *I will soon throw my arms around you, give you a loving embrace. I want to hear of your adventures, of your thoughts, of your hopes. I promise to reassure you, to give you thoughtful advice, to steer you toward a safer path through this life.*

But the words were written by Gabriel's father. A man who moved through the world with as much stealth as a sea eagle—intelligent, cunning, and always ready to strike.

Gabriel stared at the fire a moment, taking comfort in the knowledge that the letter had been sent from Catalonia. His father's journey to Cyprus could take months, depending on the weather and the time spent in various ports along the way.

With any luck, Gabriel would be on a hunting and hawking expedition high in the Troodos mountains during his father's visit to the island and their paths would never cross.

Scraping back his chair, he strode to the hearth and tossed the letter into the flames.

# CHAPTER 5

Summer 1457
Famagusta, Cyprus

GABRIEL STOOD on the deck of the galley, awaiting the appearance of the captain. Sailors scurried around him, most of them speaking Genoese. Finally, a tall, ruddy-skinned man with green eyes emerged from the hold.

"*Kalimera*. I'm Captain Drummond Fordun," he greeted Gabriel. "You've been sent by the court to pick up the falcons?"

Gabriel nodded. "A dozen of them, I was told to expect."

"That's right. They made the journey from Rhodes in good health. I'll be glad to unload them, truth be told, for keeping hawks and falcons alive is a gamble in the best of circumstances."

A vessel whose banners bore a Basque motif glided into the harbor from the glittering sea. One of the crew raised an arm and shouted a greeting to Gabriel.

He squinted, shading his brow, then grinned and returned the wave.

"Tavern of the Bee-Eater tonight?" the man called, raising his hands in a questioning manner.

"Wouldn't miss it." Gabriel glanced at the Scotsman. "I'll make the return trip to Nicosia tomorrow. I'll tend to the birds and feed them myself this evening to save you the trouble. And in thanks for your good care of the creatures, I'll buy you supper at Famagusta's finest tavern."

"The Bee-Eater's one of my favorites, too," Captain Fordun remarked. "It seems every agent of the knights prefers that tavern to all the rest."

Gabriel nodded. "That's how I learned of the place, when I worked for the Order as a guard at their sugar plantation."

"The falconer's life suits you better, I take it?" the Scotsman asked, smiling.

"I'm handy with a blade, and I have the knights to thank for that. But yes, I'd rather train a falcon than oversee slaves at Kolossi."

Captain Fordun's smile disappeared. "I'm with you there." He signaled to a crewman. "Take the falconer below and give him everything he needs to tend to his birds. They'll remain in the hold for one more night."

When the church bells of Famagusta rang the hour of vespers, Gabriel disembarked from the Scotsman's vessel and hurried though the gathering dusk.

His mother's small home in Famagusta was lost to him now. He would stay the night in a dwelling owned by his father that sat empty near the harbor. He'd passed it on the way here, and its shutters had been closed as always. A key lay hidden under a loose cobblestone in the courtyard, its location known only to him.

He had one more matter to attend to before he could relax with a cup of wine and a meal.

Hastening through the twisting lanes to the neighborhood where his mother's former home stood, he paused outside it for a moment. Though the house had a new owner, it stood empty. He stood motionless, lost in memories of his mother's soft voice, her reassuring embrace.

A voice startled him. "Gabriel?"

His hand fell to his sword. A figure shrouded in a dark blue hooded cloak stepped out from the shadows. Gabriel smiled, recognizing the monk immediately.

"Brother Pavli!"

They embraced. "I've not seen you since. . ." Gabriel faltered.

"Since your mother's funeral," the older man finished, squeezing Gabriel's shoulder. His grip was as firm as ever, even if his eyes were more sunken in his face, the lines in his brown skin deeper. "When will you move back into her house, give it life again?"

Gabriel could not meet his eyes. "It's not my house any longer."

"What?" The old man relinquished his grasp on Gabriel's shoulder. "How can that be?"

"Another man owns it now." Gabriel could not bring himself to admit he was to blame for that. Instead, he changed the subject. "How does the monastery fare?"

After Mamá's death, Brother Pavli had arranged her funeral at the Coptic monastery. As a slave, she'd been forbidden to worship in the church of her choice, but she had often sent Gabriel to the monastery to purchase eggs, cheese, and other goods for his father's household. Then, after his father freed her, she'd visited the monastery daily until she died.

"Things have been better." The monk's tone was guarded. "The Genoese take most of what we earn. But we manage." He straightened. "Are you still working for the king?"

Gabriel nodded. "Falconry suits me. We lost a leopard on a hunt recently, and now we've got to replace her. I'm on my way to the home of an Egyptian merchant who helped me with such matters in the past. From what I hear, it's a good time to be seeking favors in Alexandria. The sultan is a friend to King Jean, or at least he pretends to be."

The monk rubbed his bearded chin. "As long as the king's tribute payments continue to roll in, the sultan will leave us alone. But there's so much piracy in these waters now that trade from Egypt has dropped off. I hope the fellow you seek still keeps a home here. There are more

and more cold hearths in this city. The life bleeds from it, and I don't
see how it will ever revive."

Gabriel embraced the old man again. "It was good to see you,
Brother Pavli. I must be on my way."

"Wait," the monk cautioned him. "Remember—"

"Slowly, slowly," Gabriel finished for him, grinning. "You've been
saying that to me since I was six years old."

It was well after midnight when Gabriel stumbled back from the
tavern to his lodging, one hand wrapped around the hilt of his sword.
His purse was considerably lighter than it had been that morning. He'd
spent far too long immersed in a game of cards that had not gone
his way.

Fumbling with the key in the dark courtyard, he finally let himself
in and made his way to a small bedchamber off the kitchen where
servants customarily slept. He never lodged in the large bedroom overlooking the street, with its carved wooden bed frame and matching
wooden chest. It was his father's space, and he rarely crossed the
threshold.

Flinging himself facedown on the straw pallet that served as a
mattress, he kicked off his boots and fell into a deep, dreamless
sleep.

"Good morning, Gabriel."

The voice repeated the words twice, three times, finally pene-
trating Gabriel's consciousness as if through a heavy fog.

He scrambled out of bed and reached for his sword.

As his eyes adjusted to the weak dawn light, he made out a familiar
figure. "Father?" he whispered in disbelief.

A long, low chuckle pierced the air. "You can dispense with that
sword, boy. I'll not harm you."

Gabriel shook his head to loosen the cobwebs blurring his
thoughts. "But I just got your letter."

"The winds were favorable. I've never made such good time from
Barcelona before." His father crossed to the window and flung open

the shutters, revealing the fine stitching on his green velvet doublet and the precise angle of his carefully trimmed beard.

*For the love of Santa Maria, why does fortune favor men like him?*

Gabriel washed his face and hands in the basin on a table by the bed, then dried off with a flax towel. "Why have you come here?" His voice was as dull as his wine-soaked brain.

His father ran a fingertip along the top of a cabinet next to the wall. "This place could use a good scrubbing. Your mother's home was much nicer than this." He sighed. "Her last desire was to see you take possession of it. How you could let it slip through your fingers is beyond me."

With each word, Gabriel's mood darkened. "Surely, you didn't come all the way to Cyprus just to chastise me?"

"I've been invited to Nicosia to assist in a matter of royal succession, in truth."

Gabriel cocked his head, confused. "Succession? Princess Charlotta will take the throne when her parents die. There's nothing to dispute about that."

His father emitted a dry, mirthless sound. "Oh, but there is. Her half-brother wishes to be king."

"Jacco?" Gabriel considered his father's words in surprise. "But he's—"

"A bastard."

The unspoken words *like you* hung in the air, making Gabriel's chest prick with anger.

"There are many who think he has the making of a fine king," his father went on.

"Do you share the sentiment?"

"It's too soon to tell, but my gut tells me to bet on young Jacco. You'd be wise to do the same when the time comes."

"With what? I've no money." Gabriel rubbed his face with the towel again, trying to clear away the last remnants of sleep.

His father shrugged. "It's not my fault you gambled away your inheritance. I only offer you advice thinking of your future."

"My future?" Gabriel repeated, incredulous. "I'm a bastard. Not worthy of your name. The world will never see me as anything else."

"Your mother's name isn't good enough for you?"

A memory of his mother momentarily silenced Gabriel. Her face swollen from a beating by his father's wife, Mamá had held him tightly in the circle of her arms on the day he'd left home to work as a page for the knights.

*Never forget,* she'd murmured in his ear. *"Bayoumi" means "a man of respect." Honor your ancestors. Earn the respect of the knights, and they will give you the respect you deserve.*

"I cherish my mother's name," he ground out. "And as for your advice, I care nothing for it. All the guidance I needed as a child came from Mamá, not you. Nothing has changed."

"I will not tolerate such insolence from you in my own home." His father's voice was tight with anger. "Every advantage you've been given came from me."

Gabriel's hands curled into fists. He fought an urge to lash out with a tremendous blow.

*No.*

Violence would not bring his mother back. And it would not change his father's infuriating self-importance, his pride.

His father had never exhibited humility, at least not in front of Gabriel. And the man likely never would.

Swallowing hard, he imagined himself in the presence of falcons.

*Patience.*

"Forgive me. I misspoke, and I regret it." The formality in his voice made him sound like a stranger to his own ears. "And now I must return to court myself. I have valuable cargo for the king. You may ride along if you're in need of transport to Nicosia."

His father's expression relaxed. "I have other business to attend to here before I go to the capital. Perhaps I'll see you there."

As his father's footsteps faded, Gabriel resolved to ignore Brother Pavli's advice on the return journey. He would depart Famagusta as fast as humanly possible.

The more distance he could put between himself and his father, the better.

# CHAPTER 6

Summer 1457
Nicosia, Cyprus

A FEW DAYS after Estelle's arrival in Nicosia, Louise appeared at the bedchamber door and invited her to visit the palace gardens. They took a meandering route through the palace, with Louise patiently answering all of Estelle's questions about the people they encountered and the various sights along the way.

At one point they stopped to accommodate a small crowd of men emerging from a door near the reception hall.

"The prince's death is a hard blow," one of them was saying. "But the Latins will rise again. We shall see to it—"

The men drew up short, eyeing Estelle and Louise.

"The king's council," Louise murmured.

"Mademoiselle." A sober-faced man with dark brows and a full beard dipped his head at Louise.

"Sir Hector." She curtsied.

His gaze slipped to Estelle, and he gave her a nod as well. The others studied Estelle with curiosity but said nothing.

Continuing down the corridor, Louise said, "The worries of the kingdom preoccupy those men. I don't know if I've ever seen any of them smile."

"What does it mean that the Latins will rise again?" Estelle asked.

Louise lowered her voice. "The queen's supporters are many in number. Prince João was aligned with the Latins in this court, and he was a strong, persuasive man. Because of him, the Greek influence here was fading. His death changed that. The king's council feels his loss deeply."

They passed through an alcove decorated with blue and gold tiles. Estelle had never seen such exquisite stonework. The archways and columns looked as if they were made of delicate lace.

"But King Jean is a Latin, and the most powerful person at court," she said. "Can't he attend to this himself?"

Louise shrugged. "Let us talk of other things, my dear."

When they entered the courtyard, the heat was oppressive. Gravel paths wound past flowering shrubs, marble statues carved by ancient stoneworkers, and fountains shimmering with water. The mournful cry of a peacock rang out. Estelle shaded her eyes with a hand, admiring the brilliant plumage of the bird's tail.

"You like this place?" Louise asked.

Estelle breathed in the scent of roses, too overcome by the beauty to speak.

They passed through a grove of pomegranate and citrus trees. Songbirds fluttered from branch to branch, calling to each other. A moment later, Princess Charlotta and her half brother, Jacco, appeared from behind a fig tree, immersed in conversation. Both Louise and Estelle swept into curtsies.

"Ladies!" Jacco cried in a delighted voice.

"Rise." The princess's voice was dull, and her eyes were swollen from crying. Dark smudges beneath them spoke of sleepless nights. Her black silk gown and matching headpiece, embroidered with intricate patterns of gold thread, enveloped her like a shroud.

"My father is enchanted by the idea of a French-born girl in my retinue," Princess Charlotta's rapid Greek held a trace of hostility. "I do not share the sentiment."

In the throne room, Princess Charlotta had declared she wanted to learn French. Had she said that simply to defy her mother? Estelle herself had often done so—but mostly in her head, not aloud. The consequences of angering Maman affected everyone in the family. She had learned at a young age to keep quiet even when she was churning with frustration inside.

She studied the princess's wan face.

*Of course she's in dark spirits. She's drowning in grief.*

"Please accept my sympathy for the loss of Prince João," Estelle murmured.

"Loss?" Princess Charlotta's eyes filled with tears. "My husband was murdered. And his killer still roams free . . ."

Estelle averted her gaze as the young woman struggled to regain her composure.

"So you are truly French?" Jacco slung an arm around his sister's shoulders, his gaze on Estelle. "Or are you one of these pretenders whose ancestors last walked on French soil three hundred years ago?"

"I was born in Auvergne, my lord."

"Who are your parents?" he asked.

"My mother's people are merchants. My father's family are noblemen. Viscounts."

"Louise's father was a French viscount, was he not?" The princess's voice was steadier now.

"Yes," Louise replied. "My parents came to Cyprus after their pilgrimage to the Holy Land. They never intended to stay, but the king welcomed them to his court, and I was born within these walls. After they died, I was raised by Cypriots."

Princess Charlotta's expression tightened. "They died on the same day, the story goes. Poisoned, no doubt. Just like my husband."

A tightness took hold of Estelle's rib cage and squeezed.

"Now, sweet sister, let's not get mired in troubling memories." Jacco snapped his fingers at an attendant. "This garden is our refuge, a place to escape our worries."

The attendant approached and held out a white silk bag. Jacco removed a gleaming metallic object from its depths.

Estelle gasped. In Jacco's outstretched palm sat a falcon made of gold, its eyes two glittering rubies.

The princess bent to examine it. "I thought you were to bring a real falcon, trained just for me."

Jacco's happy expression dimmed. "The merlin is off her feed, the falconer tells me. She refuses to fly. I believe the fault may lie with her handlers, not her health. In the meantime, I bought you this beauty— the very finest specimen at the marketplace." He turned a small key in the golden bird's back.

With a mechanical whir, the bird's wings raised and lowered. Its head rotated side to side, the rubies catching the sunlight like two glistening drops of blood.

Princess Charlotta reached out a hand and stroked the bird's shiny black beak, which was made of polished stone.

"Clever," she said. "And beautiful. Thank you, brother. You know just how to lift my spirits."

"Anything for you." He handed the bird to his attendant. "And with God's grace, your merlin will be back to good health within a few days."

"My lord," Estelle ventured. "My father is falconer to the Grand Master of the Knights Hospitaller."

"Why, the knights' falconers are legendary!"

"Papa has shared his best recipes for healing possets and ointments with me. I'm sure your falconers have such remedies as well, but if I can be of any assistance, I would gladly share what I know with you."

She had spent so many years as her father's scribe that she'd memorized many of his notes, even though she had little experience handling the birds themselves.

"I'm eager to hear more, mademoiselle." Jacco glanced from her to Louise. "You both must come to supper one evening at my palace."

Louise clapped her hands together, eyes shining. "I am honored, my lord."

"You seem quite taken by our new French jewel." Princess Charlotta crossed her arms over her chest. "Perhaps the mademoiselle can be your tutor instead of mine, Jacco. If you're truly going to be head of the Latin church in Cyprus, shouldn't you know French?"

"Cyprus is for Cypriots, not Latins. I don't need French lessons. If the gossips are right, you're to be betrothed to a Frenchman soon. You'll have to speak his language if you want to find happiness in his arms."

Charlotta struck her brother on the shoulder. "That's not funny! Louis is my cousin. I can't marry him—it's a sin."

He smirked. "As you say. I'm certain we can find a use for Estelle in Nicosia, one that makes Papa happy and that you find tolerable. For our father loves us, and we don't want to displease him, do we?"

*Tolerable?* Estelle shifted her weight uncomfortably. Once again, she was being discussed as if she weren't there. But this time, she did not dare speak in her own defense.

Princess Charlotta slipped an arm through the crook of Jacco's elbow, her face stony. "Papa loves *you*, that is certain."

As the siblings strolled away, Louise took Estelle's hand. "We've been invited to sup at Jacco's table. It's a great honor—and yet you look unhappy."

"I have nothing to wear but this." Estelle gestured at her bodice and sleeves, unwilling to share her true thoughts. "Latin clothes."

Louise contemplated Estelle for a moment, toying with her pearl necklace. The ruby at its center caught the light, glowing scarlet like the bird's eyes.

"You'll wear something of mine, then. You can keep it until your own gowns are made. I'll take you to the marketplace in Nicosia soon. We can buy silk, thread, whatever you need."

Estelle nodded her thanks, still ruminating over Princess Charlotta's words. "Will the princess marry her cousin, do you think?"

"Not if her mother has anything to say about it. But the barons— the men on the king's council—want her wedded to him. And they spend their days whispering in His Majesty's ear."

"There are so many courtiers here with French names. There must be someone qualified to tutor the princess in my language. Someone other than me."

"You heard Jacco. The French nobles here have never been to

France. Like me—I've no idea how to speak true French. Bits and pieces of it, to be sure, but it's only used for contracts and such these days."

"Surely, the king would have ensured his children speak French?"

Louise shook her head. "You saw how it is between the king and queen. Princess Charlotta spent her whole life in the queen's apartments, surrounded by Greeks, until her marriage. She is a Greek girl."

"By all the saints, I don't understand this court," Estelle said. "Nor my place in it."

"Don't look so glum!" Louise smiled. "It was an honor to receive King Jean's invitation, wasn't it? Even if you must work as a tutor, it won't be for long. One day, you'll marry a Cypriot nobleman, or perhaps a wealthy merchant. So will I, if God allows it."

Signora Rosso's words flooded back to Estelle. *The truth is you're going to Cyprus to find a husband.*

An uneasiness gripped her. Perhaps the widow was not mad, after all. But if her claims were true, Estelle's parents had grievously deceived her.

"No," she blurted. "I'm going back to France one day. My future is there, not in Cyprus."

Louise took her hand. "You'll get used to this place," she promised. "You'll come to like it here. But first, you have to show the princess your loyalty. For you're not only French, but you're also pretty. She doesn't like her attendants to outshine her."

Estelle's unsettled feeling deepened. Why was Louise flattering her in this way? She'd rarely been praised for her looks, having spent her life in the shadow of her mother's golden-haired beauty. Everyone always said she looked like Papa and her older brother, Étienne.

Louise tugged her in the direction of the arched doorway leading to the interior of the palace.

A blue butterfly floated ahead of them, gliding swiftly on a current of air. A sob pressed against Estelle's chest when it flew out of sight, an insistent ache that grew more painful with every beat of her heart.

*God grant me wings.*

How she longed to follow the butterfly into the vast, cloudless sky and ride the wind back to Rhodes.

"I must send a letter to my family," she said abruptly. "I need to tell them I've arrived safely."

"Scribes and notaries are often working in the palace library," Louise told her. "They send correspondence out with couriers every week or so."

Estelle lifted her chin, a plan forming in her mind. She would write to her parents and tell them this had been a horrible mistake. When the next ship left Cyprus for Rhodes, by all the saints, she would be on it.

# CHAPTER 7

Summer 1457
Nicosia, Cyprus

WHEN THEY ARRIVED at Jacco's palace for supper, Estelle prayed she
would not trip over her own feet in the unfamiliar clothes. She kept
pace with Louise, checking the placement of her borrowed silk headpiece, smoothing the embroidered green silk of her skirt. They passed
through delicately carved archways and along marble corridors lit by
Venetian glass lamps. Following Louise's lead, she ignored the guards
who stood silently tracking their every movement.

They entered a lofty chamber where a long table stood at one end
surrounded by high-backed wooden chairs. The royal siblings were
already seated at opposite ends of the table. A group of courtiers stood
near the door, chatting in low tones. They looked up as one when
Louise and Estelle entered the room.

A male servant announced each courtier by name, then led them to
seats around the table. Estelle was last. The only place left at the table
was next to Jacco. She fought an urge to wipe her damp palms on her

borrowed silks and kept her gaze straight ahead, aware that the other supper guests had their eyes fixed on her.

*Staring can't hurt me. Soon enough they'll tire of it.*

She sank into her seat, heat rising on her neck.

"Ah! Our French mademoiselle." Jacco grinned at her, arms outstretched in welcome. "What a delight to see you."

She sat mutely, dazzled by his exuberance—and by his striking appearance. His square jaw and high cheekbones gleamed in the candlelight, and he carried himself with both power and grace. Louise had told her Jacco was an accomplished horseman and hunter, and woe to anyone who bested him in a match of strength: he hated to lose. He exuded self-assurance, just like her brother Étienne. But Étienne also harbored a reserve of humility that she saw no sign of in Jacco. Perhaps, with time, she would.

"I am honored, my lord," she murmured.

He snapped his fingers at a manservant, who scuttled away. Almost immediately, a line of servers appeared bearing silver platters heaped with food. Each platter was presented first to the princess, then to the archbishop. A royal taster then ate portions of the food chosen by the princess and Jacco.

"He's already tasted all of this in the kitchens. It never hurts to check one more time, in my view. If he doesn't keel over dead from poison or overstuffing, we shall sup with confidence," Jacco informed Estelle in a loud whisper.

"That is reassuring," she managed to reply.

*Poison.* The word scampered around her brain like a mouse trying to escape a trap.

A few moments later, Jacco and Princess Charlotta began to eat. The instant they did so, the others at the table ripped legs and wings off roasted fowl, speared chunks of lamb with their knives, and plucked grapes and oranges from heaping platters of fruit.

Estelle tentatively reached for a lone wing of a small game bird. Jacco's knife shot out and speared the wing before she could touch it. She snatched her hand back, chagrined. But instead of keeping the morsel for himself, he deposited it in front of her.

"They're like vultures, these courtiers." He glanced darkly around the table. "You must act fast, or you'll starve tonight."

He ripped a handful of grapes off the large bunch on a platter between them and offered them to her.

She smiled in gratitude.

Animated conversations rose up around the table as the meal progressed. Estelle ate a grape, relieved the courtiers' attention had shifted away from her.

"Tell me about your childhood in France." Jacco took a long pull from his wine cup. "I've never been there, more's the pity."

He leaned back in his seat, goblet in hand. Both he and Princess Charlotta drank from golden cups, she noticed. Everyone else had silver.

The man across the table, whose narrow face had something of the crow in it, with black eyes and a beaky nose, watched her with a calculating expression.

She took a deep breath, wondering what, if anything, King Jean had told his son about her. Her memories of home sustained her. She could reel off twenty beloved stories of adventures with Étienne and still have dozens left to tell. But she would never share those precious recollections at this table.

"There's not much to tell, my lord. I left there for Rhodes many years ago."

Jacco popped a grape into his mouth. "Not many French families have a reason to sail there, I'd imagine."

"The knights bestowed much honor upon my father with the position of master falconer."

"I'm sure they pay him a fine salary. They have revenues from every corner of Europe, whereas we are mired in debt." The light vanished from his eyes, and he put down his cup with a thump. "What I wouldn't give for a white gyrfalcon. The most esteemed of all the falcons. We've had a few here. But they all died." He glanced down the table at his sister. "I've had no luck with falcons of late."

"My lord, one of your father's best falconers is in Nicosia," the crow-faced man said. "He's on his way from Famagusta to St. Hilarion castle. I could ask him to assist here before he returns to the mountains."

"By all means. I've sacked most of my falconers. What good is a man in a mews who can't keep a bird alive?" Jacco turned back to Estelle. "The knights have been busy reinforcing the walls in Rhodes, I hear, ever since Constantinople fell to the Turkish sultan."

"Yes, my lord." This was the kind of talk she had no cause to be wary about. "There is always fear of the Turks attacking Rhodes Town. New towers are going up, and the walls grow thicker with each passing year."

"Built by infidel slaves, no doubt?" He drank deeply.

She nodded. "There are hundreds, my lord, and more entering the harbor all the time."

Jacco glanced at the crow-faced man. "We've got Christian captives in the East that need ransoming. If the knights possess any infidel slaves of value, we can arrange an exchange." His words tumbled out quickly as he warmed to his idea. "See the beauty of the scheme? We'll strengthen our positions with the Mamluks of Egypt and the knights at the same time—"

At the other end of the table, Princess Charlotta put down her knife with a clatter. "Such matters are best left in our father's hands."

The muscles in Jacco's face tensed. Estelle held her breath. It was as if a storm cloud passed over him. One moment his face was alight with jovial goodwill; the next, fury radiated from him like a crackling flame. A fraught moment slipped by. Then he picked up his cup and took a long swallow.

"Tell us more, mademoiselle," he said curtly. "Do you know the grand master personally? What is his palace like?"

"Yes, I know Lord de Milly. He and my father are both men of Auvergne, so they have much in common. His palace sits at the top of a hill overlooking the harbor and the sea beyond. It's the most magnificent structure I've ever seen."

Her father visited the grand master's imposing palace daily to oversee the mews, but Estelle had only entered its gates a few times, and she doubted Lord de Milly would remember their brief interactions. Admitting her insignificance to the knights seemed foolish, however.

"Rhodes Town is an odd place to bring a respectable family," the man across the table said. "It's a city of men, after all. Of knights and mercenaries and sailors."

"And brothels." Jacco smiled.

A laugh went up.

Estelle could not help the defensive edge that crept into her voice. "The town is full of merchants and their families. Just like here, we have notaries, goldbeaters, lawyers, and bankers among us. Everyone attends mass. There are so many churches the sound of all their bells tolling is like thunder. And there's beautiful art everywhere. Frescoes, paintings, statues. Some of it ancient, some made by artists trained in Venice and other places in Italy."

She thought of the Venetian artist Paolo Foscolo and his daughter, Anica, her dearest friend and language tutor. Anica was the reason she spoke Greek and Italian. The value of their daily language lessons was becoming more apparent with each passing moment in Cyprus.

"But an attack on Rhodes from the Turks will come any day," the crow-faced man pointed out. "Why does anyone of means still live there? Such folk could sail away for safer lands."

"It's true that attackers come from time to time, whether they're Mamluks, Turks, or Venetians. But the knights always defeat the invaders."

"Such talk fills my ladies with terror." Princess Charlotta's voice shot through the air with crisp finality. "It is not a woman's place to speak of such things."

Estelle recoiled as if the princess had slapped her. What had Louise said yesterday?

*She doesn't like her attendants to outshine her.*

"Nonsense." Jacco put a hand on Estelle's arm. His touch sent a shiver of apprehension through her. "I want to hear more about these attacks," he commanded. "Tell us."

A hint of menace lurked in the hard set of his jaw. She cast a glance at the princess, whose downturned mouth and narrowed eyes trumpeted her displeasure.

*Princess Charlotta isn't inclined to be my ally, but Jacco might. Perhaps if I gain favor with this man, he'll help me return to Rhodes.*

"They come from the sea, of course," she began slowly, trying to put the princess out of her mind. "Usually at night, or just before dawn . . ."

Estelle reached back into the past and grasped the threads of her old life. The eldest girl and the baby-minder of her family, she knew when to lower her voice, slow the pace, insert a dramatic pause. The rapt faces around the table told her she was winning them over. Until this moment, she had been the daughter of a lesser French noble with no fortune to her name, no one of consequence. But now she was something else.

A storyteller.

The tale she spun this evening was a variation on the same theme that had been drummed into her since arriving in Rhodes Town. Everyone in Rhodes was used to constant attacks from the sea. Whenever it happened, Estelle's father had faith that the knights would keep them safe. But each new threat from the East sent Maman into a fit of weeping. Sometimes she would threaten to sail back to France with the children. She would speak of the horrors that the infidels would inflict upon them all when the siege came, warning they would all become slaves or concubines or end up with their heads on spikes.

Papa would shake his head and hush her, tell her not to frighten the children. Estelle would take Jean-Philippe and Isabeau into another room and distract them with a game during such moments. Her mother was a tempestuous woman, prone to wild moods.

Not like Estelle.

*You have the heart of a falcon*, Papa used to say. *You are calm. You are brave.*

The hot flush that had scalded her face moments ago cooled. Her heart thrummed steadily under Louise's silk gown.

When her story ended, applause rose up from the courtiers around the table. Estelle smiled, reveling in the moment, but when her gaze slipped to Princess Charlotta, her smile faltered. The young woman's expression was icy. Next to her, Louise looked worried.

Jacco hefted his goblet in the air. "To Estelle, our delightful French mademoiselle," he cried. "A welcome addition to the court."

Estelle grasped her cup with trembling hands and raised it to her lips. The triumph coursing through her veins ebbed away. Dark thoughts descended on her mind like shrieking gulls, harsh and intrusive.

What would matter more in the days to come—Jacco's admiration or the princess's enmity?

# CHAPTER 8

Summer 1457
Nicosia, Cyprus

ESTELLE HAD NEARLY FINISHED DRESSING for the outing to the marketplace a few days later when a rap came at the door. She opened it to find the crow-faced man who'd sat across from her at supper.

*"Kalimera,"* he greeted her.

*"Kalimera."* She regarded him with a trace of wariness.

"I bring you a gift from my master, Lord Jacco." He fished a small velvet bag from a leather pouch at his waist and held it out.

"What is the occasion?" She accepted the bag.

He chuckled. "Because you pleased him, of course. With your storytelling at the supper table. Perhaps, if you are lucky, you shall please him again."

Estelle stiffened, uncomfortable at his insinuation. How could she have refused Jacco's demand that she tell her story? The king's son was obviously used to getting his way. Yet she now wished she had not spoken. For in addition to incurring Princess Charlotta's anger, it seemed she'd also made Jacco think she had a romantic interest in him.

"Thank you, sir," she said coolly. "Please convey my gratitude to Lord Jacco."

She closed and latched the door, willing her racing heart to slow.

The bag was tiny and lightweight. It nestled in her palm, inviting her gaze. She fumbled with the drawstring and shook out the contents into her hand.

It was a pearl necklace similar to Louise's. At its midpoint hung a single ruby set in gold filigree. She walked to the window and held it up. The ruby glowed, its facets catching the light.

*I should refuse this.*

Papa and Maman would never approve. Such a gift was dangerous. What would Jacco want in return?

She pushed away the thought and slid the necklace over her head. The weight of it made her skin tingle.

*Refusing his gift could be just as dangerous. Keep it, but hide it away.*

When she sailed back to Rhodes, she would have this necklace as a keepsake to remind her that, for one night at least, the court of Cyprus had fulfilled her expectations.

She removed the necklace, wrapped it in a handkerchief, and stuffed it in the bottom of her trunk.

Estelle hurried to the palace gates to meet Louise and a few other ladies of the princess's retinue, plus several maids and two guards. When the courtiers returned her greeting, she was relieved. Perhaps she'd imagined the princess's displeasure at supper with Jacco. All would be well.

"The princess hasn't had time to tell her ladies how bold you were the other night," Louise murmured, taking Estelle's arm. "She's been called away to the monastery where her mother convalesces. The queen's health grows worse by the day."

The palace guards opened the gates.

"May Her Grace recover swiftly. I hope Princess Charlotta will forgive my wagging tongue. I do enjoy telling a story . . ."

Estelle kept her voice light, as if the evening had not made much of an impression on her. As if she had no regrets about drawing so much attention to herself.

"That was obvious." The group set off into the streets, Louise keeping hold of Estelle's arm. "Try not to fret. You are the least of her worries, believe me."

The courtiers moved with confidence on the lanes they'd known since childhood. For her part, Estelle wished they would slow their pace. She did not want to miss a single detail of the bustling capital city.

Louise had told her the market was in a nearby square, around the corner from Prince João's former house. She tilted her head back, admiring elegant buildings made of sand-colored stone and white marble. As in Rhodes Town, the flat facades pressed close to the streets, concealing lushly planted interior courtyards.

Well-dressed citizens walked toward the marketplace, immersed in chatter. Vendors leading donkeys laden with goods shouted greetings to one another and exchanged news of the day. The convivial atmosphere made Estelle long for Rhodes Town, for the excitement of marketplace visits with her family.

They passed a wrought-iron gate hung with three massive Venetian glass lamps.

"The Italian merchants' quarter is through that gate," Louise said, pointing.

Estelle slowed her step. "Those lamps are lovely." Beyond the gate, homes of honey-colored stone lined the street, their polished wooden doors glinting in the sunlight.

*Signora Rosso lives through there.*

She had found the woman irritating on the voyage from Rhodes—even a bit mad. But now, after experiencing the strange world of the Cypriot court for herself, she realized Signora Rosso's declarations had contained more than a little truth. An uncomfortable feeling of remorse spread through her.

*The widow deserves my sympathy, not my scorn. I should pay her a call.*

Louise gestured in the other direction, where another iron gate stood. "And the Armenian quarter is opposite, tucked against the city walls."

A family group strolled toward them beyond the gate, laughing amongst themselves. The father held his youngest daughter in his arms. How many times had her own family ambled from their Rhodes Town neighborhood to the market street, immersed in their own world? Would they ever get that opportunity again?

"Come, Estelle!" Louise's voice interrupted her reverie.

As they approached the market square, the cries of vendors rang out.

"Can we visit the goldbeater's stall?" Estelle asked. "And the man who makes artificial birds?"

Of all the artisans Louise had described to her in the preceding days, this one intrigued her most. She wanted to meet the man who'd crafted Jacco's gift to Princess Charlotta.

"Of course. But first, we must stop for pistachio tarts and honey cakes." Louise led the group to a bakery stall under a stone arcade that was scented with cinnamon, cloves, and honey.

Once they had chosen their treats, they wandered through the crowd. A wagon with a square window cut into its side dominated a corner of the square. Garishly dressed puppets manipulated by invisible handlers bobbed and jigged in the window, prompting gales of laughter from the children gathered nearby.

Estelle's eye was drawn by a spice purveyor's stall. She drifted closer, curious to see what the merchant had to offer. The spice sellers in Rhodes Town were always irresistible to her mother, who could not get enough ginger, clove, cardamom, and cinnamon. Such goods were so costly in France they had been reserved for feast days, but in Rhodes Town, things were different.

The merchant hawked his wares in the Cypriot dialect. Estelle understood many of his words, but one phrase he used made no sense to her. He pointed to a ceramic dish of red powder and cried its name again. She moved closer still, peering at the substance.

*Dragon's blood*, she realized with a start. *Of course*. It was a mainstay of her father's recipes, proven to cure a variety of raptor ailments.

Her mind went to the princess's pet merlin. Perhaps she could buy a small measure of dragon's blood and concoct one of her father's remedies for it. If it brought the falcon back to health, she might find favor with the princess.

"*Kalimera, kyrie*," she greeted the merchant in her most polite Greek. "I wish to buy a measure of dragon's blood."

"This is the last of it." He reached for the dish. "You're in luck. One measure. Eighty cartzias."

She shook her head, frowning. "I'll give you thirty and no more."

As she spoke, something behind her distracted the merchant.

"*Kalimera, kyrie!*" he sang out, his face breaking into a huge grin.

Estelle turned her head to see a young man approach, his hand raised in greeting.

The merchant bowed. "By the Holy Virgin," he exclaimed. "It's been an age. What can I do for you today?"

The newcomer smiled. His teeth were startlingly white against his copper-brown skin, and his prominent cheekbones and strong jaw could have been chiseled by a stone mason. Estelle studied him with open curiosity. He was dressed in a doublet and hose, like a Latin man, but his curly black hair was partially covered by a Cypriot-style cap.

"We're in need of dragon's blood." The young man drew abreast of Estelle. "Give me all you can spare, if you would."

The merchant showed him the dish of red powder. "It will be my pleasure."

"But I asked for it first!" Estelle gave the spice purveyor an indignant glare.

"You said you'd only pay thirty." The merchant did not meet her eyes, but poured the entire dish's contents into a flax cloth pouch and bound it tightly. "That's insulting."

"It's the custom to haggle," she protested. "Only a fool would accept the first stated price."

The young man turned to her. "What use does a Latin woman have for dragon's blood?" he asked, a hint of amusement in his voice.

Her hands flew to her bodice. She'd reverted to her own clothes today. He regarded her in silence, a half-smile quirking his mouth, his eyes glowing at her with startling intensity. Were they green or gray? The light in the stall was shadowy; it was impossible to tell.

She finally managed to speak. "Women find the herb as useful as men, no matter where we come from."

Memories of Maman navigating crowded marketplace stalls flooded her mind. Estelle had learned to barter in Rhodes Town at her mother's side, watching Maman purchase fine cloth from merchants in Rhodes Town for shipment to various ports in Western Europe. She did not possess her mother's fiery temperament or golden-haired beauty, but she could be bold when she needed to.

"*Kyrie*," she said sharply to the merchant, the word ringing out above the buzz of the marketplace crowd. "I was first, remember?"

He ignored her.

Estelle rapped her knuckles against the table holding his wares. "From now on, I'll see to it that Princess Charlotta's spices come from some other merchant!"

He looked up, startled. "What do you mean by this?"

"I mean that if you had not been so rude, you would have become known as the spice purveyor who saved Princess Charlotta's pet falcon from certain death."

The men exchanged a bemused glance as if they had a private joke between them.

"That's quite a claim to make." The young man chuckled. "You sound like someone who can spin a tale, though. Impressive powers of exaggeration."

"How dare you mock me?" she demanded.

Without responding, he removed his purse from his belt and tipped a few silver coins into the merchant's palm. The merchant passed the pouch to him and bowed. Estelle watched the exchange with rising frustration. She could have been invisible for all they cared.

"May you melt like wax, both of you!" she snapped in French, hastening from the spice stall directly into the path of several armed men dressed in purple-and-black livery. One of them pushed her roughly out of the way in his haste to follow his companions.

She tumbled back, losing her balance. But someone arrested her fall with strong arms, his voice quiet in her ear.

"Careful, mademoiselle. These streets are full of surprises." The young man from the spice stall steadied her, grinning. "Lucky for you, I'm quick on my feet."

She wrenched free of his grasp. "I don't think you heard me in there. I told you to melt like wax!"

The French words exploded from her like cannon shot. They would have little impact on a Cypriot, but it felt good to unleash them.

He threw back his head and laughed. To her astonishment, he said in beautiful French, "I've lived in Cyprus my whole life. If I were in danger of melting, I'd have done it long ago, mademoiselle."

Flushing with indignation, she stalked away. When she found Louise and the other ladies, she could not banish the incident from her mind. Maman often told her a woman's ambitions were all too often thwarted in a man's world, but the encounter stung just the same. Why had that merchant been so eager to accommodate the fellow? He'd not looked wealthy; he'd not been accompanied by an entourage of servants. And yet he'd been treated with the deference afforded the richest noblemen.

Louise took Estelle by the arm. "I lost sight of you for a moment, my dear."

Another pair of men in purple-and-black livery ran through the marketplace, inciting cries of annoyance from bystanders.

"That bodes ill." Louise watched their progress with a worried expression.

"Who are those men?" Estelle asked.

"They work for a wealthy lord—they wear his colors." Louise shaded her eyes with a hand, studying the milling crowd. She turned to one of the guards. "Go see what's happened. And return at once to give us the news."

He bowed to her and trotted away.

Estelle stared after him, uneasy. But none of the other ladies seemed concerned.

"Ah—the artificial birds," Louise said, pointing at a nearby stall. "Shall we see them now? It will be a good diversion."

Estelle studied the rows of colorful painted birds, marveling at the ingenious placement of wings and beaks, the delicately carved legs, the gleaming eyes. She crouched to examine an exquisite reproduction of a heron. Reaching out to pick it up, she imagined the young man from the spice stall attempting to whisk it out of her grasp.

*Oooh, let him try.*

She would snatch it back with the speed of a striking snake if he dared—

"My ladies!" The guard's gruff voice startled her. "I bring you news of a sword fight. The servants of a baron loyal to the queen are brawling with a band of knights—friends of Lord Jacco, the rumor goes. The fight grows in number by the minute. It could spill over into the marketplace."

Louise sighed. "Well, there's nothing for it. Our outing is ruined."

The group began retracing their path back to the palace, flanked by the guards. The crush of people tightened in the narrow lanes as they sped their steps. Jostled on all sides, Estelle was soon separated from the others. She found herself caught up in a group of Venetian merchant wives and their servants.

"Louise!" Her shout drowned in a sea of panicked voices. "Louise!"

A large group of men in yellow-and-red livery appeared from a side lane, pouring into the street with swords clattering, their angry voices rising like a surging wave. The Venetian women veered away from the men, screaming in fright, as the men pounded past them.

At the gate to the Italian quarter, one of the women glanced back at Estelle, brow furrowed. "Are you lost, signorina? You should take shelter. These streets are not safe."

Estelle tried to steady her breath. Should she try to find the palace on her own? No, not during a violent brawl in a foreign city. Taking refuge in the Italian quarter seemed the wisest plan.

"I'm calling on a friend," she told the woman. "Do you know Signora Rosso's home?"

The merchant's wife nodded, waving her through the gate. "Follow us. And by all the saints, stay close."

# CHAPTER 9

Summer 1457
Nicosia, Cyprus

A MOMENT LATER, the group paused before a home with a dolphin-shaped door knocker.

The woman who had spoken earlier pointed at the door. "Get yourself inside before harm comes to you."

*"Grazie."*

Estelle lifted the dolphin's tail and pounded on the door as the women hastened away. A small, fearful part of her wanted to follow the group, to cling to them like a burr.

*It's quiet in this quarter, away from the madness. I'm safe here.*

The reassuring thoughts did nothing to quell the pounding of her heart.

After an excruciating delay, a servant opened the door.

"I am Estelle de Montavon, a friend of Signora Rosso," Estelle said in a rush. "There's been some trouble in the streets and I—"

"Is she expecting you?" The woman's voice was suspicious.

"She was my chaperone on the journey from Rhodes. She told me I was welcome here."

The servant admitted her and led Estelle into a cramped parlor, where Signora Rosso sat at a desk covered with ledger books, her quill and inkpot at the ready.

"You!" Signora Rosso put down the sheaf of paper she'd been holding. "Why are you here? And how did you manage to come alone? The palace guards its courtiers like precious jewels."

"There was a swordfight and the crowd panicked. I was separated from my companions."

The widow leaned back in her chair, frowning. "Violence. Always more violence."

She pointed at a nearby chair.

Estelle sank into it, grateful to be off her feet, and tried to still her trembling hands. Why was she so unnerved? Nothing had happened to her. All was well.

At the thought, tears burned in her eyes.

A sudden, unbearable longing for her family gripped her. In that moment, all she wanted was to return to Rhodes.

"I wish to leave Cyprus with the next merchant fleet to Rhodes Town." The words shot out without warning.

Signora Rosso eyed her dubiously. "What have they done to you in that palace?"

"No one has harmed me. But Prince João was poisoned by the queen's chamberlain, they say. And I've heard of others who were poisoned as well."

"What of the king? Has he found you a husband yet?"

Estelle shook her head. "I've only seen him once, and he said nothing of that. I was sent here to be a tutor, not find a husband."

"So who are you tutoring, then?"

"No one," Estelle admitted. "The princess wants nothing to do with me."

A triumphant gleam entered Signora Rosso's eyes. "See?"

"All the more reason for me to leave. They've no use for me."

The widow toyed with her rosary beads. "Your lot is better than it could be. You've not much to complain about, really."

"Surely, poison is worthy of complaint?" Estelle shot back.

"That's nothing new. Did you know King Jean had another wife before Queen Eleni?"

"No."

The widow nodded. "Soon after the wedding, the poor thing died, along with most of her ladies. A sudden illness, that was the official cause. But everyone knew they were poisoned." She held up a skull-shaped bead. "*Memento mori.* We all must die."

A queasy feeling plunged into Estelle's stomach. "Of course. But I don't want to die here."

"What do you want me to do about it?" Signora Rosso frowned. "Do I look like a person who arranges transport on merchant fleets? Besides, such travel is costly. Do you have fifteen ducats to spend? Twenty, if tariffs keep rising? Who's going to chaperone you?"

Estelle's face grew hot. She had not even thought about the price of a sea journey to Rhodes.

"I can't stay here," she whispered, bowing her head. "It was a mistake to come, don't you see?"

"Listen, girl." The widow walked around her desk and raised Estelle's chin with a finger. "There's no arguing with the fact that the Cypriot court is a dangerous place. But change is coming. If there's ever a time to influence the course of your own fate, it's during such moments."

"If it's so dangerous here, why do you stay?"

"I'll leave when the signal comes." Signora Rosso retreated behind her desk and settled into her chair with a sigh. "If you're clever, you'll wait for it as well."

"What signal?" Estelle asked in frustration.

The widow crossed herself. "You'll know when the time comes, believe me. Now get back to the palace. I'll have someone accompany you."

Signora Rosso rang for a burly servant, who glowered when she gave him his assignment. Then she waved Estelle away without another word.

Outside, the servant set off at a brisk pace. "God's bones, there's something wicked in the air," he grumbled.

Estelle had not thought to bring her dagger. But she'd had no cause today. Their group had been accompanied by armed guards, after all.

It was a quick walk through the quiet lanes to the iron gate. The bells of a nearby church rang out, marking the hour. Soon more chimes from churches all over Nicosia resonated overhead.

Twenty paces from the gate, two men sidled out from the shadows of a broad stone doorway, blocking the way.

"What's in there?" one of them snarled at Estelle, his gaze flicking to the purse at her waist.

"Leave her be!"

Signora Rosso's servant drew his sword, but the man's companion brandished a blade of his own. With surprising agility for a person of his size, the servant lunged forward and dealt a mighty blow to the man's head with the butt of his sword. The fellow toppled to the ground with a grunt.

Estelle screamed, hoping to attract attention from people on the street beyond the quarter's iron gate. But the city's bells drowned her voice with their clanging.

The man threatening her let out a low chuckle. "It seems God is not on your side, signorina." He reached for her purse.

Estelle stomped on his foot with her heel. He caught hold of her skirts. With a hard tug, she freed herself.

"You little whore," he hissed. "I'll have your purse—and then I'll have you."

"Run!" Signora Rosso's servant bellowed. "Run for the gate!"

She dashed off and burst through the gate, her lungs burning, then slipped behind a passing mule cart.

Using the cart as a shield, she peered anxiously back through the gate. Signora Rosso's servant loomed over her attacker, pummeling him and shouting obscenities. Estelle shuddered. It would not end well for that scoundrel, she had no doubt.

"Are you hurt, mademoiselle?" the man leading the mule cart asked.

Turning to face him, she drew back in astonishment. "You?"

It was the young man from the spice merchant's stall. Again, his eyes disarmed her. They were the color of the river rocks she and Étienne used to collect in Auvergne, a luminous gray.

The muscles in his jaw tightened. "What is fortune playing at, putting you in my path twice in one day? These streets are no place for a respectable young lady to wander without a chaperone. If you are indeed respectable."

"I can assure you, signor, or *kyrie* or however you are meant to be addressed, I am the picture of respectability." Estelle gave him a cold stare. "I was separated from my companions, that's all."

"Separated from your friends twice in one day? Bad luck you're having, mademoiselle." He led the mules onward. "Walk with me if you like. I have a blade, and judging by what I've seen in these streets today, I may need to use it."

After an instant of hesitation, Estelle fell into step alongside the man, watching him covertly from under her lashes. He was not much older than her, she guessed.

"I hope your sword is sharp," she said.

"I hope you don't get the chance to see me wield it," he retorted. "Where are your companions? I'll take you to them."

She bit her lip, not wanting to share anything. But what was the alternative?

"The palace," she admitted. "I live there."

He glanced at her, one eyebrow raised. "What was a Frenchwoman who lives at court doing in the Italian quarter?"

"That's a mystery you'll have to solve on your own. If it takes you out of your way, there's no need to trouble yourself walking me all the way to the palace."

"I have an errand at the palace myself, so it's no trouble."

"What business do you have there?" she asked.

"A delivery." He jerked his head back toward the mule cart, its contents hidden by a canvas cover.

All around them people streamed by, discussing the brawl and putting forth various theories as to who started it and why. As they put more distance between themselves and the Italian quarter, Estelle began to relax.

She studied her companion as they moved through the streets. This man was a stranger. She should not be in his company. She should not tell him anything, should not ask him anything—

He turned his head and caught her staring.

"What is it?" he asked.

"Nothing—I only wonder what I should call you?"

He nodded. "Gabriel Bayoumi. And your name?"

"Estelle de Montavon," she replied.

They were nearing the palace gates now. The crowds had thinned out, and the rattle of the cart's wheels replaced the tolling of bells overhead.

"When did you come to Nicosia?" he asked.

"I arrived soon after the death of the prince," she said.

"You've not been here long at all, then."

"It's been only a handful of days. Yet it feels like an eternity," she said more bitterly than she intended.

The glimmer of a smile appeared on his face. She caught a flash of square white teeth, and his expression softened around the eyes. The sudden warmth in them startled her. She did not want to look away.

"I understand," he replied. "I spend as little time in Nicosia as possible."

"Are you Latin?" she couldn't help asking.

"My father is. But my mother was Egyptian." His smile vanished.

They stopped before the palace gates.

"Where do you live if not in Nicosia?" she asked.

Instead of answering, he spoke briefly to a guard, who signaled to his companions to let them through. As they moved into the palace courtyard, Louise and a servant approached.

"Thank all the saints, you're back!" Louise took Estelle's hands in her own. "I was about to send out a party to search for you. Are you unharmed?" Glancing at Estelle's companion, she frowned. "Who is this man?"

The king's steward appeared. "*Geraki*, at last!"

Estelle gaped at Gabriel, the memory of her father using that very word echoing in her mind.

"*Geraki?* You're a falconer?" she asked.

"What news of the king's falcons?" the steward asked Gabriel at the same moment. "Are they all accounted for? And have you purchased the supplies we ordered? The dragon's blood for the princess's merlin?"

"The falcons are in good health, *kyrie*. And I've done everything you asked." The man followed the steward toward the cart without another glance at Estelle.

She broke away from Louise, trailing the men.

"You bought that dragon's blood for the princess?" she cried.

"I did," came the reply.

"Do you know Michel Pelestrine?"

"Of course." He turned, giving her a surprised look. "I work for him."

Another man in royal livery greeted the falconer. They bent their heads together, talking in the Cypriot dialect, then walked rapidly toward the stables.

"Come." Louise tugged on Estelle's hand. "We'll find you some refreshment, and then you can rest."

"No, no," Estelle protested, her eyes fixed on the retreating falconer. "Gabriel," she called. "Wait!"

But at that moment, a half-dozen mounted guards clattered through the gates into the courtyard. Their captain ordered the women inside.

Louise pulled Estelle to the palace doors. "You could have been killed, you know. Blood flows on the streets of Nicosia as we speak. You're fortunate that you stumbled upon that falconer, luckier still that he behaved honorably."

Estelle barely heard Louise's words. Her mind was on the book for Michel Pelestrine. If she could get it to Gabriel, he could deliver it to her father's friend and let him know she was on Cypriot soil.

She needed an ally, a person of influence in Cyprus. Michel Pelestrine was master falconer to the king. Perhaps he would give her the aid she needed to make her way back to Rhodes.

A cool current of resolve traveled from her belly up her spine, set her scalp tingling.

Somehow she would find the falconer before he left the palace and get him that book.

# CHAPTER 10

Summer 1457
Nicosia, Cyprus

GABRIEL FOLLOWED the king's steward past the stables and kennels to the mews. The palace mews in Nicosia was much smaller than the one at St. Hilarion castle, nestled by a courtyard abutting the high walls that separated the royal residence from the rest of Nicosia. He delivered the dragon's blood to a waiting falconer with instructions to whisk it well with egg whites before administering it to the merlin.

"Some say whisk, some say shake, some say stir," the man grumbled, seizing the leather pouch from Gabriel's grasp. "There is no right way to do it, though you at St. Hilarion think otherwise."

Gabriel ignored him. He'd learned early on that the royal falconers were a competitive bunch, all vying to be singled out as the most effective bird trainer, the most successful healer of falcon ailments. That was what he found so refreshing about Michel Pelestrine. The Frenchman seemed oblivious to the competitive nature of his work. He had a magical way with animals, whether feathered or furred, and he made quiet alliances with houndmen and hunters, overseeing large hawking expeditions with practiced ease.

In the storeroom, the steward unlocked a cabinet and withdrew a box. He shook it. The sound of gentle metallic clanging rang out.

"Tooled silver falcon bells for the king's favorite birds. They arrived from Damascus just yesterday."

They walked back toward the mule cart, which stood in the shade of a vaulted stone arcade between the courtyard and the mews.

Gabriel took the box. "How many of the birds I brought from Famagusta do you want here in Nicosia?"

From behind him, a brash voice spoke up. "Let me see them first. Then you'll have your answer."

Gabriel's heart plummeted. He turned to see Jacco striding across the courtyard, directly into the path of a stable hand carrying an enormous load of hay balanced on a pitchfork. The hay was piled so high there was no way the boy could see Jacco coming.

"Watch out!" Gabriel called sharply.

But his warning came too late. Jacco twisted out of the boy's way, then slapped him hard across the face. The boy staggered backward, dropping the pitchfork. Jacco advanced and kicked him savagely in the belly. The lad crumpled, landing on the upended pitchfork with a cry of pain.

Then the king's son wheeled and continued on toward Gabriel and the steward, striding through the scattered hay as if the encounter never happened.

Gabriel fought an impulse to help the stable hand collect himself. Instead, he bowed low. "My lord."

Jacco regarded him with a petulant air. "I don't know why I wasn't informed you'd arrived."

"Forgive me, my lord." Gabriel steeled himself for a tongue-lashing or worse. Had Jacco heard the leopard his father planned to give him was dead, stabbed in the heart by Gabriel's blade?

The king's son had been blessed with physical grace and strength, but he lacked the temperament to be a successful hunter. He was incapable of stilling his mind and body long enough to stalk, sight, and dispatch a deer. He was happier hawking, so Gabriel often found himself settling peregrines and saker falcons on Jacco's gloved wrist, and refilling his pouch of rabbit meat to reward the birds after a successful kill.

Once, on a hunt in the mountains, Jacco's peregrine had killed a bird in midair and sent it hurtling into a lake. When the servants sent to find the carcass returned dripping and empty-handed, he'd whipped their heads with a leather switch. One of the men had been permanently blinded. But Jacco had a generous streak, too. If he was happy with the hunt, he showered his attendants with gold coins and praise.

As Gabriel always did when confronted with this man-boy, he silently asked: *Which face will you show me today, my lord?*

"My sister's merlin is poorly, and no one is doing anything about it," Jacco announced. "I've sacked my falconers." He gave Gabriel a speculative look. "I could use your skills at the archbishop's palace. What say you?"

Gabriel's muscles tensed. He would never take a position in Jacco's household. But how to refuse without angering him?

"I am honored, but I've a contract with the king, my lord. Many of his favorite birds are under my care at St. Hilarion. I'm bound to take a load of precious cargo to the mews there this very day, in fact. I dare not break my promise to deliver it safely."

He jerked his head at the mule cart, praying that Jacco's distractible nature would divert him. A quick glance at the stable hand revealed the lad creeping into the shadows. Relief coursed through him.

*Good. Stay there until the danger passes.*

"What's in there?" Jacco surveyed the cart, arms crossed over his chest.

"Falcons and hawks for the hunt, from Famagusta."

"Are there any gyrfalcons among them?"

Gabriel shook his head. "No, my lord. Saker falcons, peregrines, a sparrow hawk, and a goshawk."

"How disappointing." Jacco's face fell. "I need a gift for a man of importance whose interest in falconry equals my own. He has an impressive mews, but I've heard on good authority that he desires more gyrfalcons."

"Where is this man you speak of?" Gabriel asked.

"Across the sea," Jacco said vaguely. "What does it matter anyway?" He strode toward the cart. "Come. Show me the creatures. Perhaps there are one or two that would be better suited in my mews than Papa's."

At that moment, a woman's voice echoed in the courtyard leading to the mews from the stables and kennels, stopping Jacco in his tracks.

To Gabriel's surprise, Estelle de Montavon appeared, trailed by a maid. In her hand was a wrapped parcel.

"My lord," she said, recognizing Jacco with obvious consternation. Stopping short, she sank into a curtsy. When she rose, the parcel was hidden in the folds of her skirt.

"What brings you to this place, mademoiselle?" Jacco asked. "Surely, the steward has not employed you as a falconer?"

She hesitated. "No, my lord. I—I thought to share my father's remedies for curing falcon ailments with dragon's blood. In hopes the princess's merlin might improve."

Jacco studied her with a calculating gaze. "If your father were to give the grand master a gift, what might he choose?"

"Lord de Milly has a collection of jeweled falcon hoods he's constantly adding to," she said slowly. "My father has procured a number of them. The grand master also collects falcon bells from all over the world, my lord."

Gabriel gave the wooden box a shake. "These are falcon bells."

The steward shot him a nasty look.

"Let me see." Jacco yanked the box from Gabriel's hands. He flung open the lid and examined the contents. "I think they'll do."

"There are jeweled hoods in here." Gabriel nodded toward the wooden cabinet where the box had been stored. "Perhaps you'll find a suitable gift among them."

"Send all the jeweled hoods you can find to my palace," Jacco ordered the steward. "I want them there by sunset."

"But your father has said nothing of this . . ." the steward began.

"Perhaps not to you," Jacco snapped. "If you value your good standing with the king, you would be wise to obey me without question."

The steward paled. "Of course, my lord. It shall be done as you say."

Jacco turned to the young Frenchwoman. "I thank you for the advice, Mademoiselle de Montavon. I won't forget this kindness, you have my word."

With that, he wheeled and strode away, his white silk robes flowing behind him.

Gabriel awaited an outburst from the steward, but the man rummaged in silence through the cabinet looking for falcon hoods, apparently cowed by Jacco's threat. As soon as the steward had taken what he wanted and left, Gabriel turned to their female visitor.

"What have you brought me?" he asked.

She stepped closer. "This is a gift from my father to Monsieur Pelestrine. It's important that he knows I've arrived."

A faint floral scent clung to her, drifting in his direction. He filled his lungs, trying to identify it. Rose, definitely. But something else, too, something spicy, perhaps amber oil—

In her outstretched hand was the parcel. He reached for it. Their fingertips touched, igniting a spark in his blood that heated his veins and quickened his pulse. Rattled, he pulled the book from her grasp with a little too much force.

"Forgive me," he muttered. "I'll see he gets it."

Her golden-brown eyes widening, she half smiled. A dimple appeared at the corner of her mouth. Gabriel stared at it, transfixed. He wished he had an excuse to touch her again.

"Please don't let the book out of your sight." She studied the parcel in his hands with an anxious expression, as if she regretted letting him take it.

"What's it about?" he couldn't help asking.

"Falconry."

The longer she held his gaze, the more uncomfortably warm he grew. Still, he prolonged the moment as long as he could.

"Why does it mean so much to you?" he asked quietly.

He thought he saw tears glinting in her eyes. "Because my father and I wrote it together."

"So you *are* a falconer?"

She stared at him levelly. "I would never make that claim. I'm a falconer's daughter. And his scribe. I wrote every word of that book."

He could not find his voice.

Without waiting for a response, she nodded to him and turned on her heel. "Good day to you."

She vanished into the shadows, the maid trotting to keep up. Gabriel found himself rooted to the ground, unable to move until the last traces of her intoxicating scent dissipated and the barking of hounds in the kennels jolted him back to reality.

*Gather your wits, man. Get back on the road and get out of this viper's nest.*

# CHAPTER 11

Summer 1457
Near St. Hilarion Castle, Cyprus

GABRIEL STOPPED his horse and waited for the others to catch up. Behind the mule cart, two royal guards rode side by side, their metal helmets gleaming in the afternoon sunlight. The persistent buzz of cicadas filled his ears, and a breeze stirred the dry grasses on the roadside. They were more than halfway to St. Hilarion castle, and the sun had begun its long descent toward the western horizon.

He uncorked his water sack and drank the last few drops. Draping its strap around the saddle's pommel, he shaded his eyes with a hand. Dust rose under the hooves of the approaching mules and horses, sending a dun-colored cloud into the sky.

"We're nearly to the inn," he called out. "Let's stop and water the animals there. We can have some refreshment to ready ourselves for the last push."

The men signaled their agreement and Gabriel set off again, taking his position in the lead.

When they arrived at the inn, few animals were tied up in the courtyard. It was not yet suppertime, and the midday rush was a distant memory.

Two stable boys watered their mounts. Gabriel directed one of the guards and the driver to stay with the cart while he and the other guard ventured inside.

"*Kalimera,*" he greeted the innkeeper, blinking as his eyes adjusted to the dim light of the nearly empty interior.

"*Kalimera,*" the man returned, wiping his hands on his apron.

While the innkeeper fetched them watered wine, bread, and cheese, Gabriel's gaze settled on three men sitting around a table, the remains of a meal scattered over its surface. They were evidently well into their cups, for their talk was spirited and somewhat slurred, and they kept interrupting one another to make their points.

The guard said, "They've no place to be, by the looks of it. Must be nice."

One of the men, whose back was to Gabriel and the guard, slammed his cup on the table. "If it weren't for me, my village would have no meat!" he said. "I risk my life to set those snares and traps."

Gabriel was sure he recognized the man's voice.

The guard looked at Gabriel sideways. "Poacher," he whispered.

One of the group noticed the guard's livery and put a hand on his companion's shoulder, giving it a shake.

"What are you on about?" The man turned, clapping eyes on the guard. He lapsed into silence.

The innkeeper bustled up with a tray. "Where will you take your refreshment?" he asked.

"Bring it outside and share it with the others," Gabriel said to the guard. "Stay with the cart."

Instead of following him, Gabriel approached the three men at the table.

The poacher peered up and smiled in recognition. "Master Gabriel!"

Gabriel returned the smile. This man owned olive groves and a rabbit farm near the ancient abbey of Bellapais. Gabriel had not been aware the fellow also dabbled in hunting and trapping, but it was no surprise. Many Cypriots did.

"Share a cup of wine with us," the man invited him.

"I'll sit for a moment." Gabriel pulled up a stool, and the innkeeper plunked down a cup for him.

The others studied him with suspicion. "A royal falconer, are you?" asked one.

Gabriel inclined his head. "I need to eat. I need a roof over my head. So I work for the king. But I'm a Cypriot, same as you."

The farmer filled Gabriel's cup with wine. "This falconer buys rabbits for the king's birds. He makes my rabbit farming venture worthwhile. Some weeks he buys a few dozen, some weeks more than that. My most valued customer, understand?"

"So why risk it all with snares and traps?" one of his companions asked.

The farmer scowled. "As if you're innocent of such things."

It was forbidden to hunt wild game on the king's lands without permission, and few commoners were granted such privileges.

"We all do what we must to feed our families," Gabriel said in a neutral tone, sipping his wine. "But it's best if you keep such things to yourselves. Even in an empty tavern, there are eyes and ears. Not all of them friendly."

The farmer's expression turned sheepish. "Enough about that. You've come from Nicosia, am I right?"

Gabriel nodded.

"What news of the court? Has the queen's chamberlain been strung up for murdering Prince João?"

"I've heard nothing of that." Gabriel put down his cup.

"What about the princess? I heard the grief is killing her, poor lady."

"She is in good health, from what I could gather." Gabriel leaned his elbows on the table. "There was talk that the king already plans another husband for her, a man from the West."

All three men looked disappointed.

"Why can she not wed a Cypriot?" the farmer complained. "Our kingdom is threatened on all sides *and* from within. We've the Genoese

lording over Famagusta, the Mamluks sending their spies and pirates
from Alexandria to attack our seaside villages, and the Turks bearing
down on us from the north. And what does the French king do? He
taxes us, imposes his rules, and spends gold on himself."

The third man spoke up. "If only the king's son weren't a bastard.
Lord Jacco'd make a fine king. He's brave, he's intelligent, he's a
Cypriot, by God. One of us!"

"He is half-French," Gabriel pointed out.

"So?" the farmer said. "It's just the matter of his birth that compli-
cates things."

"His father could legitimize him," the third man suggested. "It's
not uncommon. I met a nobleman's son in Limassol who took his
father's name and made a fortune for himself after he was declared
legitimate. His mother was common-born, a housemaid from Nicosia."

Gabriel shifted uncomfortably on his stool. These men knew
nothing of his private history. But he, too, was a bastard unfit to
receive his father's name. Yes, his father had done some valuable things
to prepare Gabriel for the future: had him tutored with his half-brothers, sent him to work for the Knights Hospitaller when he was a lad,
made a sailor of him on one of the family's ships. But the most useful
step of all, legitimizing his birth, had never been discussed.

"What do you think?" The farmer's voice penetrated the tangle of
thoughts in his mind.

"Forgive me," Gabriel apologized. "What was the question?"

"Do you think the king would legitimize his son, make him his
heir?"

"As long as the queen has breath in her body, that will not happen."
He stood. "I've a great hill to climb, and sunset approaches." More
quietly, he added, "I suggest you head home now, too, and go out the
back. The guards I travel with are not friendly to poachers."

The three men scrambled up and made their farewells, then
skulked through the kitchen.

Outside in the courtyard, the guard said, "One of those men was a
poacher. I'm going to report him, get the reward. Where's he from, did
he say?"

The king's steward offered gold to any man who reported a known poacher. Gabriel knew many poachers and had reported none of them. He had been hungry enough in his youth to know the desperation a parent felt when confronted with empty-bellied children. His own mother had stolen food on more than one occasion to feed him, and he would do the same in her predicament.

"He said he's on his way to Paphos," Gabriel offered, coming up with the lie on the spot. "He's done with poaching and is throwing his lot in with a fishmonger."

The guard gave him a perplexed look. "From poaching to fishing? That's an odd switch."

His gaze flicked to the inn. For a moment, he looked ready to stride back inside.

Gabriel nodded. "Said he's getting old and his legs can't take tramping around the woods any longer. His friends paid for his meal. He's got no coin. Even if we reported him, the king would get nothing for our effort."

"But I would get a reward for reporting him."

The guard was very young, Gabriel realized. He probably knew little of the inner workings of the court.

Probably.

"Not true." Gabriel took his horse's reins from a stable boy and tossed him a thin silver coin. "The perpetrator has to be brought in, witnesses have to be rounded up, there's a meeting before the burghers of Nicosia. Scribes, notaries, lawyers. The whole thing takes months."

The enthusiasm waned from the man's expression. "Let's get on the road," he said in disgust, turning away.

Sweat trickled down Gabriel's back as he swung into the saddle.

He did not know the rabbit farmer well, in truth. And yet he had lied for the fellow. He just could not bear to see common Cypriots like himself ground down by the nobility. There were so many dangers in this world, so many injustices. If he could tip the scales even a tiny bit in his peoples' favor, he couldn't resist doing so.

*Interfering with the problems of others will get you into serious trouble one day, Gabriel.*

He could almost hear his mother's voice in his ear as he rode away from the inn. She'd warned him on this count many times. Not that he'd listened.

Spurring his mare to a gallop, he swept up the crest of a rise in the road, making sure the way was clear ahead. A gust of wind tugged at his cap, set his sleeves billowing.

He signaled the guards to proceed and sat motionless in the saddle, unable to put his mother's warning out of his mind.

# CHAPTER 12

Summer 1457
Nicosia, Cyprus

LOUISE AND A MAID carrying baskets of fabric appeared one morning not long after the marketplace excursion. Estelle ushered them into her chamber, still clutching the towel dampened with rose water she'd been washing with.

After the maid deposited the fabric on the bed, Louise dismissed her and shut the door, turning to Estelle with a broad smile.

"You can choose anything you like and my seamstress will make it into a Cypriot-style gown. Yellow, pink, violet, scarlet . . . What shall it be?" She picked up a length of camlet cloth, made of silk and wool woven together. "This burnt orange would look pretty with your hair."

Estelle touched it with a fingertip, marveling at its softness. Maman often purchased such fabrics, and she knew how costly they were. "I will pay you, I promise."

*With what? You have a very light purse and no work.*

"I'm in no hurry to pocket your coin." Louise held up a length of deep purple silk. "This would be lovely on you, too."

Of all the choices, it was the one that drew Estelle's eye. She'd always loved the color.

"I like it best."

"It's decided, then. While you wait for a new gown to be made, perhaps we can make some adjustments to the Latin clothing you brought." Louise crossed the room and flung open the wooden trunk that lay beneath the window. "Where are your underthings?" She began rummaging through the contents.

"Wait." Estelle went to her side. "Let me—"

Louise rocked back on her heels, something small and glittering clutched in her hand. "Where did you get this?" She turned it over in her palm. "It's so much like my own."

Estelle's heart pounded faster. "It was a gift. From Jacco. His servant brought it the morning after our supper."

"It was obvious you charmed him that evening." Louise put a hand to her throat and pulled aside her high-necked blouse, revealing her own pearl-and-ruby necklace. "Yours is not quite as big as mine."

Her voice carried a brittle, harsh note. Was it triumph? Pride? Estelle could not be sure.

"The day of Princess Charlotta's wedding feast, I sat beside Jacco and made merry with him. I got him dancing, then laughing. This necklace was delivered to me the next morning." Louise's eyes shone at the memory. "Jacco rewards those who entertain him—but he also expects much of them."

Estelle's mind darted to the crow-faced man, to the insinuation he'd made about her pleasing Jacco.

"What does he expect?" she asked, dreading the answer.

"His interest is like a rainstorm—powerful one day, gone the next. All I know is this gift means there's more to come between the two of you." Louise dangled the necklace from her fingertips, considering it. "If we fix one of your blouses to be high-necked in the Cypriot style, you can wear it without anyone knowing."

Estelle bit her lip, more confused than ever about Jacco's intentions. The sparkling ruby in Louise's hand caught the light, glowing from within.

"It doesn't feel right to wear it," she admitted.

Louise slipped the necklace over Estelle's head. "Nonsense. It's not often one experiences a gesture of kindness in this court." The hard edge had vanished from her voice.

All at once, Estelle understood that Louise, for all of her lightheartedness and frivolity, suffered just as she did in this strange place. She squeezed her friend's hand in gratitude.

"The sooner you look like the rest of us, the sooner you'll feel like one of us." Louise pulled a blouse from the trunk and examined it. "This will do," she said with assurance. "I'll sew the edges of two seams together so the neckline extends above your collarbone. Do you have a needle and thread in the trunk?"

The palace chapel's bell tolled the hour, its gentle rhythm seeping under the door. Estelle bowed her head, thinking of her family. At this hour, the children would be assembling in the courtyard with their mother's French maid, learning songs and stories. Maman had put the maid to work as a tutor for them all when they arrived in Rhodes, worried they would lose their grasp of their native tongue.

*I'm French. I'll never be one of you, no matter how you dress me. Soon I'll be sailing back to Rhodes, to my family, to everything and everyone I've left behind.*

Estelle found her sewing kit in the trunk. "Afterward, will you take me to the library? I've written a letter to my parents that needs to go with a courier to Rhodes."

Louise pushed open a door and Estelle followed her through it into a large, airy chamber.

The walls were lined with shelves filled with leather-bound volumes. The ceiling itself was painted sapphire blue and spangled with gold stars. Several tables were occupied by men bent over open volumes, some of them with quills in hand, inkpots at the ready.

"You can leave now," Estelle told her friend, smiling. "I can see this won't be a quick inquiry—for I love books, and I have not seen so many in one place since I was a young girl, when my father worked for a count in Auvergne."

"Did the count have a library to rival this one?" Louise asked.

"Nearly as grand. His lady wife, the countess, needed help writing letters when her hands grew stiff with cold in the winter. I was invited into their library to help her on many occasions."

"A child serving as scribe for a countess?" Louise raised an eyebrow.

"I had a particular talent with a quill and ink early on."

The reason she'd been taught to write at a young age was painful to recall, and a hard lump ached in her throat as the memories flooded her. When one of Estelle's younger siblings had died, Maman's grief had been all-consuming. She'd retreated to her bed, barely eating or drinking, engulfed by sorrow.

At his wit's end, Papa had taken Estelle and Étienne to the mews every day to escape the atmosphere of gloom in their home. Étienne had reveled in learning the care and feeding of falcons. For her part, Estelle had been mesmerized by her father's writing desk and his hobby of crafting quills from the birds' feathers.

She swallowed. "My father relied on me to transcribe his notes and write correspondence."

"You must have an endless well of patience." Louise shook her head. "I hate writing. Each time I put a quill to paper, the ink smears or I break the nib. When you are finished here, come to my chamber and I'll arrange some fittings for you with my seamstress."

Estelle bade her friend farewell. She turned her gaze back to the books, her fingertips tingling. She longed to run her hands over each volume, pull them from the shelves one by one.

A man dressed in a pale blue silk tunic walked in her direction. Estelle recognized him as the notary from her journey to Nicosia.

"Mademoiselle! We meet again." His French was smooth and fluid.

"Signor Derian, *bonjour*."

"What brings you to the library?"

"I've a letter to send to my parents in Rhodes Town, and I was told couriers could be found here."

Signor Derian nodded. "A Catalan fleet leaves Limassol in a fortnight for Rhodes. I'm gathering correspondence to bring to the ship's captain before he sails." He held out a hand. "The letter?"

She handed him the square of sealed linen paper. Its contents were brief. She had described the odd world of the Cypriot court, her idleness and lonely existence, and her desire to return to Rhodes. On the face of it, she'd written "Cédric de Montavon, master falconer, palace of the grand master, Rhodes Town."

Signor Derian studied the lettering. "Signora Rosso did not lie," he said. "You write as well as a royal scribe."

"Thank you."

"Where did you receive such training?"

"My father, at first. Then I practiced on my own."

He studied her with sympathy. "I'm sure it is difficult to be separated from your family, to be surrounded by people who don't speak your language."

She fought an impulse to confide in him, to share her troubles.

Signora Rosso's words echoed in her ears.

*Trust no one.*

"I'm surprised to hear you speak French so well when so few people here do," she said.

There. Now he would have to speak about himself, not her.

"Not many of the notaries here can speak it as it's meant to be spoken." He tilted his head toward his companion, who was immersed in his work, oblivious to their conversation. "I'm Armenian. My people are more entwined with the French heritage of the court than most on this island, and I've a brother who lives in Provence. Have you seen our quarter near the marketplace in Nicosia? The most beautiful streets in the city, some say."

She nodded. "I saw the gates when I was in town for market day."

"Ah! How did you like the excursion?" he asked. "I often see the princess's ladies at the marketplace, buying treats and trinkets."

"I enjoyed it very much until a brawl put an end to our amusements."

"That must have frightened you."

"It did," she admitted. "But I was pleased to have an outing all the same."

Speaking French was like drinking from the cool stream that fed the lake in Auvergne where she had grown up—a pure, delicious relief.

"Are we permitted—I mean, do you think I could . . ." Her gaze flicked to the books lining the walls.

"Read these books?" He chuckled. "By all means."

He tucked her letter into the purse at his waist and returned to his seat. Opening the leather-bound record book before him, he turned the pages under another man's watchful eye. They spoke quietly in the Cypriot dialect as they pored over sales, agreements, and contracts.

Such record books were familiar to Estelle because both her father and mother worked frequently with notaries. Papa for his endless purchases of falcons and all that was needed to sustain them; Maman for her fabric exporting enterprise.

The thoughts of her parents made tears well up again. She blinked them away. Perhaps now was not the time to sit and read in view of all these men. Sorrow seemed to strike at the worst moments lately, when she needed to put on a brave face.

Padding to the door, she slipped out, making for Louise's chamber.

She was nearly there when the steward's voice rang out in the corridor behind her. "Mademoiselle!"

"Yes, *kyrie?*"

He strode toward her, rummaging in a satchel at his waist.

"A letter has come for you."

Estelle stared at him in surprise. "For me?"

"A Hospitaller ship arrived in Limassol last night, and riders brought in the correspondence from Rhodes this morning." He thrust a square of paper at her and bustled off.

Back in her own chamber, Estelle went to the window and held the letter up to the light.

*Mademoiselle Estelle de Montavon. Royal Palace of Nicosia, Cyprus.*

Papa's hand, familiar and dear, had formed this script.

With a rush of anticipation, she broke the seal.

A tiny object fluttered to the floor from the folded page. Bending down, she realized it was a scrap of paper cut into the shape of a heart, stained pink with beet juice.

*Isabeau.*

She'd taught her small sister to craft such things not long ago.

Smiling, she returned her gaze to the page, devouring her father's words. When she reached the last line, her hand began to tremble. She sank to her knees, the words blurring on the page.

*No. No, Papa. This cannot be.*

A Hospitaller galley bound for France had gone down in a storm soon after it left Rhodes Town. Its hold had contained Maman's latest shipment of cloth of gold, camlet fabric, and silks destined for France. Much of the family's savings had been bound up in those fabrics, Papa wrote. After the shipwreck, he'd taken out a loan from the Florentine bank to make ends meet, but Estelle's salary as a tutor in the Cypriot court would be essential in the coming months. He concluded with instructions for entrusting coin with the Hospitaller couriers who regularly visited Nicosia.

*Dearest child, we need your earnings to help pay off this debt.*

The letter drifted to the floor. She stared unseeing at the pomegranate tree outside the window, ignoring the parakeets flitting from branch to branch. After they'd left France, her grandfather in Toulouse had sent the family money each summer. But he had died some months ago. Until now, his gifts of gold had allowed Papa to avoid becoming indebted to moneylenders.

A memory of the Kastellania, the Rhodes Town prison, rose unbidden in her mind. Papa had once been unjustly detained there, and it had nearly broken him. Would he be relegated to the same fate again if he could not repay his debt?

*Never.*

Bending to retrieve Papa's letter, Estelle folded it into a tiny square and stuffed it down the front of her bodice.

Her mind went to the men diligently copying texts in the library. Her talent with a quill was indisputable. And Signor Derian had once offered her work as a scribe. Perhaps he would take pity on her now, extend the offer once more. Would he even remember that conversation, the day Estelle arrived at the palace?

She steadied her breath and wiped her eyes.

She would cast aside her sorrow, relinquish her desire to escape the palace. She would make a place for herself in Cyprus, and earn the gold her family needed to avert financial disaster.

*Find Signor Derian, retrieve the letter you gave him for Papa, and ask him for work.*

Squaring her shoulders, Estelle took a deep breath and swept through the door.

# CHAPTER 13

Autumn 1457
Nicosia, Cyprus

SEVERAL WEEKS after Papa's troubling letter arrived, Estelle woke as usual to the sound of parakeets chattering in the pomegranate tree. She rose and spent a few moments admiring the purple silk gown a seamstress had delivered to her last night. She'd visited Louise's chamber a half-dozen times for fittings, and yesterday's had been the final one.

*Now I'll look like them. If only I could feel like a Cypriot, too. Perhaps the loneliness would ease.*

While she dressed, her thoughts strayed to the necklace. Louise would ask about it, as she always did. Despite her friend's encouragement, Estelle kept it locked in her trunk. The knowledge that her parents would not approve of the gift made her uneasy.

Since the day she'd received her family's urgent news, Estelle had adopted a routine that was beginning to feel comfortable. Each morning she went to the library to transcribe notes and copy pages from record books for Signor Derian; each evening she supped with Louise and other ladies of the court. She'd sent her first wages to Papa with a courier of the Knights Hospitaller and had made arrangements to send another bag of coin in a month's time.

As she had each morning since that day, she fell motionless for a moment. Bending her head, she murmured a prayer of thanks to all the saints for the Armenian notary's kindness. He'd not only remembered his offer of scribe work; he'd enthusiastically hired her the day she came to him seeking employment, blinking back tears, the words scraping against her throat. His calm, reassuring presence had given her the confidence to enter the library each morning since then and write with a steady hand.

As she adjusted her headwrap, Estelle's mind strayed to a familiar worry. Princess Charlotta had ignored her since they'd supped with Jacco. The princess spent most of her time attending to her mother, whose declining health was a subject of daily gossip among the courtiers. If Estelle never got the opportunity to befriend her, would she be dismissed from the court altogether? Now that she was earning gold, Estelle had to maintain her position as a scribe until Papa's debt was resolved.

The palace chapel's bells began to toll, interrupting her thoughts. Slipping a fresh fig into her purse, she went to the library. When she pushed open the door, she was surprised to see that none of the other scribes or notaries had arrived.

Instead of getting to work copying the water-stained record book Signor Derian had assigned to her earlier in the week, she approached the north wall, where books written in French were shelved.

Running her fingertips over the titles, Estelle selected a slim volume whose leather cover was stained by time and neglect. A faint gold leaf stamp decorated its face, but she could not make out the pattern.

"*Chronique des jours sombres,*" she read aloud from the title page.

*Chronicle of Dark Days*. Who had written this?

Intrigued, Estelle hunched over the book at one of the oak tables. The script was well-crafted but cramped, the words crowded together in neat, close lines. Reading French was like dancing, laughing, singing

—completely immersive. It took her far away from Cyprus. All the way back to the land of her birth.

*The Mamluks took the king captive twenty-seven days ago,* she read. *The countryside is scorched, fields trampled, homes reduced to ash. I have not cowered in fear during these long days. I am far too busy. Our fortress on the sea is strong and well provisioned, and we are ready to defend it.*

Estelle shivered, imagining the horrors of war. Who was this writer? Was the tale true, or a fabricated story?

She smoothed the page where someone had folded down a corner long ago. Papa had taught her never to mar the pages of a book, and whenever she copied falconry texts for him, she had taken great care to preserve the integrity of the paper or parchment.

"Poor book," she murmured aloud. "They haven't treated you well, have they?"

On the next page, the writer had drawn a three-leafed clover, a heart, and a fleur-de-lis, loosely grouped together in the upper left-hand corner, before continuing the narrative.

*We have secured all the kingdom's things of value, hidden them away. Some of the treasure is close, safe within these stone walls.*

The door swung open. Estelle glanced up to see Signor Derian enter the chamber. She slipped the book into her lap, feeling oddly protective of it.

"Mademoiselle." He shut the door behind him.

"Will you be working today, Signor Derian? I was beginning to wonder where everyone was."

His expression was tense. "I've your wages. And I've something else for you."

"My wages?" She shook her head. "You're not due to pay me for nearly a month, monsieur."

He smiled sadly and handed her a small bag of coin, then produced a note from the pouch at his waist. Its red seal was thick and elaborately stamped. As she accepted it, Estelle heard a flurry of voices in the corridor.

"You will need to find work with another notary, I'm afraid," Signor Derian said. "I won't be in court for some time."

"What's happened?"

He shook his head. "A sad affair. The queen's chamberlain was murdered by two Sicilian cutthroats."

"Her . . . her chamberlain? The man who is like a brother to her?"

"Yes, the very same."

She clamped her mouth shut, repressing a dozen more questions, and broke the note's seal. The words were written in Greek.

*Mademoiselle—I've left for Rhodes, and your stories of the place make me hopeful. Be so kind as to write me a letter of introduction for your father. With his help, I'll soon be hawking with the grand master. Though I regret leaving just when we were becoming acquainted, I know we will meet again soon. I'm afraid my sister will be hard to win over in the meantime, but you've already captured my affection. When I return and take my rightful place in Cyprus, you'll find nothing else matters. Yours, J.*

Below Jacco's elaborate initial was a crudely sketched crown.

Estelle read the lines again, her mouth growing dry.

*My rightful place . . .*

"I haven't seen Lord Jacco for weeks," she said slowly. "I thought he was on a hunting trip."

Signor Derian plucked the note from her grasp, then set out a quill, inkpot, and sheet of linen paper on the table. "Please write a note to your father. I must be on my way."

Estelle hesitated, thinking of the necklace, of Jacco's attentive behavior at his supper table. The truth was Jacco had been nothing but kind to her. There was no reason to refuse his request. She dipped the quill's nib into the inkpot and began to write.

Waiting for the ink to dry, she raised her gaze. "Why must you leave?"

His expression clouded. "I'm a friend to Lord Jacco. Now that he's angered the queen, it will be dangerous for my family to remain in Nicosia. With God's grace, we'll be back before too long."

"I wish you safe travels. And you have my gratitude, monsieur. The coin you've paid me has meant everything to my family."

The tension in his expression eased a bit at her words. He stowed her note in his satchel.

"You should return to your chamber at once, mademoiselle. Who knows what else might happen today?"

Estelle snatched up the little leather-bound book and followed Signor Derian out the door. He nodded a farewell and hurried away. Guards marched through the palace in pairs, their swords clanking at their sides. Hastening to her chamber, Estelle caught snippets of conversation from the courtiers streaming past.

"Princess Charlotta asked Jacco to avenge her husband's death," a woman nearby hissed to her male companion. "And he complied."

"The Bastard wants the throne for himself," he replied. "Woe to anyone standing in his way."

*I cannot believe this gossip. I will not.*

Estelle turned in mid-stride and raced to Louise's chamber. Louise would know the truth. After all, she had lived in this court her entire life. She was a trusted member of the princess's retinue.

But when she arrived there, the door was open and a servant was cleaning the fireplace.

"Where is Louise?" Estelle asked the woman.

The servant wiped her forehead with the back of a hand. "I've no idea. She was here last night, but this morning she'd vanished, along with her maid. All her things are gone, too."

"But that can't be . . ." Estelle trailed off. It was true. There was no trace of Louise's personal things. The silver tray where she kept her perfume, hairbrush, and other toiletries had vanished, and the trunk where she stored her clothing had disappeared, too.

The servant crossed herself. "This place will turn my hair white, by the saints."

Estelle's knees wobbled. She reached for the doorway to steady herself. "Louise is my friend," she murmured, more to herself than to the servant. "My only friend."

The woman spat in the hearth. "Then you must pray that no harm has come to her."

Estelle edged through the door, the woman's words echoing in her ears.

She rushed back in the direction she came, so overwhelmed by Louise's disappearance that she lost her way. Hurrying down an unfamiliar corridor, she turned a corner and found herself in the courtyard garden.

The black-clad princess and a small group of ladies in silks were gathered in the shade of a fig tree, heads bent together. They looked up as one when she came into view. Estelle sank into a curtsy.

"Your Grace."

"I have no need for a thief in my retinue." Princess Charlotta stared at her with haughty displeasure. "Remove yourself at once."

"What?" Estelle recoiled in astonishment. "Your Grace, I've stolen nothing."

"Louise sent me a note this morning," the princess countered. "You coveted her pearl-and-ruby necklace, and then you stole it."

"I did not, Your Grace," Estelle protested. "She lent me a gown and a headpiece, but no jewelry—"

"Lies," the princess cut in crisply. "You were seen entering her chamber several times recently, my servants tell me."

"For dress fittings, Your Grace."

*God help me, I'm being watched at all hours.*

"Do you have in your possession such a necklace?" the princess demanded.

"Yes," Estelle admitted. "But it was a gift. It's not Louise's. I can fetch it now and show you."

"A gift from whom?"

Estelle swallowed hard. Revealing the truth seemed dangerous, but what choice did she have? "From—from Lord Jacco."

The princess and her ladies stared aghast at Estelle as if she had just announced she had the plague.

"Another falsehood, and an audacious one at that," the princess said in a curt voice. "Where is Louise? I'll bring her before me. We shall have the truth from her lips—and from yours. If you continue to spew lies, you will not like the consequences, mademoiselle."

"But she's left, Your Grace. I went to her chamber just now, and all her things are gone."

"That's not true. It can't be." Even as she spoke, the princess's confident expression faded. "Where would she go?"

A man Estelle recognized as Sir Hector de Chivides, one of the barons in the king's council, strode into the courtyard and made straight for Princess Charlotta. He bowed.

"Your Grace."

"What is it, Sir Hector?" A note of annoyance flickered in her voice. "Where is my brother? We're to meet with my parents this afternoon."

"He left in the night. He and his guards scaled the city wall in the Armenian quarter, then rode for the sea. Word is he's sailing to Rhodes."

"Leaving me to confront my mother's fury alone." The princess's face paled. "You've heard the lie the gossips have spread. Now even Mamá believes I told Jacco to have her chamberlain murdered! I never did, I swear it. I only said I wished—"

"The king and queen grow impatient for their audience with you." A note of warning lurked in Sir Hector's deep voice. "Come."

Princess Charlotta's ladies closed in around her like a swarm of glittering bees. They followed in her wake, leaving Estelle alone under the drooping branches of the fig tree.

The princess turned. She pointed at Estelle, said something to the baron. He stood motionless a moment, staring at Estelle, then spoke to a pair of guards. The men split off from the group and marched to Estelle.

"You're to be confined in your chamber," one of them growled. "Come with us."

Though she was outside, she felt trapped below decks in a wildly pitching ship, at the mercy of a storm-tossed sea. She followed the guards through the palace, her legs dragging like lead weights, her breath shallow.

The door to her chamber shut behind her. Wood scraped against wood as it was barred from the outside.

What were the penalties for thievery in the kingdom of Cyprus? Would she be publicly flogged? Lose a hand? Be thrown in a dungeon? She shook her head in an effort to banish the panicked thoughts.

*I have the heart of a falcon.*

Estelle went to the window, eyes fixed on the blue sky above the courtyard. In her mind's eye, she took the shape of a peregrine launching into flight. Her powerful wings beat the air, propelling her over Nicosia to the sea, the golden hills and pale sand of the beaches falling into shadow. Higher and higher she flew, hurtling north to Rhodes on the wind, gliding away from Cyprus forever.

Staggering backward, she sank onto the bed. Such fantasies were useless. She had no hope of escape—and even if she could return to Rhodes, what help could she provide her family then? She pressed her fingers against her eyelids.

*Think. Think.*

She must clear her name, then find a new source of coin.

It was the only way forward.

# CHAPTER 14

Autumn 1457
Nicosia, Cyprus

THAT NIGHT, Estelle was completely alone. Not even Antonia came to her door. There was nothing to eat in her chamber. A half-full pitcher of watered wine was her only sustenance.

*How long will they leave me here? What would Papa do? Maman?*

Her father was a patient man. But Maman was impulsive, guided by emotions. Which was the better choice? To wait or to act?

She tried pounding on the door and calling for help. The guards outside silenced her with threatening shouts each time.

The next morning at dawn, she put on her underclothes, then tied the purple silk gown and a gauzy black headpiece into a bundle.

Carrying a stool to the window, she studied the courtyard for movement. Satisfied it was empty of servants and courtiers, she dropped the bundle over the windowsill. It landed with a soft thump on the ground below.

The pomegranate tree's limbs extended so close to her chamber they rustled against the shutters at night. She studied them with critical eyes, gauging their strength.

As a young girl, she'd followed Étienne up oak and apple trees in Auvergne, his steady voice tempting her with the promise of an abandoned bird's nest filled with pale blue eggs or the sight of clouds shaped like dragons.

She stepped from the stool to the windowsill. Longing for the agility of a child, she took hold of the thickest branch and pitched her weight forward.

The branch sagged under her, but did not break. She clung to it fiercely, heart thundering.

*Don't look down. Don't panic.*

With slow, painstaking movements, she edged toward the trunk. Slithering from branch to branch, she descended the tree with little grace. Finally, she reached solid ground.

She stood catching her breath for a moment, then dressed quickly in the weak dawn light. With trembling hands, she adjusted the black headpiece. From the back at least, she would look like a Cypriot. Perhaps she could make it to her destination without being detained.

It was not much to hold on to, but it gave her a measure of courage.

Estelle moved through the palace silent as an owl, staying in the shadows. When she neared the kitchens, she retrieved some coins from her purse.

The smell of frying onions and sausages made her stomach rumble. Approaching a servant who had just emerged from the kitchens carrying a tray laden with flatbread, cheese, and fruit, she opened her palm, displaying a flash of silver.

"Will you give me some of that bread and show me to Sir Hector de Chivides's chamber?" She sweetened her request with a pleading smile.

If he had the power to imprison her, perhaps he also had the power to set her free. At the very least the man was a Latin, like her—and the only member of the king's council who had ever acknowledged her existence.

The woman balanced the tray on a nearby chest and accepted the coins. Nodding at her basket of bread, she said, "Take two pieces and follow me."

Estelle gulped down mouthfuls of the warm, rosemary-scented flatbread as they walked, her hunger dissipating with each stride. When they came to an intersection with another corridor, the servant paused. Estelle could just make out the form of an animal at the end of the corridor.

"Sir Hector's chambers are the last doors on the right. His hound guards the place. I'm afraid to go down there, myself."

The hound rose and turned in their direction, studying them in silence, then settled on its haunches. It was a massive animal, with a thick neck and long legs. Estelle bit her lip, considering him, then summoned her resolve.

She and Étienne had once been Papa's little shadows, trailing their father through the Count de Chambonac's mews, stables, and kennels. They'd learned much at his knee, not least of which was the right way to approach an unfamiliar hound.

"Can I have another piece of bread, please?" Estelle pitched her voice very low.

The servant acquiesced, then hefted her tray and disappeared.

Estelle tossed a bit of bread toward the hound. "Here's a treat for you, fine fellow."

A low growl reverberated through the air. After nosing the bread, the hound snatched it up. She tore off another chunk, moving cautiously forward.

"Such a strong, handsome boy you are." She threw it in his direction.

The hound gobbled the bread, then gave Estelle an expectant look.

She scattered the last crumbs behind her and rapped on the door, praying Sir Hector was within. The hound snuffled around her feet, licking the marble floor.

"Yes?" a deep voice rang out.

Relief flooded her. "Sir Hector, I bring a message about the Knights Hospitaller in Rhodes."

The door opened with a creak. "What's this?" he asked, a towel draped over his shoulder. He wore a shirt and hose, but hadn't yet donned a doublet. His eyes narrowed as he studied her. "You were accused of theft by the princess."

"Falsely accused. I am a woman of noble birth, the daughter of the master falconer to the Grand Master of the Knights Hospitaller." Her voice gathered strength as she spoke. "Lord de Milly would be greatly displeased to learn I've been imprisoned here with no food or drink."

"How did you get past the guards?"

"I climbed down the pomegranate tree in the courtyard," she said flatly.

His eyes dropped to the hound, whose tail had begun to wag. "And you somehow charmed my hound. Continue."

"I know you are a man of honor, Sir Hector. That's why I've come to you. As an ally of the knights yourself and a champion of the Latin cause, you will want to hear what I have to say."

He shifted his weight, considering her words. Then he waved her inside his parlor. "Be quick about it. I've an audience with the king at eight bells."

A manservant with a doublet in his arms eyed her from the bedchamber doorway.

"That can wait." Sir Hector dismissed the man and turned to her expectantly. "Well? What is your message?"

"Firstly, I am no thief. I should not be punished for a crime I did not commit. Secondly, if you wish for news of Lord Jacco's stay in Rhodes Town, I can get it for you. He intends to befriend my father in order to gain access to the grand master's ear. The council should know my well-being is of particular interest to Grand Master de Milly, for he and my father are great friends. And because I've served as scribe to Lord de Milly for many years."

That last claim was a lie, yet it rolled easily off her tongue.

Pulling a sheet of folded linen paper from her purse, she held it up.

"It's a recipe to cure a common ailment in hawks and falcons, my lord," she said. "I wrote it from memory last night. I have dozens more recipes at the tip of my tongue. In Rhodes Town, I kept all the records for the grand master's mews."

This, at least, was partially true. In Rhodes, she'd transcribed her father's notes each evening, rendering them legible.

Sir Hector did not look impressed. "The Bastard is free to visit Rhodes as long as he likes. I've no doubt he will attempt to charm the knights. Indeed, I'm quite sure they'll find him amusing. But he will not inherit the crown; his sister will. And as for your scribing talent, it means nothing to me."

*Try a different tack. Quickly.*

Estelle held his gaze. "I was invited here for a reason, Sir Hector. I was meant to be a tutor to Princess Charlotta. She wants nothing to do with me, yet I need a salary. That's why I've come to you. I must work, my lord."

He crossed his arms over his chest, a frown furrowing his brow.

"My value to this court is twofold," she went on, emboldened by his silence. "I can teach your future queen French, the one language that will help her forge strong connections to the Latin world—the knights and the kingdoms of the west." She brandished the recipe again. "And as you see, I am the equal to any of your royal scribes. Use me for the talents I possess, Sir Hector. There is a place for me in this court, I promise you."

He studied her for a long moment. Then he crossed to a small table holding a pitcher and two cups. He poured a thin stream of wine into both cups and handed her one.

"I agree that the princess must learn French. In fact, it was the council's idea to invite you to join the court. We learned of you from your father's falconer friend Michel Pelestrine. King Jean approved the plan at my urging. After Princess Charlotta married Prince João, I realized she would never learn Portuguese and he would never learn Greek. His French was fluent, though. We needed a French-born tutor for the princess so she could communicate with her husband. But now he's dead and she's back at her mother's side, a thoroughly Greek girl. With an all-too-apparent dislike of you, mademoiselle."

"Why have I been left to fend for myself?" Anger hardened Estelle's voice. "You say it was the council's idea to bring me here, yet you all ignore me!"

He sipped from his cup and indicated she should follow suit.

*Don't trust him or his wine.*

She pretended to sip.

"Recent events have proven quite challenging. Prince João's death. Then the chamberlain's." He sipped again. "Securing a new betrothal for Princess Charlotta has been our most pressing matter."

"Who has been chosen?" she asked.

"The princess's cousin, Louis of Savoy."

"Savoy?" Estelle repeated in surprise.

Her beloved brother Étienne had traveled to the Duchy of Savoy at age twelve to join the household as a page. He'd risen in the ranks of service to the duke as the years passed; he now served the family as a knight.

"The House of Savoy is French, my lord," she said. "Clearly, the princess needs a French tutor, now more than ever. She needs *me*, Sir Hector."

An infuriating look of amusement took hold of the nobleman's face. "And yet she believes you to be a thief."

"If we could just find Louise, this matter would be resolved—"

Sir Hector raised a hand. "Your accuser has not vanished. She's gone to join the household of Lord Jacco's mother."

*Louise in the service of Cropnose? She never would have gone willingly.*

"But why?"

Sir Hector shrugged. "The Bastard has formed an attachment to her, I suppose. He sees the world as a chessboard of his own making, mademoiselle. In his view, we're all pieces to be shuffled around at his whim. He likely told her to stir discord between you and the princess. And if that is true, he's succeeded."

"Will the princess be informed of this game of his? Or is she to believe I'm a thief forevermore?"

He chuckled. "She'll be told. Whether it changes her opinion in the end is up to you."

*An impossible task. How on earth will I ever begin to find favor with Princess Charlotta?*

The palace chapel's bell began to toll.

"Ah! Eight bells." Sir Hector went to the door and poked his head out into the corridor. After a murmured conversation, he turned back to Estelle. "For the time being, you'll continue to work in the library as a scribe. Speak to the steward about your salary. My valet will accompany you. Good day, mademoiselle."

The hound whined as she exited the chamber door, and she stroked his velvety ear, whispering a farewell.

Following the valet through the palace to the steward's quarters, Estelle felt as unsteady on her legs as she had the day she arrived in Cyprus.

They passed several courtiers, all of whom gave her curious glances. She forced herself to meet the eyes of each passerby.

*They cannot harm me. I belong here now.*

She spooled out the calming thoughts with each step she took, imagining the words taking shape above her head, as solid and graceful as if she'd hand-lettered them on a page.

The valet rapped on the steward's door. When it opened, he exchanged a few words with the man. Then the steward looked her in the eyes. For the first time since her arrival, she had the feeling he truly saw her.

"It seems we overlooked the matter of your salary, mademoiselle." He beckoned her forward. "Come in."

# CHAPTER 15

Spring 1458
Nicosia, Cyprus

A BIRD with gleaming blue feathers settled on a windowsill, cocking its head at Estelle. She looked up from her work, watching it preen in the sunlight. It was a bee-eater, she was fairly certain. Louise had told her that last summer, when they were walking in the courtyard arm in arm one afternoon. During the first bloom of their friendship.

One of the other scribes cleared his throat, startling the bird. Wings beating the air, it vanished into the branches of a fig tree.

Estelle weighed her quill in her hand. It had the look of a saker falcon's tail feather. Her father favored those when he cut and trimmed his quills by the fire on a winter's evening. He went through them quickly, for he wrote with a heavy hand. She'd often found piles of discarded quills by his writing desk, their nibs crushed. Her thoughts strayed to the falconer Gabriel Bayoumi. Did he make his own quills, too? The king possessed hundreds of hawks and falcons. If Gabriel had the inclination, he could make as many quills as he wanted.

She dipped the quill into the inkpot and got back to work. She had ten more pages to copy in this record book before she could leave today. Then another week before she could collect her wages and send them off to Rhodes with an agent of the knights.

In his last letter, Papa had told her it would take another year at least to pay off his debts. If she could just befriend Princess Charlotta, that year would pass in the company of women. She would speak French all day long. An overwhelming urge for companionship racked her, sudden as a gust of wind. She lifted the quill from the page, fearing she'd smear the ink.

*Stop daydreaming about things that will never come to pass. Steady your hand.*

All winter, she'd spent her days copying manuscripts in this library and thinking about people who weren't there. Papa. Maman. Étienne, Jean-Philippe, Isabeau. Her friend Anica in Rhodes. Gabriel. Papa's friend, the mysterious master falconer of Cyprus, Michel Pelestrine.

*Will I ever meet him?*

Then there were the people she tried not to think about. Signor Derian. Louise. Jacco. Signora Rosso. They invaded her thoughts so relentlessly she gave up one day and invited them in.

*Make yourselves comfortable in my mind. Can I offer you refreshment? I beg you, don't do anything to unnerve me, not when I'm scribing.*

She formed a perfect, sinuous S. Dipped the quill again.

The door opened and shut with a soft thump. Estelle did not take her eyes off her work.

"Mademoiselle de Montavon," a man said.

She put down the quill. "Yes?"

"Sir Hector calls for you. You're wanted in the king's study."

The walls of the king's study were covered with tapestries depicting scenes of the hunt; the floor was made of rose-colored stone set in pleasing patterns. And the windows opened to a lush courtyard, a private world Estelle had never known existed.

The king sat surrounded by his council at a polished walnut desk.

He was even heavier than she remembered, his eyes dark pinpricks in his bloated face. A silver platter before him was piled with spun-sugar concoctions.

Sir Hector nodded to her. They'd barely spoken since her brash appearance at his chambers last autumn. But he'd been true to his word; she worked steadily as a scribe now. As the steward was quick to remind her, she also lived in a well-appointed chamber, had her own maid, and never lacked for food or drink. Each month, she sent home a bag of coin on a Hospitaller ship. She'd had a second gown made, in emerald-green silk this time, and had grown used to dressing in the Cypriot style. If it weren't for the fact that she'd been shunned by the princess and her ladies ever since Louise's false accusation, court life would be satisfying indeed.

"Ah! Here she is, our young French mademoiselle." The king gestured her forward, popping a treat into his mouth. A dusting of powdered sugar settled on his beard.

"Your Grace." She sank into a deep curtsy.

*Will I finally be a tutor to the princess after all?*

He swept a ring-laden hand in a circle. "Have you met my advisors? My most loyal men?"

"Sir Hector and I are acquainted, Your Grace."

The other men of the council studied her with cool, shiny eyes. She'd come to think of them as a conspiracy of ravens, clad in black and bearing somber tidings. One of them, a gangly man with sharp features and a downturned mouth, cleared his throat.

"Indeed, Sir Hector has taken an interest in your future, mademoiselle," he said. "As have I."

"Yes, Lord Chimi," said the king. "You've been most helpful of late. And so has my dear friend Lord Podocataro. A more loyal courtier never walked the earth."

A barrel-chested man stepped forward. His teeth were yellowing, and there were deep lines around his mouth and eyes. He reached for Estelle's hand and bowed over it, pressing his lips to her skin.

"How enchanting to meet you, mademoiselle." His French was barely comprehensible.

Estelle forced herself to remain still.

"Do you enjoy sweet treats, mademoiselle?" His question resonated through the chamber, floating up to the wood-paneled ceiling like a curling plume of smoke.

A servant approached with a tray and offered it to her. She removed her hand from Lord Podocataro's grasp and selected a sugared almond.

"Please eat it. Do not be shy." Lord Podocataro and the other men watched her, waiting until she placed the nut in her mouth.

She chewed and swallowed, gazing around uneasily.

*Am I being poisoned?*

The king chewed another treat with his mouth open, smacking his lips.

"What if I told you there is a place on this island where sugar syrup flows like water?" Lord Podocataro's voice dropped to a low, intimate murmur. "A place where you will find enough sweetness to satisfy every craving."

*What does he mean by this?*

She sought Sir Hector's gaze, hoping for reassurance.

"Lord Podocataro has honored you, mademoiselle, by considering you for his bride." Sir Hector's expression was inscrutable. "And the king himself has offered a substantial dowry."

The air escaped from Estelle's lungs. She stood very still, sure the men could hear the battering of her heart against her rib cage.

*Dear God, this cannot be. A betrothal?*

She looked wildly around the room, searching for an escape. But she was surrounded by a wall of men.

*Breathe. Think. Fight.*

"You are fortunate, mademoiselle," King Jean said airily. "Lord Podocataro is an esteemed citizen of Cyprus, a loyal servant of the crown, and a wealthy man. His sugar farm near Paphos is rivaled only by the knights' plantation at Kolossi."

"My father's permission is required for a betrothal, Your Grace. After all, I am not a ward of this court."

A collective gasp went up from the council.

"You are being given a greater honor than any court lady of your rank could hope for." The king scowled. "Show your gratitude, if you please."

Signora Rosso's words on that long-ago sea journey pounded in Estelle's brain. *If you're lucky, the king will give you to one of his favorites.*

She raised her chin, ignoring the heat on her cheeks.

"It is up to my father to decide if this honor will be mine, Your Grace."

Lord Chimi gave her a scathing look. "Lord Podocataro's family has been loyal to the crown for generations. There is no man in the kingdom who would make a better husband for you."

"My lord, this is a matter that requires negotiation. My father must be notified at once." Estelle's mouth was so dry she could barely push the words out.

"Mademoiselle, I grow tired of your protestations." The king's voice rose in annoyance. "You have been treated with the utmost generosity in my court. Of course, my council has informed your father of this great honor. We await his response, but I've no doubt he will give the arrangement his blessing."

The king extended his hand, waiting for her to kiss his ring. When she hesitated, Sir Hector loudly cleared his throat.

Reluctantly, she bent over the king's outstretched hand.

Lord Chimi smiled thinly. "Good girl. Once the arrangements are made to Lord Podocataro's satisfaction, you will sign the marriage contract."

She straightened her shoulders. "With all due respect, my lords, I cannot sign anything without my father's permission."

A thick silence settled over the chamber. The hostility radiating from the king's council was palpable.

Estelle's future husband studied her with shrewd dark eyes. His gaze ran up and down her body, assessing, judging. Though he was old enough to be her grandfather, he had an assurance to his stance that gave him an air of command. The idea of him possessing her, forcing her into the marriage bed, made the skin on the back of her neck prickle.

*I would rather swim back to Rhodes than marry you.* She pressed her mouth into a thin line, silencing the insolent words.

"You will not regret our union, mademoiselle. I vow it."

She backed out of the king's presence, her heart writhing like a water-starved fish.

She could recall nothing of the long walk back to her chamber. Once inside, she barred the door and leaned against it, her pulse roaring in her ears. The urge to weep nearly overwhelmed her, but she forced away the tears.

*Think, don't cry.*

This betrothal could never go forward. Papa would not approve. She would write him at once, send the letter with a Hospitaller agent. And she would seek out Sir Hector, plead her case. He had shown her sympathy once. Surely, he could do it again. If he refused to help her and the betrothal proceeded, there would be only one solution.

Escape.

Estelle sought out Sir Hector at mass in the palace chapel the next morning. He usually lingered after the service to chat with other members of the king's household for at least a few moments.

She did not listen to a word of the mass. She twisted her fingers together, rehearsing her words. Though she usually sat in one of the pews farthest from the door, this time she sat in the last row, next to the aisle, ready to spring up the moment he passed.

Several of the princess's ladies sat in the row across from her. She ignored their sidelong glances and whispers. The princess herself was absent. She usually attended Greek Orthodox services with her mother at the monastery.

Breathing in the aromas of incense and beeswax, Estelle tried to calm her mind. When mass ended and Sir Hector strolled past her down the aisle, she rose and moved quickly to his side.

"My lord," she murmured.

He glanced at her, eyes narrowed. "What is it, mademoiselle?"

"Why did Lord Podocataro choose me for his bride? I've no title, no lands, no property."

"Where is your gratitude, mademoiselle?" he demanded. "We've secured you a great honor with this arrangement."

"I am simply attempting to understand how this betrothal plan came about."

"Lord Podocataro has dipped into his own coffers many times to support the crown." Sir Hector leaned closer, his voice hard and precise. "His household is filled with bastard sons, but no legitimate heirs. When we learned he has always coveted a Frenchwoman in his bed, we naturally thought of you. If Lord Podocataro sires an heir with you, mademoiselle, you'll be the most favored wife on Cyprus. Dripping with jewels. From what I hear, your family relies on your salary. With this marriage, you can pay off your father's debts for good. Think on it—and trouble me no further with your complaints."

He turned away.

Estelle sagged against a marble column, steadying herself. Several ladies of the queen's retinue stood nearby, studying her with curiosity. They were part of the contingent that had moved to Cyprus after Constantinople fell to the Sultan of Turkey several years ago, and though they never attended Latin mass, they often appeared afterward for the social hour. She felt the weight of their judgment, saw the disdain in their eyes. No matter how she dressed, no matter how beautifully she spoke Greek, she would always be a Latin interloper in this court.

She took a breath and stood tall.

*I'll find a courier for my letter to Papa today. But how long can I wait for his answer?*

# CHAPTER 16

Spring 1458
Nicosia, Cyprus

ANTONIA BUSTLED into Estelle's chamber a few days later bursting with gossip. "Lord Jacco is back from Rhodes. Have you heard?" She set a tray of bread and fruit down on the table with a thump. "His men killed the Viscount of Nicosia as soon as they arrived on Cypriot soil, and now the high court is deciding his fate."

From her perch on the bed, Estelle took that in with a measure of skepticism. Antonia did like a good story. She picked up her hairbrush. "Who told you this?"

"The steward. He said to carry on with our work as if nothing had changed, but I've never seen so many guards patrolling the palace. Lord Jacco brought a great many soldiers and valets with him. People talk of them attacking the queen! You know how he hates her."

Estelle dropped the brush on the bedcovers, anticipation rushing through her. Perhaps with this new crisis in court, the king and his council would forget her impending betrothal.

"When will the high court make its decision?"

Antonia rolled her eyes. "It doesn't matter what they decide. Lord Jacco appeared in the palace this morning and went straight to the king's chambers. I heard him laughing as he strode along the corridor; the steward saw him embrace his father the moment he entered the royal apartments. When he left here, he told the steward he'd be back tomorrow to plan a hunt with the king. He can do no wrong in King Jean's eyes; that's the truth of it."

Estelle barely heard the servant's final words. "Back tomorrow?" she repeated. "What time, did he say?"

Antonia gave her a knowing look. "The queen's pain keeps her up all night, and she sleeps until noon these days. He'll come in the morning, I warrant. He'll have his father's full attention that way. Such a handsome man, Lord Jacco is, with a smile that could blind the sun." She winked. "You've fallen under his spell, too, haven't you, mademoiselle? Many in the court could say the same."

Estelle kept a neutral expression. "Braid and pin my hair, please. I have something to discuss with Lord Jacco, as it happens. When he arrives at the palace tomorrow, fetch me from the library."

Smirking, Antonia reached for the hairbrush.

The next morning, Estelle sat fidgeting in the library, unable to focus on her work. Two scribes sat at a table near the courtyard window, talking in low tones about expenses and salaries. When Antonia appeared in the doorway, Estelle nearly knocked over the inkpot in her haste to leave the chamber.

"He's with the king now," Antonia told her as they hurried through the corridors. "I don't know how you'll get a moment to speak with him, for a crowd has gathered near the king's apartments. Can't tell his enemies from his friends, not these days. They're all curious, that's certain."

Estelle stood at the edge of the crowd, smoothing her skirts. "Thank you, Antonia. You may go."

"You'll tell me if I miss anything interesting, won't you, made-moiselle?"

"Of course."

As Antonia reluctantly trudged off, Estelle fixed her gaze on the courtiers. Sidling closer to a pair of men she recognized as members of the king's council, she strained to overhear their conversation.

"Sir Hector's to be Viscount of Nicosia now," one said. "No one hates the Bastard more than he does. And yet he went to Lord Jacco and begged him to put in a good word with the king."

The other man let out a sharp exhalation. "I suppose I should go to the archbishop's palace and grovel to the Bastard myself. Who knows what he could do for me?"

Estelle absorbed their words with a growing sense of determination. What if she did the same? Lord Jacco already liked her. He could influence the king on her behalf.

*This idea of betrothal to Lord Podocataro could be dissolved with a few words from him.*

She threaded her way through the assembled courtiers, intent on reaching the front of the group. If Jacco spied her upon leaving his father's apartments, he would surely engage her in conversation. After all, he'd gone to Rhodes with her letter of introduction to Papa. Her father had written that Lord Jacco had participated in several hawking expeditions there during the past several months.

The doors to the king's apartments opened, and several guards and valets spilled out. Jacco was not among them. Some of the assembled courtiers groaned in disappointment.

"Where is Lord Jacco?" one woman cried.

A valet paused in mid-step. "Even his lordship needs refuge from this busy court from time to time. Trouble him no further today. The queen is very ill, and Lord Jacco is deeply troubled by her pain."

The council members near Estelle made sounds of indignation.

"No one hates the queen more than the Bastard," one of them griped. "Her pain brings him mirth, not sorrow."

Estelle wheeled. If Jacco truly needed a refuge, perhaps he'd gone to the garden courtyard where they'd first met. He had described it that day as a beloved retreat.

She walked as fast as she could, her silken skirts whispering over the stone floor. In the garden, she went straight to the fig tree.

Jacco stood surrounded by attendants in the shade of the tree, his white silk tunic immaculate. His voice assailed her ears, loud and aggrieved.

"What do you mean, no camels? I'll spend two hundred ducats from my own purse. What's a hunt without camels to carry our tents?"

Estelle pressed a hand against her breastbone, trying to slow her heart. Hope and foreboding mingled in her mind.

Jacco fell silent when he recognized her. "Is that you, mademoiselle? How elegant you've become, dressed like a Cypriot maiden."

"My lord." She curtsied, smiling. "You've returned from Rhodes."

He beckoned her forward. "Those knights know how to make a man feel welcome."

"Papa told me you enjoyed his hawking expeditions in the Rodini Valley." She forced herself to speak in a bright, conversational tone. "I'm glad my letter of introduction was helpful."

He grinned. "A good fellow, your father. I saw how easily he speaks with the grand master, and something struck me." Jacco's gaze grew serious. "If I spoke better French, I could have Lord de Milly's ear, too."

*Now. Now is the moment. Speak.*

"I could be your tutor, my lord. It would be easily done. You're so intelligent, a quick study. You'll speak excellent French in no time, just like my father and Lord de Milly."

"Clever girl. You're far more valuable as a French tutor for me than as a broodmare for old Podocataro."

Estelle grew very still. So he had already heard of the plan.

"The betrothal has been forced upon me, my lord. My father has not given his permission for the marriage, but Sir Hector and the other barons will not let the matter rest."

Jacco stayed quiet, considering her with an appraising gaze.

One of his attendants spoke into the silence. "If the mademoiselle must marry, there are many other French speakers in Nicosia who can teach you, my lord."

Jacco scoffed. "They claim to speak French, but it's garbled and strange, an old way of talking. It's not like hers." He pointed at Estelle. "Or Lord de Milly's. I need to speak that kind of French to be treated like an equal by the knights or any other ally in the West."

He dismissed his attendants, then took her hand. She allowed him to pull her closer, feeling like a fish on a line.

"Poor little mademoiselle. You would be miserable in old Podocataro's bed. Your beauty would be wasted on him. He can barely see."

"Perhaps you could tell that to the king," she suggested. "He would listen to you, my lord. Then I would be free to teach you French each day from now until your fluency exceeds mine."

Jacco laughed. "Is that a promise?"

He raised her hand to his lips and brushed the tip of each finger against his mouth, never taking his eyes from hers.

Estelle's breath stilled. She nodded slowly.

"Then it shall be done. Podocataro will have to find another bride."

"Thank you, my lord." She bowed her head, desperate to break their gaze.

*What have I just agreed to?*

How quickly fortune's wheel spun when powerful men turned their attention upon her.

"It's decided, then. We shall meet tomorrow under this very fig tree for our first lesson. Mark my words, you shall be paid well for your instruction." He relinquished her hand and rummaged in his purse. "I do have one condition. You must wear the gift I gave you each time we meet. Is the necklace still in your possession?"

Ducats dropped from his fingers and clinked together in her cupped hands, cooling her skin.

"Yes." She swallowed. "But the barons will be angry about this. The betrothal was their idea."

A bitter smile curved his mouth. "Worry not. The barons will soon be occupied by far more urgent matters. The queen's health, in particular. The poor woman is in dreadful condition."

The malice in his voice reverberated in the air between them. Estelle shrank back, repulsed, as his face contorted like a grotesque death mask.

"Sir Hector and the rest of the Latin council claim I hate our queen, but that's a lie." He managed to sound both offended and dismissive at the same time. "She and I both have Greek blood and Greek pride. Once she's gone—unless someone's brave enough to stop them—those dried-up vultures will banish every Greek in the court and turn this kingdom back to Latin ways."

"Who could stop them?" She couldn't help herself. The words just tumbled out.

Jacco tapped a finger on his chest. "I think you know."

# CHAPTER 17

Spring 1458
St. Hilarion Castle, Cyprus

GABRIEL RUBBED the cypress-wood hutch with linseed oil until it shone. When the task was done, he wiped his brow with a sleeve. He'd been working nonstop in dusty, hot conditions since dawn. A movement near the door caught his eye. Turning, he saw a stable boy who often hung around the mews.

"Run and fetch me some water," he called. "I'll let you help with the afternoon feeding later."

Quick as a hare, the boy loped off to do his bidding. Gabriel made a habit of looking out for the youngsters in the mews and stables. His memories of being shipped off as a page for the knights at their fortress of Kolossi were still raw. He'd been barely twelve and small for his age. No one had abused him there, but no one had been kind either. That's why he always went out of his way to treat these boys as little brothers.

Kolossi. A strange, lonely place on a windswept plain overlooking the sea. Dominated by its monstrous sugar mill, where the canes cut down by slaves were processed into syrup and powdered sugar. He had been betwixt and between during his time there. Not a nobleman's son groomed for knighthood, as some pages were. Yet he'd had some advantages. Though he was a bastard, his father's status as a wealthy man and long-standing agent of the order had given him more standing than most boys of illegitimate birth. And his language skills made him valuable to the knights, many of whom were French.

He hadn't come into his growth until he was sixteen. Within a few seasons, he shot up in height, grew broad in the chest and shoulders. It was then that the sergeant who supervised him at Kolossi decided he'd make a fine guard and sent him off to train with a sword and shield. By that time, he'd nearly forgotten what it was like to be greeted with affection by a loved one, to share a confidence. He'd honed the skills of impassive observation he'd developed during his early years, watching his mother navigate life as a slave and being helpless to protect her.

But the emotions boiling under the surface had grown hotter with each passing year. He'd fought them off with every scrap of willpower he possessed. Feelings were dangerous; reacting to them could bring disaster. He'd seen it happen. Worse, he'd made it happen.

The longer he worked as a falconer, the better he became at controlling his feelings. And he genuinely enjoyed reporting to Michel Pelestrine, a just and fair man. So he was content here, in this rambling castle overlooking the impossibly blue sea.

And yet.

His thoughts strayed to the young woman Estelle, to her golden-brown eyes, her confident voice telling him she was her father's scribe. She knew things he knew. About falcons and how to handle them, how to heal them. What other woman in Cyprus possessed such knowledge? Perhaps that was why he couldn't get her out of his thoughts. His mind lingered on her faint floral scent. The way she moved through the world, graceful and determined.

Would he ever marry? He'd not given the idea much thought, in truth. But something about Estelle made him think of a shared future. What would life be like with a woman like her at his side?

The idea made his heart pump a little faster. Then he shook his head, chuckling at the absurdity of it.

What could he possibly offer a woman in marriage, other than his love? He had nothing. Even though falconers were not taxed and incurred much envy from the king's other servants because of it, his salary was modest. He owned no property or land. He often slept in the mews to tend to sickly raptors.

"A foolish notion," he muttered, shaking his head as the boy trotted up with a leather water gourd.

"My thanks." Gabriel winked at the little fellow, then drank deeply.

By God, the water here in the mountains tasted good. Cold and fresh. He offered the gourd to the boy. "You?"

The boy looked sheepish. "I already had some."

"Good." Gabriel smiled. "There's plenty more where that came from."

The boy examined the oiled hutch. "Why are you cleaning everything?"

"Lord Jacco is back from Rhodes. He and the king are coming here for the spring hunt soon. We have much to do before they arrive."

The boy's eyes grew round. "What will they ask of me?"

"Nothing special," Gabriel assured him. "Just do what you always do, and stay out of Lord Jacco's way. Now off with you."

Before he could get back to work, the blare of a distant trumpet made him grow still. In a moment, the pounding of hooves outside the castle walls shook the earth.

Gabriel emerged from the mews, wiping his hands on a rag. The gates creaked open, and a stream of horsemen cantered into the keep, wearing the colors of the king.

"The queen is dead!" they shouted. "The queen is dead!"

Servants and courtiers gathered around the messengers. Hounds surged around their legs, barking with excitement.

Gabriel saw a rider who looked familiar. "What happened?"

The man dismounted, handing his reins to a stable hand, who led the horse to a water trough.

"The queen went to visit her favorite monastery not long ago, then her health took a turn for the worse. She died there. It's not a surprise; she was poorly for years."

This was true. The few times Gabriel had glimpsed the queen, she'd been reclining in a litter, carried from place to place by attendants. Though she could not walk, she still managed to dominate the court, bringing in her own courtiers from Morea in the north and pouring gold into the Greek churches and monasteries on the island. Gabriel still wasn't sure he believed the tale that she had bitten off her rival's nose when she discovered the woman in bed with King Jean. Jacco's mother wore a veil, he had seen that with his own eyes. But whatever she concealed underneath it was a mystery.

"And her guards? What of them?"

The man snorted. "What would you have done in their place?"

"Gotten on the next ship out of here."

"That's just what they did—along with most of her supporters. Many fled to Venice. The palace is half-empty now."

A thought struck Gabriel. "What of the hunt?"

"Canceled. The king is in mourning, and as for his son . . ."

"Celebrating?"

The guard grinned. "You said it, not me." He glanced at the doorway leading into the castle's lower floors. "Is there a table for us? I'm starving."

"Go ahead," Gabriel said. "You'll find plenty to eat in the kitchens."

He watched the man stump across the keep, his mind still reeling with the news. What now? They'd been preparing for an elaborate hunt—it was to have lasted a fortnight, possibly longer. Part of him was disappointed, for he loved venturing into the mountains. But he was also relieved. When the king and Jacco were around, no one could relax, not even for an instant.

His attention was drawn by an animated conversation between two guards of St. Hilarion and one of the riders who had just arrived. He and Michel Pelestrine joined the knot of men at the same time.

"Do you think Lord Jacco had a hand in the queen's death?" one castle guard was saying.

The rider scoffed. "Whether poison caused her death or not, she was not going to last much longer."

The first guard said, "It's not as if he's incapable of such a deed. His cutthroats killed her chamberlain. And he ordered the murder of the Viscount of Nicosia, too."

Gabriel had heard this. Apparently, Jacco considered the viscount responsible for stripping him of his title of archbishop, and when he returned from Rhodes, he and his men had set upon the poor fellow's house, found him there, and murdered him.

"He's a bastard," the other guard said with a derisive sneer. "He'll never wear a crown."

"Still, he has his supporters," Gabriel said.

"My father's a valet for the king," the rider said with an air of self-importance. "He's mentioned nothing of Lord Jacco taking the throne. He told me Princess Charlotta is the official heir. When she becomes queen, her new French husband, Louis of Savoy, will be king."

"King consort, you mean?" Gabriel asked.

Consorts did not wield the power of a true king or queen, and he imagined any foreign husband of the princess would fall into that category.

The rider shook his head. "No. He would become the one true king. It's part of an agreement the barons made with the House of Savoy."

Gabriel exchanged a sober glance with the guards.

"The kings of Cyprus have always had French blood," Michel pointed out. "What's the difference between a Lusignan and a Savoyard king?"

"The difference is the Lusignan kings have ruled Cyprus for hundreds of years, whereas a Savoyard is a foreigner, like you, monsieur."

A feeling of protectiveness rose up in Gabriel's chest. He eyed the men, casting about for something to say.

"Well, for all our sakes, we'd better hope the new king brings an army with him," he finally managed. "There's sure to be another attack soon, whether from the Mamluks, the Turks, or the Genoese."

"The Venetians are none too pleased with us either," added the rider. "The crown's debt to Venice grows with every passing year." He coughed and spat. "My throat is full of dust from the journey. I'm ready for refreshment."

The rider strode toward the kitchens, and the guards dispersed to their stations.

Michel turned to Gabriel. "What's that about the king's son wanting the throne for himself? There can't be any truth to that gossip." There was a worried look in his eyes.

Gabriel's mind went to the conversation he'd had with his father in Famagusta last summer. What had resulted from his visit to Nicosia? Had he agreed to support Jacco if he made a bid for the throne? He'd heard nothing from his father since then.

"I heard the same rumor in Famagusta," he said. "At the harbor. And again in Nicosia."

Michel nodded. "Are there Cypriots who would help him seize the throne?"

"So I've been told." They entered the supply room. Gabriel blinked as his eyes adjusted to the dim light. "Shall we start dismantling the traveling hutches and storing all the supplies?"

Michel reached for the nearest box of leather jesses. "Let's keep them at the ready. Summer approaches. The king's never missed a summer hunt, not as long as I've been here." He thought for a moment. "Last night, I got word that a merchant fleet with a shipment of saker falcons from Crete is headed to Limassol soon. I thought I'd have to hire guards to bring them here since we were to be away, but now I'd rather have you do it. With hired guards, it's always a gamble."

"I'll be happy to fetch the falcons," Gabriel replied. "And even happier to keep them alive."

# CHAPTER 18

Summer 1458
Nicosia, Cyprus

FROM THE FIRST moments of their time together, Estelle had to admit Jacco was a quick study and a good mimic. Reading frustrated him; the act of grasping a quill and scratching out letters on a page turned his mood sour. All he wanted was to speak her language with authority, to be as charming in French as he was in Greek or the Cypriot dialect.

The first afternoon in the garden, they sat on a carved marble bench in the dappled shade of the fig tree, shielded from the glaring sun. As they practiced verb conjugations, a female peacock pecked aimlessly at the base of an oleander shrub nearby.

"Why must peahens be so ugly?" Jacco asked, reverting to Greek.

"Perhaps we should dress them in silks and jewels," Estelle responded in French.

He laughed. "*Très amusant, mademoiselle.*" His gaze fell to her throat. "Where is *your* jewel? Did you wear it?"

She pulled the necklace from beneath her blouse. He studied it with satisfaction.

"I knew it would suit you," he said. "It would look better with a Latin-style gown, though. You must still have one amongst your things."

She chafed under his scrutiny. "I only wear Cypriot clothing now."

"But the queen is dead. It was because of her that you changed your style of dress." His tone was cheery and matter-of-fact.

Court gossips whispered that Jacco had orchestrated the queen's death. He certainly did not seem saddened by the loss. He may have shared Greek heritage with his father's wife, but respect? Affection? Love? No. If anything, his spirits were heightened, his smile broader, since her death.

The more time Estelle spent with Jacco, the less she trusted his words.

He reached out to finger the hem of her silken sleeve. "Why not revert back to the French way? If I were king, I would let everyone wear exactly what they wish." He gripped her wrist, his eyes smoldering with intensity. "Especially you."

*If I were king.*

She sat motionless, unable to breathe until he released her. Sir Hector's warning rushed back in that instant. Jacco saw the world as a chessboard of his own making, the nobleman had cautioned her. Was she simply a pawn in some grand scheme of Jacco's? Did he plan to make her his servant? His concubine?

She bit her lip, forcing the disturbing thoughts away.

*Jacco is your only ally here. Whatever happens, do not jeopardize his favor.*

As summer progressed, the weighted significance of his words began to fade. Jacco threw around references to his imagined future as a king so often, and so casually, that Estelle barely noticed his insinuations. She left each tutoring session exhausted, for his temperament was overwhelming —a dizzying combination of exuberance and barely suppressed anger.

Each time he said anything that made her muscles tight with tension, she put a hand to her purse. It was heavier now. The day when she'd found him under the fig tree, Jacco had poured ten ducats into her hands. Whenever she'd seen him since then, he'd given her something of value—coins, a pair of earrings, a length of silk embroidered with gold thread.

She'd sent the ducats to Papa, along with a letter describing the betrothal plan, begging him to forbid the marriage. Though Jacco had assured her he'd put things right—and, indeed, none of the barons had mentioned the betrothal since their encounter in the king's study—she was wary of relying solely on Jacco's word. Surely, as soon as Papa received the letter, he would resolve the matter.

In the meantime, the queen's death had thrown the court into disarray. Most of the Greek courtiers who'd served her had disappeared. King Jean and the barons were now occupied with planning Princess Charlotta's marriage to her cousin Louis of Savoy and entertaining the foreign emissaries who had traveled to Nicosia for the queen's funeral and still lingered here.

Still, a small voice in her head whispered the same words over and over.

*I am nothing but a pawn in Jacco's game. What does he have in store for me next?*

On a sultry day in midsummer, Jacco and Estelle followed a garden path around orange trees and rosebushes, discussing horses, hunting, and hawking. In a rapid blend of French and Greek, he described his plan to establish falcon farms in Cyprus.

"Why transport falcons across the sea when we can raise them ourselves?"

She nodded, seeing the sense of the idea.

"If I were king, I would set this plan into motion *immédiatement.*" Jacco flapped a hand at the far end of the courtyard, where the princess and her entourage of ladies gathered in a grove of pomegranate trees. "My sweet sister. It's good to see her taking some air. She has been trapped indoors far too often these past weeks. Let's greet her."

Estelle hesitated. She'd grown used to the women's dismissive stares, but she still hated their scrutiny.

"They don't like you." Jacco nodded. "I know how that feels. But you still must try to gain my sister's favor. Once she warms to you, the rest of them will."

"It is kind of you to say, my lord, but your sister believes I'm a thief. That's why she dislikes me."

He frowned. "Is it true?"

If Louise did live in his mother's household, he'd never acknowledged it, and Estelle had no wish to incite his ire by bringing up the matter herself.

"I was accused of stealing a necklace from Louise. The one you gave her. The one that looks much like this." She gestured at her throat. "I did not take it. But the princess does not trust me any longer."

"Come." He took her hand and tucked it in the crook of his elbow. "I'll convince her to like you again."

Estelle began to tuck the necklace under her blouse again. Jacco caught her hand in his.

"No. Leave it. Let them see."

She reluctantly complied, then allowed Jacco to lead her to the group of women. All of them curtsied to him except for the princess, whose red-rimmed eyes looked tormented.

"What have the barons done to you now?" Jacco gathered his sister in his arms.

"It's not just them," the princess burst out. "Papa says I must marry my cousin, even though I'll go to hell for it. Mamá said I'll be cursed! But I have no choice. It's all arranged."

One of the women began weeping at the princess's words. Another crossed herself, murmuring a prayer.

Estelle had heard that on her deathbed the queen had forced her daughter to promise never to marry Louis. In the Greek Orthodox religion, the marriage of first cousins was an unforgivable sin.

And now Princess Charlotta must break her promise to her

mother. A twinge of sympathy gripped Estelle at the thought. All women, even princesses, were subject to the whims and schemes of men.

Jacco kissed his sister's head. "You won't go to hell, dearest sister. None of this is your fault. You'll marry under Latin rites, with a Latin mass. In the Latin church, one can get a special dispensation to marry a cousin. It's not a sin."

The princess pulled back from his embrace, her tearstained face showing a glimmer of hope. "Truly?"

"Of course." He turned to Estelle. "Isn't that right, mademoiselle?"

Estelle nodded, though she knew nothing of the matter. "Yes."

Princess Charlotta's eyes narrowed in suspicion. "Why should I believe her? One of my ladies accused her of theft. Sir Hector told me to let the matter drop, but I still don't trust her." Her gaze fell to the gold chain around Estelle's neck. "That's the necklace she stole!"

"Being accused of something is different from being guilty of it," he asserted. "And Estelle is not guilty. I know."

"How would you know the truth?" the princess demanded.

"Because I gave her that necklace. Louise had a similar piece, but it's no longer in her possession. She pawned it in Nicosia. The pawnbroker, a Venetian, informed me of the transaction, and I purchased the necklace from him. I'll bring it to the palace to prove the truth of this."

"Why did Louise tell me the mademoiselle stole it from her?" Princess Charlotta asked.

Estelle stood rock-still, waiting for Jacco's reply.

"Perhaps she was jealous of my affection for Mademoiselle Estelle. Envy makes people act in unfortunate ways." He bent his head toward his sister. "If you can bring yourself to speak to the young mademoiselle again, it would be in your best interest."

"Why is that?"

"Because you're soon to wed a Frenchman, and I don't exaggerate when I say that your French is terrible."

She glowered, her arms crossed over her chest.

Estelle endured the princess's hostile stare with as much dignity as she could muster. Once Jacco's French was fluent, he'd likely discard her with as little concern as he would a broken quill. But today, his approval was like a protective shield infusing her with strength.

She returned the princess's gaze with new assurance.

*You're not yet sixteen,* she thought. *Widowed before your marriage was a year old. Now you've lost your mother. You're betrothed to a cousin you've never met—and fear you'll burn in hell for it. I wouldn't trade places with you for all the gold in the world.*

"Your Grace," Estelle ventured. "I would be honored to teach you alongside your brother."

"Perhaps from time to time." Princess Charlotta's expression relaxed a little.

"It's decided!" Jacco grinned. "You'll soon be speaking French as beautifully as I do."

The princess returned his smile. Her ladies followed suit. The tension in Estelle's body dissipated like a receding tide.

"Your Grace!" A man's voice rose up from the shadowy arcade leading into the palace. "Your Grace!"

The king's steward hurried toward them, trailed by a pair of guards. "Princess Charlotta. My lord. The king has fallen ill. He's taken to his bed. He asks for you both."

The siblings exchanged a stricken look. Princess Charlotta took her brother's arm. They trailed the steward and the guards along the gravel path, the women forming a pack behind them.

Estelle stayed rooted in place as their footsteps faded, the sun beating down on her head, a single thought catapulting through her brain.

*This is the moment Signora Rosso spoke of. Everything is about to change.*

# CHAPTER 19

Summer 1458
Nicosia, Cyprus

ESTELLE STOOD at the back of the cool, candle-lit cathedral with the other mourners, tracking the movements of the highest-ranking nobles as they exited the great doors. Antonia had found her a black silk gown and headpiece in the wardrobe of a Greek courtier who'd fled to Venice after the queen's death. In this costume, Estelle melted into the crowd with ease.

When she caught sight of Sir Hector and Lord Podocataro walking together along the main aisle of the nave, she edged behind a column and stood perfectly still. After a few moments, she joined the long line of people filing outside.

Standing at the top of the steps, blinking in the sunlight, Estelle thought she heard a man call her name.

*Please, God, don't let it be one of the barons.*

Then she sighed. The entire court was required to swear fealty to the new queen following the funeral mass. Even if she evaded the men here, she would undoubtedly encounter some or all of them later today.

"Mademoiselle de Montavon?" An unfamiliar man stood in the sun a short distance from the cathedral steps, squinting up at her.

She descended the steps, keeping several strides between herself and the stranger.

"You look like your father; I could not have missed you." The man's black doublet and hose were identical to those of most of the Latin-born men in the crowd. He had a round face and a close-trimmed beard. "I'm called Michel Pelestrine." He bowed. "It is a pleasure—and a relief—to finally make your acquaintance, Mademoiselle de Montavon."

"I was beginning to doubt you even existed," she said in wonder. "Did you truly recognize me by my resemblance to Papa?"

He smiled. "In part. Gabriel Bayoumi described your features to me exactly. I never realized he was so observant. Do you recall meeting him? My best under-falconer. He delivered the book from your father."

"Yes, of course." Heat pricked at her skin. Her mind jumped to Gabriel's glowing gray eyes, his confident stride.

"I wish I'd been free to visit you here earlier. But the king's pleasure was to keep me in the mountains with the falcons and leopards, ready for the hunt," Monsieur Pelestrine went on. "I had no choice in the matter, I'm afraid."

"Leopards?" she asked, glancing around at the dispersing crowd. The barons and Lord Podocataro were walking purposefully away from the cathedral, following the gilded oxcart that bore Princess Charlotta and her ladies back to the palace.

*No, not princess. The moment King Jean died, Charlotta became queen.*

He nodded. "Great cats from Africa. They run faster than horses. The kings of Lusignan use them for hunting. Something I never imagined before coming to Cyprus. But then, there are many things here that have surprised me since moving from France."

She nodded. "I understand the sentiment."

"May I accompany you to the ceremony?" he asked. "It looks as if all of Nicosia is off to swear fealty to their new queen. We'd better not be the last ones in the queue. Don't want to make a poor impression."

Estelle couldn't help smiling. "Queen Charlotta's impression of me couldn't get much worse, I'm afraid. But for your sake, I'll speed my step."

Outside the reception hall, courtiers clustered in small groups, waiting their turn for an audience, the low hum of their conversations rising and falling.

Estelle sensed a presence next to her.

"Mademoiselle, what a pleasure." Lord Podocataro swept into an elaborate bow.

"My lord."

"Ah, Monsieur Pelestrine." He turned to the falconer. "It seems our hunting and hawking is continually delayed. Perhaps autumn will be a luckier time. When the queen's betrothed arrives from the West."

"Yes, my lord," the falconer replied. "That is my hope as well."

Lord Podocataro sought Estelle's gaze. "The events in court of late have disrupted our own plans, too, but soon that shall be rectified."

"Oh?" She looked back at him levelly, trying not to imagine his plum-colored lips pressed against hers.

"You shall learn more when you pledge your oath to our queen, mademoiselle." He murmured a farewell.

Monsieur Pelestrine looked at her sideways. "You're acquainted with his lordship?"

"The king and his barons tried to force me into a marriage with him without my father's knowledge or permission." She kept her voice low and even. "With Lord Jacco's support, I've managed to put the matter behind me."

"Lord Podocataro doesn't seem to think so." Monsieur Pelestrine's tone was slightly alarmed now.

*Jacco has quashed the betrothal. I have no need to worry. Yet Lord Podocataro looks so smug.*

Estelle's thoughts were interrupted by the clang of the gong. Monsieur Pelestrine's name was called.

"I'll return directly to St. Hilarion castle after my audience with the queen," he told her. "Write to me there if you need my assistance or counsel."

He disappeared through the doors to the reception hall. Estelle distracted herself from the tense atmosphere of the chamber by counting to one hundred.

When she reached sixty-three, Jacco emerged from the reception hall and walked in her direction.

She had not spoken with him since the day in the courtyard when Sir Hector came to inform them of the king's illness. Since the king's death, the daily rhythm of life had been thrown off. Would their lessons resume? She dearly hoped so. Despite her uneasiness in his presence, she needed his generosity and his protection.

"Come to pledge your allegiance to my sister, have you?" Jacco asked.

Estelle nodded, glancing at the doors to the reception hall. Men hovered at the threshold, talking amongst themselves.

"How they covet my sister's favor," he muttered. "But none can deny I was the first to swear my oath to her. The moment Papa died, I placed his ring on her finger, still warm from his own hand. My rightful place is in there at her side, fending off that pack of barons." Jacco leaned in, his breath hot against her cheek. "One day, I shall have a court of my own. There will be a place for you in it, Estelle."

She shifted her weight from one leg to the other, glancing across the chamber at Lord Podocataro. "The betrothal plan—you spoke to Sir Hector about it, my lord? The barons have been silent on that account since we began our tutoring sessions. I've no reason to worry?"

Jacco's lips turned up at the corners, but there was no warmth in his eyes. "Sir Hector is in my debt, mademoiselle. He'd be a fool to cross me now, I assure you."

An attendant announced her name.

"Go on," Jacco urged. "Show my sister your loyalty."

When she passed into the reception hall, the barons fell silent, watching her approach. On the dais, Queen Charlotta's small form was dwarfed by the massive throne. Her dark eyes burned in her pale face.

Estelle curtsied.

"Rise and swear your oath," said the queen.

"I pledge fealty to you, my queen." Estelle stood tall. "I promise never to cause you harm, to defend you in good faith and without deceit."

Sir Hector ascended the steps and whispered into the queen's ear. She nodded without expression.

"Do not look so despondent," Queen Charlotta said to Estelle. "You will soon depart from this court, mademoiselle."

For an instant, Estelle imagined herself standing at the prow of a merchant galley cutting north to Rhodes through the sapphire waves.

"Your marriage to Lord Podocataro will take place in a month's time." The queen's face was impassive. "It is all arranged."

All the air escaped Estelle's lungs. "But, Your Grace, Lord Jacco told me he had discussed the matter with Sir Hector. There will be no betrothal."

"I recall no such conversation." Sir Hector snapped his fingers, and a servant climbed the steps with a leather-bound book in his hands. "You yourself have accepted the marriage proposal. Do you not recall?"

He opened the book and thrust it toward her. Estelle recognized a notary's florid signature at the bottom of the page. But that was not the place where the baron pointed. Next to it, someone had written her name in script she did not recognize.

"No," Estelle protested. "I never signed it. That is not my hand."

Lord Chimi stepped forward. "Are you accusing the royal notaries of dishonesty?" His voice crackled with hostility.

"I am telling you the truth." The words rang out, more loudly than she'd intended. "I would never sign a document without reading it first. What's more, my father has not given his permission for this marriage!"

Queen Charlotta glanced at Sir Hector and the other members of her council. None of them returned her gaze. A flicker of irritation—or was it anger?—washed over her face. "And yet the barons wish to see the matter through. You are dismissed, mademoiselle."

Outside the reception hall, the assembled courtiers parted to let her through, staring at her with open curiosity. There was no sign of Jacco.

How angry he would be if he knew what had just transpired.

She made a quick, fruitless search of the courtyard garden, then tracked down the steward in the entry hall and asked if Jacco was still in the palace.

"Lord Jacco has been escorted to his home by the queen's guard." The steward's voice was low and tight.

"Why?"

"There are rumors of an uprising by his supporters, mademoiselle. When power changes hands at court, things are never certain. It would be foolish not to prepare for the worst."

He was already turning away, distracted by some shouted question from an approaching courtier. Outside the gracefully arched windows, servants swung shut the exterior shutters one by one. Estelle caught a glimpse of crossbowmen assembling in the courtyard. A regiment of guards marched past the great doors, the sun glinting off their helmets. Then servants closed and barred the doors and a shadowy gloom descended over the entry hall.

*This is a palace no longer. It's a fortress now.*

She returned to her chamber and unlocked her trunk. Unearthing the necklace, she weighed it in her palm. Louise had once told her there were pawnbrokers in Nicosia. How many ducats was the necklace worth? After a long moment, she stuffed it back in its hiding place and found the worn little journal she'd taken from the library so long ago. Beneath it was another book she'd borrowed. The author was a Frenchwoman named Christine de Pizan.

*I'll have to return these before I—*

She realized she was preparing herself to flee Nicosia.

No reply from Papa had come. Whether he approved of her marriage or not, whether she would be able to find work in Rhodes upon her return to help repay his debts—these were questions she could not spend more time pondering. She was a prisoner here with few opportunities to escape. Perhaps Jacco was imprisoned, too. His influence over the barons was clearly not as powerful as he'd imagined.

She crossed to the window, extending a hand to touch the pomegranate tree.

Like a burrowing insect, Signora Rosso's admonition gnawed at her.

*The truth is you're going to Cyprus to find a husband. If you marry well, your whole family benefits.*

Estelle willed the words away, imagined them tumbling over a cliff's edge into a raging sea. Papa and Maman would forgive her for leaving Cyprus. They would never approve of a marriage to an elderly stranger —nor would they want her to stay in this murderous, poisonous court.

*Even if I did marry Lord Podocataro, would he let me send gold to Papa and Maman? I know nothing of the man's true character. But if he conspired with the barons to have my signature forged on that betrothal agreement, I want nothing to do with him.*

She made up her mind. She would find a way to leave Cyprus on the day of the queen's coronation.

# CHAPTER 20

Autumn 1458
Nicosia, Cyprus

ESTELLE FOUND a place near a group of courtiers outside Santa Sophia, the sun pounding her skull. She longed for a breeze to cool her face. Behind the richly dressed members of the court thronged hundreds of citizens. Excited chatter rose up from the merchants, artisans, and other commoners gathered in the square. Now that the coronation ceremony was finished, the people were eager to get a glimpse of their new queen.

She studied the crowd carefully, straining to hear the conversations around her. When a flurry of Italian rose up from a merchant family nearby, anticipation flooded her. As soon as the ceremony ended, she would follow that group back to the Italian quarter and go straight to Signora Rosso's home.

Around her throat, tucked beneath the folds of the white silk under-blouse Louise had helped her alter, hung the necklace gifted her by Jacco. Every coin, every valuable she possessed, was somewhere on her body or concealed within her purse and clothing. Her dagger was affixed to her belt, hidden beneath her silk cloak.

This was the last time she would ever see Santa Sophia cathedral.

Across the square stood several bearded men in Greek-style robes. With a start, she realized one of them was the crow-faced man who'd delivered the necklace to her so long ago. He met her gaze and she looked away, her pulse quickening. Jacco himself was nowhere to be seen, but that was no surprise. He'd been confined to his palace by the barons. She'd heard some of his servants had lost their lives in skirmishes with the queen's guard, and their heads were now displayed on spikes for all to see on the Bridge of the Pillory.

Her attention was soon diverted by the noblemen of Cyprus emerging from the cathedral with their wives and children, their silks and jewelry gleaming in the sunlight. A procession of priests, bishops, and abbots followed. She'd heard there were dignitaries from as far away as Rome and Savoy amongst the celebrants, including representatives of the pope and the King of France.

Finally, Queen Charlotta appeared in the doorway, her slight body framed by the imposing stone portal. The jewel-toned portraits of icons in two niches on either side of the jamb echoed the rich red of her silk gown and the vibrant blue velvet of her ermine-lined cloak. As she moved forward, seed pearls embedded in her gown caught the sun, and the rubies and sapphires in her golden crown glittered. She descended the steps trailed by a half-dozen ladies-in-waiting. A hush settled over the crowd.

Two attendants led a white horse draped in cloth of gold to the base of the steps. Sir Hector extended an arm to the queen and helped her into the saddle. The clop-clop of the horse's hooves on the cobbles echoed overhead.

As the queen's horse passed before Estelle, several pigeons took flight across the square, their wings churning frantically. The horse shied and nearly reared up. Queen Charlotta threw her hands around the pommel to steady herself. Her crown slipped from her head, smashing against the stone. A stark metallic clang pierced the quiet, floating up to the bell tower of Santa Sophia and vanishing into the brilliant blue sky.

All around Estelle, people crossed themselves and gasped in horror.

"Oh holy Virgin," muttered the woman next to her. "That bodes ill for the poor queen."

Sir Hector dove for the crown and snatched it up. With a bow, he handed it to the queen. She pushed it down over her brow, her expression taut with anxiety.

The attendants clucked to the horse, and it plodded forward again. The crowd was restless now, the solemnity of the moment shattered.

Estelle glanced skyward. The pigeons flew higher and higher, heading west. Her gaze fell to the crow-faced man. His bony face broke into a smile.

As soon as the queen's entourage left the square, he scurried to Estelle's side. "Mademoiselle."

Behind him, another man approached, weaving through knots of citizens and courtiers. She stood taller, her breath hitching in her throat. It was the falconer Gabriel Bayoumi. He strode with a loose-hipped grace that mesmerized her.

"You saw it with your own eyes—the girl is cursed and will never rule this kingdom," Jacco's man said to Estelle with an air of smug assurance.

The words barely penetrated Estelle's consciousness. She kept her gaze on the falconer.

"Those who stay loyal to the queen will soon regret it," the man went on. "The rightful king will take his place on the throne before long, mark my words."

Gabriel drew up at Estelle's side. She smiled at him. Though she barely knew the man, she felt an odd mixture of exhilaration and comfort in his presence.

"Something frightened those pigeons." He studied the crow-faced man with a cool look, one hand resting lightly on his sword's hilt.

"Indeed. Birds startle so easily."

"Even well-trained ones," said Gabriel. "I watched them find their way home—a short journey to the archbishop's palace. Normally, such pigeons fly much longer distances."

"I know nothing of that." The man's expression tightened. "I dearly hope our new queen is not unduly troubled by the bad omen."

He made his excuses and slunk away.

"I haven't seen Jacco yet." Estelle turned to Gabriel. "Would he truly snub his sister on her coronation day?"

"The barons had the queen order Jacco to confine himself at home. There's talk of an uprising by Jacco's men."

"And you believe this rumor? Nicosia feeds on gossip."

"I know men of power who will throw their lot in with him, and most common folk feel the same way." Gabriel dropped his voice. "The crown falling from the queen's head is more than bad fortune to them. It's a sign that she's not fit to lead."

"But she'll soon wed again," Estelle pointed out. "Surely her new husband will bring his own army with him."

Gabriel nodded. "If he shows himself to be a worthy leader, Queen Charlotta will find more supporters, I have no doubt."

"Including you?" she asked.

"Perhaps." His gray eyes drew her in, emitting a fierce, intelligent light. "What about you?"

"I want to get off Cyprus," she said, avoiding the question of loyalty. She searched the crowd for the Italian merchant family. They were still in the same spot. "I've heard ships leave regularly from Limassol."

"Now is not the time to travel," warned Gabriel. "Jacco won't be content until he's sitting on the throne. That means war is coming. And with it, violence—especially toward women."

She squared her shoulders. "I'm supposed to marry an old man a few weeks from now. I won't do it. This is my chance to return to Rhodes—there may not be another."

People were beginning to disperse now. A regiment of royal guards appeared on the far side of the square, striding toward Jacco's residence.

"Why are you here?" she asked abruptly. "Surely, an under-falconer does not receive invitations to coronations while the master falconer stays away?"

"I had a matter to attend to in Limassol. I retrieved a shipment from a Scots privateer who works for the knights."

"You saw Master Fordun?"

"The truth is I'm here because he gave me something for you," Gabriel said. "A letter from your father."

Estelle's hand flew to her mouth. Tears pricked at her eyelids.

"Calm yourself, mademoiselle," he murmured. "There are eyes everywhere."

Over Gabriel's shoulder, she spied the Italians heading away from the square. Collecting herself, she gestured after them.

"Will you accompany me to the Italian quarter? I have to pay a call there. We can walk with that group, and you can give me the letter out of view."

Gabriel looked a bit surprised but nodded gamely.

They followed the family, drawing close enough to hear their conversation. The group was abuzz with gossip about the coronation and rumors of Jacco's plans.

Estelle and Gabriel trailed them through the gates of the Italian quarter, then paused on a quiet corner. Gabriel handed her the letter. She broke the seal with care. Studying her father's familiar scrawl, she held her breath.

Though she was certain Papa would not approve of the betrothal scheme, a tiny thread of doubt still tugged at her.

*What if Signora Rosso's mind is not addled after all? What if she spoke the truth? Did my parents send me here to find a husband?*

Papa's words quashed those thoughts with dazzling finality. He had gotten all the coin she'd sent, praise all the saints. She read the final lines of the letter twice, savoring them.

*I have heard nothing of this betrothal from King Jean,* her father had written. *I do not grant permission for the union. Return to Rhodes with the next Hospitaller fleet. I've written to Michel Pelestrine as well, asking him to look after you until you manage to get off the island. I beseech you, my beloved daughter: do not travel alone. Use whatever coin you have left to hire armed companions and a maidservant for the journey. Cyprus is no longer safe.*

She swayed, suddenly light-headed.

*Cyprus has never been safe, Papa.*

Gabriel helped her settle on the step of a nearby doorway.

"Is it bad news?" He shaded her from the sun with his body.

She shook her head, unable to stop the flow of tears, and smiled up at him. "Just the opposite. I wrote them about the king's plan to marry me to a Cypriot nobleman, and Papa forbids the betrothal. My family wants me back in Rhodes."

# CHAPTER 21

Autumn 1458
Nicosia, Cyprus

ACCEPTING GABRIEL'S EXTENDED HAND, Estelle stood. Something warm ignited within her at his touch, seeping through her veins like a draught of hot, spiced wine. She looked at their entwined fingers, wishing she could find a reason to keep hold of him.

"Let's go." Her voice was throaty, roughened by emotion.

*A letter from Papa will do that.*

*But it's not just the letter. It's more.*

The truth was something shimmered in the air between her and Gabriel—something she could not name, an irresistible force.

His gaze was on their linked hands, too. He stood motionless, slowly bringing his eyes up to meet hers.

*He feels it, too. He must. I can see it—*

She released his hand with reluctance and moved forward. It was better not to dwell on such thoughts.

He fell into step with her. "Who do you seek in this quarter?"

"A widow. My chaperone on the journey from Rhodes."

The air in these narrow lanes was dank and fetid. When they reached Signora Rosso's door, Estelle's knees shook. What if the woman refused to help her?

She raised the iron knocker and thumped it against the door. No one responded. All the windows were shuttered and latched.

"We can ask for her there." Gabriel crossed the lane to a home with its shutters flung open. When a servant answered the door, Estelle inquired about Signora Rosso.

"She's gone." The woman wiped her hands on a soot-stained apron. "Two days ago, the signora and all her servants vanished. Headed for Limassol harbor, I heard. Ever since the king died, people have been leaving. There are twelve cold hearths in the Italian quarter now."

*Death brings change.*

They walked back to the gates and turned in the direction of the palace.

Fifty paces ahead, a regiment of the queen's guard trooped across an intersection, the strike of their boots on the cobblestones making Estelle's stomach lurch. Gabriel put a hand on the hilt of his sword, his expression tightening.

Estelle thought of the dagger hidden beneath her cloak.

*Please, God, let this not be the day I'm forced to use my weapon.*

There was an air of unrest in the city, that was certain. Rather than celebrating their new sovereign's coronation, the citizens were disappearing into their homes, latching shutters and barring doors.

When they reached the Armenian quarter, dozens of guards were massed at the gates.

"Why are they here?" she asked Gabriel.

"They're likely trying to keep Jacco's friends from congregating at his palace."

Signor Derian was an associate of Jacco's. Had he returned from his journey? Would he rise up against the queen?

"But the queen is the rightful heir to the throne. She's been crowned. Why can't we have peace?"

Gabriel shrugged, his gaze straight ahead. "The people want a strong ruler. Queen Charlotta has little experience of the world. She's sixteen, if that. Not much more than a child."

"But Jacco has not seen twenty winters himself. What does he know of the world?"

"Cypriots would rather place their faith in a man than a girl."

He flicked a glance at her as if awaiting a rebuttal. But she simply nodded.

"I see," was all she said.

More guards filled the street ahead.

"Three hundred men are assembled at the Bastard's palace," their captain shouted. "If you are attacked, show no mercy!"

Gabriel shielded Estelle with his body as the men pounded past them. She could swear the cobblestones below her feet vibrated with the force of their boots striking the earth.

When the way was clear, Gabriel sped his step. "The palace is the safest place for you," he tossed over his shoulder. "Hurry."

Estelle struggled to keep up. She could not return to the palace. But where else would she go? They passed a convent. The thought occurred to her that she could take refuge there. In the next instant, she dismissed the idea. A convent was a cage, too, with none of the trappings of a palace. Perhaps the best solution was to head straight for a harbor.

"If I can catch up to Signora Rosso," she mused aloud, "I can book passage on the ship she's taking."

Gabriel gave her a strange look, but said nothing.

"You said you have another cargo of falcons to transport," she said in desperation. "So you've a mule cart at your disposal. You can take me to Limassol!"

He glanced at her sideways and chuckled.

"Why are you laughing?"

"I'd never risk the falcons' health or my own life by taking an unessential journey on the eve of an uprising. And even if you get to the harbor, who's to say you'll find a ship there or this woman you speak of? Perhaps she's already left. How will you find a trustworthy shipmaster? Alone, you'll be lucky to find safe lodging—you may end up forced into a brothel."

Estelle's despair hardened into anger. "I will not marry an old man, a stranger, and live out my days in Cyprus. I'm going back to Rhodes. This is my chance!"

"Who is your betrothed?" Gabriel asked in a mild voice. "I've lived on this island my entire life. I probably know the man."

"He farms sugarcane on the other side of the island, near Paphos. He's a widower called Lord Podocataro."

"I know of him. He's three times your age, but he's rich. You'll live well."

"How would you like to be married off to an old woman?" she spluttered.

"If she were rich, I wouldn't mind," he said cheerfully.

"You know nothing of what I suffer," she shot back. "You mock my misfortune."

"I know more of suffering than you imagine." His tone was sober now. "The world is a harsher place for women than for men, I'm the first to admit it."

The palace gates loomed before them. A guard approached, his helmet shining in the sun.

Estelle hung back, grappling with a powerful urge to run.

"You're luckier than most," Gabriel said quietly. "Make the best of your situation."

"Is this what you say to the women in your family?" she demanded.

"I've no sisters, and my mother is dead." His expression was unreadable. "But she was a slave when I was born. And I can tell you she did make the best of her situation."

Estelle took that in, shocked into silence.

"Help me," she managed to say. "For the love of God and all the saints, help me."

He gave a barely perceptible shake of his head. "The safest place for you at this moment is within the walls of the palace. You must trust me on this. Violence is about to erupt in Nicosia, mademoiselle."

The guard had nearly reached them now. One of the gatekeepers called out a greeting to Gabriel.

Estelle looked into his eyes one more time. The resolve she saw there made her heart twist.

*Please.*

Her mouth was so dry she could not even push the word out. Not that it would have mattered if he'd heard it.

For the moment the massive gates began to swing open, Gabriel spun on his heel and walked away.

# CHAPTER 22

Autumn 1458
Nicosia, Cyprus

ESTELLE WALKED past stone-faced guards and gossiping courtiers, her ears buzzing with the agitated chatter of a hundred restless people. Many of the queen's adherents had retreated here after the coronation, fearing violence from Jacco's supporters in Nicosia. Richly dressed nobles gathered everywhere she turned, a flock of glittering, preening birds. The corridors, the courtyard garden, the great hall—there were no empty spaces in the palace today.

Finally, she arrived at Sir Hector's chamber. A torch just outside his door cast a pool of light over his hound, who sat still as a statue at the threshold. Estelle fished a dried apricot from her purse and held it in her outstretched palm, murmuring a greeting. He stood and stretched, a gleam of recognition in his dark eyes, and lapped the morsel from her hand.

As she raised her hand to knock, the door flew open, revealing Sir Hector and Lord Chimi.

"Sir Hector." Estelle looked straight at him, ignoring the other man. "I have important news to share from my father—"

"God's teeth. Our kingdom is on the brink of civil war." Lord Chimi pushed past her into the corridor. "There is nothing more important than that. Come, Sir Hector, the captain of the queen's guard awaits our command."

"Please." Estelle put her hand on Sir Hector's sleeve. "My father has written." She pulled the letter from her purse. "He forbids the marriage with Lord Podocataro. He wants me to return to Rhodes immediately."

Lord Chimi sighed loudly. He snatched the letter from Estelle's hand and held it to the torch.

"No!" she cried, horrified.

"By all the saints!" Sir Hector reached for the letter, but it was already engulfed in flames.

"How dare you?" Estelle balled her hands into fists. "You had no right!"

"You are the one with no rights here, mademoiselle." Lord Chimi could barely contain his rage. "The council has shown you nothing but generosity, and still you whine at Sir Hector like a mosquito buzzing in his ear. We should have you publicly flogged for your insolence."

"You've sworn your loyalty to the queen, mademoiselle." Sir Hector's tone was blunt but calm. "Do your duty by her and prepare to wed. Jacco the Bastard may have shielded you from this marriage while it suited him, but he will never wield power in this court again."

Estelle's blood surged with anger. "I remind you I am not a ward of this court. My father is my guardian. He wants me home, and I'll leave on the next ship to Rhodes."

Lord Chimi burst out laughing. "Your innocence is only exceeded by your dim-wittedness, mademoiselle. The palace is more closely guarded than a dragon's lair. You are not going anywhere until your marriage day, and after that, only with your husband's permission."

Sir Hector shouted an order to someone within his chambers. A valet appeared and took Estelle by the elbow. The hound growled deep in his chest.

"You'll be accompanied to your chamber, and I advise you to keep out of the trees this time," Sir Hector said. "I pray Lord Podocataro can summon the patience to treat you kindly, for he holds your future in the palm of his hand."

A few days later, the palace had begun to empty of terrified nobles, though crossbowmen and heavily armed guards still marched through the corridors and blocked the palace doors. Jacco and his men had indeed staged an uprising, but it had failed. Dozens more heads adorned spikes on the Bridge of the Pillory, a grim warning to his remaining supporters. And Jacco himself had fled to Egypt, seeking aid from the sultan. With his departure, Estelle's last vestige of hope had disappeared. Her only ally was gone—and with him, her source of gold.

A knock at her door one morning revealed an unwelcome sight: a wedding gown. The seamstress laid her work out on the bed. Silver thread edged the headpiece; tiny seed pearls decorated the sleeves and hem of the red silk gown.

Estelle had been given no information about her upcoming nuptials, only that her betrothed would journey to Nicosia for the ceremony and take her with him back to Paphos.

The seamstress cleared her throat. "I won't be paid if you're not pleased."

"It is a beautiful gown," Estelle said honestly, even if her hollow voice was unconvincing.

As soon as the woman left her chamber, she went to the window. The scent of jasmine drifted inside, filling her lungs with sweetness. Birdsong and the buzz of insects pulsed through the air.

Her thoughts darted to Paphos, to Lord Podocataro, to what awaited her on the far side of Cyprus. She took hold of the branch that had been her escape route from the chamber once before, gripped the sun-warmed wood with all her strength. Could she flee again? Disguise herself as a servant? Slip out the palace doors with tradespeople, perhaps?

A pair of guards marched directly under her window, interrupting her feverish thoughts. At the same time, a pounding commenced on the door, nothing like the gentle rap of the seamstress a few moments earlier.

Estelle tensed. "Who is it?" she called.

"The queen's guard," came the gruff response. "You've been summoned to meet with Her Grace."

In her study, the queen sat at a table flanked by Sir Hector and Lord Chimi.

Estelle swept into a curtsy.

"Your Grace," she said. "My lords."

Queen Charlotta looked even more wan and drained than usual. She regarded Estelle without expression.

"Your nuptials approach," she said finally. "My servants arranged for your wedding dress. Did you receive it?"

"I did, Your Grace. But I respectfully remind you that my father forbids this marriage and calls me home. He wrote me a letter to that effect. Lord Chimi took the letter from me and burned it."

The queen turned to Lord Chimi with a questioning look.

"The girl is spinning falsehoods, my queen." Lord Chimi held up his hands in a gesture of innocence.

Estelle tried to catch Sir Hector's eye to no avail. He stared at a point somewhere over her head.

"Lord Podocataro is eager for a son," Lord Chimi said. "The mademoiselle looks healthy and strong; with God's grace, she'll soon give him what he wants."

Estelle swallowed her distaste at his words.

"We have other, more pressing matters ahead of us." The queen returned her gaze to Estelle. "No doubt you've heard my brother is across the sea, trying to gain favor with the Sultan of Egypt. He seeks the support of the Knights Hospitaller as well."

Estelle nodded. Gossip about Jacco was the primary topic of the servants and courtiers. She was heartily sick of it.

Lord Chimi cut in. "How well does your father know the grand master of the knights?"

An urge to grossly exaggerate her father's relationship with the grand master seized Estelle. To tell them Lord de Milly himself forbade the wedding—that going forward with it would displease him so greatly he would withdraw the knights' support for the Kingdom of Cyprus.

*Careful, now, careful. Which choice leads me back to Rhodes? Stirring the pot or befriending the queen?*

"Papa is frequently called upon by the grand master for advice," she said. "He plans hunts for the knights and trains falcons for Lord de Milly to keep in his chambers."

The two men exchanged a glance. Sir Hector leaned over and whispered in Queen Charlotta's ear.

"I have important correspondence to write in French to Lord de Milly," the queen said. "I need your knowledge of the grand master and his ways to forge a strong connection with the man. The notaries and scribes say you display a fine hand with a quill, mademoiselle. You'll help scribe my letters, and you'll tutor me in French as you did my brother."

After ignoring her, shunning her, and accusing her of theft, Queen Charlotta was finally inviting her into the royal retinue? How long would Estelle hold the illustrious positions of royal tutor and scribe before her marriage? A week? Two?

*This is madness.*

A year ago, when Estelle had been a newcomer to this court, she would not have hesitated a moment. She'd have accepted the queen's words with gratitude and pride. She knew better now. An urge to laugh at the absurdity of the situation bubbled up in her chest and choked her. She bowed her head, calmed her mind.

Scrambling for the right words, she raised her chin. "I am grateful, Your Grace. But I will soon leave the court to marry. Perhaps a delay of my wedding would be prudent. In the interest of helping you with this endeavor, I mean to say."

"How insolent," Lord Chimi snapped. "Your wedding will proceed as planned."

Queen Charlotta ignored her advisor. She leaned forward in her chair, fixing Estelle with a long, contemplative look, and said, "I assure you we will make the most of the time we have, mademoiselle."

Estelle visited the queen every day for the next week. They went over verb conjugations, simple phrases, and vocabulary. Queen Charlotta had a strong Greek accent and not even a basic grasp of French grammar. But at least her attitude had shifted. She *wanted* to learn French now. And despite her poor skills, she listened attentively to Estelle's explanations and repeated the words and phrases presented to her without complaint.

Through it all, Estelle longed to bring up the topic of the betrothal, to somehow turn the queen to her side. But Queen Charlotta's attitude during the lessons was remote and formal. She would not be inclined to help unless she trusted or liked Estelle, that was certain. It was too soon to ask. And yet there was not much time left before Estelle's opportunity to change the course of her fate vanished forever.

One day, with no warning, Queen Charlotta said, "Do you ever think about your friend Louise?"

"I know she lives in the household of Lord Jacco's mother."

"She accused you of theft." The queen watched Estelle intently from beneath her long black lashes. "Aren't you angry? You must despise her."

Estelle shrugged. "I wonder why she left so suddenly. Perhaps she had no choice in the matter. There's much I don't know about what happened to her, in truth."

"You want to learn more before you make a judgment." The queen sounded envious. "The barons wish I were more that way. They always urge me to choose a wise strategy; they say I'm too impulsive."

"Strategy?" Estelle repeated.

Queen Charlotta waved a hand at a side table where a chess game sat. "Since my father died, my council has endlessly lectured me about plotting one's actions ahead in order to outwit one's opponent. When my parents were alive, no one ever encouraged me to play chess, study the rules of war, or master diplomacy. Now, with a kingdom to command, I am suddenly expected to have the education and experience of a man."

Estelle stared at her in astonishment. There was a wistfulness in the queen's tone, a fragility. And a perceptive intelligence Estelle had not seen her exhibit before.

Gabriel's words loomed in her mind. *Cypriots would rather place their faith in a man than a girl.*

"I can play chess. I would be honored to be your partner in the game," Estelle said. "Your Grace, there is a book in your library I believe you might find helpful. It's by a Frenchwoman, Christine de Pizan, and it describes the art of war."

The queen's eyes held a gleam of interest. "A book about war, written by a woman? What is it called?"

"*The Book of Deeds of Arms and of Chivalry.* It describes all the details of preparing a castle for war, arming soldiers, feeding them—"

"Tomorrow, bring the book to me and read it aloud," the queen interrupted. "You can translate the important bits into Greek. And we can play chess together."

*She's warming to you. Ask her now.*

"It will be my pleasure, Your Grace. And, if I might, I'd like to ask you—"

The palace chapel bells rang out to mark the hour.

"The barons return for another meeting with me soon." Queen Charlotta gripped the edge of the table, the animation draining from her face. "I must prepare."

Estelle stood and bowed. "Till tomorrow, then," she said in French.

The queen nodded. *"Oui, à demain."* She held up a hand. "Wait." Opening a cypress-wood box on the table, she pulled out a familiar object. "Here. It belongs to you."

"Someone went through my things?" Estelle reached out a hesitant hand and plucked the pearl-and-ruby necklace from Queen Charlotta's grasp.

She had hidden it away in her trunk as soon as she returned from the Italian quarter after the coronation, vowing she would find a way to pawn the necklace and book passage on a ship for Rhodes. Perhaps she'd forgotten to lock the trunk with her usual care. She'd been distraught, after all, overwhelmed by the day's events.

"Of course. You were once painted as a thief by someone I trusted. I had my jeweler compare this necklace to the one Louise pawned. As you had insisted, there were two necklaces that looked very much alike. Jacco gave you each a slightly different version of the same design."

Estelle nodded, keeping silent.

"I was quick to believe her accusation, and I regret it," the queen went on quietly. "I've been too trusting my whole life—until my husband was poisoned, I thought betrayal was something that happened to other people less fortunate than myself. Now I know better. I no longer see the world through the eyes of a child." She tilted her head to one side, her eyes narrowing at the sound of footsteps in the corridor. "The barons are here. You may go."

# CHAPTER 23

Autumn 1458
Nicosia, Cyprus

A FEW DAYS LATER, Estelle arrived in the queen's study to find Queen Charlotta standing at the window, dressed in blue silk. She appeared rested, energized. And eager.

"Today we write to the knights of Rhodes," she told Estelle. "It's time I make an ally of Lord de Milly. I can only hope my brother made a poor impression on him during his months there."

The notary at a table in the corner tapped a quill on his inkpot and cleared his throat.

She flung him a hard glance. "What is it, then?"

"Your Grace, I've some correspondence for your signature. The council wants this letter on the next ship to Venice."

The queen stalked to the table. The man laid out a letter before her. She studied it, frowning.

"Mademoiselle," she said over her shoulder. "Do you read Italian?"

"Yes," Estelle replied. "Not as well as French, but I can understand most of what I read."

"Then translate this letter for me. It's to our agent in Venice."

The notary gave Queen Charlotta a wide-eyed look of befuddlement. "But, Your Grace, the barons have approved the message—"

She crossed her arms over her chest. "I have not, though. And I will no longer sign anything that hasn't been translated for me. Is that clear?"

He nodded slowly, a sheen of sweat forming on his brow.

Estelle came to the table, read the letter quickly, and summarized the contents aloud.

"It requests a delay in payment of the debt owed to Venetian interests due to the king's death and the costs of hosting the coronation."

"Is there any mention of my brother? The uprising he incited? His escape to Egypt? His attempt to befriend the sultan?"

Estelle shook her head. "None, Your Grace."

"Then I shall not sign the letter." The queen glanced at the notary. "And because it seems my councilmen look the other way when false signatures appear on their notaries' record books, I shall destroy it." She took up the letter and tore it into small pieces. The bits of linen paper drifted to the floor, scattering like ash.

"Your Grace!" The notary's face turned scarlet.

"The barons invited you here, and I grow tired of your presence." Queen Charlotta pointed at the door. "Out with you!"

He gathered his things, cowed, and scuttled away.

"Spies," she said curtly as he vanished into the corridor. "They come in every guise imaginable." She sought Estelle's gaze again. "You're not here simply because you know something of Lord de Milly, mademoiselle. You were brave enough to defy my councilmen when they presented that false signature on the marriage contract. My father rarely defied them. My mother hated them. She said they would try to control the kingdom through me. Some of them are good men, with the best interests of the kingdom at heart. Lately, though, I wonder which of them are truly loyal."

Estelle regarded her with amazement.

*How I've underestimated the queen. She is far more sophisticated than I imagined. Despite her youth.*

"Now, let us turn to the matter of my correspondence," Queen Charlotta said crisply. "Lord de Milly once lived in my kingdom. He was grand commander of Cyprus for the knights when I was born. He was at my christening, in fact. I will remind him of this in my letter."

The queen's confidence seemed to grow with every passing day. When they weren't discussing the Knights Hospitaller, practicing French grammar, or playing chess, they spent hours poring over Christine de Pizan's *The Book of Deeds of Arms and of Chivalry*.

"What do you recall of Lord de Milly?" the queen asked her one afternoon.

"My father thinks he is a kind, just man. He kept Rhodes Town safe from plague when I was a child. Most of his attention is fixed on reinforcing the walls of the city and preparing for war. The Turks and the Mamluks both made attacks while I lived there, and the Venetians, too."

Queen Charlotta nodded, a look of intense contemplation on her face. "Attacks always come from the sea, no matter who is behind them."

"Yes," Estelle agreed. "Papa says the reason the knights keep control of Rhodes is their fleet. They hire privateers and mercenary soldiers to fight their battles at sea."

"We've had horrible violence in Cyprus, and if we could stop the invaders before they even come ashore—"

A deep voice from the door made Estelle jump. "Discussing matters of war, are you? A curious pastime for a pair of women."

Sir Hector strode into the chamber and bowed to the queen.

"Why isn't our military fleet larger?" she asked him.

"The kingdom is in debt, your grace. Ships and soldiers are costly."

"If we'd spent the kingdom's wealth on ships and soldiers instead of jewels and hunting expeditions, my grandfather King Janus would not have been taken captive during the Mamluk attack all those years ago. It's because of his ransom payment that our coffers ran dry."

"I see you've been reading the histories. Unfortunately, we cannot change the past, Your Grace." Sir Hector's tone grew impatient. "Now may we turn to the news of the day?"

Queen Charlotta's expression lost its enthusiasm. "As you wish."

"The matter involving the mademoiselle is resolved, Your Grace."

They both turned to Estelle. She endured their stares uneasily.

"You are not eager to wed," the queen said to her. "It's obvious."

"No." Estelle's tone was more defiant than she'd intended. "I hate the idea, in truth."

Queen Charlotta let out a short laugh. "You'll be relieved to know, then, that you won't be marrying Lord Podocataro after all."

Estelle's knees wobbled. "But how . . . ?"

"A different bride has been found for him." Sir Hector delivered the news in a bored monotone, as if he were discussing taxes and tariffs. "Of French extraction, just like you. And about your age as well. He's pleased with the substitution."

Estelle looked from him to the queen. "Who is she?"

Queen Charlotta's expression grew hard. "Louise. Jacco stole her away from my court and installed her with his mother. He filled her head with lies. Promised her she'd be his consort one day. He told her to accuse you of stealing her necklace to make me mistrust you."

Sir Hector spoke up. "Cropnose is a spiteful mistress, and those in her household are miserable. It took very little prodding to get Louise to admit to the Bastard's manipulations, I assure you. She was only too happy to accept Lord Podocataro's offer of marriage."

Estelle absorbed his words with a wariness that had become all too familiar. Had Jacco truly influenced Louise in this way? One thing was sure: Louise had often spoken of her desire to marry a wealthy nobleman.

"But what does this mean for me?"

"You've become too valuable to cast off into the countryside," the queen declared. "I need you here. Until my betrothed arrives from Savoy, my attention must be fixed on forging stronger bonds with our allies. Especially Lord de Milly. Your help will be indispensable."

Estelle nodded in gratitude, desperate to believe the queen's words. "Thank you, Your Grace."

Her relief was tempered by the sober awareness that even if she wasn't about to become a man's property, she was still trapped in the Cypriot court.

*Find a way out while you're in her favor. Who knows when she'll cast you aside?*

Sir Hector made a sound of impatience. "Mademoiselle, are you quite well? By the saints, she's gone pale."

"Yes, my lord. I am well." Estelle's voice was steady now. "And honored to assist the queen in this endeavor."

She locked eyes with Queen Charlotta, and for the first time she saw a flicker of warmth in the young woman's gaze.

"I must implore you, Your Grace, to consider this: my family returns from Rhodes to France in a year's time, and they want me at their side. Lord de Milly has approved the plan."

*God forgive me for this lie.*

Estelle's family did plan to return to France one day, though she had no idea when the opportunity would arise. She knew one thing with bone-deep certainty, though: tying her future to the knights would offer the best chance of returning safely to Rhodes.

*I am missed. I am remembered. I am loved.*

She repeated the words over and over in her head like a prayer, drawing strength from them.

Sir Hector harrumphed. "Until the Bastard is captured and imprisoned, the threat to our queen's crown grows more dangerous every day. None of us can have any hope of fulfilling our personal ambitions in the meantime, not least a foreigner like yourself."

"How many times must I say it?" Estelle asked in frustration. "I am not a ward of this court, my lord. Holding me here against my will makes a prisoner of me."

"You've sworn fealty to me," the queen said. "And you are paid for your work. That makes you my courtier."

"I regret to say I have not received a salary since the king's death, Your Grace."

Queen Charlotta gave Sir Hector a pointed stare. "Go along to the treasury, my lord. Fetch a fine fat purse for the mademoiselle, if you please. She and I will get started on my letter to Lord de Milly."

Looking slightly stunned, he made for the door.

Estelle picked up a quill, her mind racing back through the conversation that had just unfolded. The queen's mention of her future husband was intriguing. Estelle's cherished older brother, Étienne, was a knight for the House of Savoy. A jolt of hope shot through her. Could her brother's destiny lead him to Cyprus as well? The thought made her smile.

"You cannot hide your happiness." The queen's expression softened. "Your relief at being freed from the betrothal is plain to see. And worry not, mademoiselle. Once Jacco's ambitions are turned to dust, you will return with your family to France, just as you desire."

Estelle murmured her thanks, one eye on the door. Would Sir Hector truly return with gold? Or would guards rush in and seize her? Either event was equally conceivable. Her body taut with tension, she tried to concentrate on the queen's words and put the quill to paper.

*If the gold is delivered, I'll abandon my plan to escape—for now. But how do I keep it safe? They've gone through my things once. They likely will again.*

A short time later, Sir Hector returned and presented her with a leather sack bulging with heavy coins. For the rest of the afternoon, it sat on the table by the inkpot, irrefutable proof that the queen had bent the man to her will. And when their work was done, Queen Charlotta picked up the sack and placed it in Estelle's hands herself.

"No one will take this from you, mademoiselle. Your things were searched on my command, but you have nothing to fear on that account any longer."

Walking back to her chamber, Estelle made up her mind.

*So be it. I'll write Papa and tell him all is well; I'll send him my earnings once more; I'll be as indispensable as Queen Charlotta wishes me to be.*

*This is the reason I journeyed to Cyprus, by God.*

*To be at her side.*

# CHAPTER 24

Summer 1459
Nicosia, Cyprus

THE QUEEN PUSHED ASIDE the French texts and flopped back in her chair, fanning herself with a piece of linen paper covered with conjugated verbs. She closed her eyes and let out a long sigh.

"Do you feel ill?" Estelle blotted the sweat from her brow with a handkerchief. The heat was oppressive today. Not a breeze stirred in the courtyard, and the sun beat down outside with relentless force.

"I feel . . ." Queen Charlotta opened her eyes again, ". . . tired of being in this study, in this palace, in Nicosia. I want fresh air; I want a view of the sea; I want amusements and games to occupy me until my betrothed arrives."

"Where might you go?" Estelle asked cautiously, glancing at the guards by the door. They looked half-asleep.

"My father used to go to St. Hilarion for his leisurely pursuits. Hunting, primarily. I don't like to hunt, but I enjoy the castle."

Estelle's mind flew to Gabriel. He would be at St. Hilarion unless he was off on a hawking expedition with Monsieur Pelestrine.

His coldness when they'd parted on the day of the coronation had wounded her. But the truth was she'd behaved like a spoiled child. Her cheeks grew hot as she recalled her desperation to flee Cyprus. At the time, her actions had seemed warranted. Now she saw herself through his eyes and understood why he would want to put distance between them.

*I want to see him, no matter the consequences.*

The thought triggered an ache in her, a longing that made her breath quicken.

"Why not go, then?" she asked, careful to keep her tone neutral. "Perhaps we could take all of these things with us." She indicated the books and papers strewn over the table with a sweep of her hand. "We can continue our studies there."

"We?"

Estelle smiled. "The idea of a castle, a view of the sea—it's appealing."

Queen Charlotta looked up as a servant entered carrying a silver pitcher and two Venetian glass cups filled with chunks of ice.

"Lemon tonic." She let out a sigh of pleasure as the woman poured their drinks. "And ice from the highest reaches of the Troodos mountains. That will cool my blood."

"The Savoyard contingent won't arrive until autumn," Estelle said. "There's time to go if you wish, Your Grace."

"Yes." The queen waited until the servant exited the chamber to speak again. "If the barons let me."

"But you're their queen!"

Queen Charlotta's expression drooped. "They tell me I must learn to rule, then dismiss my ideas. If they had their way, they'd take full command of the kingdom until Louis arrives."

"They agreed with your idea to reinforce the coastal fortresses in case Lord Jacco attacks," Estelle reminded her.

"But they refuse to send envoys to Egypt. Jacco has made a home for himself there. He whispers in the sultan's ear while we do nothing. It could be our downfall." The queen took a sip of her drink, then put her cup down with a thump. "I'll go, and I don't care what they say. And you'll accompany me."

Although the queen tried to keep her entourage small, the barons' concerns about security won out in the end. A plodding train of mule carts hemmed in by mounted guards ambled from Nicosia to the castle on a rugged hilltop overlooking the sea. At the center of it all, Queen Charlotta rode in a converted oxcart whose cushioned interior was lined with red silk. And seated among her ladies-in-waiting was Estelle.

The queen's inner circle had once been walled off from her like a defensive tower, and now she lived at the heart of it. Though none of the other women had befriended her in the way Louise had, they were uniformly pleasant and polite. They simply followed the lead of their queen, she understood now. Queen Charlotta's loyalties were theirs.

*Within a few months, I've transformed myself from outcast to confidante. The queen has kept her word; my salary is generous and paid without fail. I must be careful, though, for fortune's wheel spins quickly in this court.*

"How the cart rattles," the queen complained, shifting on her cushioned seat. "Who will help me pass the time?"

"Let's talk of Christine de Pizan's book," Estelle suggested.

The queen brightened. "Excellent idea. You begin."

The two of them discussed at length the administrative details involved in preparing for and surviving a siege, down to the number of crossbow bolts to stock and the amount of food required per day to feed a garrison of five hundred men. The other ladies, bored by talk of requisitioning supplies and bolstering defensive perimeters, dozed in the stupefying heat.

Finally, they emerged blinking into the glare of the sun, the blue canopy of the sky gleaming overhead. Estelle's spirits rose at the sight of the castle's soaring towers and crenellated walls, its unobstructed view stretching to the sea. Finally, she was free of the palace, the capital, and the scheming courtiers whose poisonous gossip fouled the air. Next to her, the queen glowed with excitement. She greeted the steward of the castle and acknowledged the rest of the staff with a torrent of high-spirited Greek.

The steward beckoned to a man in the line of servants, and when he stepped forward, Estelle recognized Michel Pelestrine.

He bowed deeply to the queen. "Your Grace."

She inclined her head. "I don't wish to hunt during my stay here," she informed him. "But when my betrothed arrives in the autumn, he will want to plan many such outings, I've no doubt. You should begin your preparations now."

Monsieur Pelestrine nodded. "It shall be done."

She tilted her head to one side. "You are a true Frenchman," she observed. "Like the mademoiselle. I hear it in your voice."

"Yes, Your Grace." He glanced at Estelle.

Queen Charlotta followed his gaze. "Do you know this man?" she asked Estelle.

"He is a friend of my father's, born and raised in France, like myself."

"Ah?" The queen studied him with new curiosity. "You shall come to supper one evening, then, monsieur. I wish to learn more about France and the French."

"It would be my pleasure, Your Grace."

Estelle searched the ranks of servants for Gabriel, but he was nowhere in sight. Following the queen into the castle, she tried to brush off the disappointment she felt.

*Don't think of him. It's better to keep a clear head.*

Their days began with early morning walks surrounded by guards. They watched the foamy sea churn far below and picked anemones and poppies in a glade near the castle. In the woods near the castle, songbirds trilled from dawn to dusk, accompanied by buzzing, chirruping insects. Estelle and Queen Charlotta practiced their French on these outings, the other ladies trailing behind them, chattering amongst themselves in the Cypriot dialect.

Upon their return to the castle, they sat in the grand salon with its bank of windows overlooking the sea, continuing their work while the queen's other attendants embroidered and gossiped. One afternoon, Queen Charlotta sent away the other ladies, irritated by the complaints of a young woman whose monthly courses were causing her undue suffering.

"All women endure such pains," said the queen. "I don't know why she thinks hers are so much worse."

Estelle set down the book she'd been about to open. "In Rhodes, there was a woman physician, an Italian, who studied medicine at a school in Salerno. My mother used to go to her for tonics that would help ease such pains."

The queen looked at her with a trace of surprise. "Did her potions work?"

Estelle nodded. "My mother would not pay for such things unless she found relief from them. She's sensible that way."

The queen's gaze fell to the book in Estelle's hands. "What do you have there?"

"I discovered it in the palace library long ago. A journal, I think. All in French. I thought we could read it today."

"Very well." Queen Charlotta leaned back in her chair with an expectant look.

She listened to Estelle read each line aloud, then mimicked the sounds as best she could. Her strong Greek accent had not waned since their study of French began, but at least her vocabulary was growing and her comprehension of grammar had improved.

When Estelle paused for a moment, the queen reached for the book. "I believe this was written by a courtier who served my grand-mother Queen Charlotte, the wife of King Janus. He was taken captive by the Mamluks during a battle. My grandmother had died a few years before the Mamluks invaded, but her ladies from France stayed in Cyprus to care for my father and his sisters. When my grandfather was taken captive, the court retreated to Kyrenia with as much treasure as they could carry, and Nicosia was overrun." The queen rose and strode to the windows, still clutching the book. "We can see Kyrenia fortress from here."

Estelle followed her. The massive stone walls of the fortress were

visible where the land met the sea. Seawalls extended from the fortifications to create a small protected harbor.

"The reinforcement work at Kyrenia is nearly done," the queen
said. "I hope I won't be forced to take refuge there, but if I must, it
will be ready."

She opened the book to the next page. Like many of the previous
ones, it was decorated with hearts, fleurs-de-lis, and three-leafed
clovers. The entry began with the single word *Courage*. The writer had
garnished the *C* with elaborate swirls, leaves, and flowers. Within the
sickle-moon shape of the letter itself, she'd sketched a woman's face.

Queen Charlotta touched the image with a fingertip. "Did she
draw herself here, I wonder?"

"Perhaps she did."

The tiny image conveyed a sober, calm expression.

"What does she write next?" the queen asked, handing the book to
Estelle.

Estelle ran her fingertip over the lines of script. "Here she says: *We
have sent some of the most precious things elsewhere on this island, to humble
places out of view of everyone in the world except God.* She describes a beautiful place, a peaceful refuge where a king, a falcon, and a knight
protect the kingdom's treasures under their eternal gaze." A thought
struck her. "Perhaps it's a secret message. She's telling the reader where
to look without giving the location away. She says it rests under the
gaze of the king. Could that mean an image of King Janus? A portrait
or fresco, perhaps?"

"Yes, why not?" Queen Charlotta said. "I've seen frescoes picturing
the king and queen in a church, or perhaps a monastery."

"Which one?"

The queen shook her head. "I was very young, and I don't recall
much about the place." She peered at the French words, frowning.
*"Belle . . ."* she said aloud. *"Pais."* She looked up, eyes shining. "Bellapais!"

Estelle stared back at her uncertainly.

"Bellapais Abbey." Queen Charlotta's voice thrummed with excitement. "It's not far from here. The abbot was at my coronation. Bellapais is where I saw the mural of King Janus and the falcon—I'm nearly
certain."

"And the knight? Did you see his image, too?" A thrill ran over Estelle's skin.

"I don't remember. Does she reveal anything more about the treasure she's hidden on later pages of the journal?"

Estelle shook her head. "It ends when King Janus is ransomed. Nothing further is mentioned of the things they hid away."

"I must collect our kingdom's wealth in the event of an attack, and the monasteries are full of treasures. Though I've put a call out to the priors and abbots to turn over their valuables to me, many will keep what they can for themselves." The queen hesitated. "I may be forced to send riders out to collect what they can. But it's difficult to know who to trust. Perhaps I'll reward those who bring back the most valuable items."

"What about me, Your Grace?" The words tumbled out in a rush. "I'll go to Bellapais and discover the truth."

*If I'm gifted jewels or gold from the scheme, Papa's debts will vanish overnight.*

The queen studied her with narrowed eyes. "You?"

"Who has a better chance of discovering the treasure, if it exists?" Estelle smoothed a hand over the worn cover of the little book. "All the clues about its location are in here. Perhaps there's something I missed. I'll read it all again."

"I wish I could go myself." There was a distinct note of envy in Queen Charlotta's voice and a trace of the wistfulness Estelle had heard in her tone once before.

A valet entered the chamber. "Your Grace, a message from your council has come. They soon leave Nicosia and will join you here to discuss matters of diplomacy."

The queen's mouth tightened. "Very well." She turned to Estelle and dropped her voice. "They won't like the idea of sending riders out for the wealth of the monasteries."

"Then keep the idea secret, Your Grace. The barons seem adept at withholding information when it suits them. Surely, as our ruler, you're entitled to some secrets of your own."

Queen Charlotta chuckled, a radiant smile transforming her expression. "A wise strategy, mademoiselle."

# CHAPTER 25

Summer 1459
St. Hilarion Castle, Cyprus

ESTELLE ENTERED THE COURTYARD, skirted a hay pile by the stables, and slipped inside the mews. She was instantly overcome by memories of following her father into such places as a young girl.

As she did when she was a child, she played a game. She studied the birds in their hutches, identifying them by size, coloring, and body shape. Some of the birds were hooded, their eyes concealed from the world. Others regarded her solemnly in the dim light. Papa always talked to his falcons, using a calm, melodic tone. She mimicked it now, stopping to address each bird in turn.

"Saker, good day to you," she said. "And merlin, too. Ah, a sleek peregrine. And saker again. And—poor thing—gyrfalcon." She stopped, shaking her head at the sight of the bird's disheveled gray feathers. "Dear old girl. You've survived this awful heat. I wish I could bring you some snow."

A voice spoke behind her in Greek. "What business do you have here, mademoiselle?"

She whirled.

It was Gabriel.

Estelle stood tall and looked him in the eyes. She saw a wariness there, an aloofness that made him seem a stranger.

She nodded at the gyrfalcon. "She's suffering. From the cliffs of Norway to the relentless sun of Cyprus—it's not an easy transition."

"Yet the demand for them from kings and sultans never wanes." His tone was softer now. "What else do you know of raptors?"

"I know that sakers do well in this climate because this is their home. They nest in Crete, perhaps here in Cyprus as well. I know that peregrines are superior hunters, but they can be moody and delicate. Merlins are often chosen as pets. My father trained a peregrine and a merlin for the grand master of Rhodes, and Lord de Milly sometimes keeps them in his study when he works." She glanced at the gyrfalcon again. "Have you tried dragon's blood mixed with egg white and *manus Christi* to help cure what ails this one?"

*Manus Christi* was a curative made with rose hips that her father often used in his work.

"Getting her to feed at all is the problem. We have plenty of dragon's blood. If I could coax any down her gullet, I'd be a lucky man indeed."

"There are other recipes in the handbook from my father that might help. Papa used his own knowledge and added instructions from a Greek falconer who is revered on Rhodes."

"Agapitos Kassianos?" Gabriel asked, looking truly astonished now.

She nodded. "None other."

"I've studied the pages of your father's book, but I don't read French as well as I speak it."

Reverting to her native language, she asked, "How did you come to learn it?"

When he replied, his French was soothing and rich, like honey to her ears. "My mother spoke many languages. She taught me what she knew. She spoke French as beautifully as you."

Heat traveled from Estelle's neck to her face at the compliment.

She dropped her gaze, overcome by an awkward shyness, and cast about for a reply. Nothing came to mind.

"Why have you come to St. Hilarion?" Gabriel asked.

"I'm scribe and tutor to the queen now."

He raised an eyebrow. "What about your marriage plans?"

She flinched at his query, the memory of their last conversation looming in her mind. "Canceled."

"So you got what you wanted in the end."

Estelle bristled. "I want to leave this place. That's never changed."

"I don't see you hurrying to do so," he remarked, looking her up and down. "Dressed in silks. Following your queen around her kingdom. Why would you leave? Who knows what rewards you might be handed?" He half-smiled, but his eyes did not hold any warmth.

She squared her shoulders and spoke sharply. "I'll have you know I'm sailing back to France with my family as soon as Lord de Milly releases Papa from service. The queen has given her blessing to the plan."

She thought she saw a glimmer of disappointment in his eyes but dismissed the notion when he spoke again.

"When will that happy day come?"

His mocking tone stung.

"Not soon enough." Though her family did plan to return to France one day, Papa had written that he might have to extend his contract with the knights in order to pay off their debts.

Gabriel studied her in silence, his expression impassive.

His rudeness when they last met flooded back to her. He'd witnessed her darkest moment, then walked away with no good-bye, no words of comfort or reassurance.

She would not let him get the better of her this time. Her station in life had changed drastically since then. She was tutor and scribe to the queen—and he was a simple under-falconer, born to a slave. How dare he question her?

The gyrfalcon flapped her wings, perhaps startled by Estelle's flare of emotion. Papa had taught her that raptors felt and reacted to their handlers' emotions with some sort of inner compass that humans did not possess.

*Oh, for the freedom and power to glide away from here as silently as a falcon. Who can grant me that?*

Spinning on her heel, she made for the door. But she was confronted by the sight of a man entering the mews.

"Mademoiselle Estelle?"

It was Monsieur Pelestrine. He glanced beyond her down the row of cages. "You've been waiting here alone? My apologies. I'd no idea."

She looked over her shoulder. Gabriel had vanished. Turning back to Monsieur Pelestrine, she took in a breath.

"I miss my father and his falcons. It was good to have a quiet moment in the mews."

He searched her face, looking worried. "Your marriage must soon approach."

Estelle shook her head. "I will not marry. For now, anyway."

"Please understand I have no influence in this court. I'm an outsider, a foreigner with no power here." A look of shame crept over his face. "Your father has asked me to do what I can to protect you. Forgive me. There's little I can do, but if I'm ever afforded the opportunity, I will act on your behalf."

She regarded him with empathy, her heart warming toward him. "I understand all too well your predicament, monsieur."

His troubled look eased.

A horse's high, plaintive whinny rose from the stables. "The queen will miss me soon," she said, using the sound as an excuse to turn away. "Good day, monsieur."

He bowed his head. "Good day."

# CHAPTER 26

Summer 1459
St. Hilarion Castle, Cyprus

AT SUPPER ONE NIGHT, Michel Pelestrine was seated next to Estelle. The queen, at the head of the table, questioned him about his past in France and his connections in the falcon trade. In broken but earnest Greek, he made his responses. Estelle listened quietly, her respect for this thoughtful, soft-spoken man growing with every word he uttered.

He truly did seem worthy of her father's friendship, and she was glad she'd given him the falconry handbook. In her first lonely months at the palace, she'd clung to the idea that Monsieur Pelestrine would serve as her protector in the kingdom of Cyprus. As the months wore on with no word from him, a small, bitter part of her had wished she'd withheld the gift. Now she was grateful to have kept her promise to Papa.

At one point, discussing the trade in fine wool fabrics in the same region where her father had been raised, she asked him a question in French instead of Greek. He responded in kind. Remembering the

Queen would not be able to comprehend his rapid French, Estelle leaned closer to Queen Charlotte and quietly translated for her as he spoke.

The queen's eyes grew round. "You are his voice," she marveled. "I've never had an interpreter give me the words at the precise moment they are spoken. The custom is to wait until the speaker finishes, then after a pause give me the words in Greek. I find my mind wanders while the speaker talks, then I forget details of the original conversation after all the pausing. In truth, I despise it." She gave a determined nod. "Let's do it again, only this time in Greek. I'll begin."

Turning to Monsieur Pelestrine, Queen Charlotta asked him a question in rapid Greek. Estelle translated aloud in French as quickly as she could. When he responded, she reversed course, translating his French into Greek this time. The queen's smile was radiant.

"You will always be on hand when I communicate with Frenchmen." She raised her cup and saluted Estelle with it. "Now I know how easy it can be, I'll not go back to the old way."

Estelle raised her glass, too, glowing under the praise.

After the meal, musicians played tunes from a codex of music written for King Janus and the first Queen Charlotte long ago. At Queen Charlotta's urging, the courtiers danced. Cool air streamed in through the bank of windows facing the sea. A sheen of moonlight on the black water glimmered in the distance.

Monsieur Pelestrine appeared at Estelle's side. "Would you do me the honor?"

She put a hand on his outstretched arm, and they took their positions in the center of the room alongside half a dozen other couples.

Estelle's only experience of dance was at home with her family, and it had usually involved rolled-up rugs and shouts of laughter from her younger siblings. Until Étienne left for Savoy at twelve, he'd been her partner, and their parents had taught them both what they knew about courtly dancing. She drew on those hours of instruction now as she dipped and swayed in time to the music, approaching her partner, then drawing back from him.

"Are you glad you've stayed on in service to the queen?" she asked as they circled one another, palm to palm.

He hesitated. "Yes, for now," he finally said. "And you?"

They stepped back a few paces, held up the opposite hands, and turned in the other direction.

"I've found my place in this court," she admitted. "I'm not as unhappy as I once was."

"You're in the queen's favor now." He smiled. "Her best interpreter, from the sound of it."

She stood still while he walked a slow circle around her in time to the music. "French tutor and scribe, too." A ripple of pride rushed through her as she spoke. "And, I believe, friend."

He sobered. "A courtier is never a monarch's friend."

"Why do you say that?"

"The kingdom—her throne—is all she cares about," he said quietly, making a tighter circle around her. "And it is at grave risk. The closer you are to her, the more danger you're in."

She kept her face expressionless, not wanting to draw any more attention to them.

"Jacco is making offers," he went on. "Bribing anyone of influence to join his cause, promising money, titles, lands, properties."

Estelle rested her hand on his arm, and they paraded along the line of paired dancers, stepping lightly in a slow rhythm.

"Has he come to you?" she asked when they came to the end of the line.

"I am not a man of influence." His voice was matter-of-fact as they returned in the opposite direction. "And you?" he asked. "Where do your loyalties lie?"

She thought about the note she'd received from Jacco, about the necklace. His blunt words to her during their tutoring sessions and at the oath of allegiance. The truth about Louise, finally revealed. Now Estelle's loyalty to the queen deepened by the day. After nearly two years of hating her existence here, she enjoyed being a courtier. Fortune's wheel had indeed turned in her favor, and she wanted to relish every moment of her good luck.

Estelle circled her dance partner, studying him with critical eyes.

How would Michel Pelestrine know what it was like to be in a position of such intimate confidence with a monarch? He was isolated here at St. Hilarion, with his falcons and other beasts of the hunt. He knew nothing of true court life.

The music ended, and she dropped into a curtsy.

Rising, she looked him in the face. "I am faithful to our queen."

A royal courier entered the chamber accompanied by the queen's valet. After a brief consultation with them, the queen summoned her steward, who clapped his hands for attention.

"Subjects of the queen, I beg you, hear these tidings. The queen's betrothed, his illustrious lordship Louis of Savoy, arrives in Cyprus in a week's time, if the winds are favorable. Be advised we prepare to leave St. Hilarion for Nicosia tomorrow."

Monsieur Pelestrine accompanied Estelle back to her seat. The queen beckoned her closer.

"I'll need you more than ever now." There was a nervous glint in the monarch's eyes. "Until my betrothed learns Greek, I'm sure there will be many delicate matters that require a French translator." She nodded at the barons, who stood nearby in a loose circle, deep in conversation. "They'll want to choose a translator for me. But they interfere with too much already. I won't let them interfere with my marriage."

"Of course, Your Grace. I'm happy to assist you." Estelle paused. "And Bellapais? Shall I arrange the outing right away?"

"Bellapais? No, no, that must wait for another time. I need you at my side, don't you see?"

The queen's tone was almost plaintive now, her large eyes pleading.

"I won't leave you, I vow it, Your Grace."

Estelle felt the weight of someone's gaze. Lord Chimi had her in his sights, his brow furrowed in an intense look of disapproval. Not long ago, she would have been struck with worry by the sight. But tonight, she stared back steadily until he looked away.

*I've come between the council and their queen, and they resent me for it. Especially him.*

What could they do to her, those men? They would look for a way to separate her from Queen Charlotta, she had no doubt. Perhaps they would accuse her of some false betrayal in hopes of turning the queen against her. She thought of the chessboard in the queen's study.

Étienne had taught her to play when they were small. He'd always encouraged her to plan several moves ahead.

She studied the barons from beneath her lashes, trying to imagine their thoughts.

*What will they plan? How will I prepare for it? I must be ready.*

The men would despise Estelle even more if they knew what the queen had just asked of her. Once Louis of Savoy arrived in Cyprus, she would be more closely entwined with Queen Charlotta than ever.

Her eyes fell to her lap, and she smoothed the repeated pattern of gold embroidery that decorated the emerald green of her skirts, repressing an urge to smile.

*Won't they be surprised?*

# CHAPTER 27

Spring 1460
Nicosia, Cyprus

ANTONIA TIGHTENED ESTELLE'S HEADWRAP, then tugged her sleeves into place.

"Ouch!" Estelle stepped away. "Hurrying is one thing. Torture's another."

The maid snorted. "When was the last time you were called to the queen's study, mademoiselle? Especially this early?" She tipped a dish of raisins and almonds into a leather purse. "Here. You'll faint if you don't eat, what with all that scribing and talking you do."

"Interpreting," Estelle corrected her, tying the purse to her belt. "It's not the same as talking."

"By the Holy Virgin, it all sounds the same to me." Antonia stood back and surveyed her, arms crossed. "You look fresh as a rose and smell as sweet, mademoiselle."

"Thank you."

It was a short walk to the queen's study because Estelle's quarters had been moved closer to the royal apartments when they'd returned from St. Hilarion all those months ago. The queen had wanted her nearby, accessible at all hours. But everything had changed when Louis of Savoy arrived with his vast entourage of attendants, including interpreters of his own. Instead of being called upon at all hours to translate for the royal couple, Estelle was relegated to the background. She occasionally helped the queen with letter-writing and interpreting, but more often found herself sitting alone at a table in the library, translating letters from allies in Western Europe into Greek.

*Perhaps today will be different. Perhaps today the queen has decided she wants me by her side again.*

She waited outside while a guard announced her, then entered at the queen's command. Her heart sank when she saw King Louis sprawled in a chair near the window, his eyes closed. He looked boneless, ready to slither off the chair onto the rug beneath, and his sallow skin made him appear unwell. Glancing at the queen, she saw the monarch was engrossed in the study of a letter.

Aside from the two helmeted guards at the door, no other attendants were present. Normally, the king's personal translator interpreted his French for the queen. Estelle admired the man for his tact and quick mind. She eyed the door, willing the translator to appear.

"Mademoiselle." The queen nodded to her, gesturing to the seat next to hers. "We have a letter to write."

Estelle took her place at the table, where linen paper, an inkpot, and a quill had been laid out for her.

King Louis opened one eye. "Praise God, someone who speaks French. What have you brought me, mademoiselle? Sweets? Playing cards?" He shifted in his chair, picking at a loose thread on his sleeve. "Anything to alleviate the boredom. The dullness of this court is maddening."

Estelle's mouth grew dry. She tried to organize a polite Greek reconstruction of his words in her mind. But the queen didn't wait for her to translate.

"Help me compose a letter to Lord de Milly, my dear husband." Queen Charlotta used her most cajoling tone. "He must hear from you on this matter. It will galvanize him to know your thoughts, to hear this appeal in your voice."

King Louis sighed when Estelle finished translating the queen's words into French. "I cannot think of anything to say. I haven't had milk-fed veal in three days. My blood is weak because of it." He looked around peevishly. "Where's my valet? He should be back by now. He was to bring me a tonic."

Queen Charlotta's mouth compressed into a flat line, her expression tightening. Her reaction confirmed what Estelle had suspected for some time: the queen's powers of comprehension in French far exceeded her ability to speak the language.

Somehow, though, the queen kept her voice light. "My darling, you shall have your veal soon. Sir Hector will arrive any moment and he promised to bring some with him."

As Estelle interpreted the words, the king's face hardened in a scowl. "That's what you said yesterday."

A Savoyard valet entered carrying a silver goblet. "Your Majesty, a hot, sweet tonic, just as you ordered."

King Louis sat up in his chair. "Praise the saints." He took the goblet and sipped, then made a face. "It's barely warm. Go fetch me another, hotter this time."

"My apologies, Sire." The man retrieved the goblet and bowed.

Queen Charlotta slapped a hand on the table. "You have been here for months. You should know how long it takes to walk from the kitchens to my study with a hot drink. Make it scalding this time or you'll lose your place as valet."

"No!" King Louis protested after Estelle's translation, looking distraught. "He plays cards better than the others. I need him in my chambers."

A look of molten fury seized Queen Charlotta's face.

*The poor queen. This marriage is not what she imagined. And he is not the king we needed.*

Queen Charlotta's hopes for a strong partner in love and life had frayed with each passing day since Louis of Savoy's arrival. In some ways, Estelle realized, the queen was worse off with this husband than she had been ruling alone.

The valet scuttled away, nearly colliding with several members of the queen's council as they entered the study. When they spotted Estelle, their expressions soured.

Their coldness to Estelle had not waned over the winter. Lord Chimi was blatantly rude to her. Sir Hector was aloof and dismissive. The others were ravens rasping at her from a tree. Annoying, sometimes menacing, but generally harmless.

"Did you fetch the veal?" King Louis asked Sir Hector.

"It's being sent to the kitchens now." The man's deep voice was soothing and patient, as if he were speaking to a small child. "You'll have your fill today, tomorrow, and the next."

"God is good!" The king beamed. "You've done well, Sir Hector."

"My spies in Alexandria have sent a letter saying war is coming to our shores," the queen said when the council was assembled around her. "Jacco has the full support of the sultan. I wanted to send envoys to Egypt a year ago and enlist the sultan's support myself, but you counseled me not to." Her voice crackled with anger. "When we finally sent them, it was too late. Therefore we should begin by telling Lord de Milly the truth: our diplomatic efforts have failed, and we are on the brink of war."

"No, let's begin by saying our delegates to Egypt were nearly victorious but were felled by a plague," said Sir Hector. "Not by a failure of diplomacy."

"Not plague," said Lord Chimi. "Tell Lord de Milly it was poison. God knows it could have been."

Sir Hector scoffed. "But a plague is raging in Egypt."

"Poison will make more of an impression." Lord Chimi stood over Estelle. "Begin!"

Estelle did not pick up her quill. Instead, she looked at the queen.

The young woman's face was taut with anxiety.

*There is no turning Egypt to her cause, not anymore. Queen Charlotta's only hope for support lies in the West.*

The realization struck Estelle in her very core.

Sir Hector gestured at Estelle's quill. "Mademoiselle, why do you not write my words?"

"She is to write *my* words. Poison, not plague." Lord Chimi glared at Sir Hector.

Estelle's muscles tensed.

"What is it Lord de Milly and the rest of the knights care for more than anything else, mademoiselle?" Queen Charlotta's voice was rough with lost sleep.

A wave of hostility rushed toward Estelle from the barons. She kept her eyes on the queen.

"Christendom." Estelle's breath grew shallow as she pushed out the words. "Preserving all of Christendom. And protecting the innocent. In times of war, all the citizens of Rhodes Town are welcomed into the grand master's palace."

She imagined her father placing a well-trained peregrine falcon on Lord de Milly's gloved wrist. The grand master's smile of thanks, his thoughtful questions, his reasoned answers. She'd heard countless stories from Papa about the man's wisdom, his fairness, his strong leadership. None of these men could claim insights into Lord de Milly's character the way she could. Slowly, she regained her composure.

"Yes." The queen nodded thoughtfully. "If the sultan takes Cyprus, he will strike a grievous blow at Christendom everywhere. Everything the Lusignan kings have struggled for, all we've gained in the name of God—it will crumble into dust if we have no support from the Order of St. John, from the pope, from all our Western allies." She gestured at the paper, waving her hand in an imitation of writing.

Estelle took up the quill, dipped it into the inkpot.

She ignored the barons, maintaining even pressure with her nib, forming each word with great care.

As had become their custom, Queen Charlotta spoke the words aloud in Greek, then Estelle translated them into French so the monarch might hear how her phrases would sound on the page. The men peered over her shoulders and interjected frequently, editing the queen's turns of phrase or choice of words. Each time, Estelle interpreted their statements aloud for the queen. Only when Queen Charlotta approved the changes did Estelle dip her quill into the inkpot and write again.

Despite the awful tension in the room and the constant interruptions by the council, Estelle wrote steadily.

"Tell Lord de Milly the court is retreating to Kyrenia fortress," the monarch said. "We've reinforced the structure, and it is well provisioned. We can withstand a siege. And if our shores are invaded, no subject of mine will be turned away from Kyrenia. It will be a place of refuge for all."

Estelle gave a start of surprise, cracking her nib. She locked eyes with the queen, and a look of knowing passed between them.

*Christine de Pizan. The Book of Deeds of Arms and of Chivalry. This is what we studied together.*

Discarding the ruined quill, Estelle snatched up a new one and gave the queen a nod of encouragement.

"But to win the coming war, we shall require aid," Queen Charlotta went on. "We need ships to sail from Rhodes with fighting men and more provisions. We need gold to finance all our efforts. Jacco has raised an army of Mamluks, and they sail for Cyprus any day. My spies say a hundred ships will be in the fleet, perhaps more. Finish it thus: Your assistance is urgently required. If you wish to preserve Christendom, you must act on our behalf, Lord de Milly."

Estelle fought to keep a tranquil demeanor as she wrote. Jacco's bid for the throne was no longer a distant threat. A fleet of warships could be gliding silently through the sea from Egypt at this moment, ready to attack. Once on Cypriot soil, his army would quickly grow in number —after all, he already had many supporters here—and lay waste to the homes and possessions of those loyal to the queen.

Estelle did not want to think about what his soldiers would do to people like herself.

"Next," Queen Charlotta said, "a letter to the pope."

"But your husband failed to visit His Holiness on the journey from Savoy," Lord Chimi said. "The pope is not inclined to help you now. A diplomatic mission must be sent with gifts that will mollify His Excellency. These things take time to progress."

King Louis roused himself. "I didn't wish to be late to my own wedding, monsieur! I had no choice but to bypass Rome."

"Send diplomats to the pope if you must, but they will carry our appeal with them, and they will leave immediately." The queen looked at Estelle. "We must also write to my father-in-law in Savoy. He must send more men to defend the crown. We don't have nearly enough to withstand the sultan's army."

Lord Chimi snorted. "The Duke of Savoy has sent his fleet elsewhere, I'm afraid. I've learned two Savoyard ships are anchored in Genoese waters."

The valet returned with a steaming goblet, distracting King Louis from the mention of his father.

"He'll take action when he learns my husband's life is at stake," the queen said flatly.

"You don't speak for the king," said Lord Chimi.

A jolt of energy surged through Estelle. She fought a powerful urge to spring up and slap Lord Chimi across the face. Instead, she sent a silent plea to Queen Charlotta.

*Don't waver, I beg you. Put him in his place, my queen.*

Queen Charlotta rose. "How dare you?" Her hands curled into fists. "I am your sovereign. You would do well to remember that, my lord."

Lord Chimi gave a shallow bow. He did not appear the least bit contrite. "Apologies, Your Grace."

King Louis gulped the steaming liquid from his goblet and smacked his lips. "Ah. This is just as it should be." He gave Lord Chimi a stern look. "My queen and I are of the same mind on this matter. We shall send letters to my father and to the captains of the fleet he sent to Genoa. I'm certain my Savoyard kin will answer our call."

Estelle watched the ink dry on the page before her, the king's words echoing in her ears. Her brother Étienne had not been among the contingent of Savoyards who'd arrived in Cyprus in the autumn. She'd questioned a few of King Louis's courtiers and learned Étienne was alive and well. Once she'd seen what a poor leader King Louis was, she'd wept with relief to know her brother's fate would not be dictated by the man.

She flicked her gaze to the queen. The joy she had exhibited at St. Hilarion was gone. Would it ever return? Instead of being comforted by an able and strong husband, Queen Charlotta was as alone as ever, fending for her kingdom, enduring a harsh litany of advice from her councilors, trying to determine a course that would protect her crown.

"To the pope, then, Your Grace?" Estelle balanced the quill between thumb and forefinger, gripped by a profound feeling of respect. Queen Charlotta's love for her kingdom was limitless, as was her determination to keep her throne.

*I hope I can exhibit the same courage in my darkest hours.*

Queen Charlotta nodded. "Yes, to Pope Pius."

The barons glowered. Estelle forced them out of her mind, concentrating purely on the effort of translating Greek to French, then putting the quill to page and writing with all the grace she could muster.

# CHAPTER 28

Spring, 1460
St. Hilarion Castle, Cyprus

"AH! THERE YOU ARE." The steward of St. Hilarion beckoned Gabriel forward.

The scent of crushed herbs rose up from a silver bowl on the steward's desk, mixing with the aroma of beeswax from the candles burning on every surface. As usual, Gabriel was unsettled by the opulence on display in the castle. He'd grown up all too familiar with poverty and hunger. He found the disparity between Cyprus's royal residences and the squalor of its poorest neighborhoods deeply disturbing.

"Monsieur Pelestrine tells me you once worked for the Knights Hospitaller at their sugar plantation."

Taken aback by the comment, Gabriel was slow to answer. "That is correct, sir."

"In what capacity did you work at Kolossi, then?"

"First, as a page. Later, as a guard."

"You were given military training?"

Gabriel nodded. "Years of it."

A gleam of curiosity entered the man's eyes. "What twist of fate took you from guard at Kolossi to the mews of St. Hilarion?"

"I left the employ of the knights to pursue a family matter." Gabriel paused, caught on a memory of his mother's hand clinging tightly to his own at Famagusta Harbor, at the delight on her face when he pointed at a merchant galley destined for Alexandria anchored near the docks. That day, he'd seen a rare glimpse of joy in her eyes.

Pushing the image away, he met the steward's gaze again. "When that was resolved, I crossed paths with Michel—Monsieur Pelestrine. He offered me work in the royal mews, and as I had no other employment at the time, I accepted his offer."

"I see. Your combat experience may be useful in the months ahead. Over the next fortnight, we'll be moving most of the contents of this castle to Kyrenia fortress, including the falcons. You and Monsieur Pelestrine will be overseeing the birds in their new home. Queen Charlotta may use them as gifts for her allies, so they must be kept in fine form."

"Is there a mews in the fortress?"

The steward shook his head. "The falcons will be housed in the stables." Before Gabriel could protest, he raised a hand. "It's far from ideal, but neither is the situation we find ourselves in. The roads may no longer be safe, though we must travel them. Rumor has it that Jacco the Pretender is recruiting gangs of cutthroats to terrorize those loyal to Queen Charlotta all over the island."

"The Pretender? Is that what they're calling him now?"

"The Bastard, the Pretender—he's one and the same. It will not be long before his agents learn the court is abandoning Nicosia; I've no doubt they will soon head our way." The steward gave Gabriel an up-and-down examination. "You wear a dagger. You also own a sword, I assume?"

"Of course."

"I advise you to wear it at all times. You may well be called to use it in defense of the court and its possessions."

Though no one else was in the chamber, the steward dropped his voice. "I called you here alone with a particular question in mind. We'll be hard-pressed to feed the people in Kyrenia, let alone the animals. If you are asked to lead men from the fortress in search of food, will you do it?"

Gabriel squared his shoulders. "I've heard Kyrenia has underground passages, ways to gain entry or make an exit undetected. If I'm to lead such missions, I'll need to know those routes. I won't put myself in harm's way by using the main gates, especially if we're under siege."

"God willing, there will be no siege." There was a hint of anxiety in the steward's voice. "But your request is reasonable. It shall be honored."

"In that case, I'll gladly fetch provisions whenever necessary," Gabriel promised.

Michel was bent over a traveling cage, securing the leather straps that would bind the structure tight on the journey to Kyrenia. He stood as Gabriel approached.

"What did the steward want of you?" he asked, wiping sweat from his brow with a sleeve.

"Testing my loyalty, more or less. And gauging my skill with a blade, in case it's ever needed."

Michel studied him for a moment but said nothing. He dug in the purse attached to his belt and withdrew a sealed letter.

"A messenger came while you were gone. Left this for you."

Gabriel nodded his thanks. He broke the seal and held the square of linen paper up to the torchlight. He read the message twice, then held a corner of the paper to the torch.

When he dropped it on the stone floor, Michel watched it curl in on itself, shriveling to a blackened twist of ash. Then he raised his eyes to Gabriel's.

"Not good news, I take it."

Gabriel took a moment to answer. "Again, it all comes back to loyalty."

"Let me guess. Jacco has made you an offer."

"And not the first one either. How did you know?"

Michel gave him a lopsided smile. "Even I've heard he's been recruiting for his group of agents. Or, as a guard referred to them yesterday, his demon-sired whoresons."

Gabriel made a sound of mock outrage. "You truly think I'd join them?"

"You were born and raised on this island. You know it better than most men. You've got courage; you've got skill with a blade. You speak a half-dozen languages. Jacco is no fool. He's pursuing the men who will put him on the throne, and he's buying their loyalty."

Gabriel shifted his weight from one leg to the other, uneasy. "His power is growing, that's certain. The Sultan of Egypt has lined his pockets with gold and given him an army."

"They're rumored to be at sea as we speak." The torchlight danced on the Frenchman's face, revealing a sheen of sweat. "They could land any day."

"Have you received an invitation from the pretender, as well?"

"No. I have none of your talents. Whether that makes me lucky or doomed, I'm not certain." Michel let out an unconvincing laugh.

"You're a fine master falconer. The finest I've met."

Now Michel's laugh was genuine. "But how many master falconers have you met in your lifetime, my friend?"

Gabriel returned his grin. "Enough to know what makes a good one."

Michel's gaze returned to the row of traveling cages. "We've got much to do before morning. We'd best get back to this before the torches burn out."

As Gabriel crouched before a cage and began testing the wooden joints, his mind returned to the letter. He'd been promised not only gold, but a house and land. In return, he would have to become a spy. There'd been no mention of the gang of cutthroats. Jacco was an intelligent man. He understood Gabriel was much more valuable to him within the queen's retinue, inside the walls of Kyrenia fortress, than roaming the countryside terrorizing her supporters.

Gabriel felt no allegiance to Queen Charlotta. She wasn't much more than a girl, and, from what he could see, she was under the control of the barons, just as her father had been before her. He'd hoped her new husband would prove to be the leader Cyprus needed, but from what he heard of the man, that hope was unfounded.

The promise of a home and land was tempting. Still, would it ever materialize, even if Gabriel agreed to the scheme? The thought of Jacco having unchecked power did not sit well with him. The idea of pledging loyalty to him, becoming his servant, was disturbing. There'd been a rumor that the king had tried to legitimize his only son; he'd brought the idea before the High Council of Nicosia, but died before the councilors gave their answer. Even if they'd been inclined to approve the idea, Jacco's alliance with the Mamluks of Egypt had destroyed his chances of a peaceful transfer of power. Christianity in the Kingdom of Cyprus would likely meet its end if he seized the throne now, for he was beholden to the sultan of Egypt.

There was no right answer.

Gabriel wound a strip of leather around an unsteady corner of one of the cages, then tested its strength. It held.

Nodding in satisfaction, he moved on to the next cage.

Each time his mind returned to the letter, his hands stilled and his breath quieted. It was not his way to ruminate, but he'd never faced a predicament this tangled before.

By the time the torches burned out, Gabriel knew one thing: he was not ready to make this decision. He would put off answering as long as he could.

# CHAPTER 29

Summer 1460
Kyrenia Fortress, Cyprus

THE FORTRESS of Kyrenia stood sentinel at the edge of the sea, its hulking stone walls both a symbol of refuge for Cypriots and a warning to invaders. Watching carts and wagons roll through the iron-reinforced gates, Estelle made a silent tally of people and animals.

She turned to Antonia. "How will we all fit?"

"The fortress could house every citizen of Nicosia," the woman replied. "You'll see once you explore the place, mademoiselle."

Estelle turned in a slow circle, examining the massive walls for signs of weakness. She saw nothing but solid stone. Thanks to the queen, this structure had been thoroughly reinforced as soon as Jacco had left for Egypt. It would take a long, sustained effort—and plenty of cannons—to weaken those walls. As the heavy gates thudded closed behind the last cart, her muscles clenched. If this place was a refuge, why did she feel trapped?

To distract herself, she surveyed the inner harbor. Several armed galleys were anchored there. Cannons were mounted along the high seawalls, pointing at the waves. The sight was reassuring. If enemy ships attempted to blockade the harbor, they'd be blown to bits by cannon shot.

Most of the kingdom's wealth now lay within these thick walls, locked away in secret vaults. The courtyard was heaped with trunks and wooden boxes containing the rest of the court's possessions, now waiting to be unpacked.

"Come," she said to Antonia. "We have much to do before we sleep tonight."

The first week passed quickly. The courtiers and servants did what they could with tapestries, small furnishings, and ornaments to soften the stark, gloomy chambers of the fort, but they could not mask the true purpose of the structure: to withstand a siege.

Estelle slept in a chamber with several other members of Queen Charlotta's retinue. She shared a bed with a woman who talked incessantly about war and often woke screaming from nightmares.

For her part, Estelle was consumed by her work and grateful for the distraction. She was called upon often to translate and write correspondence for the queen. If she'd had nothing to do, like her bedmate, her mind would be roiling with darkness, too.

Within these thick stone walls, she could only imagine birdsong, the chirp of crickets, the soft riffle of wind through a fig tree's leaves. Here, she caught glimpses of the sea and sky, the occasional soaring gull or wayward pigeon. Wind forced its way through chinks in the stone with a low, persistent moan that burrowed into her skull.

More unsettling still were the faint cries rising up from the dungeons beneath the fortress, twisting though gaps in stone and mortar, fighting their way skyward. Enemies of the Lusignan kings had always been imprisoned in this fortress, other courtiers told her. This was where the treacherous were tortured, where spies were interrogated, where traitors lost their heads.

Whenever she heard those ghostly sounds, she prayed for the poor souls who made them.

*Please, God, forgive them, whatever they're guilty of.*

"Estelle." The queen's voice was strained and raspy these days. If she had smiled since her wedding day, Estelle had not witnessed it.

"Yes, Your Grace?" Estelle looked up from the letter she was writing to the Grand Commander of the Knights of St. John, the man who oversaw the Order's properties in Cyprus.

"Tonight, my servants arrive here with all the treasure of St. Hilarion castle, including the most precious falcons from the mews."

Estelle put down her quill. "Are the falconers with them?"

"The castle's entire household is on the move. Every member of my court, from the most powerful lord to the lowliest servant, must come to Kyrenia." The queen's shoulders slumped. "For I cannot defend them if they do not."

Indignance shot through Estelle. Why did the queen have to shoulder the burden of defending this kingdom alone? If only her husband would assemble an army, make a plan to defend the island. Instead, he complained about the lack of comforts in the fortress, the dearth of entertainments.

"Few abbots or priors have heeded my call to bring their valuables to us. You have a dozen notes of command to write next, ordering them to deliver their possessions to Kyrenia. My couriers will ride for every monastery on Cyprus tomorrow at dawn. We shall start seeing a procession of holy men arriving at Kyrenia with all haste, if God hears my prayers. And even if He does not, my guards can be most persuasive."

Estelle nodded, her heart sinking. Already, her writing hand was stiff from too many hours spent scratching out words on a page. She tried not to think about the fact that she'd be paid nothing for the work.

In the months since the queen began preparing for war, she had eliminated salaries for her essential attendants. They'd all been promised gold once the Pretender was dealt with and the kingdom was functioning normally again. Until then, they would economize as the queen herself must.

Estelle kept most of her remaining coin in her purse, attached to her belt at all times. She'd hidden a stash of ducats in a hollow between the frame and the bottom of her traveling trunk. But here in the fortress, she had no need for money. She was housed and fed by the Cypriot court.

*Soon,* she reminded herself, *this will all be in the past.*

Her family would leave for France one day, and she would be with them. The queen had assured her more than once she would be released from service when the time came.

Squaring her shoulders, Estelle got back to work.

Several hours later, she eyed the pile of correspondence before her with glassy indifference. As the wax seals cooled, Queen Charlotta absently ran her fingertips over the mother-of-pearl tiles embedded in the table's surface.

A servant poured wine into a Venetian glass cup for the queen. She gestured to him to pour one for Estelle, too.

"You've done well, mademoiselle." Queen Charlotta raised her cup. "You don't complain; you don't weep. Your skills cannot be faulted, neither as a scribe nor a translator. I am fortunate to have you by my side. I cannot say the same for all my other ladies."

Estelle bowed her head, taken aback by the compliments. The queen rarely expressed appreciation aloud.

"Thank you, Your Grace," she finally managed to reply.

They both drank.

A few days later, as evening fell and the sky turned amber, the first of the priors and abbots arrived. Among them was the abbot of Bellapais Abbey.

Estelle was called in to meet him.

"Long ago, some of the kingdom's treasures may have been hidden in abbeys and monasteries around the island," the queen told him.

"The mademoiselle discovered a book that describes such hiding places. I believe one may be at Bellapais."

Estelle took up the volume and read portions of the little book aloud. As she translated the text into Greek, the abbot's attention kept returning to the sack of silver candlesticks, incense burners, and other ornaments he had brought from the abbey.

"We've murals and frescos, to be sure," he said vaguely when she finished. "But all in a state of decay. If we had more funds, of course, we could restore them."

"Do not conceal anything from me." The queen's voice was icy. "You will not like the consequences."

"I know the abbey better than anyone, Your Grace. I'll return there and make an investigation of the walls for you. After all, I belong there, not in this fortress."

Queen Charlotta had told Estelle before the abbot arrived that he was rumored to keep concubines in the abbey. Here in the fortress, he would truly have to live as a monk.

The queen stared at him for a long moment. "Where is your record book?"

"Locked in my residence at Bellapais, Your Grace."

"Give me the keys to the abbey," she commanded.

He put a hand to the iron key ring at his waist, a horrified expression on his face. "Your Grace!"

"Now."

Slowly, he unhooked the key ring from his belt and laid it on the table.

"Retire and rest, abbot." The queen's tone calmed. "You must be fatigued after your journey."

With downcast eyes, he trudged from the chamber.

"I don't trust him," Queen Charlotta said to Estelle. "I would guess he's held some goods back for himself."

"I could go to Bellapais myself, as we once discussed." The idea of escaping the fortress even for one day sent pinpricks of excitement up Estelle's spine. "I can keep my seat on a horse. My brother and I used to ride together on the count's lands in Auvergne. I could bring a pair of your guards with me, and—" Her thoughts jumped to Gabriel. Their last few encounters had been frustrating and painful. She recalled the wariness in his expression, his mocking words.

*No, not him.*

Her mind settled on Michel Pelestrine, the only man in Cyprus she was confident she could trust.

"I'd like the master falconer of St. Hilarion castle to come along, too. My maid, Antonia, is strong and sensible. She can be my companion. We'll be there and back again in one day, if all goes well."

The queen took a long breath before responding, her eyes never leaving Estelle's face. "You look forward to this outing."

"Yes."

"You may rise."

Estelle stood, her buoyant mood seeping away.

"There are many among the court who believe the Pretender's star is ascending, and they are mesmerized by its glow." The queen got to her feet, too. "Jacco took a liking to you, gave you a fine gift, directed the full power of his charm your way. Did he ask for your loyalty, too?"

Estelle held her gaze. "I swore fealty to you, my queen."

"Every day, people loyal to me turn tail and pledge their allegiance to my bastard brother. I've seen too many times in this court the consequences of betrayal—it sickens me. Much more of it will turn my heart to iron."

Sorrow radiated from Queen Charlotta like a feverish heat. She looked frail, worn down, aged beyond her years. Estelle yearned to embrace her, to offer words of comfort.

But a fierce gleam in the queen's dark eyes made her uneasy. Estelle stayed motionless, sure the wild pounding of her heart was audible.

For a long, agonizing moment, Queen Charlotta said nothing. When she finally spoke, her harsh voice snaked through the air like the flicking point of a whip.

"If you ever betray me, mademoiselle, your life will be forfeit."

# CHAPTER 30

Summer 1460
Kyrenia Fortress, Cyprus

GABRIEL HELPED UNLOAD the traveling cages from a mule cart. He signaled to the oldest stable hand.

"Find a steady partner and carry these two at a time into the stables, then put them into the stalls against the far wall," he directed the lad. "There's a coin in it for you if you take extra care. I don't want the birds jostled, and if you drop one, your master will hear of it."

"Yes, *kyrie*." The boy tugged at a companion's sleeve.

Michel returned from his meeting with the garrison commander. His normally cheerful expression had sobered. "A group of servants from St. Hilarion made for Nicosia and pledged their loyalty to Jacco as soon as we left the castle. The commander told me dozens of the queen's attendants have done the same."

Gabriel shook his head. "They're likely doing it out of fear. Queen Charlotta's supporters in the east are being strung up, beheaded, their homes ransacked, their gold pilfered. Jacco's agents show little mercy."

Michel's face paled. "Surely, that's just gossip."

"I wish it were." Gabriel wiped his sweaty brow with a sleeve.

"You won't be pleased to hear what I have to say next, then."

"What do you mean?"

"I've been commanded by the queen to accompany Estelle de Montavon and her party to Bellapais Abbey tomorrow. Apparently, the abbot held back some treasure there. The mademoiselle seems to know where it is. Or she thinks she does."

"I'm better suited for such a job," Gabriel protested. "You're not skilled with a blade."

Michel raised an eyebrow. "Don't hold back now. Tell me what you truly think of my swordsmanship."

"I only say it because the roads are more dangerous with every passing day." Gabriel aided the boys with the next cage, admonishing them to navigate the uneven cobblestones with care. "Now that the queen has abandoned Nicosia and St. Hilarion, Jacco's men will be bolder in their tactics. They've stuck to the east of Cyprus so far, but they'll soon move our way."

"You seem to know a lot about their activities." Michel's eyes held a question. In the bustling courtyard of Kyrenia fortress, surrounded by the queen's staunchest supporters, he would not dare voice it.

"I'm a Cypriot," Gabriel replied. "I make it my business to know because I dearly hope to stay alive. I owe you much, friend. You can't go to Bellapais without me." He pointed at the boys, who were trotting back from the shadowy confines of the stables. "I suppose we'll have to assign them to help keep an eye on the birds while we're gone. Why were you chosen for this outing?"

"Estelle de Montavon asked for me specifically. She must have her reasons. God knows I can't stay here while she rides out to those hills. I could never face her father again if I did."

Gabriel took in his friend's words, frowning. That French girl intrigued him, but she was also infuriating. She'd sought his aid, claimed to want nothing more than to escape Cyprus—until she'd wormed her way into the queen's favor. Now she was enjoying her privileged position, becoming as imperious as the queen herself. It annoyed him, and if he had a chance to tell her so on this ridiculous journey, he would.

A galley entered the harbor with its banners rippling in the wind. Distracted from his thoughts, Gabriel shaded his eyes, watching the crew maneuver it into position, readying to drop anchor.

"Let's pray these ships keep coming, for how the queen plans to feed everyone in this fortress is beyond me."

He glanced at the open gates, where a stream of people, animals, and carts filed into the courtyard under the glare of the sun. Michel followed his gaze.

"It will be hard enough to feed the people," the Frenchman agreed. "What about the falcons? Meat will be near impossible to get the longer we're trapped in here."

"There's enough to last them a week or so," Gabriel replied. "After that, I'll take care of it. I've my sources."

Michel searched his eyes again but said nothing.

"Boys!" Gabriel called. "There's a sausage in it for each of you if you step up the pace. We don't want to be standing here until night falls."

The stable hands grinned at the mention of sausage.

Michel chuckled. "You know how to motivate a lad, that's certain."

"I remember all too well what it was like to be a growing boy with an empty belly," Gabriel said softly.

"Let's get the rest of these cages in." Michel gestured at the nearest one. "Give me a hand?"

Gabriel helped Michel lift the cage. As they carried it past the horses and mules to the farthest stalls, where the rest of the cages stood, his mood plummeted. The air was stale in here, the shifting torchlight weak. The cages would have to be stacked one atop the other. Far from ideal conditions for raptors.

"Discouraging, isn't it?" Michel removed his cap and ran his fingers through his hair. "But the commander told me the queen plans to send most of the falcons across the sea as gifts to her allies. So this won't be a problem for long."

"Good." Gabriel smiled at his friend. "Because there's a whole host of new problems coming."

# CHAPTER 31

Summer 1460
Kyrenia Fortress, Cyprus

ESTELLE WATCHED Antonia settle uneasily on her horse.

"You have ridden before, haven't you?" she asked, taking the reins from the stable boy and handing them up to the maid.

"Of course." Antonia gripped the reins so hard her knuckles turned white.

Estelle sent the stable boy to fetch her own horse. She turned her head at the sound of voices coming from the harbor. When she recognized Sir Hector and Lord Chimi approaching from the dock, she groaned inwardly. Sir Hector's hound trotted alongside his master, his large paws silent on the cobblestones.

She thrust a hand in her purse and came up with a biscuit.

As the men passed, Sir Hector nodded a greeting. Lord Chimi did not acknowledge her. The hound came closer and nuzzled her hand. She laughed and held out the biscuit. Crumbs sprayed the ground as the hound devoured it, then snuffled at her cloak.

"What's this?" Sir Hector's deep voice was tinged with indignation. "He never leaves my side."

"You should have him whipped," Lord Chimi returned.

Another voice rang out. "Whipping a hound for accepting a treat won't end well."

Estelle drew in a sharp breath.

*Gabriel.*

The falconer emerged from the stables leading a horse. His gaze slid from the men to Estelle, and his gray eyes were cold.

She bent down. "Go along, boy," she murmured in the hound's ear. "Mind your master."

With one more hopeful sniff at her hand, he bounded after Sir Hector.

Gabriel thrust the horse's reins at Estelle.

"I thought you were a falconer, not a stable hand." She smiled.

His stony expression did not change. "If you hadn't planned this fool's errand, I'd be spending the day with my hawks. Instead, here we are."

"You're joining us?" she asked. "There's no need if you don't wish to come along."

"No need? You leave me with little choice."

Michel Pelestrine hurried out from the stables, smiling broadly. "Mademoiselle de Montavon, what a pleasure to see you again."

"Thank you, monsieur. Your presence will be most welcome on the journey."

Gabriel made a noise that sounded like a strangled cough and vanished into the stables again.

She gave Monsieur Pelestrine a questioning look.

"His mood will lighten once we get on the road," the Frenchman assured her.

"I don't care what his mood is like." Estelle swung into the saddle. "Shall we be off?"

The rising sun set the sea aflame as their party rode through the fortress's gates. Estelle's heart soared. It was glorious to feel the sun beating down on her brow and watch the wind ruffle her horse's mane. She longed to urge her mount into a gallop, to taste freedom for a day. She and Étienne had ridden on the count's lands too many times to count when they were children, racing through meadows and along the shores of the lake where swans paddled under shifting clouds.

Shading her eyes with a hand, she spied the towers of St. Hilarion castle outlined against the blue sky on a distant peak. Then her gaze lingered on the road to Nicosia snaking through a notch in the craggy mountains to the south. Would she ever travel that road or see the capital again? It was unlikely. Even if the queen moved her court back to Nicosia once the threat of siege passed, Estelle would not be in her retinue. Soon she would sail away from Kyrenia, back to Rhodes and her family. The thought of leaving Cyprus made her feel even lighter, more exuberant.

"Which of these mountains are we heading to?" she called out to Monsieur Pelestrine, who rode alongside Gabriel a few paces away.

"Buffavento," he replied, pointing. "Throne of the winds. There's a ruined castle on it, see?"

She shifted in the saddle, studying the serrated peaks.

"We're riding all the way there?" she asked in dismay.

"Bellapais Abbey is tucked in a valley well below that peak. It's not far," he assured her.

Her gaze shifted to Gabriel. He stared straight ahead. His displeasure at being part of their group showed in the rigid tension of his spine, the hard set of his jaw. Despite his prickly temperament, she was reassured by his presence on this outing. Without the falconers along, she would have to place all her faith in the pair of guards who rode at the head and tail of their party, silent and stern-faced.

Next to her, Antonia chattered as they rode past groves of cypress and carob, orchards planted with olive trees, vast stretches of lemon and orange trees that were bare of fruit.

"Everything edible has been harvested and sent by mule train to Kyrenia," the maid said when Estelle expressed disappointment at the fruitless groves. "You'll be glad for that when you get back to the fortress, mademoiselle."

Each homestead they passed between Kyrenia and the abbey was quiet. The inhabitants and their animals had likely fled to the fortress,

Antonia declared, though some may have retreated to higher ground, taking shelter in the mountains until the threat of war passed.

It was not a long journey, but the way grew steep as they neared the abbey. Mist cloaked the upper reaches of the mountains, and a gentle rain began to fall as they climbed a steep curve through terraced vineyards, their mounts slowing with the effort. A village appeared in her sights, and beyond it rose the graceful spires of Bellapais Abbey.

Estelle caught her breath, mesmerized.

Without realizing it, she pulled on the reins. Her horse stopped. Antonia, who had been a little ahead of her, didn't notice and kept moving along.

She studied the soaring rooflines of each building, admiring the fine craftsmanship, the stone curves and arches softened by wind and rain. This could have been built by French stonemasons. In fact, it likely had been. Tears burned in her eyes, sparked by a fierce longing for home.

Hooves pounding the earth disturbed her reverie. She swiped at her eyes with the hem of her cloak.

"What is it?" Gabriel cantered up, his voice laced with irritation. "Why do you linger here?"

She gathered herself. "I—I didn't realize I had stopped."

"Keep up," he commanded. "Each moment we delay makes this outing riskier."

Estelle straightened in the saddle. "It won't happen again." She urged her horse into a trot. "Why are you angry at me?" she asked when she was abreast of him.

He did not turn his head. "You think of this as a marvelous adventure. I think of it as an unnecessary risk."

"We're helping the queen prepare for war. It's our duty. And if it feels like an adventure, too, what of it?"

He was silent a moment. "The first few times we met, you struck me as intelligent. But now I'm not so sure."

"Why do you say that?"

"You've been sheltered like a bird in a gilded cage in the palace for years now. You've seen little of what men can do for the sake of money or power. I pray to God that you don't pay dearly for your innocence—and the rest of us don't suffer because of your choices."

His words stung more than she wanted to admit. "I'm not as innocent as you think, *geraki*. I've seen violence. I've had to survive this world just as you have."

He watched her, one eyebrow raised slightly, and kept silent. Was that a smile playing around his mouth?

A current of fury rippled through her. "Do you mock me?" she demanded.

Digging his heels into his mount's belly, he galloped away without another word. Startled, Estelle's horse broke into a canter. She clung fiercely to the saddle's pommel to keep herself upright.

"Coward!" she shouted at Gabriel.

The wind snatched the word and flung it to the heavens. She gulped for air. When was the last time she had shouted at anyone? She'd done it rarely, when her younger brother Jean-Philippe's mischievous ways led him toward danger, or a heavily loaded donkey veered too close in a crowded Rhodes Town street.

Slowly, her anger gave way to resolve.

*Gabriel Bayoumi is unfathomable. Every moment you spend thinking about him is wasted.*

She would savor this break from the fortress, from the endless preparation for war. It would take more than a few cutting words from a surly falconer to dampen her spirits.

# CHAPTER 32

Summer 1460
Bellapais Abbey, Cyprus

A THIN PLUME of smoke rose from within the abbey complex. At least one soul had stayed behind when messengers warned of the coming war.

Estelle dismounted and fumbled with the keys. She inserted the largest one into the lock and, after a bit of fiddling, heard a dull click.

Swinging open the gates, she led her horse in, and the others followed.

"Don't worry," she said brightly to Gabriel as she locked the gates again. "I wouldn't dream of putting us at risk."

She made a great show of testing the gate to demonstrate it was secure. He said nothing, just turned his horse's nose and trotted away. While the others dismounted and turned to her expectantly, he rode around the corner of the church.

*Ignore him. He's clearly here to judge, not help.*

"First, we'll go to the library and the abbot's quarters and search for the record book." She looked at Monsieur Pelestrine. "After that, we have another task."

There was no point explaining to Antonia and the guards what they were truly after, especially if they found no treasure.

One of the guards hauled a bucket up from the well in the center courtyard and began watering the horses. The other accompanied her, Monsieur Pelestrine, and Antonia to the nearest doorway. Trying one key after another, Estelle found the correct one. They passed through the dark, musty refectory and discovered a corridor leading to a barren dormitory. Back in the corridor, they found another door leading to the library. Cabinets lined the walls, but all of them were empty.

"To the abbot's quarters," Estelle said.

They crossed the courtyard again to a generously sized building beyond the church. None of Estelle's keys worked in the door's lock.

One of the guards smashed through the shutters on a ground-floor window, then disappeared inside and opened the door from within.

"Someone is living here," said Antonia as they ventured inside. "It smells of fresh smoke."

Monsieur Pelestrine went to the hearth. "I see a live ember."

There was a scurrying sound overhead.

"Stay here," said the guard, disappearing upstairs.

A moment later, he clattered down the stairs, pulling a woman by the arm. She scolded and screeched in the Cypriot dialect. As soon as she spied Estelle and Antonia, she collapsed on her knees, begging them to protect her from the men.

"They won't hurt you," Estelle said. "Calm yourself. You're safe with us. Why are you here alone?"

"I'm the abbot's housekeeper," the woman said though her tears. "He told me to stay here and protect his things until he returned."

Estelle took in the woman's kohl-rimmed eyes, the gold thread edging her purple headpiece, and the velvet slippers on her feet.

"No servant I've seen wears gold thread and velvet," Estelle said. "Even at the palace in Nicosia."

"The prior is a generous master," the woman retorted.

"It's obvious you're more than a servant to the man," Antonia said, yanking the woman to her feet. "We're about to be attacked by

Mamluks, in case you haven't heard. So out with it before we're all strung up by our heels and roasted alive."

The woman sniffled. "Yes, I warm his bed. I'm not the only one. Of the monks here, only a few followed the rules."

Monsieur Pelestrine nodded. "I'd heard that, but I'd hoped it was just gossip."

"You know what we say in Cyprus." Antonia nodded sagely. "Two things spread quickly: gossip and a forest fire." She trained her gaze on the woman again. "Where are they all now?"

"Fled for the mountains, mostly. Some went to Kyrenia. I'd rather rot in here than in that fortress." She crossed herself.

"Where does your master keep his valuables?" Estelle asked.

No response.

Antonia reached out and pinched the woman's forearm. "Devil got your tongue?" she asked.

"Ouch!" the woman yelped. "We—he has no valuables. He took them all to Kyrenia."

"Search the house," Monsieur Pelestrine told the guard.

The guard thudded up the stairs again. Furniture scraped across the floor. Something heavy fell, followed by muffled cursing. "Nothing there," he reported upon his return. "An empty cabinet and a chest of oak. I'll check the cellar and the kitchen."

Estelle watched the woman's face. When he said *cellar*, a look of panic washed over it.

"We'll go with you," Estelle said.

She followed the guard, Antonia on her heels.

The kitchen revealed nothing of value. In the cellar, though, there were two locked cupboards in the shadows beyond a stone archway. The guard smashed the locks with an axe. One cupboard held books, the other silver plates and a magnificent set of tooled silver candlesticks that had once been inlaid with jewels, all of which had been pried out.

"These can go to the queen." Estelle found several canvas sacks on a broken stool and handed one to Antonia, who started stuffing the valuables into it. The guard turned to go.

"Wait." Estelle thrust a sack at him. "Help me with these books."

"The kingdom needs books to fight a war?"

"It does," she assured him, picking up an armful of volumes. "Books can be every bit as valuable as silver."

Back upstairs, Estelle told the woman they would pay her to cook them a meal. After some coaxing, she revealed a stash of vegetables and grain and started a fire in the hearth. Estelle told Antonia to stay and help her.

Then she signaled to the others. "To the church."

Inside the church, she momentarily lost sight of her purpose, admiring the beauty of the structure's sweeping nave and the jewel-toned glass in the windows. The guard crossed himself, then ambled slowly down the center aisle.

Estelle and Monsieur Pelestrine walked the perimeter of the church, entering the shadowy transepts, searching the walls by candle-light. Flakes of paint showed places where frescoes had once adorned the walls. In the chancel beyond the ornately carved wooden altar, Estelle stumbled on the uneven stone slabs and nearly fell. Then she gasped, her eyes fixed on the ground.

"A tomb," she said.

Monsieur Pelestrine swept his arm over the stone floor, his candle's flame revealing the carved outline of a knight clad in armor.

Footsteps behind them made Estelle whirl, her nerves heightened by the discovery.

Gabriel strode toward her, an oil lamp in one hand. "I found this in the kitchens."

"Thank the saints." She smiled in gratitude. "Some light just when we need it."

He did not return her smile.

"We found a knight's tomb," Monsieur Pelestrine said. "There are likely more all over the chancel."

The guard retreated outside. The coo of a pigeon high in the vaulted ribs of the nave drifted through the chilly air.

Estelle retrieved the journal from her satchel and held it up in the lamplight. "This is the reason we made the journey here. Servants of King Janus hid some of the kingdom's treasure in holy places around

Cyprus during a war many years ago. Queen Charlotta and I believe some of it may be here."

Michel took that in, a look of slowly dawning excitement on his face. Gabriel scowled.

"You risked our lives because of some musings in a book?" His voice was full of barely contained anger. "This scheme would be absurd in the best of times, but now? When the kingdom is on the brink of war? It's—it's—"

Michel cleared his throat. "It's worth exploring, and we're here, so there's no use arguing about the merits of the plan now." He looked at Estelle. "Where to next, mademoiselle?"

She took in a steadying breath, avoiding Gabriel's gaze, then crouched low to examine the stone underfoot. A close inspection revealed a half-dozen more flat funerary slabs embedded in the floor.

"The journal said the treasure was watched over by King Janus, a falcon, and a knight," Estelle told the men. "Perhaps it's here under these knights' tombs."

Gabriel held the lamp higher, illuminating flakes of white, blue, and black paint on the wall.

"See there?" Estelle pointed at what looked like three black half-moons. "Could those be a falcon's talons?"

Gabriel held the lamp higher. "Yes. And above, I see the curve of a wing." His voice was calm now.

Estelle turned and walked in a direct line from the falcon to the opposite wall, where a sarcophagus stood. The top portion was a carved effigy of a knight, his arms crossed over his chest, cradling a sword.

She retraced her steps to the middle of the chancel and looked at the shadowy back wall. "Can you shine the lamp up there?" she asked, but Gabriel was already closing the distance to her side.

With the aid of his lamp, they discerned the forms of a kneeling man and woman.

"King Janus and the first Queen Charlotte," Estelle said in a hushed voice. "The journal said the treasure was watched over by the king. Perhaps that means it's underneath his image."

All three of them looked at the bare stone floor below the image of the king. No funerary slabs were in evidence here. The stone was dulled by layers of dust, the seams around each slab darkened with grime.

"But there's nothing here," Monsieur Pelestrine said in disappointment. "Nothing at all."

Estelle turned the book's pages, her mind working furiously. Gabriel looked over her shoulder in silence.

*What did I miss? What did she tell us that I cannot see?*

Gabriel set the lamp down on the floor. Kneeling, he swept his fingertips over the stone, beginning with the slabs against the back wall, then working his way out.

"What are you doing?" Estelle asked.

He did not respond. Methodically, he continued his task.

She regarded him in confusion for a moment, then realized what he was after. Sinking to her knees, she ran her hands over the stone. After a few moments, she felt a divot under her fingertips, then another. She studied the imperfections carefully.

Monsieur Pelestrine brought the lamp closer.

"Look." Estelle rubbed her fingers over the imprints of a heart, a three-leafed clover, and a fleur-de-lis. "The same pattern as in the book."

Gabriel withdrew his dagger from its sheath and inserted the tip between that slab and the one next to it. With quick movements, he worked it back and forth. He glanced up at Estelle.

The excitement she saw in his eyes made her pulse surge.

"This mortar is loose." He dug deeper into the crack.

"Keep at it," she urged him.

Monsieur Pelestrine knelt at Gabriel's side. The two men worked at the seam until, with a grunt of effort, they pulled the stone slab from its foundations.

A dark cavity opened up below them.

Estelle could not help herself.

She dropped to the floor and thrust an arm into the yawning abyss.

# CHAPTER 33

Summer 1460
Bellapais Abbey, Cyprus

ESTELLE'S HAND made contact with something soft. Was it skin? Stifling a yelp, she closed her fingers around the object and pulled it out. She set it gingerly on the floor.

"A velvet sack." Gabriel weighed it in his hand. "Filled with . . . pebbles?"

Estelle poked her arm into the cavity again. "There's something else down here." Her fingertips brushed against something hard and coarse. "I can't quite grasp it." She sat up and brushed off her hands. "You have longer arms, *geraki*."

He regarded her with an expression of incredulity. "What kind of lady rolls around on the floor of a church searching for treasure?"

"The kind with a falconer for a father and a stout heart," Monsieur Pelestrine replied.

Gabriel lay down and rooted around in the darkness, then extracted a canvas-covered item. "It's heavy."

They all eyed their discoveries in silence.

"Only one way to find out what's inside," Monsieur Pelestrine commented.

"Supper is ready!" one of the guards called, crossing the threshold into the church. "I found a jug of wine in the cellar, too."

"And a bat." Antonia stepped inside. "Though it was dead, praise the saints."

Estelle stood, arranging her skirts over the sacks while the men pushed the stone slab back into position.

"What were you looking for in here?" the guard asked. "Buried treasure?"

He laughed at his own jest, and Antonia joined in with enthusiasm.

"We're on our way," Estelle told them. "We'll follow you out the door."

She picked up the velvet sack and concealed it under her cloak, then handed the canvas-wrapped parcel to Monsieur Pelestrine. "Will you stay with these things in the abbot's study while we sup with the others? I'll bring you food. Then, after they're asleep, we'll see what's inside."

He smiled at her in the flickering lamplight. "Have you always had a knack for thinking ahead?"

"Perhaps I have. I never knew it until I got to Cyprus, though."

They returned to the abbot's house. Monsieur Pelestrine retreated to the study with their finds, while Estelle and Gabriel joined the others in the kitchen for vegetable stew and barley washed down with wine.

When the guards retreated outside to patrol the grounds, Gabriel filled a bowl for Monsieur Pelestrine. As the Frenchman ate, Estelle read the journal aloud before the fire. Monsieur Pelestrine and Gabriel pulled their stools closer and listened with rapt attention until Antonia trundled into the room. She'd been eating her meal alongside the abbot's mistress in the kitchen and was now bursting with gossip.

"According to her, monks fathered most of the children in the village." She squatted by Estelle's side. "This place is anything but holy, if you ask me."

"How did the abbot escape punishment by the Church?" Estelle asked absently, her mind on the velvet sack. How much longer would they have to wait to reveal its contents?

"Jacco is more interested in seizing the throne than overseeing the island's Latin churches," Gabriel said. "If this were a Greek Orthodox or Coptic monastery, there would have been more discipline."

"That's another thing," Antonia said. "Some of the families from the village have already pledged their loyalty to Jacco. He sent agents promising the villagers protection if they swore fealty to him."

Estelle's stomach tightened. "When did they come?"

"Not a week ago. Some of the villagers went away with them."

"Went away?" Gabriel asked sharply. "Or were taken away?"

Antonia shrugged. "She said they went willingly. The Pretender has promised to free serfs all over Cyprus when he comes—and I've heard that from plenty of folk, not just the abbot's woman. The common people have been forced to serve Latin nobles as far back as anyone remembers. They'd rather have a Cypriot for a king than Queen Char-lotta's foreign husband." She turned to Estelle with a panicked expression. "Please don't tell the queen."

"Your loyalty is not in question," Estelle assured her.

But Antonia's gaze slid away from hers. For a moment, Estelle wondered if the woman was doubting her own decision to follow the queen from Nicosia to Kyrenia.

Kyrenia was the safest place on the island, the most well-fortified structure in Cyprus. But for a fleeting instant, Estelle imagined it surrounded by soldiers firing cannons, by ships aiming their guns and arrows at the high walls of the fortress.

Would the fortress prove to be a sanctuary or a trap?

When she looked up and met Gabriel's somber gaze, she could swear he knew what she was thinking.

The abbot's mistress offered Estelle and Antonia a bedchamber. The guards refused beds, preferring to keep watch until their party left again at dawn. Monsieur Pelestrine and Gabriel rolled out pallets before the hearth in the abbot's study and bade Estelle a good night. Upstairs, she tiptoed into the bedchamber. Antonia was already snoring on the straw-stuffed mattress.

As soon as she was certain Antonia's snores were genuine, Estelle crept downstairs to find Monsieur Pelestrine asleep on a blanket near the hearth. Gabriel sat up, staring into the fire. Next to him lay the velvet sack and the canvas-covered parcel.

He glanced up at her approach and gave her a barely discernible nod. She sat on a nearby stool, wrapping her cloak around herself. Outside, a gentle rain sifted down. Gabriel poked the embers with a stick. A flame licked upward, dancing in the draft.

"What if we return to Kyrenia, give those things to the queen, and there's nothing but pebbles and wood inside?" His tone was blunt.

"Bar the door," Estelle said.

He got up in one fluid motion, crossed to the door, and latched it.

Under half-lowered eyelids, she watched him pad back to the hearth and lay another log on the embers. He crouched low and blew on the flames, coaxing them higher. There was a grace about Gabriel, a supple litheness, that mesmerized her. Even his rudeness today could not shatter the invisible force of attraction humming between them, as much as she hated to admit it.

Monsieur Pelestrine stirred.

"Should we wake him?" Gabriel asked.

Estelle shook her head. "Let him sleep."

She picked up the velvet sack. Inside it were several small leather purses. She untied the drawstring of one and tipped the contents into her palm.

"By God and all the saints," Gabriel breathed. "They could be glass, but if they're truly rubies, the queen will be glad to have them."

Estelle stared at the glittering gems in her hand, astounded. She couldn't contain an enormous smile. "It's as I dreamed it would be."

He rolled his eyes. "Such fancies can lead you into trouble."

"You truly have a gift for spoiling the mood of a joyous moment, don't you?" she asked. "I saw the excitement on your face when you pulled that canvas sack from the darkness. You can't deny it."

Gabriel folded his arms across his chest and allowed a grin. "It was a thrilling moment, I won't lie."

Her pulse leapt when he said that. She held his gaze, drawn in by the genuine warmth in his eyes, until a sudden shyness descended upon her.

She weighed the gems in her palm for a moment, considering them. Papa's debts would be canceled if she kept a few of these aside. She could sew them into her skirts. No one would know—

"Tempting, isn't it?"

Gabriel's quiet words stung like the prick of a needle. She flushed, muted by a creeping sense of shame. Carefully returning the rubies to the sack, she opened the other small sacks in turn. Sapphires, amethysts, and pearls glowed up at her.

"They're not pebbles," she whispered.

He nodded. "Tie them off again, and we'll have a look at the other parcel."

She secured the small sacks and set them aside, then picked up the heavy object. "There are so many layers of canvas. Whatever's underneath is smaller than I first thought."

After much unwrapping, finally the canvas was off.

In her lap lay a crown of gold inlaid with rubies the size of pigeon's eggs.

Estelle found her voice. "No wonder it's so heavy. This is solid gold."

She held it up so it caught the light of the fire. It was dulled by age and neglect, but the rubies reflected the glow of the flames, seeming to crackle with heat.

"It's a crown of flame." Gabriel reached out to trace the outline of the large central ruby with his fingertips.

A log shifted, making Estelle flinch. Gabriel's fingers brushed the back of her hand. Nervous energy shot through her at his touch.

"Perhaps it once belonged to the first Queen Charlotte," she said. "But why didn't her ladies retrieve it after King Janus was ransomed?"

The falconer's lips parted as he prepared to respond, and she found herself wondering what it would be like to kiss them.

"They must have had a reason," Gabriel said. "It was a time of chaos and violence. My mother was taken captive at the same time as King Janus, by Christians who brought her to Cyprus."

"Why?"

"Retaliation for King Janus's capture. The Christians sought revenge. A group of knights slipped into a wealthy part of Alexandria and kidnapped as many rich folk as they could find. My mother and her family were among them. Most of them were ransomed after King Janus was returned to Cyprus."

"But not your mother."

He stared at the flames, his tawny skin gleaming in the firelight. "No."

"How old was she?"

"Not much more than a child."

Estelle shuddered. "Long ago, when I was a young girl, I narrowly missed the same fate. But my captor was foiled before any harm came to me."

Gabriel looked at her with a mixture of shock and disbelief. "Truly?"

The dark memory tightened its claws, constricting her breath. When she spoke again, the words had to fight their way out. "I—yes. Forgive me. I don't know why I told you. I've never told anyone, in truth." She took in some air. "How terrible for your mother. And for her family. No child should be taken captive, and I suppose I understand that better than most people. I returned to my family unhurt, and for that I have the saints to thank."

A muscle flickered in his jaw. "My mother was not so fortunate. She never saw Alexandria again."

"What happened to her?" she asked softly.

Gabriel poked the fire with the stick. In profile, his face looked carved in stone, like the marble statues of gods from ancient times scattered around the island of Rhodes.

"A Latin man made her his slave. I'm the only child of theirs who survived. She died not long after he freed her."

The raw pain in his voice warned her not to question him further.

She dropped her gaze to the crown. "We'd better wrap this up again."

He helped her spool the layers of cloth around it. The fire blazed companionably, finally giving off a bit of heat.

"Thank you for coming along, even though you thought this was a fool's errand," she said. "Now we know the journey was worth it."

He let out a wry laugh. "Once we're safely back at Kyrenia, I'll tell you if I agree."

# CHAPTER 34

Summer 1460
Near Bellapais Abbey, Cyprus

As soon as the dawn sky brightened, their party set out. Monsieur Pelestrine carried the sack of jewels in a pannier strapped to his horse's saddle. The crown was in a battered leather satchel slung over Gabriel's shoulders. None of the others knew what they had found besides the books and valuables they'd seized in the abbot's home. Those items were strapped to one of the guard's saddles.

The exultant mood Estelle had experienced on the ride here yesterday was gone. She could not banish the thought of Jacco's agents fanning out over the island, recruiting supporters and terrorizing those loyal to the queen. She tried to calm herself by studying their surroundings: the foothills and plains sweeping to the coastline, the sea gleaming like burnished pewter in the distance.

*Enjoy the beauty. Soon, you'll be trapped in the fortress again.*

Three crows launched from the highest branches of an olive tree, their harsh cries breaking the quiet. Estelle's horse shied. She gripped the saddle's pommel tightly, shushing her mount with soft words. When she looked up, the view to the sea was marred by dark shapes on a slight rise in the road ahead.

Horsemen.

"Be on your guard!" she shouted to her companions.

Gabriel tore the satchel from his shoulder and spurred his horse to her side.

"Take this. Ride into the cover of the woods." He turned to Antonia and Monsieur Pelestrine. "Stay with Estelle," he commanded them.

Wheeling, he spurred his horse to the guards, and the three of them cantered onward.

Estelle dug her heels into her horse's belly. "Follow me!" she cried.

"I won't leave your side," Monsieur Pelestrine shouted from behind her.

"Holy Virgin, protect me!" Antonia's voice rippled overhead, carried by the wind.

*We must get off this road.*

Estelle guided her horse into an olive orchard. She could hear nothing but the thud of hooves in the soil as they careened between two rows of trees. The satchel bounced and thudded against her ribs. Reaching to steady it, she did not see the branch bearing down upon her. It tore off her headpiece, scratching her face. She couldn't help crying out in pain.

The horse swerved, unnerved by her scream. The reins burst from her grip. The animal careened through the orchard, then tore across a stubble field. Clinging to the pommel, she spoke soothingly to the horse until it slowed.

She twisted in the saddle. Antonia and Monsieur Pelestrine were nowhere in sight.

*At least I've put a good distance between myself and the bandits. Please, God, let the others be close behind.*

She entered a mixed forest of carob and plane trees. Birds flitted from branch to branch above, serenading her with haunting whistles.

Spying a dark copse of pines ahead, she spurred the horse on. Its hooves were silent on the soft forest floor. Dismounting, she patted her mount's nose, whispering words of praise and thanks.

*Where are the others?*

The men could be dead by now or forced into Jacco's army. Antonia —what would they do to her? The thought made her eyes burn with tears.

*It's my fault they're here at all.*

A branch snapping nearby made her seize with terror. The attackers were here. Hunting for her. Wresting her dagger from its sheath, she weighed it in her hand. A dagger against a man's sword would be laughable, but it was all she had.

Through the shrubs, she saw a man astride a large black horse. His short cape and dark cap marked him as a Latin. Behind him ranged three more mounted men, all dressed in the light-colored tunics of the Cypriot style.

Rummaging in the satchel with shaking hands, she pulled out the crown and looked around desperately for a place to hide. Leaving her horse, she slipped deeper into the shadows.

Twenty or so paces away, she edged behind a stout pine. A tree had fallen long ago nearby, its rotting stump covered with leaves and branches. She jammed the crown as deeply as she could under the debris, then pressed herself against the pine tree and began to pray.

Her pursuers found the horse a moment later. They whooped at their discovery, crowing in the Cypriot dialect.

Estelle tensed, awaiting discovery.

But in the next instant, the men retreated. They led their mounts out of the pine grove, their voices fading with every step. She sagged against the tree, trembling with relief.

An utter stillness descended.

And then a voice spoke in Greek, accented by some Latin language. "So. The horse did have a rider."

It was the man in the short cape, studying her from a dozen paces away, his hand resting on his sword's hilt. In the dimness, his features were not fully clear to her. But something in the set of his jaw, the arrogant sweep of his gaze, was familiar.

She had seen this man before. But where?

He took a few steps in her direction.

She backed away, every instinct in her body screaming at her to run. "Who are you?"

He chuckled. "A lucky man indeed. You're lovely."

He reached for her. She screamed, the force of it tearing at her throat, and his hand snaked out and struck her so hard she fell backward to the earth, directly atop the crown. Struggling to right herself, she inadvertently kicked the crown from its hiding place.

"What have we here?" He caught the canvas bundle with his foot and eyed it with interest.

Fear swept over her. Now she knew who this man was.

"Nicolau Baldaia." Her voice was hoarse but steady. "You should be in hell, not walking the earth."

His surprised expression twisted into astonishment. "Have we met?"

She took advantage of his befuddlement to stand. Somehow she still had hold of her dagger, and she tightened her grip on it.

"Remember the girls in Rhodes Town? The ones destined for your ship, the ones you planned to take across the sea?"

He went stone-still. "The falconer's daughter?"

"Thanks to my father, I am alive and well."

His astonishment was quickly replaced by a sneer. "And all grown up. You don't have your mother's golden beauty, but there's something irresistible about you all the same. Why did I want to give you to some other man? I should have kept you for myself."

He reached for her. With a sudden strike, she thrust the dagger at his arm and felt it meet flesh. He bellowed in anger. Tearing the blade from her grasp, he tossed it aside. His hand closed around her arm like a band of iron.

"Estelle?"

Relief coursed through her at the sound of Gabriel's voice.

"I'm here!" She frantically lunged in an effort to free herself.

The Catalan pushed her to the ground, scooped up the crown, and stalked toward Gabriel.

"Gabriel!" Estelle shouted. "He's coming for you!"

She scrambled to her feet and snatched up her dagger.

*If he attacks Gabriel, he'll feel the sting of my blade again.*

But the two men did not draw their swords. Gabriel spoke to the Catalan sharply, gesturing at the wrapped crown, but the man shook his head and kept his grip on it. The Catalan stepped forward as if he meant to strike Gabriel, but the falconer held his ground as though he dared the man to try it. A moment later, the Catalan turned away and vanished into the forest.

Gabriel hurried to Estelle's side. "Are you unhurt?"

She nodded, spying blood on his sleeve. "Your arm is wounded! And Monsieur Pelestrine?"

"He's hurt, too, worse than me. We must get him to Kyrenia."

"The others?"

"The guards are dead—and the men took Antonia with them."

"Do you know that Catalan? Is he an agent of Jacco's?" Estelle searched his face, struck by a horrifying thought. "Perhaps you're in league with him. Why else would he walk away without a fight?"

"Yes, he's an agent of Jacco's. No, I'm not in league with him." Gabriel jerked his head at Estelle's horse. "While you question me, Monsieur Pelestrine bleeds on the roadside. We must hurry!"

A few moments later, they found Monsieur Pelestrine slumped near the sprawled bodies of the guards, his shoulder leaking blood. Estelle did what she could to bind it with strips of her underskirt. Then she and Gabriel helped him back on his horse. She tried not to think about the crown and the gems.

The queen's parting words came back to her.

*If you ever betray me, your life will be forfeit.*

She cast a glance at Gabriel. He had not even tried to get the crown away from the Catalan. Was that betrayal? Would she tell the queen what she'd seen him do? Would she share her suspicion that Gabriel was in league with the man?

Watching him tend to Monsieur Pelestrine with a steady gaze and gentle, sure hands, she knew in her heart she could not. Whatever the consequences, she would keep her doubts to herself.

"Did Antonia go with them by choice?" she asked him.

He shrugged. "There are many on the island who support the Pretender. She could be one."

"But she's been a loyal servant of the court for years."

He turned on her. "That means nothing. Survival becomes more important than loyalty when war strikes. You'll learn that soon enough."

"Do you think we have a chance of getting the treasure back?"

"It's gone," he said flatly. "We won't see it again."

A nervous flutter started beneath her collarbone. "What if the queen thinks we took it, hid it somewhere for ourselves?"

He frowned. "Why would she think that?"

"She fears betrayal by those closest to her—rightfully so."

Gabriel drew in a long breath and let it out with a single controlled exhalation. "The three of us are the only ones who saw the crown and the jewels. Say nothing of them. Say we found silver plate and candlesticks under the floor and in the abbot's house, and the bandits took those things. That's an easier loss for her to bear."

Monsieur Pelestrine let out a moan. "Let us be off," he rasped.

Estelle stood frozen, a question spinning relentlessly through her mind.

*What will I tell the queen?*

Gabriel leaned closer, his voice low and tight. "The longer we wait, the longer you worry, the closer to death he is."

# CHAPTER 35

Summer 1460
Kyrenia Fortress, Cyprus

THE HORSES CLATTERED over the drawbridge and into the heart of the fortress. Dozens of soldiers dressed for battle milled about the court-yard. Several mule carts were being loaded with shovels, spikes, and other tools. The shouts of men and the strike of metal on stone filled Gabriel's ears.

"What's happening?" he called to a guard.

"The king is sending out a regiment to dig up the roads leading to Kyrenia. Plan is to make it harder for Jacco the Bastard and his Mamluk army to approach."

Nervous energy surged up Gabriel's spine. "Have the invaders landed?"

"They say it's a matter of days."

Gabriel reached for the Frenchman's bridle. Estelle slid from her saddle and rushed to help him. Together, they supported Michel as he slid awkwardly from his horse. A stable hand made to take her place, but she shooed him away, looping the falconer's arm over her shoulders.

"Let's take him to the stables," Gabriel shouted through the clamor. "All my healing remedies are with the falcons, and I want to stay at his side."

A pair of royal guards approached. "You're needed in the queen's study, mademoiselle," one of them said to Estelle.

"One of you help the falconer into the stables, then."

Her steady gaze and crisp, authoritative voice gave the guard no alternative but to obey.

*This is a world of men preparing for war, and yet she seems so calm. How can that be?*

As she walked away with the other guard, Gabriel could not get the thought out of his mind.

Gabriel made Michel as comfortable as possible on a cot in an empty horse stall. He did what he could for the falconer's wound that night with the materials he had on hand. First, he bathed it with wine, then he daubed it with an ointment made of honey, beeswax, and medicinal herbs and wrapped the Frenchman's shoulder with a clean linen bandage. With the help of a bribe, he secured beef soup and bread for his friend. He spent the rest of the night caring for the falcons and snatched a few hours' sleep before dawn lit the sky and the fortress roared back to life.

That evening, after a full day of tending to and feeding the birds, he returned to Michel's side with another round of soup and bread. The Frenchman had slept on and off all day. He seemed a bit feverish, and his wound oozed fresh blood, but he had an appetite. After he ate, he nodded off. Seated on a stool at his side, Gabriel trimmed and shaped tail feathers into quills with a sharp knife. He glanced up when he heard someone approach.

At the sight of Estelle de Montavon, his pulse ticked up a notch.

"How is he?" She knelt at the falconer's side, studying the bandage. "It bleeds too much."

"There are few herbs and fewer clean bandages to be found in this place. I sent two stable boys searching for a physician, and they claim there are none to be found."

"One of the king's valets was supposed to find you last night. I gave him supplies to bring along for Monsieur Pelestrine. He never came?"

"I've not seen any of the king's servants nor any supplies."

She dropped her voice. "Everyone was surprised that the king ordered the roads to be torn up. It was the first order he's given to prepare the fortress for war. I suspect it was the queen's idea, in truth. But last night, King Louis talked of hunting and hawking, not defending Kyrenia from a siege. The valet was to arrange it with you."

Gabriel's hands stilled. "Do you jest?"

"I wish I could."

"God help us. Who else will help the queen defeat Jacco? Will the Knights of St. John heed her call for aid?"

"Lord de Milly demands gold in exchange for ships and soldiers. More than she has."

"What will you do?" he asked.

"Do I have a choice?" Estelle put a hand on Monsieur Pelestrine's forehead. "I'll obey my queen's command. You, on the other hand, are thinking about survival. That Catalan did not let you go without a fight for no good reason. I ask you again, where do your loyalties lie?"

Gabriel stared at her without answering for a moment. "I stand with the queen," he finally said, then tilted his head at Michel. "And I owe much to this man. I won't abandon him now."

Two stable hands hurried by, chattering anxiously about the coming siege. A hooded peregrine falcon shrieked and beat the air with her wings, perhaps frustrated by the confines of her cage. Gabriel tucked his knife away and went to her, speaking softly in the language of his mother's people.

"Will you find something to ease his pain and clean his wound?" he asked over his shoulder when the falcon quieted. "He needs more help than I can give."

Estelle nodded and rose. "I'll be back."

When she returned after dark with wine, more bandages, and a needle and thread, Gabriel surveyed the supplies with gratitude.

"Where did you find those?" He pointed at the neat pile of flax strips in her basket.

"My underclothes." She removed the bloodied bandage on Monsieur Pelestrine's shoulder. "Can you prop him up?"

Gabriel did as she asked. She poured wine over the wound, prompting a groan from the Frenchman, then examined it closely.

"It's deep, but not jagged." She threaded the needle. "That's something."

"Shouldn't you find a physician to do that?" Gabriel asked.

"I've had no more luck on that count than the stable hands. I've seen my father do this a hundred times on falcons and other creatures. When he needed my help, I gave it."

Michel's eyelids fluttered open for an instant. His eyes were bloodshot and glazed by pain.

Gabriel held the flagon of wine to his lips. "Drink, my friend," he whispered. "It will do you good."

The falconer took a few sips. At Gabriel's encouragement, he forced down one more. He eyed Estelle and her needle, then turned his head away.

"Do what you must," he muttered.

When it was done, Michel dozed. Estelle and Gabriel took turns swigging from the flagon, listening to the rise and fall of voices, the clatter of hooves, the shouted orders of naval officers and trumpet blasts on galleys in the harbor. Here, tucked away behind the falcons, they had a tiny enclosed world, a quiet place to await the horrors of war.

"You said you owe much to Monsieur Pelestrine." Estelle shifted on her stool. "What did you mean by that?"

Gabriel drank again and jammed the cork stopper into the flagon. "He gave me my livelihood."

"Did he hire you?"

"He took a chance on me. I was caught up in some trouble in Nicosia. He came upon me, drunk out of my mind, lolling on the street, with no home, no work, no money. He brought me to my senses, set me on my feet, and when I thanked him in French, he took me under his wing."

"Did you know much of falconry?"

Gabriel laughed. "Not a thing. But Michel was a Frenchman in need of a translator, and that I could do."

Estelle smiled in understanding. "It's a valuable skill."

"My French isn't perfect—"

"I disagree," she broke in. "To hear you speak, one would think you'd been born in France."

He smiled, offering her the wine.

"What language did you speak to the falcon earlier?" She took a sip.

"Coptic."

"I thought Egyptians spoke the language of Arabs."

He nodded. "Yes, we do, for we've no other choice. But some of us still speak Coptic. My mother taught it to me. When I speak it, I remember her gentle nature, and it seems to calm the falcons."

Michel moaned aloud and thrashed his legs.

Gabriel took off his tunic, folded it, and slid it under the Frenchman's head. His own shirt was ripped where he'd been cut on the upper arm.

"Your injury needs tending, too." Estelle put out a hand to touch his arm, but he pulled away.

"Careful, woman," he growled with mock irritation. "Stay away from me with that needle."

"It could fester." She placed the lamp on a wooden box in a corner of the stall and beckoned to him. "Can I at least clean and bandage it?"

In answer, he pulled his shirt over his head and presented his arm to her. She hesitated, staring at his bare torso. A ripple of shame shot through him.

"Well?" he demanded. "Surely, you've seen ugly scars before?"

"I see nothing ugly before me."

There was a hint of tenderness in her voice that made heat rise in his chest. Or had he imagined it?

She traced the latticework of silver-white scars on his chest and belly with a fingertip, her touch so gentle it felt like a soft breeze. His muscles tensed.

"Do they hurt?" she whispered.

He shook his head. "Not anymore."

Gabriel longed to interlace his fingers with hers, to pull her into his embrace. Not for the first time, he wondered what it would be like to kiss her.

She fumbled for the wine flagon and poured a thin stream on the wound. The scarlet wine coursed over his skin like blood. With a fresh strip of cloth, she blotted the liquid, frowning.

"It's shallow," she said after a moment. "You're lucky." Taking up another long strip of cloth, she twisted it around his arm and tied it off at the ends, then handed him the wine flagon. "A bit more of this will help, too."

He accepted the wine. "Thank you. For the wine and the care. You're kinder than I thought."

"What is that supposed to mean?"

"You seemed to care for nothing and no one but yourself when I first met you. Now I know differently."

"I could say the same about you," she retorted, tossing her head.

"We're more alike than you'd admit." Grinning, he handed her the flagon. When she took it, her skin brushed his. He kept his hand where it was, enjoying the sensation.

Estelle's eyes shone in the candlelight, her lips curving in a smile.

Without making the conscious decision to do so, he bent his head and kissed her lightly on the mouth. Then he pulled back, chagrined. "Forgive me."

But she did not scold him or turn away. Instead, she put a hand on his chest, over his heart.

"Again," she whispered.

He hesitated, glancing at Michel. The falconer snored softly, oblivious to the world.

He turned back to Estelle, leaning close. "Gladly."

Her warm lips on his ignited a flame in his very core. He'd told himself the reason Estelle de Montavon occupied so much space in his mind was because she infuriated him. But that wasn't true, he admitted now. It had never been true.

He loosened her headwrap and set her long hair cascading down her shoulders. She took one of his hands and brought it to her lips.

The soft pressure of her mouth pressed against his palm made his entire body throb with desire.

"Gabriel." She said his name like a term of endearment, like a secret caress.

He buried his face in her hair, breathed in her scent, luxuriating in the aroma of flowers and a mysterious elixir of spices.

A distant boom rumbled, startling them apart.

"Was that thunder?" She snatched up her headwrap, her eyes wide.

"It's not raining." He reached for his shirt. "I'll go outside and see what's—"

A tremendous crash sent stones tumbling to the earth outside. Horses whinnied nervously up and down the stables. The falcons shrieked in distress, batting their wings against their cages. Michel awoke.

"What is it?" he asked blearily. "What's happening?"

Another boom sounded, reverberating through the air, burrowing deep into Gabriel's bones.

"Cannon shot." His throat constricted with dread. "God help us."

Men shouted in the courtyard. Trumpets blared. The deep bass of a drumbeat echoed in his ears.

A soldier rushed through the stables, rousing anyone who still slept. "The Bastard's army is here! We're under siege!"

# CHAPTER 36

Summer 1460
Kyrenia Fortress, Cyprus

THREE DAYS after the siege began, Estelle hurried through the corridors past flickering torches and silent guards. There was time to check on Monsieur Pelestrine before reporting for duty in the queen's study. She stood at the doorway to the courtyard, steeling herself for chaos.

A thunderous explosion tore from a cannon mounted on the parapets as she emerged into the bright sunlight. Pressing her hands over her ears, she kept to the perimeter of the courtyard. A movement in the harbor caught her eye. Pausing, she saw two new galleys were anchored there. The sight gave her hope. These ships must have arrived in the night.

*Santa Maria, thank you. Some help at last.*

Heartened, she slipped through the stable doors, heading straight for Michel Pelestrine's cot. Gabriel sat vigil over him, trimming a feather into a quill with his small knife.

"How does he fare today?" Estelle knelt and took Monsieur Pelestrine's hand in hers. "I'm surprised he can sleep through the siege."

Gabriel looked sheepish. "I found some poppy milk for him."

"How did you manage that?"

He shrugged, grinning, the dance of light in his gray eyes distracting her.

She flushed, thinking of their kisses, her recklessness on the first night of the siege. His warm skin under her fingertips, the hard muscles flexing in his chest and arms. The beauty of his finely chiseled features.

*I want to trust him. But can I?*

Her mind went to the forest, to the strange encounter with Nicolau Baldaia. Something had passed between the two men that day; she was sure of it. Why else had the Catalan sheathed his blade and walked away when no other men of their party had escaped unscathed?

She banished the thoughts, retrieving a flagon of wine and some bread and cheese from a satchel under her cloak. "This should please him when he wakes."

"Cheese," Gabriel remarked. "So that's what they're eating in the royal apartments. Out here, we've seen nothing but hard biscuits since our return. I'll soon be sent out to fetch provisions, no doubt. The garrison must be fed if they're to fend off Jacco's army much longer."

Though keeping Monsieur Pelestrine in the stables had seemed an odd choice, Gabriel had insisted. Now Estelle understood why. It was the only way he could watch over his friend day and night. She touched the Frenchman's forehead and cheeks, relieved to find his skin cool. Perhaps, if she prayed hard enough, he would evade infection.

"I'll keep bringing cheese as long as I can. Why would you be sent in search of food? You're no soldier. You'll be killed!"

"I was a guard for the Knights Hospitaller before I was a falconer." Gabriel added his trimmed and shaped feather to a small pile next to him, then picked up another one and twirled it in his fingers. "There's no need to worry on my account. I can take care of myself."

She studied the feather in his hand. "A saker falcon's tail feather if I'm not mistaken."

"I sometimes forget you weren't always a courtier." With a few deft movements, he cut and shaped the feather's nib. "You know a thing or two about falconry, as well."

He added it to the pile of trimmed quills, and thrust them out to her.

"What's this?" she asked in surprise.

"For your work. A scribe needs fresh quills all the time."

She closed her fingers around the feathers, overcome by gratitude. Raising her gaze to his, she said, "The first night of the siege, when we . . ."

He cradled her cupped hands in his. "When we did this?"

Gabriel kissed her with an intensity that made her breath grow ragged. She leaned into his warmth, exulting in the pleasure of his touch.

A series of booms rang out from the artillery mounted on the fortress's walls, thrumming like the beats of a bass drum in Estelle's chest. She pulled back from Gabriel uneasily as the horses stamped and whinnied in response. Several raptors shrieked in distress, flapping their wings and rattling their cages.

"The poor animals," Estelle said. "I wish they weren't trapped in here."

"A few will soon make their escape," Gabriel replied. "Queen Charlotta ordered us to select two falcons for her husband as pets."

"He should be thinking of war tactics, not pets," she muttered.

"Judging by the number of men abandoning the queen for Jacco since King Louis arrived, I'd wager you're not the only one to say that."

"Will you see that Monsieur Pelestrine eats and drinks? I must get back to the queen." Estelle hesitated, holding up the quills. "My father used to prepare these for me from his falcons' tail feathers, and the sight of them brings me joy."

His expression softened into a smile. "I'll remember that."

She hurried back through the stables, flinching at the sound of a distant boom.

As she retraced her steps through the courtyard, a massive explosion shook the earth. A cascade of stones struck the ground with terrifying force nearby. Soldiers shouted orders from the parapets, their voices mingling with the frantic blare of trumpets. Cannons discharged one after the next, high above her. Laced through it all were the agonized screams of injured men. Her heart pounding, she crawled toward the nearest wall and curled against it. These stones, at least, were solid.

A hand squeezed her shoulder. "Estelle!"

She blinked, struggling to focus her gaze, and found herself looking into the shadowy eye slit of a Savoyard knight's helmet. He huddled over her, his chest plate and chain-mail shirt covered with a thick layer of dust. He repeated her name, his voice familiar as air, as sunlight.

*Étienne?*

The word hummed in her throat, trapped by dust and terror.

Her brother helped her stand.

"But how did you get here?" Estelle sagged against him, nearly losing consciousness.

He carried her through the doorway to the fortress's interior and gently set her down. "Are you hurt?"

"My head hurts, but I'm fine otherwise. You?"

"Never better." He removed his helmet.

"You've become a man," she marveled, reaching out to touch his beard.

"And you're a woman. Time will do that." His mouth quirked in a smile, his brown eyes radiating happiness.

She'd been his little shadow during their childhood in Auvergne, toddling in his footsteps through the meadow near their home on the count's lands, helping Papa in the mews at his side, learning to ride first a pony and then a horse under his watchful eye. He had been her kind protector from the day she was born until he left them for Savoy and an uncertain future. Now, as miraculous as it seemed, she had been given the gift of his presence once more.

"Estelle!" Gabriel emerged through the doorway from the court-yard, his sword clanking at his side.

Barely giving Étienne a glance, he gripped her by the arm. "Are you injured?"

"No." Relief coursed through her. "You're still in one piece, praise the saints. And Michel?"

"Fine. Though he couldn't sleep through that one."

"Who's this?" Étienne gave the falconer an up-and-down assessment, frowning.

"Étienne, this is. . . a falconer, Gabriel." Estelle jumped as another shower of rocks thudded against the cobblestones outside. "And, Gabriel, this is my brother Étienne. He fights for Savoy."

Gabriel's eyes widened in surprise, but he recovered quickly. "Welcome to Kyrenia, monsieur."

Étienne acknowledged his words with a curt nod.

"Dear brother," Estelle said firmly, "I owe my life to Gabriel. As does our father's good friend Michel Pelestrine. I hope that gives you a bit of ease."

"You'll have to tell me all the details when our lives aren't balanced on a knifepoint," Étienne returned. "I went out to the galley to fetch more of my things and thought the world was coming to an end. That was the biggest explosion I've ever witnessed."

"You arrived with the new galleys in the harbor," she said, nodding. "How did the captains evade attack from the Mamluks—"

Two guards burst through the doorway. "We need physicians!" one of them shouted. "The injured are being brought down from the parapets now."

Étienne thrust his helmet on his head. "I'll help carry the wounded."

Gabriel fell into step with him. "So will I."

"I'll fetch physicians." Estelle turned away as the men headed for the doors. "God protect you all!"

# CHAPTER 37

Summer 1460
Kyrenia Fortress, Cyprus

HER EARS RINGING and a band of pain tightening around her forehead, Estelle went to the infirmary that had been set up in the fortress's great hall. She informed the physicians on duty they were needed in the courtyard. One man volunteered to go; the other stayed where he was.

When she gave him a questioning look, he said, "If we both die today, there is no hope for the injured."

She could not argue with that. Hobbling down the corridors to the queen's study, she spied Sir Hector and other members of the council just ahead. Sir Hector's hound padded behind the men, his tail between his legs.

*Poor boy. He must be terrified by the noise.*

The barons filed into the chamber, leaving the hound outside. She rummaged in her purse and came up with a scrap of cheese. As she passed the hound, she slipped it to him.

Inside, the men of the council surrounded King Louis and Queen Charlotta at their table, cawing and jabbering until Estelle wanted to scream at them for silence.

"We can all agree this latest blast was the worst yet," the queen said wearily. "We've lost nearly twenty men, and many more are injured. How did they do it?"

"Their cannon was mounted to a Greek church a good distance off, but its aim was true. The Pretender's artillery men were lucky." Lord Chimi always seemed to know the most about Jacco's tactics and offered frequent opinions about how the royal couple should counterattack.

"We will not hold out much longer if they wreak destruction of that nature upon us," the queen said flatly. "The ships from Genoa that arrived last night were a blessing, but they carried mostly provisions. No matter how much biscuit and wine we hoard, provisions are useless if we cannot fight off Jacco's army."

Estelle glanced at King Louis. He picked at a hangnail on his finger, frowning. "Some of my father's best knights were in the fleet. I, for one, feel heartened by their arrival. My gaming table will finally be put to good use."

"What good are thirty knights against five hundred Mamluks and dozens of cannons?" Lord Chimi demanded. "We need hundreds more soldiers and better artillery."

"Translate the letter from Lord de Milly again," Queen Charlotta said to Estelle. "The part about Western leaders and his promise to us."

Estelle did as she was asked. Each line or two, either the queen or the barons interrupted her.

"He claims to have written to the pope, to the French king, to the Duke of Burgundy and the rest entreating them for gold and soldiers," said Sir Hector. "But how long will that take? We need aid now."

"My father-in-law will send aid." Queen Charlotta glanced at her husband. "He's sending ships and soldiers and money besides. Isn't that right, my dear?"

The king raised his eyes to hers. The contrast between his dull gaze and his wife's agitated energy startled Estelle, as it always did.

"I've asked him to do so, yes. He might need more persuading, though. If need be, I can always return home and cajole him over roasted boar and a Burgundian red. I've half a mind to do it now. The poverty of our situation is impossible. I'm king!" His petulant tone grated on Estelle. "Why must I live like this?"

The irritation emanating from the barons was thick in the air, and Estelle couldn't blame them for it. She saw it all clearly now. The barons—and most of the other powerful Cypriots—had never entertained the idea that Queen Charlotta would actually rule. When her father died, they had filled her ears with their schemes, striking a wedge between her and Jacco. Once she was married again, they'd planned to rule using Louis of Savoy as their pawn.

How furious they must be that King Louis had proved to be useless, and Queen Charlotta was their best hope at salvaging the kingdom of Cyprus.

"Continue, mademoiselle," the queen told Estelle, taking her seat again.

"Yes, Your Grace."

Estelle began reading aloud, translating the letter from French into Greek.

"Wait!" Louis held up a hand. "I hate that part. When he says he wants you to come to Rhodes and he'll send more ships and soldiers to protect us—but *only* if I stay here. It's unfair!"

Queen Charlotta sighed. "But don't you see, my darling, that if you leave Cyprus, the Pretender will claim your throne. The people will remain loyal to us if you show them your courage, for you are the one true king."

"What's the use of staying?" King Louis flopped back in his chair. "This fortress is crumbling around us, stone by stone. We shall never regain what has been lost."

Queen Charlotta twisted in her seat to face her husband. "You cannot lose faith now. We're the God-ordained rulers of this kingdom. In time, we'll have a son and he'll be king after us."

"Yes, an heir," said Sir Hector, crossing his arms over his chest. "That would go far to assure the people that their kingdom will persevere."

"When will our son arrive, my dear?" King Louis asked his wife, his face brightening. "Do you have any news on that front?"

She blanched. "You shall be the first to know when that happy day comes, my darling."

*Dear God and all the saints. This is hopeless.*

Estelle put a hand to her mouth, wondering for a frantic moment if she had spoken the treasonous words aloud. But no one looked her way.

"The Knights Hospitaller would look more favorably on your request for ships and soldiers if you could offer them something in return," Sir Hector said to the queen. "Have all the monasteries turned over their wealth to the crown?"

"The abbots and priors presented me with various items in silver, and my riders found a few valuables that had not been accounted for. All of it shall be given to Lord de Milly, along with some of my own jewelry," the queen replied.

Lord Chimi's attention swiveled to Estelle. "You led a party to Bellapais Abbey. You lost two guards on the return journey and came back empty-handed. Who exactly was behind the attack?"

"Jacco's agents, my lord. Led by a man who sowed evil in Rhodes Town when I was a girl. A Catalan called Nicolau Baldaia."

"You know him?" The queen looked at her in surprise.

"Unfortunately, yes. He made life difficult for many in Rhodes Town, including my family."

"What slipped through your fingers on the road?" Lord Chimi persisted.

"Silver plates and candlesticks, my lord."

The time to mention the crown and jewels had passed. Still, Estelle felt a stark uneasiness at withholding information from the queen.

Lord Chimi eyed her with disdain. "That was an ill-fated choice, letting the young mademoiselle lead a party into the mountains."

Queen Charlotta ignored him, turning to Estelle. "I shall accept Lord de Milly's invitation to visit him and make my case to him personally. You'll accompany me to Rhodes as translator."

Estelle grew very still. The letter slipped from her hand and fluttered to the floor.

For three long years, she'd longed to return to her family in Rhodes. But her beloved brother was now in Kyrenia. Gabriel was here, and her connection to him deepened by the day. And what about Michel Pelestrine?

*I cannot leave them. My heart will shatter.*

"Perhaps she's unwilling to accompany you, Your Grace." Lord Chimi's voice cut through the panicked thoughts in Estelle's mind.

*There's no other choice. I must go. But not without Monsieur Pelestrine.*

Despite the pounding headache, despite the roaring in her ears, she gathered herself and retrieved the letter. "Thank you, my queen. And I wonder if bringing the grand master a gift of falcons might be worthwhile? He loves them so."

The queen stared at her for a moment, nodding slowly. "An excellent idea."

King Louis pouted. "But not the falcons I'm selecting as pets. I've yet to see the best ones. I think the falconers are holding them back."

"My king," Estelle said, "just this morning a falconer told me he was examining all the birds, selecting the very finest specimens for you."

"Some good news at last," the king said, beaming.

Estelle regarded the queen again. "Your Grace, might I suggest the French falconer accompany us to Rhodes? He'll ensure the falcons survive the voyage."

"I thought he was injured," the queen objected.

"Yes, but I'll look after him on the voyage. My father told me Lord de Milly specifically requested to meet Monsieur Pelestrine."

She held her breath, the lie burning her tongue. The medical care was superior on Rhodes, with its hospital filled with experienced physicians, surgeons, and nurses. If she could just get Monsieur Pelestrine there, the burden of responsibility she felt for the man would ease. Healing ointments, wine, food—such supplies were scarce here. His chances of surviving this siege were quickly fading.

"An excellent idea," said the queen.

A valet burst into the chamber, panting, two guards close on his heels.

"What is your business here?" Queen Charlotta demanded.

"A messenger brings news." He bent, hands on his knees, struggling to catch his breath.

"Where is he?" The queen pushed back her chair and stood.

"He collapsed from exhaustion, Your Grace," replied one of the guards. "In the harbor. But his story is already making its way around the fortress."

"What does he say?" King Louis demanded.

When the valet raised his head, Estelle saw a glimmer of fear in his eyes. "The Pretender has already converted many Cypriots to his cause, both knights and peasants. Everywhere he goes, he gives serfs their freedom, and . . .and—"

"Out with it, man," the king said crossly.

"The Pretender's agents are pillaging the homes of your loyal supporters in Nicosia as we speak. Many of your friends have been murdered, my queen. Their heads are on spikes for all to see. The capital city is lost. All of Cyprus save this fortress is under his control!"

Queen Charlotta's face crumpled. She covered her eyes for a moment, her shoulders shaking. The king paled. He glanced nervously at the barons, then at his wife.

"God save them," the queen said finally. "God save all of us."

When she was dismissed, Estelle managed to stand and back away from the royal couple without stumbling. She had eaten nothing today, and her stomach cramped with hunger. The sounds of screams rose in her memory like breaking waves, crashing into her brain relentlessly until she could not bear it any longer.

Staggering down the damp, musty corridor toward her chamber, she began to weep.

# CHAPTER 38

Autumn 1460
Kyrenia Fortress, Cyprus

ESTELLE STOOD next to Monsieur Pelestrine in Kyrenia harbor, shivering in the wind despite the wool cloak she wore. It was oddly quiet. The siege had ended abruptly a few days earlier when the Mamluk army retreated with no warning and no explanation.

The queen's spies had ferreted out the reason. Apparently, the Sultan of Egypt was near death. His soldiers dared not be absent during the transfer of power lest they fall out of favor. So despite Jacco's pleas for them to stay and destroy Kyrenia, they had sailed back across the sea to Egypt.

When and whether they would return was a mystery, but Jacco's remaining forces still controlled most of Cyprus.

Monsieur Pelestrine sat on a wooden trunk next to her, his arm in a sling. Though he was still quite weak, his wound hadn't festered, thanks to Gabriel. Glancing around, Estelle saw the falconer bent over a traveling cage, securing its waxed canvas cover. The merlin within the cage was hooded and quiet. She'd noticed the birds were rarely agitated around Gabriel. He had the same quality of calm that her father exhibited with falcons and hawks.

He must have felt her eyes upon him, for he rose and walked toward them.

"They're all lashed to their perches," he said to Monsieur Pelestrine. "The meat for their feedings is in the black trunk."

He tipped his head at the luggage stacked on the dock.

"My thanks to you," the Frenchman replied. "Where you've been finding meat these days is a mystery I'd like unraveled."

"You'll have a fine day for sailing." Gabriel ignored Monsieur Pelestrine's comment. He smiled at Estelle, his gray eyes glowing. "The wind is crisp, the sky is clear."

"It looks like our captain has arrived." Monsieur Pelestrine pointed at the harbor entrance.

A galley glided in from the sea, green-and-purple banners rippling on its mainsail mast. When the captain appeared on deck, her spirits soared.

"It's Master Fordun!" she exclaimed. "Oh, for the love of all the saints, let him be the one taking us to Rhodes Town. He was in the convoy that brought me here."

"He's said to be the best the knights have." Monsieur Pelestrine squinted against the glare of the sun. "As fine a soldier as he is a sailor. I'll feel better about this journey if we're in his hands, that's certain."

Gabriel studied the Scotsman's galley with an expression of relief. "It'll make me breathe easier, too."

His gaze slipped to Estelle again. There was something in his face that made her heart thud faster. A tenderness she'd only witnessed in him a few times. The sight made her long to throw herself in his arms, melt into his embrace.

"Estelle!" Étienne hurried along the dock, weaving around piles of luggage and supplies. He thrust a small sack at her. "There's a letter for Papa and Maman in here. And something for our brother and sister. Give them my love."

"How did you extricate yourself from the king's side?" she asked him, taking the sack.

Since the siege ended, Étienne had found himself enlisted as a player at the king's gaming table every day.

"He grew tired of me winning."

Gabriel regarded Étienne with interest. "You served King Louis in Savoy, I gather?"

Étienne shook his head. "I was first a page, then a knight for the House of Savoy. But I rarely saw Lord Louis—forgive me, King Louis. I worked mostly for his father, the duke. I've spent more time with King Louis in the past few days than in the previous ten years."

"And?" Gabriel asked.

Étienne gave him a long, considered look but said nothing.

Monsieur Pelestrine spoke up from his perch on the trunk, his voice raspy and thin. "A wise king would send out an army now, in the Pretender's moment of weakness, and destroy him."

"Brother, I serve as scribe and interpreter for the queen," Estelle said quietly, leaning close to Étienne. "I am sorry to tell you this, but she's a better king than her husband."

The muscles in his jaw tightened. "I've only been here a short time. I'll see for myself what the king is made of."

"Yes," Estelle said sadly. "You will. I'll pray for your safety every day until I return."

"I forbid you to return, sister." He took her hand, his expression solemn. "This is your chance to escape. Things will only get worse here, believe me."

Gabriel nodded. "It's quiet for the moment, but Jacco will be back to sack Kyrenia as soon as he steals enough gold to pay for a new army. Your brother is right, Estelle. It would be madness to return."

"I can't abandon you. I won't." She looked from her brother to Gabriel, fighting tears.

"It doesn't feel right to me, either," said Monsieur Pelestrine. "Why did I get the chance to leave Kyrenia while you're stuck here, awaiting Jacco's next move?"

Estelle exchanged a glance with Gabriel. She had told him of her ploy to get Monsieur Pelestrine back to Rhodes, but no one else knew the truth.

He put a hand on the falconer's good shoulder. "You're doing your part for the queen by bringing our best raptors to the grand master. May God protect you and keep you well."

The Frenchman stood with difficulty and embraced him. "I owe you much, my friend."

"Farewell, Estelle." Gabriel's voice struck her like a hammer blow. "May God and all the saints protect you."

The air rushed from her lungs.

*I will see you again. I must see you again. I could not bear it if something dreadful happened to you . . .*

She looked straight at Gabriel, desperate to voice her thoughts aloud. He gazed unwaveringly back, his sober look tempered by a softness around the eyes, a warmth that eased her sorrow just a little.

Somehow she knew he understood.

When the galley glided into the harbor at Rhodes Town as dusk was falling five days later, Estelle could not contain the tears sliding down her cheeks. No explosions shattered the air; no distant booms signaled cannon fire. She exulted in the commonplace sounds of fishmongers crying their wares, gulls shrieking overhead, the gentle slap of waves against the seawalls.

Telling the queen's attendants that she would ride with Monsieur Pelestrine to the grand master's palace, she oversaw the placement of the raptors' cages in a mule cart, then helped the Frenchman onto the bench.

"We'll go to the palace by way of the hospital," she informed the driver.

"But I've been ordered to take you directly to the palace," he protested.

She passed him some coins. "And you will—after we stop at the hospital."

Monsieur Pelestrine looked at her in confusion. "What's this you speak of?"

"You're not recovered yet. You'll stay in the hospital for a few days."

He began to protest.

She raised a hand. "I'll take care of the birds and deliver them into my father's capable hands. He'll present them to Lord de Milly in your place."

His protestations dwindled as the cart wheels creaked into motion. Within a few moments, his head sagged to her shoulder and he began to snore. Estelle pushed back her hood so she could take in the familiar sights of Rhodes Town. The cart rolled to the Street of the Knights, one of her favorite locations in the compact harbor city. The hospital sat at the street's lowest point, near the city walls and the harbor. Inns and knights' residences lined the street as it swept up a gentle incline to the gates of the grand master's palace.

The cart eased to a halt at the hospital doors. A red dragonfly settled on one of the mule's bridles, wings glimmering in the sunlight.

Estelle smiled. "Good day to you, dragonfly."

For one exquisite moment, the horrors of Kyrenia vanished from her mind.

Inside the palace gates, the cart rolled past the shadowy arcades lining the perimeter of the courtyard, past rows of ancient marble statues that had been painstakingly cleaned by the knights and displayed for all to see.

The doors to the mews were ajar. Estelle slipped inside, her eyes adjusting to the dim light. With a start, she recognized the form of her father bent over a table strewn with equipment.

"Papa!" Estelle raced forward and flung her arms around him.

"God in heaven! You've returned to us." He returned her embrace, his voice gruff with emotion.

"How are Maman and the children? I've missed you all so."

"They're all well, praise the saints." Papa examined her face with care. "You're not a girl any longer, are you?"

"I left childhood behind the day I sailed away from Rhodes for Cyprus. I've learned to manage very well on my own." She disentangled herself from him. "And, lest I forget, I've brought some falcons and a hawk for the grand master. You'd best have your helpers bring them inside."

He went to the door and surveyed the cart and its contents, then ordered two under-falconers to unload it.

Turning back to her, he sighed, clearly struggling for words. "I never would have agreed to let you go had I known what it was truly like in that place."

Though she'd counseled herself during the sea voyage to keep her bitterness to herself, it rose up anyway.

"Why did you send me there, Papa?" she beseeched him. "How could you?"

He caught her hands in his. "Your mother and I thought it was an honor, the king's invitation. King Jean wrote to me after I sent Michel Pelestrine to him. Saying how he valued having a born-and-bred Frenchman in his court. He told me his daughter was soon to wed a Portuguese prince who spoke only Portuguese and French. He said Princess Charlotta spoke Greek, not French, and needed a tutor. Michel had told him about my family, how I had a daughter who was about the same age as his. Michel himself was happy in Cyprus. He saw no reason for us to refuse the king's invitation."

"Monsieur Pelestrine lived at St. Hilarion, a castle in the mountains." She shook her head. "He knew nothing of life at court in Nicosia."

"I had no idea at the time how little he understood of the court nor how far away he would be from you." Papa's shoulders slumped. "Forgive me. I truly believed he would watch over you and keep you safe."

Estelle took that in, struggling to contain her emotions. There was so much more she wanted to say. But one thing stood out above all else. A question that had haunted her for too many years. It was time to seek an answer.

"Signora Rosso said you were sending me to Cyprus to find a

husband. I did not want to believe her. But I've carried her words with me all this time, hoping they were a lie."

Estelle fought tears, waiting for her father's response. His expression registered first shock, then anger.

"That woman has a wagging tongue. She filled your mother's head with fancies about wealthy Cypriot noblemen, but our intention was for you to be companion to the princess, as the king had promised. The betrothal was a surprise to us both, and not a pleasant one." He gripped her hands tighter. "We were frantic with worry. All we wanted was your safe return to Rhodes. After the king died, we wrote to Queen Charlotta many times asking for her to release you from service. And she never responded."

A slow burn of fury ignited in Estelle's chest. Perhaps the queen was just as cruel in her own way as Jacco.

"I was angry at you for a time, I'll not deny it," she admitted. "Especially when the betrothal was arranged. But once Gabriel gave me your letter, my dark feelings vanished."

"Gabriel?" His brow furrowed.

"He works with Monsieur Pelestrine. He's been . . . helpful to me. To us both. Monsieur Pelestrine was gravely wounded in a roadside attack on Cyprus, during an outing I'd planned. I've delivered him to the hospital in Rhodes Town. He's made some improvement, but conditions in Kyrenia grow worse by the day. He would not have survived there much longer."

Her father nodded. "Praise the saints the king allowed him to return here."

"King Louis had nothing to do with it, Papa. Monsieur Pelestrine is alive thanks to Gabriel, but I had to get him on that ship from Kyrenia. If I'd failed . . ."

Papa studied her with sympathy in his eyes. "You felt responsible for him."

"Yes."

"When will you visit the rest of the family?" he asked.

"Tomorrow, perhaps?" Estelle remembered the letter from Étienne in her purse, then decided not to mention it. She'd wait and surprise them all with the letter and her news of him. "I'll ask Queen Charlotta if I can join you for supper. I can't promise anything, though. She seems to require my help at all hours."

"You were always quiet as a girl. People assumed you were shy. I knew better. I knew you had a core of steel inside. But now—" Papa shook his head, chuckling. "That steel? It's starting to show on the outside, too."

# CHAPTER 39

Autumn 1460
Rhodes Town, Island of Rhodes

THE NEXT MORNING, she accompanied Queen Charlotta to her meeting with Lord de Milly and served as translator for the queen during the negotiations.

The grand master's face lit up when her father brought forth the falcons Michel Pelestrine and Gabriel had chosen. Then the queen's attendants presented him with silver goblets, platters, scepters, and other valuables retrieved from Cypriot monasteries. A group of musicians played passages from the famed Codex written during the time of King Janus and the first Queen Charlotte.

When one of the grand master's servants entered and whispered in his ear, he smiled broadly at the queen.

"Your Grace, our prayers have been answered," he said. "Two ships from Savoy approach Rhodes Town harbor. Your father-in-law is true to his word, it seems."

The queen cried out in delight. "I must go to the harbor at once."

But when she rose, she sank into her chair again, the color draining from her face.

"Perhaps not," she said in a more subdued voice. "The journey has taken a toll on me."

"Let us call for refreshment." The grand master studied the queen in concerned silence. "Rest, Your Grace, and we'll take up this business again tomorrow and welcome our Savoyard visitors."

"Thank you, Lord de Milly." The queen smiled weakly. "King Louis and I are most grateful."

After accompanying the queen and her attendants to their apartments, Estelle hurried through the palace to the mews. When she got there, her father was deep in conversation with a cloaked woman.

The woman turned at her approach. *"Ma chérie!"*

"Maman!" Estelle hastened to her mother and fell into her embrace.

"Seeing the two of you together again makes my heart soar." Papa's voice cracked. "I wasn't sure it would ever happen."

Maman kept hold of Estelle, weeping. "We never should have let you go. I blame myself. I was flattered by the king's invitation; I won't lie. And by Signora Rosso's stories of noblemen who would make you fine offers of marriage."

"Offers?" Estelle let out a short laugh. "I only wish I had been shown that courtesy."

"We've nearly finished paying off our debts, and the grand master says we may return to France next year. You'll be at our side, darling girl."

Estelle wiped her mother's tears away with the hem of her cloak.

"I'm safe now, Maman. Let's find comfort in that." She smiled. "You never used to visit the palace when I lived in Rhodes Town. Is this a new habit?"

"Your father told me yesterday you'd returned. Do you think I slept a wink all night? Then this morning I heard the news that Savoyard ships approach Rhodes Town. Étienne could be with them! How could I stay away from you and keep that news to myself?'

Papa grinned. "If we have both Estelle and Étienne back at once, the little ones will burst with excitement."

Estelle fumbled in her purse. "Étienne is not with the Savoyard fleet. He's in Kyrenia." She held the letter out to her parents. "This is from him."

Her parents' joyous expressions faded.

"God save him. How can that be?" Maman clutched the letter to her chest. "He'll be killed!"

A peregrine falcon nearby shrieked and strained against her leash, wings churning the air.

"Hush, you'll frighten the falcons." Papa put a steadying arm around Maman.

The heavy footfalls of guards at the door startled them all into silence.

"Mademoiselle, return to the queen's apartments at once. She demands your presence," came the gruff order.

"Go," Papa told Estelle. "We'll await word from you."

She kissed her parents and followed the queen's guards back to the queen's apartments. One of the men held an oil lamp to light their way, his shadow lurching like a drunken giant on the stone walls.

Queen Charlotta lay in bed curled on her side, attended by two ladies-in-waiting who had accompanied them on the journey. A pair of nuns stood nearby.

Estelle went to the bedside, unnerved by the queen's hollow-eyed stare. "Your Grace."

"My son and heir," Queen Charlotta whispered. "Dead before he even had a chance to live."

Estelle sank to her knees, stunned. "Please accept my deepest sympathies, Your Grace."

"I told no one in Kyrenia. If I had, the barons would not have let me leave. And Lord de Milly is my greatest ally—I had to come here!"

"Of course." Estelle reached for the queen's hand, then stilled herself. It was not appropriate for a courtier to touch a monarch uninvited, even in moments of crisis.

"Stay by my side tonight. In the morning, I'll keep my appointment with Lord de Milly. Afterward, we must write to my husband." Queen Charlotta shifted her position, wincing. "We'll tell him all is well and I am enjoying the hospitality of the knights. He must know the grand master is happy with his gifts and is looking favorably on our request for aid. We'll say nothing of this." She gestured at her abdomen.

Estelle nodded. "As you wish, Your Grace. With your permission, I can send for the woman physician I once told you about. Signorina Giuliana may have a remedy to ease your pain."

"Yes. Please."

*Has the queen ever used that word in my presence before?*

Estelle asked the nuns to fetch the Italian physician. They hurried away at once.

Queen Charlotta fixed her with a serious look. "You've been true to me when many others have not. I'll not overlook you when the royal coffers fill with gold again. And you may stay on in Rhodes Town with your family when I return to Cyprus. I'll miss you dreadfully. But I'll honor your wish and release you from my service."

She reached out a hand to Estelle.

Estelle took it. "I have been happy to serve you."

It was mostly true. There were many days when she *had* been happy in Queen Charlotta's court. That summer at St. Hilarion had been truly joyous. But her pride had swelled too much; it had kept her from finding a way out of Cyprus sooner, before the horrors of war descended on the island.

"There is a question that troubles me, Your Grace," she ventured. "My father said after he learned of the betrothal planned for me, he sent you letters asking that I be released from your service. But he never got a response. Why?"

The queen looked at her blankly. "I did not receive his letters, mademoiselle. Before my mother died, she intercepted all of my correspondence. She only let me see what she deemed to be appropriate. After her death, the barons continued the practice. For my protection, they told me." Her eyes narrowed. "They withheld too much. It has cost me dearly. Since the court retreated to Kyrenia, I've had the captains of the Savoyard fleet board incoming ships, retrieve messages, and deliver them to me out of sight of my council."

Estelle nodded slowly. "And the barons accept this?"

"Remember all our days studying Christine de Pizan's book?" the queen asked softly, keeping hold of Estelle's hand. "That knowledge gave me the courage to defy the barons. If you hadn't read it to me—translated it for me—I might have failed. You've helped me more than you know, though I haven't rewarded you properly for it. Have faith, mademoiselle, for I assure you I will."

Estelle regarded their linked hands, the queen's words resonating in her mind.

Queen Charlotta had fought for her throne with a fierceness and tenacity beyond her years. She navigated a world of powerful men every day, bending them to her will, cajoling them to join her cause, sacrificing her own health in the name of her kingdom.

Estelle raised her eyes to the queen's tearstained face. The monarch's hope for an heir had been extinguished, but there was still hope for her throne.

"Thank you, my queen. You honor me."

She went to the window, every muscle taut with tension. She could now rejoin her family, take up the threads of her old life in Rhodes Town, find work here, and earn the ducats her father needed to pay off the last of his debts. And yet instead of relishing this news, she was more troubled than ever.

Her mind careened back to the thunderous explosions shaking the walls of Kyrenia fortress, the screams of injured soldiers.

*I never want to see Kyrenia again.*

But Étienne and Gabriel were still trapped within that stark, miserable cage of stone. How could she abandon them now?

Outside, dusk gathered, sending long shadows over the grand master's gardens. The mournful cry of a peacock echoed through the cooling air. The cloudless sky darkened, revealing a silvery latticework of stars. She watched the night sky unfurl, taking comfort from its beauty.

From the bed, Queen Charlotta let out a long sigh.

*Remember what Michel Pelestrine said. The closer I am to the queen, the more danger I face.*

# CHAPTER 40

Winter 1461
Rhodes Town, Island of Rhodes

ESTELLE WALKED Signorina Guiliana to the door of the queen's apartments. "Thank you, signorina. Your remedy not only helped her sleep, but her color is back today, too."

The physician slipped her cloak on and took up her satchel. "She's young and strong. And she knows she can conceive now. With God's grace, she'll soon find herself with child again."

Estelle shut the door behind her and leaned against it, closing her eyes. She'd slept in the queen's sitting room last night. Perhaps *slept* wasn't the right word. She'd tried to find a comfortable position on the cushions she'd piled near the hearth, worrying about Gabriel and Étienne while the fire died a slow, sputtering death.

Luckily, the queen had taken a tonic administered by Signorina Guiliana and had slept soundly for most of the night. Her attendants now helped her dress, readying her for a meeting with the Savoyard captains of the galleys that had sailed into Rhodes Harbor yesterday.

Estelle smoothed her skirts and returned to the sitting room. Just as she finished settling the cushions in their proper places, Queen Charlotta appeared in the doorway, leaning on the arm of a lady-in-waiting.

"My servants tell me the Savoyard ships bear three hundred knights and soldiers, and their holds are packed with provisions for Kyrenia fortress." The queen's eyes sparkled with excitement. "If Lord de Milly and his knights honor my request for another ship, soldiers, and supplies to support our efforts, we'll have a fearsome army at our disposal."

"Jacco's numbers have never been weaker." Estelle's fatigue vanished. "If we hurry back now—before he rallies more Mamluks to his side—the Savoyard troops can retake Nicosia."

"We?" Queen Charlotta's gaze turned inquisitive. "You're staying in Rhodes, mademoiselle. Though I wish it weren't so."

Estelle's thoughts went to her family, then inevitably back to Kyrenia, to the men she'd left behind.

*If I stay in Rhodes, will I regret the decision till the end of my days?* This question had tormented her all night. Another question struck her now. *Have I done everything in my power to help Gabriel and Étienne?*

If she stayed here, one thing was certain: she could do nothing more for them. The thought was unacceptable.

She lifted her chin. "Once Nicosia is retaken and Jacco is ousted, I'll leave your service. But this is not the moment, I'm sure of it. That is, if you'll still have me."

"If I'll still have you?" The queen shrugged off her attendant and gripped Estelle by the shoulders. "You don't know how happy you've made me, Estelle de Montavon. You'll not regret this choice." She dropped her voice. "We won't have to write that letter to my husband. We'll soon sail into Kyrenia harbor with an army. I can think of no better way to bolster his spirits than that."

Once the decision was made to return to Cyprus, Estelle barely had a moment to think about her choice. She spent the next few days at the queen's side, overseeing supply lists, discussing plans with the captains of the Savoyard fleet, and writing letters of thanks to each knight in Rhodes Town who had supported Queen Charlotta's cause.

The eve of their departure was sunny and unseasonably warm. Only the faintest sea breeze rustled the branches of oleander shrubs and citrus trees in the city's gardens, and the sky was crisply blue.

Arm in arm with Papa, Estelle walked from the palace through the streets of Rhodes Town to their house, lost in memories of all their wanderings here when she was a girl. The island had never felt like home before she'd left for Cyprus. Now, strangely enough, it did.

When they entered the house, it seemed much smaller than she remembered. Her small brother and sister scampered around her like puppies, screeching with delight.

"Who are these giants?" She wrapped her arms around both of them at once. "What have you done with Jean-Philippe and Isabeau?"

"We're them!" Jean-Philippe said indignantly. "We've just grown."

Isabeau took Estelle's hand and planted a kiss on it. "We're tiny giants," she confessed. "Especially me."

Her mother bustled into the entry hall with Christine, the maid who had been with the family since Papa and Maman were married.

After Maman kissed Estelle, Christine enveloped Estelle in an embrace and took her cloak. "What a lovely woman you've become." She beamed, wiping tears away.

Maman studied Estelle's clothing, frowning. "These Cypriot styles confuse me, I must say. The cloth's weave is impressive, and I love the blend of silk and wool. But all the tucks and drapes! I prefer a fitted bodice and a low, square neckline myself."

"My life was easier in Cyprus when I dressed the way they dressed, so I was pleased to do it." Estelle accepted a cup of wine from Papa.

"The table's set in the courtyard," he said. "We're lucky to have such a fine day. Let's sit a while and eat before it gets dark."

Outside, they sat on benches at the olive-wood table. A kitchen maid brought out platters of fish, rice, and roasted vegetables, scenting the air with ginger and saffron.

Estelle saluted her parents with her cup. "To your health," she said. "I'm grateful we're all well and together again."

"Except for Étienne," Jean-Philippe said mournfully. "He should be here, too."

Isabeau nodded. "Yes, he should."

"Now that you're back, we can plan our return to France." Maman spooned some rice into Isabeau's bowl. "I've already started making inquiries with the merchants at the marketplace. There's a ship captain from Provence who spends his winters here. He'll likely be the one we sail home with next summer."

"First, though, I'll take you to meet a notary who needs a scribe." Papa speared a chunk of fish with his knife. "He's newly arrived from Toulouse, of all places. He knew your grandfather—in fact, he worked with him for a time. Your return must have been written in the stars, my girl."

As the evening wore on, the children finished eating and grew bored with the adult conversation. They slipped away in pursuit of a lizard scuttling across the courtyard.

Estelle watched her parents talk and eat and sip their wine. Their banter had always mesmerized her. Her mother got fiery at times, and this table had been the site of many tearful arguments. Yet her parents' enjoyment of one another was never in doubt—nor was their mutual respect.

It would be cruel to let them go on thinking she was here to stay. She had to speak, and soon.

Pulling two small objects from her purse, she held them out to her siblings.

"Spinning tops from your brother," she said. "Sent with love."

The children raced to her side, squealing. They took the wooden tops to the entry hall, where oil lamps cast a golden glow on the smooth stone floor.

Satisfied they'd be distracted for a time, Estelle faced her parents. No soft preamble came to mind, so she simply plunged in.

"I won't be staying in Rhodes Town. I'm returning to Kyrenia with the queen."

"Absolutely not," Maman said without hesitation. "We won't let you go. It's bad enough Étienne is in that den of wolves."

Papa put his wine cup down and regarded Estelle in silence.

"In Rhodes, I can do nothing to support Étienne if bad fortune strikes," she said. "I'm more than a scribe and a translator for the queen. I'm her advisor, too."

Maman snorted. "Advisor? Your imagination runs away with you, my dear."

"I don't exaggerate. She relies on me. She offered to release me from service, but what she truly wants is me at her side. She's promised me gold, too, in addition to the salary I'm owed. All of that will help you pay off your last debts, perhaps even pay for the journey back to France next summer."

Papa shook his head slowly. "But Kyrenia is besieged. Cyprus is overrun. It grows more dangerous with every passing day."

"Jacco's army has abandoned him," Estelle asserted. "This is the moment to attack him, and the queen has more than enough troops to succeed. He's doomed."

"How can you be sure?" Maman asked. "Nothing is certain. We never know what is about to change our fates, whether it's a storm, a fever, a chance encounter with a madman. We cannot foretell the future—that's all we can be sure of."

"I agree with your mother." Papa sipped from his cup again. "You're our child and in our charge. We can forbid you from going."

Estelle grew quiet. A feeling of deep calm spread through her. "I'll always be your daughter. But I stopped being a child the day you sent me to Cyprus. I've made my own decisions for many years now, and I'll keep doing so." She stood. "I plan to lend my support to Queen Charlotta one more time. When she vanquishes her brother and the throne is safe, I'll return to Rhodes, I swear it."

Maman rose to her feet, too. Her blue eyes were wet with tears. But instead of unleashing a torrent of protests, she held her tongue, struggling to remain calm. Estelle watched her with wary anticipation.

Papa sighed. "Sit, the both of you."

They settled back on the benches.

"I suppose we're to blame for this show of independence." His voice held a trace of chagrin. "We sent you into that viper's nest. We were fools to do so. And somehow you survived."

"I survived because of you both," Estelle said gently. "Everything you've ever taught me, everything you've ever shown me—I used all of it in Cyprus. There were many days I told myself I had the courage of a falcon, even if my knees shook with fright."

Maman reached across the table and took her hand.

"Do you still have the blade I gave you?" Papa asked.

"Yes."

"Is it with you now?"

Estelle shook her head. "I'm not permitted to wear it when I'm with the queen, and I'm with her most days."

"Promise me you'll carry it every time you leave her side, from this day forward."

"I promise."

He laid his hand over hers and Maman's. The evening quiet was only broken by the children's laughter drifting from the entry hall. Overhead, stars winked in the darkening sky.

# CHAPTER 41

Winter 1461
Off the coast of Cyprus

ESTELLE CREPT above decks and padded through the shadows to the stern as the Hospitaller vessel glided through ink-black waves, its silk banners whispering in the breeze. Lord de Milly had donated a galley and a hundred soldiers to their cause, and it raced alongside the Savoyard galleys aided by a favorable wind.

They were not headed to Kyrenia fortress, not yet. The grand master had urged Queen Charlotta to begin her reconquest of Cyprus by taking back the harbor and fortress of Paphos, which had been under Jacco's control for months. This way, the Pretender would have no port in which to shelter Mamluk ships if they returned. Seeing the sense of the proposition, the queen had agreed.

As they neared Paphos harbor, the Savoyard ships took the lead. The Hospitaller galley hung back. It would stay well out of range of crossbows and cannons since the queen was aboard.

From her vantage point on the deck, Estelle could make out the fortifications jutting over the harbor, the faint illumination of torches flaring here and there in the darkness. The castle and fortress would not be easy to breach. But now, with two Savoyard vessels and hundreds of additional soldiers in her retinue, Queen Charlotta was emboldened. Her men would retake Paphos—or die trying.

Estelle held her breath as groups of soldiers dispersed over the gunwales of the galleys into small boats waiting to ferry them to shore. The slap and gurgle of waves masked the noise of oars dipping into the water. Mist drifted up from the sea, filling her lungs with a damp chill.

*Santa Maria, protect our soldiers.*

Shouts echoed over the water from the castle; first, a few voices raised in alarm, then a growing chorus of panicked roars. More torches flickered to life atop its highest towers. More Savoyards disembarked from the fleet, rowing silently ashore to join their comrades in the attack.

A light touch against her foot made her jump. Estelle glanced down. The galley cat pressed against her, its sleek body glowing pale gray against the deck. Then, tail flicking, it leaped away into the blackness.

The cries of men grew louder. A cannon boomed.

"Into the hold with you, mademoiselle." The crewman's voice was harsh in her ear. "What in God's name are you doing up here?"

"The queen asked me to be her eyes and ears above decks." The lie slid out like quicksilver, silencing the man.

*I would rather take my chances in the open than be trapped down there— may Santa Maria protect me.*

Estelle was stunned at how quickly the queen's forces overwhelmed the castle and other fortifications of Paphos. After installing a captain and a reinforced garrison to guard the port, the monarch ordered her retinue back to Kyrenia.

They arrived victorious in Kyrenia harbor, the lamps fixed to their masts casting an eerie sheen on the black water.

As the vessels dropped anchor, a great cheer went up from all aboard. The guards on the parapets whooped and bellowed from above, their calls mingling with the celebratory blares of trumpets.

Disembarking from the galley amidst exuberant chatter, Estelle swept her gaze over the figures hurrying through the harbor. By the flickering light of lamps and torches, men unloaded their gear. Others poured out from the interior to greet the newcomers and offer help.

"Looking for someone?"

She turned, startled. "Gabriel!"

His confident and graceful stride made her breath falter. She fought an urge to embrace him.

"It's truly you." A broad smile creased his face. "I never thought I'd feel a moment's joy in this place again." He stepped forward, catching an overstuffed satchel as it slipped off her shoulder. "I hope our friend remained behind in Rhodes?"

"You'll be pleased to know Monsieur Pelestrine in good hands there. He's recovering nicely."

In the wavering torchlight, Gabriel's face sobered. With a barely perceptible motion, he extended a hand, interlacing his fingertips with hers.

"Why did you return?" he asked.

Now that she was back in Kyrenia with a victorious army, her fears for Gabriel and Étienne seemed vaguely ridiculous. Though Jacco still controlled much of Cyprus, including Nicosia, his power was waning. Paphos was proof.

"The queen needs me. And she offered me a reward for my continued service." Estelle gripped his hand tightly, then let it go. "My family can use the gold."

"Your family sent you back here?" A thread of anger darkened his voice. "That's madness!"

"No. It was my choice." Before he could speak again, she added, "Paphos is retaken and the tide is turning. The queen wants King Louis to lead an attack on Nicosia and take back the city. Jacco's bid for power will soon be over."

They followed the stream of soldiers toward the inner reaches of the fortress.

"Nicosia is overrun and ransacked," Gabriel told her. "The heads of

Queen Charlotta's supporters rot on spikes all along the Bridge of the Pillory, their houses torn apart, their wealth stolen. And Jacco's supporters there grow in number by the day."

"The queen has many more soldiers now—at least a hundred mercenaries hired by the Knights of St. John and three hundred from Savoy."

"These men don't know Cyprus," he said tersely. "They'd be picked off like herons in a hunt if they were to venture into the hills."

She shook her head, thinking of Étienne. "No. Don't say that, please."

They were nearly at the stables now. Two torches burned on either side of the doorway, and they stopped beneath one.

"Estelle!" Her brother hurried toward them, sword clanking at his side.

"Thank God you're safe." Étienne folded her in his arms. "Did the queen force you to return? In my letter, I told Papa and Maman not to let you out of their sight."

"I'm no child, Étienne." Estelle removed herself from his embrace. "I returned by my own choice. Our parents were not happy with my decision, but they accepted it."

She did not add that she'd also promised them she would use all her influence with the queen to protect her brother.

Gabriel held out Estelle's satchel. She reached for the strap, her hand lingering on his.

"Of course. You've followed your heart straight back into hell." Étienne's stony gaze settled on Gabriel. "It should have been obvious to me the day we met. She's here for you."

"I told her not to return," Gabriel ground out. "I don't want her here any more than you do."

Étienne fell into a brooding silence.

Estelle was suddenly conscious of her exhaustion after the events of the past several days. All she wanted was to escape the tension between the two men and go to bed.

"Étienne," she entreated her brother, "what if our places were reversed? If I were stuck here while you sailed away to safety?" She turned to Gabriel. "My brother's not wrong. You have a place in my heart, it's true. How could I leave either of you to the fates? I had to come back. Whatever my favor with the queen is worth, it may help you both survive this accursed place."

Gabriel's expression softened. Her brother studied the two of them, frowning.

"You should get inside, Estelle," Étienne said gruffly after a moment. "The company of men, especially at night, can be dangerous."

"Yes, you're right."

Estelle took a last look at her brother and the falconer illuminated in the glow of the torchlight, side by side, and smiled. For this moment, all was well in the world.

# CHAPTER 42

Winter 1461
Kyrenia Fortress, Cyprus

*DEAR GOD, protect my brother.*

To Estelle's consternation, the words appeared bold and black on the page. She cast a furtive glance at the queen and her council. None of them were looking at her. Quickly, she pressed the nib of her quill hard against the page, crushing it. Ink smeared across the words she'd written.

"My queen, forgive me." She held up the ruined quill.

"Begin again. It's not much to rewrite yet."

Estelle reached for another sheet of linen paper and a new quill. This letter was destined for the King of France, entreating him for aid. And each sentence uttered by the queen was torn apart and rebuilt by the barons.

How any of them could concentrate today was a mystery. King Louis and several hundred men had ridden away from Kyrenia yesterday at dawn, intent on retaking Nicosia. Étienne had been among them.

Gabriel, thank all the saints, was not.

Estelle had passed a sleepless night praying for her brother's safe return. Her eyes burned with fatigue. She imagined the queen had not gotten much rest either.

Forcing herself back to the matter at hand, she dipped the quill in the inkpot.

Then the calm in the windowless room was shattered. Trumpets and horns blared from the fortress's walls with the force of a gale roaring in from the sea. Queen Charlotta sprang up from her chair.

"That's the signal to open the gates," she said grimly.

Estelle dropped her quill and stood. "Surely, that's not the king and his men. They can't be back already."

The barons were already pushing open the heavy door. Estelle and the queen followed them to the courtyard doors, a pair of guards in their wake, and burst through into chaos.

"Étienne!" Estelle launched herself into the melee of soldiers, horses, and royal guards filing into the fortress's courtyard from the open gates. A litter bearing two injured men scraped along the stones nearby. She approached, her heart in her throat, praying neither of the injured were her brother. When she was satisfied she didn't recognize them, she wheeled and wove through the crowd, calling her brother's name.

"Sir." She tugged on the sleeve of the king's valet, who led his master's black horse toward the stables. "How many more will come?"

He squinted against the sun, glancing her way. "Many were left behind. They were ambushed at the Pass of St. Catherine."

She kept pace with him. "Were any taken prisoner?"

He nodded. "Some of the knights pressed forward so the king could make his escape. They were taken."

Her heart dropped. "Savoyards?"

"Yes." He tugged the horse's reins and moved on.

Estelle stepped into the shadow of a wall and pressed her spine against the stone. Horrible thoughts pushed through the barrier she was trying to erect in her mind.

She screwed her eyes shut, willing them away.

*He may yet be safe. He may be hiding in the mountains. He may be—*

A guard's rough cry jolted her out of her thoughts. "Make way for the king!"

Queen Charlotta and King Louis walked by. The king was supported by two guards, his complaints to Queen Charlotta audible despite the noise of hooves on stone, the clatter of weaponry, the shouts and cries of the injured.

"Praise God you were not hurt, my dear," said the queen.

"Why our spies could not foresee this ambush is beyond me," her husband whined. "Their heads should be on spikes. Instead, you pay them with gold from my own coffers, rewarding them for their treachery."

The queen's face was hard. "If anyone has betrayed us, I shall root him out and hang him by his feet. I vow it to you."

"They took some of my best knights prisoner," he went on. "I'd be dead if it weren't for those men, and as God is my witness, I'll never sally forth from this fortress without them again."

His strident voice faded as they and their entourage disappeared inside.

Estelle straightened her shoulders, her knees trembling, and surveyed the wreckage of King Louis's army.

Some of his best knights. Was Étienne one of them?

There was still time for him to appear. There were still men trickling into the gates, some of them limping, some sobbing. A few supported their wounded comrades, trudging grimly through the glaring sun.

"Étienne!" She plunged into the crowd, screaming for him. "Étienne!"

A voice spoke in her ear. "He's not here."

She spun around to confront Gabriel.

"How do you know?"

"Because I've been looking, too."

She swallowed. Her throat was raw from shouting, from holding back tears.

"What can I do, Gabriel?" she asked, her voice breaking. "How can

I help him?"

He led her into the shadows by the stable door and took her hands in his. "If he's been taken prisoner, there's still a chance. You have the ear of the queen and her favor. If anyone can intervene on his behalf, it's her. Think carefully, though, about how you'll address the matter. Jacco does not take kindly to threats, and if the queen makes demands he finds unreasonable, he may strike out at your brother in retaliation."

Estelle took a gulp of air, then another.

"From what I hear in the queen's chamber, Jacco never deals with prisoners in the same way," she said slowly. "Some are beheaded, some hung by their feet, some bled to death with daggers. And others are given gifts, money, property, titles. Some become his agents and close confidants."

Gabriel nodded. "I know a few men who've received such treatment. If he finds a man particularly entertaining or brave or comely, he'll forgive nearly anything. That could work in Étienne's favor."

"But Étienne doesn't know any of that," Estelle pointed out. "He's only just arrived. He speaks no Greek. His disadvantages are many."

Several nuns whom Queen Charlotta had enlisted as nurses bustled past them carrying bandages and jugs of wine.

"The queen was losing supporters before this happened." Gabriel tightened his grip on her. "Now that Louis has failed to retake the capital, she will lose many more. Your loyalty has never been more important than at this moment. Go to her, remind her of how much she values you. How much your brother means to his king. I know you have the courage. I've seen it in you many times."

She studied their joined hands, his long, graceful brown fingers wrapped around her smaller wheat-colored ones.

Conscious of all the eyes in the courtyard, the men patrolling the fortress's walls, she reluctantly pulled free of his grasp. "If she refuses to help me—"

Her throat closed up, trapping her voice. She imagined Étienne's body bleeding, abandoned on a rocky slope, picked over by vultures . . .

"You're not alone." Gabriel's words cut through her anguish, fierce and steady. "I have little to offer you, but whatever I have, it's yours."

A muscle fluttered in his clenched jaw, and she realized that despite his veneer of calm assurance, he was as worried as she.

# CHAPTER 43

Winter 1461
Kyrenia Fortress, Cyprus

Estelle returned to the queen's study to find the monarch sitting at the table in silence. The king was absent, but Lord Chimi and two other men of the council stood near her. The only other people in the room were the guards posted at the door.

She curtsied. "Your Grace."

"Mademoiselle." Queen Charlotta's face was pensive, her head tilted at a slight angle.

The men studied Estelle without speaking. Lord Chimi's eyes held a trace of smugness. He flattened his lips as if he were repressing a smile.

Estelle caught sight of the quill on the floor, recalling she'd dropped it when the trumpets sounded. She went to retrieve it, but the queen held up a hand.

After the drama of the day's events, the queen must have been exhausted. Yet her face did not betray fatigue. Instead, her expression was taut and cold. This was not the moment to ask for a favor.

But Étienne needed help now.

*Open your mouth and ask before you lose your nerve.*

Before Estelle could compose the words, Queen Charlotta waved a creased rectangle of linen paper at her. "My bastard brother has written me a letter."

Estelle regarded the page in surprise. It was covered with a familiar blocky script.

The queen tossed the letter on the table. "He killed Sir Hector de Chivides, my most long-standing advisor and Viscount of Nicosia. One of the few noblemen in my kingdom whose loyalty was never in doubt."

Estelle recoiled. "How can that be?"

"Sir Hector left the safety of Kyrenia fortress to procure some veal for the king several days ago. He never returned."

"A trusted spy has just arrived from Nicosia," Lord Chimi put in. "He saw Sir Hector's head on a spike."

Estelle stared at him in horror.

"My councilman Lord Synglitico left Kyrenia the same day Sir Hector did," the queen continued. "He went straight to Jacco and advised him of Sir Hector's errand for the king, told him where the poor man was staying. At least that is my brother's claim."

Lord Synglitico had been the most reserved of the queen's advisors. Estelle had often wished the others were more like him, taciturn instead of strident. His mild exterior had concealed a deeply scheming mind, she now realized.

The queen snatched up the page again. "My brother did not spare me any details. *As soon as dawn broke,* he wrote, *I mounted my horse and fell upon Sir Hector as he emerged from his lodging, and with great satisfaction I killed him and severed his head, dear sister.*"

Estelle's determination wavered as the words assaulted her ears.

*Find a way to speak! Étienne's life balances on the point of a blade.*

"Your Grace, I—"

"I'm not finished." The queen's voice was dangerously low. "He goes on: *Treachery lurks everywhere, even before your very nose, sweet sister. The*

*young Frenchwoman in your midst found a priceless crown and jewels at Bella-*
*pais Abbey and tried to steal them. My trusted Catalan agent, Nicolau Baldaia,*
*intercepted her and retrieved the crown and jewels, which are now in my posses-*
*sion. Be wary of her. She is as dangerous as a knight in her own way, for she and*
*the Catalan have a long and twisted history."*

Estelle staggered back, astounded. "But these are lies!"

The queen advanced on Estelle, radiating fury. "I wondered if you were holding something back from me that day. You used that journal to find my family's gold and jewels, and then you gave the treasure to Jacco's cruelest agent? What did you owe the man? What did you do for him?"

"He is my enemy, Your Grace! I owe him nothing. I despise the man. We did find a crown and jewels, but when the Catalan's men attacked our party and he stole it all from us, I was afraid to tell you what had slipped through our fingers. I didn't want to disappoint you. Forgive me—"

"The time for forgiveness has passed," Lord Chimi hissed. "It was Sir Hector's mistake to invite you to this court, and we've been paying for his error far too long."

"Jacco is trying to tear us apart," Estelle pleaded with the queen. "He's destroying the trust between us with lies. Too many have fallen victim to his schemes, Your Grace. It's an evil game he plays, and we cannot let him win!"

The queen's lips quivered. For a moment, Estelle saw her resolve falter.

"Enough of your falsehoods," Lord Chimi cut in. "Guards, remove this woman from the queen's presence."

The two guards standing by the door leaped forward, their hands clamping around Estelle's elbows.

"Not to her chamber. She'll stop at nothing to escape confinement. She once jumped from a window in the palace at Nicosia." Lord Chimi stepped closer to Queen Charlotta. "For the sake of your kingdom, keep this traitor from our midst!"

The queen's eyes narrowed. "I tire of your voice harping in my ear. It's no secret you've never accepted the mademoiselle's role in my court, Lord Chimi. You've always hoped she would lose my favor."

He paled. "She's a foolish girl who has some talent with a quill. Taking her counsel is dangerous, especially when your trusted advisors are on hand to guide you, Your Grace."

Estelle watched the queen in trepidation.

*Will she defend me? Or will she crumble?*

The news of Sir Hector's death still tainted the atmosphere in the chamber. Had Jacco truly beheaded the man himself? What lengths would he go to in order to win the throne?

Queen Charlotta's tight-lipped expression revealed nothing. She considered Lord Chimi's words for a long, excruciating moment.

"My brother was once my greatest champion. Now he decorates the bridges of Nicosia with the heads of my supporters." Her voice was resigned, underscored with sadness. "Will there be any end to the betrayal in my court? I've no choice, it seems, but to mistrust those I once held in the highest esteem." She turned her gaze on Estelle. "Guards, take her to the dungeons. See that she is kept apart from the others and treated with consideration. Mademoiselle, you had better pray my brother's accusations will be proved false."

# CHAPTER 44

Winter 1461
Kyrenia Fortress, Cyprus

WHEN THE EVENING passed with no sign of Estelle, Gabriel grew restless. He paced around the stables with an oil lamp, checking on falcons and horses, cleaning jesses and hoods, inventorying what little remained of their healing remedies and dried rabbit meat. Some of the birds were ill. Several had died in recent days. He was relieved each time he found a dead raptor at the bottom of a wooden cage. One less mouth to feed. He'd rather lose them quickly than watch them slowly starve.

At dawn, he visited the kitchens to make some inquiries. No one remembered seeing Estelle when the queen and her attendants were served supper the previous evening. But one young maid looked troubled by his query. When he slipped her a few coins, she opened up.

"I saw the mademoiselle with a pair of guards yesterday."

"Where were they taking her?"

The girl shrugged. "I was going upstairs while they went down. But she looked frightened. I've never seen her look that way before."

A tightness clamped around Gabriel's chest. He hurried through the fortress in search of a guard he'd befriended. When he spied the fellow by the armory, he pulled him into the shadows for a quiet word.

"Was there any talk last night amongst the guards about one of the queen's ladies?" he asked.

"Some highborn lady was taken into the dungeons, I heard. A Frenchwoman. She's a traitor. Or that's what they say."

Gabriel gripped the man's arm. "Are you certain?"

"Why would I lie?" The fellow shook him off.

"Forgive me." Gabriel passed him some coins. "I'll not forget your help."

As he retreated from the armory and made his way through the interior of the fortress, he questioned two more guards who were only too happy to confirm the first man's story. He stumbled onward, contemplating the improbable truth that Estelle had been imprisoned in the hellish underground layers of the fortress.

It was immediately apparent to him what he would have to do.

Gabriel crept though a cramped, dripping tunnel and into a cave that was ankle-deep with seawater. He fought his way toward the light, cursing the tides. At least he would make it out before water completely filled the cave. When he returned, he'd take a different route. There were other ways into Kyrenia that did not rely on a sea cave for entry. At this point, he knew them all.

He moved quietly through the countryside, staying well off the road. He did not pause to rest. Every moment wasted was a moment Estelle could be tortured, or dying, or dead. He had no choice but to press on.

When he entered the gates of Nicosia late that afternoon and fumbled a coin out of his purse for the toll, he mentally mapped out the quickest way to the palace and walked in that direction. But passing over the Bridge of the Pillory, he regretted the decision. It was lined with metal spikes, each bearing the gruesome remains of a human head. All supporters of Queen Charlotta and her foreign-born husband. All murdered for their loyalty to the crown.

The head at the very end of the row was so fresh it still leaked blood. He gave a start of recognition. The grotesque face of Sir Hector de Chivides stared blankly at him, frozen in a scream.

Fighting off nausea, he dropped his chin and stared at the road ahead.

*Why in God's name did you have to look, man?*

His throat was dry as dust and his feet throbbed by the time he arrived at the palace. But he had made good time—in the end, that was all that mattered.

Jacco sat on his father's throne, arms crossed over his chest. He looked Gabriel up and down, his gaze assessing and critical.

"I was surprised when you did not respond to my initial queries. You could have had a place in my mews long ago." His white robes were shot through with gold thread, and the back of the throne was draped with cloth of gold. "I always enjoyed our forays into the mountains. The other falconers and huntsmen spoke so highly of you. They said you are intelligent, brave, you know when to speak and when to stay silent. For God's sake, man, you could have been a great asset to my court—could still be. Frankly, I thought you would jump on my offer. Surely, a fellow who gambles away his inheritance would not turn down such generosity. And yet . . ."

His smile vanished.

"Forgive me, my lord."

"My king, you mean to say." Jacco's gaze was baleful.

"My king." The words scraped against Gabriel's throat. How he longed for a cool drink. Anything to soothe the dust from his parched lips, to renew his spent energy. "There has been no opportunity to compose a reply. The chaos in the fortress of Kyrenia—it's overwhelming."

A smirk tugged at Jacco's mouth. Gabriel had guessed he would revel in that bit of news.

"Tell me more. I would dearly love to know how my sister and her husband fare."

"As far as I can tell, my king, Queen Charlotta is beholden to the whims of her council. As for her husband, he is far more interested in falcons and other amusements than war."

Now Jacco's smile flashed wide in his bearded face. His eyes sparkled. "Yes! That is what others have said. He's a fool, that man. Better suited to a gaming table than a throne."

Gabriel studied Jacco with apprehension. What next? He waited in silence, not wanting to turn the man's mood dark again.

"Why have you come?" Jacco asked abruptly.

Gabriel swallowed. "To pledge my loyalty to you. There is no future with the king and queen. Cyprus belongs in your hands."

Somehow he managed to produce the lies in a smooth, clear voice.

"Excellent." Jacco signaled to an attendant, who handed Gabriel a small pouch.

"I am a generous benefactor to my loyal men," Jacco went on. "I always pay them well. And I expect much in return."

"How can I serve you, my king?" Coins clicked together in the pouch, strengthening Gabriel's resolve.

"First, as an informant and messenger. My attendant will give you messages to deliver to other spies within Kyrenia. I'll have you return weekly with reports on the queen's plans."

Gabriel nodded. "I vow it will be done."

Jacco held up a ring-laden hand. When he spoke again, his brisk, jovial tone turned hard. "If you betray me, your head will join the others on the Bridge of the Pillory."

Gabriel barely heard the threat. His fingers wrapped around the bag of coins. From their weight, he knew they were gold. He could pay off the guards and feed Estelle for a long time with these funds. But better would be to arrange for her release. How much gold would that take?

"There is more," Jacco said crisply, interrupting his thoughts. "I've had my agents inquire about your time at the sugar plantation of

Kolossi. It seems you made quite a name for yourself in the employ of the knights. By all accounts, you were a skilled guard, and more than once you killed for them."

"Only when my own life or that of my comrades was threatened." Gabriel shifted on his feet, uneasy.

"Once my sister and her husband are dead, I will give you a list of names. Men who resisted or outright refused my call. One by one, you'll pick them off. Under cover of darkness, slipping through the shadows of the seashore, the forests, the highest mountain peaks. You'll make the last of Charlotta's supporters so terrorized that they'll rue the day they ever pledged fealty to her."

Gabriel swayed, sickened by the man's words. Informant, spy—those were roles he could abide. But assassin? Never. Killing to satisfy another man's thirst for revenge was something he could not do. He would rather kill Jacco himself than be the man's assassin.

He stared unblinking at the Pretender, conscious that his thoughts could get him executed on the spot.

"As you command, my king."

# CHAPTER 45

Winter 1461
Kyrenia Fortress, Cyprus

THE GUARDS LOCKED the cell and vanished with their torches, leaving Estelle in utter darkness. Her heart skittered like a moth batting against a shutter, frantic to reach the light. She stood trembling, trying not to wail aloud. A rancid stench filled her lungs.

The drip, drip, drip of water on stone burrowed into her brain. The distant slosh of waves ebbed and rose, a whispery reminder that this fortress was perched at the edge of the earth. Wind, tides, storms—there was no escaping the wild moods of the Mediterranean in this place. Here, in Kyrenia's deepest, darkest depths, the sea threatened to rear up and swallow her in its foaming jaws.

Estelle had never tried to describe the horrifying feeling of suffocation she endured every time she found herself in an enclosed space. But now she had no choice but to face it.

The worst moments of her life had been experiences of entrapment.

Once, on the long-ago sea voyage from France to Rhodes, when the captain would not allow children above decks; later, when she had been taken from the streets of Rhodes Town against her will, bound, and stowed in a dark place until her rescue. Then the long nights trapped in airless cabins on the voyages between Rhodes and Cyprus.

Now, in the dungeons of Kyrenia fortress, she raised one hand and spoke the word aloud.

"Entrapment."

Her voice rattled like a dry reed in the wind.

She said it again, louder and clearer this time, one hand held aloft.

"Entrapment."

Estelle caught the word and closed her fist, crushing it.

She imagined the ritual of dipping her quill, touching it to linen paper, and producing graceful black letters. Her hand swirled and paused, swept up and down, weaving the letters into a word that hung unseen in the dark before her.

*Entrapment.*

With one forceful ejection, she blew the air from her lungs.

In her mind's eye, the word scattered, each letter sailing through the bars of her cell, tumbling along a draft into the corridor, then snaking through an arrow slit into the sky.

Her heart settled a bit. She pushed back her shoulders.

*Courage.*

Time was passing. It had to be. Was it still night? Or had dawn come? There was no way to know. It seemed as if she'd been in here for ages, but perhaps it had only been hours.

Eventually, she would have to move, explore the confines of her tiny cell, but she'd been unable to budge from the spot where she'd last seen a flicker of light through the locked gate that led to the corridor. Her feet were sore; her knees ached. She was hungry.

Kyrenia fortress had been low on rations for a long time. The king and queen and their remaining courtiers still ate fairly well. She had once been one of those fortunate individuals. The other inhabitants were lucky to get dry, crumbly grain biscuits doused in broth or dipped in ale, with the occasional fresh vegetable or bit of meat smuggled in from the outside world. Gabriel had told her about the lengths he went to in order to secure meat for the falcons. He traipsed into the mountains at least once a week for rabbits or game fowl. How he returned safely each time was a mystery.

He would have expected her in the stables. Was he worried? Would he search for her?

She pushed away hope. What could Gabriel possibly do for her if he did discover her whereabouts? He had some influence outside this place—after all, he'd been able to source meat when others could not; he'd walked away unscathed from that roadside attack near Bellapais Abbey—but within its walls he was an under-falconer, the illegitimate son of a Latin man and his Egyptian slave.

A tremulous moan floated by in the darkness, followed by a cry for help. Then sobs. Deep, guttural sobs that wrenched at Estelle's heart.

"Shut up, you devil!" someone shouted.

The sobs quieted, but did not cease.

Light appeared through a hatch in the corridor's door, casting a pale glow on the stone floor in front of her cell. The guards' station must be right outside the door. They talked for a while about how bad the food was in Kyrenia. Then they began arguing over a game of cards. One of them had a hacking cough.

Soon she would be coughing, too. It was so damp down here. So cold. She wrapped her arms around herself, wishing she'd worn a cloak to the queen's chamber.

Glancing around, she realized she could now see the outline of a plank atop two boxes that served as a bed. Gingerly, she padded across the wet stones and sank down. It was a relief to sit. She studied her surroundings. A rivulet of water trickled down a seam in the opposite wall, culminating in the drip that was her constant companion.

An anguished groan rose up, echoing with deep, sinister finality.

Estelle shuddered. That hadn't even sounded human.

She knew, because the queen's ladies gossiped about such things, that Kyrenia's dungeons housed some prisoners in oubliettes—holes in the ground accessible only by trapdoors. Other poor souls were

doomed to die in iron cages affixed to the walls of sea caverns underneath the fortress.

*At least I'm not in an oubliette or in a cage at the mercy of the tides.*

There were other women in the dungeons. As the hours passed, she
heard them fighting. Screaming and cursing at one another in shrill,
desperate voices. She pressed her hands over her ears, trying to muffle
their terror, rage, and madness.

Were they fighting over food? Belongings?

*Don't think about them.*

Thank God the queen had ordered her to be imprisoned apart
from the other prisoners. She was afforded the luxury of solitude,
tucked at the end of a long row of cells.

*It could be worse.*

Some time later, perhaps a few moments, perhaps a day, a key
turned in a lock. She held her breath, watching the corridor door swing
open. But when she saw a familiar figure emerge from the gloom, her
heart soared.

"Gabriel!" She sprang up and went to the bars of her cell, reaching
for him.

Behind him, a guard muttered, "Make it quick," and vanished
through the doorway.

As the heavy door swung shut, Gabriel leaned close. "Are you hurt?"
he asked, his voice strained. "Did they hurt you, by God?"

His apprehension tore at her.

"No, no," she assured him. "I'm hungry and cold and tired of
listening to the madness down here, but I'm well."

He cupped her face with his hands. She pressed herself against the
iron, yearning for the warmth of his touch. When his lips found hers,
she kissed him with a ferocious need she hadn't known she possessed,
clinging to him with all her strength.

"Gabriel," she whispered after a long moment. "How on earth did
you get in here?"

His white teeth glimmered in the dimness, revealing a smile. "It's
amazing what a man will do for a bit of meat in difficult times."

"You bribed the guards?"

"I gave them some of this." He pulled a wrapped object from his pouch and handed it to her. "Dried rabbit and oatcakes that've seen better days."

Eagerly, she unwrapped the food and began to devour it. "The best meal I've ever eaten," she said between bites. "Thank you."

He watched her consume it in silence. When she was finished, he pulled something else from beneath his tunic. It was a small flagon of wine. He uncorked it and handed it over.

"This should help me sleep through the screaming tonight." She took a grateful swallow.

"Why are you in here?" he asked.

"Because of a Catalan who tried to destroy my family in Rhodes many years ago. I'd thought—hoped—he was dead. His name is Nicolau Baldaia. He's the man you saved me from after Bellapais," she said. "The one you let escape, who took the crown. Jacco told Queen Charlotta that I was in league with the Catalan, that I gave him the crown and the jewels. And the queen believed the story."

Gabriel was silent a moment. When he spoke, his voice was low and rough. "Why would she believe anything Jacco says—or his agent for that matter?"

"So many have deserted and betrayed her. She has little faith in those who remain and much mistrust."

"What did the Catalan do to your family?"

"He—" she broke off. "It doesn't matter now, it's over. What matters is Étienne. If he's still alive, Jacco may have imprisoned him somewhere. Will you search for him?"

The door creaked open, and the guard stumped inside. "Come now," he said gruffly to Gabriel. "You've been here long enough."

Gabriel extended the wine flagon. "A few more minutes?" he asked in a pleading voice.

"As long as it takes me to drink this," the guard returned, "and I'll stand here as I do it."

Gabriel rested his forehead against Estelle's between the bars. "I can do little for you or Étienne in here," he told her quietly. "But outside the walls of the fortress, there are people I know who might be able to help. I'll pay the guards to bring you food every day until I return."

She kissed him. "May God and all the saints protect you and keep you from harm."

"Finished!" The guard smacked his lips and belched.

"I'll be back for you," Gabriel vowed in a hoarse whisper. "Be brave."

"I always am." She tried to keep her voice light, to conceal the fear lurking just beneath the surface.

Again, that flash of a smile. "I know."

# CHAPTER 46

Winter 1461
Kyrenia Fortress, Cyprus

THE FAMILIAR CREAK of the door sent a stab of fear into Estelle's gut. She bolted upright, not that she'd ever truly slept on her slab of wood. Occasionally, she'd drifted off, felt herself teetering on the brink of sleep, and then jolted awake in a panic. She forced her mind to memories of times gone by, her childhood in Auvergne, the wildflowers in the meadow on the count's lands, the swans in the lake. Étienne taking her hand when they had to walk to the château, because he knew she feared it. Papa, trimming falcon feathers into quills for her, teaching her to dip the pointed tip into ink, then apply it to linen paper or parchment with gentle pressure.

And Maman, her blue eyes crackling with laughter, with anger, with excitement. Her boldness when she stalked through the marketplace in Rhodes, bartering with merchants and artisans, running her fingertips over bolts of wool, cotton, and silk.

Estelle herself had worked hard all these years to be bold and brave like her mother. To all outward appearances, she'd succeeded. A veneer of courage protected her from the world. Yet in her heart, she was often paralyzed by terror. No one but Étienne knew it, and he'd left for Savoy when she was a young girl. After they moved to Rhodes, she kept her fear to herself. But that small voice within her, the one that issued commands whenever fear struck—it knew.

As if she'd summoned the voice with her thoughts, it spoke to her now. Silently, assuredly.

*Courage.*

The guard appeared in the corridor, followed by a man holding an oil lamp. Its glow illuminated his face when he turned toward her cell.

Her muscles tensed when she recognized his features.

"Lord Chimi?" she said in disbelief.

"On my signal," he told the guard.

The guard grunted in response and retreated through the door, pulling it not quite shut.

"Mademoiselle." Lord Chimi moved to the iron bars. "Are you well?"

She lifted her chin. "As well as one can be in this place."

"You've been here a fortnight. You must be starving." His careless tone belied any consideration his words might have held.

She would be starving if it weren't for Gabriel. Thanks to his bribes, she'd been given enough food to keep from wasting away. He'd brought a whole jug of wine once, and she took a few sips morning and night, rationing it in case no more such gifts arrived.

"I still live, as you see."

"Brave one, are you?" Lord Chimi's dark eyes glittered in the lamplight.

"Why are you here?" She crossed her arms over her chest.

"I have good news."

*Don't believe him. The court of Cyprus is a viper's nest.*

"The king wishes to speak with you."

"King Louis intervened on my behalf?"

"Not him. The rightful king."

*Jacco.*

When Estelle found her voice, she said, "You work for him?"

"The pay is better," he replied. "And he is our future. The only hope we have for Cyprus."

"Why does he want to help me?"

Instead of answering her question, he posed one of his own. "Do you wish to save your brother's life?"

She gripped the bars. "Of course. What do you know of him? Where is he?"

Lord Chimi's lips stretched back in a mirthless smile. "The love of a sister is a sweet thing to witness. Dame Fortune is on your side today, mademoiselle. Your brother is in the custody of the king. If you come with me now, you have a chance to save him. If you don't, his head will be on a spike by morning."

She stared at him, aghast. "Let's go, then."

"I thought as much." He stepped away and rapped on the door.

The guard appeared and unlocked the door to her cell.

"Follow me," he growled. "And keep quiet."

Estelle took an unsteady step forward. Could this be a trap? Could they be leading her to an oubliette? To an iron cage in a sea cave? She looked at the walls of her cell. Though she hated this place, she had been safe in here.

With these two men holding her fate in their hands, what lay ahead?

"What's the delay?" Lord Chimi demanded. "Don't you want to be free of this place?"

She forced herself to put one foot in front of the other.

The guard led them down a series of unfamiliar corridors, past locked doors and bricked-in archways, past the occasional flickering torch. She tried to memorize their path but soon grew disoriented.

Finally they reached a low door in the wall of a vast, empty store-room. The guard turned to Lord Chimi.

"Remember what I said. You'll walk straight ahead; the third passageway on the left is where you'll turn. When you get to the other side, you'll come out into a sea cave. The tide is fairly low, so you should have no problem getting to dry land."

"Should have?" Lord Chimi repeated, a note of irritation in his voice. "You were paid to ensure we encounter no problems."

"The tide is not a problem," the guard retorted. "But the longer you take to get there, the higher it will be. Make haste!"

Lord Chimi ducked and vanished through the doorway into the blackness. Estelle looked from the door to the guard, overcome by terror.

"Go," the guard ordered her. "Quick as you can, and don't lose sight of him. You need the light he carries."

She scrambled through the doorway. Hunched over to clear the low ceiling of the tunnel, she scurried after Lord Chimi, his form outlined by the glow of the lamp.

What had the guard said? Walk straight ahead, third passageway on the left.

It was musty and damp in the tunnel, and there was an unpleasant scent in the air—a sharp, acrid smell.

Like blood.

*Ignore the smell. Breathe through your mouth.*

"Son of a whore!" Lord Chimi burst out ahead of her. He dropped low, one hand to his head. He must have bumped his head against the rough stone ceiling.

One passage.

Two passages.

Her back was beginning to ache with the effort of bending over.

There was a muffled thump. Lord Chimi cried out, and the light vanished.

"What the devil?" he muttered. "This cursed place."

She could see nothing in the utter blackness that descended.

*And neither can he.*

Estelle kept quiet. She put a hand out and felt her way along the left side of the wall. She could hear him scrambling around, righting himself, the scrape of the metal lamp against stone. A clatter when he dropped it again.

All she wanted was to put distance between herself and this odious man.

She was passing him now. If he reached out, his hand would collide with her body. She pressed herself against the wall, slid as sinuously as a snake, prayed she would not trip and fall and reveal herself.

"Where are you?" he said suddenly, his voice so close she almost screamed.

But she kept control of herself, kept creeping quietly forward, trailing her left hand along the damp stone wall.

"God above, where've you gone?" His footsteps sounded in the dark, coming after her.

The third passageway.

She turned down it.

His voice faded behind her. She breathed a bit easier when she heard the rustle and sigh of the sea. Emerging into a cave, she drew in a long breath of briny air. Water licked at her feet and ankles.

Raising her skirts, she plunged forward.

She exited the cave onto a narrow stretch of sand abutting the rocky shore and picked her way over the stones to higher ground. Breathing hard, she climbed a bluff overlooking the sea, the fortress of Kyrenia looming in the distance. The moon hung suspended in the velvety sky, casting its pale light over the waves.

*I'm free.* An urge to run rose up in her, a rush of energy so powerful she nearly succumbed to it.

*No. Your fate lies in Nicosia. With Étienne.*

The only way forward was to walk right into the web of spider's silk Jacco had constructed to trap her.

"Mademoiselle." A voice nearby made Estelle flinch.

Slowly, she turned.

Two men approached, torches in hand. Her heart flailed wildly against her ribs.

Of course there would be others involved in this scheme.

"The king awaits," one of them said.

"Where is your guide?" said the other, peering beyond her at the sea cave.

"He fell behind."

"God's teeth! Where is she?" Lord Chimi struggled up the slope, arms flailing. When he reached her, he cuffed Estelle across the face so hard she nearly fell.

Planting her feet wide, she ignored the pain and looked past him to the other men. "I'm eager to meet with the king, and we have a long ride ahead of us." By some miracle, her voice was steady. "Shall we go?"

# CHAPTER 47

Winter 1461
Nicosia, Cyprus

THE DOOR to Estelle's former bedchamber shut behind her. Crossing to the window, she tried to open the shutters. They would not budge. Apparently, they were barred from the outside.

She made a quick survey of the space. The bed linens were clean and inviting. If only she could bathe and rest for a while, get out of her filthy, wet clothes. She had not slept in the rattling mule cart from Kyrenia, afraid of what Lord Chimi might do if she drifted off.

The door opened again. She whirled.

"*Kalimera*, mademoiselle!" Antonia bustled across the threshold.

"Antonia? You're alive!"

"And why wouldn't I be?" Antonia deposited towels and a pitcher on the table. "The king treats all his servants well." She poured water into the basin and retrieved a square of fragrant soap from a sack. "Poor thing. What a sight you are, with those dirty clothes and that bruise on your face! You've been mistreated by the queen's agents, haven't you?"

Estelle put a hand to her cheek. It was tender to the touch. With the maid's help, she removed her clothes, washed, then dried off with the towels.

Antonia brushed Estelle's wet hair, clucking her tongue. "So thin! When did you last eat?"

"Sometime yesterday. Or perhaps it was the day before."

Antonia retrieved a wrapped object from her sack. "Here. A fig-and-pistachio biscuit sweetened with honey."

Estelle devoured it.

"Holy Virgin! Don't choke now." Antonia hovered over her with a worried look. "There's no wine to wash that biscuit down with, I'm sorry to say."

Estelle wiped crumbs from her chin with the back of a hand. "I've no need for wine."

"It's time," the guard called from the corridor.

Antonia crossed to the wardrobe and flung it open. Hands on her hips, she studied the contents. "The purple-and-gold silk brocade, I think. Yes. Purple suits you very well."

"What's the delay?" The guard's voice was irritable.

"May you be eaten by eagles, sir! She's not dressed yet." Pulling out the dress and matching sleeves, Antonia marched to the bed. "I know you don't like help when you're dressing, but we're in a bit of a rush."

Numbly, Estelle allowed herself to be dressed.

"Your shoes are ruined." Antonia retrieved a cypress-wood box from the wardrobe and removed a pair of kidskin boots. "These should fit."

"Where did these things come from?"

"The king, of course. He thinks of such details. A very generous man."

Jacco's forces had swept through the island confiscating the goods and wealth of every citizen known to support his sister. Many of the inhabitants of those households had been murdered.

She smoothed her dress and studied the soft leather boots peeking out from beneath her skirts.

*Whose gown is this? Whose boots are these?*

"Thank you, Antonia," she said. "I'm glad you're being well treated here. May God protect you."

Jacco sat on the throne, resplendent in white silk embroidered with gold. Next to him perched a woman in a pearl-encrusted red gown, a matching veil over the lower half of her face. Her eyes, elaborately enhanced with kohl, were fixed on Estelle.

Courtiers stood in small groups, talking in hushed tones. Estelle sensed a presence on her right and turned to confront a familiar face.

"Louise?"

The young woman's lips tugged upward in a tight smile. Her cheeks were fuller than Estelle remembered. Her pregnant belly pushed against the soft folds of her blue velvet gown, and three strings of pearls adorned her neck.

"You look elegant." Louise's gaze swept over Estelle. "Though your face could use some powder. That's an ugly bruise."

Estelle could summon no words.

"Aren't you going to speak to me?" Louise demanded.

"Why did you do it?" Estelle managed to ask. "Why did you tell the queen I'd stolen your necklace?"

"Look at our king." Louise's gaze slid to Jacco. "How handsome he is."

In that instant, Estelle understood Louise was under his control.

"And your husband?" she asked. "Are you content with Lord Podocataro?"

"Of course." Louise's voice lost its energy. "He buys me all manner of silks and jewels. And when our son is born, he shall buy me a home and a vineyard, too."

"He was one of Queen Charlotta's staunchest supporters, I thought," Estelle said. "At least when I was meant to wed him, that was my understanding."

"My husband was loyal to King Jean, not his daughter. And now he supports the rightful king."

Lord Chimi and Lord Podocataro appeared from behind a marble column, immersed in conversation. Lord Chimi had changed into a green silk tunic and hose, a velvet cap atop his head.

"Together again." There was a trace of bitterness in Louise's voice. "How happy they must be."

"What do you mean?"

"They were childhood friends. As close as brothers. Lord Chimi lost his fortune some years ago and owed my husband a great deal of money. He paid off his debt in two installments. The first was me. My husband's wife died, and he wanted a young Frenchwoman to replace her. Lord Chimi offered him you first. But when the queen decided she had other uses for you, he turned to me."

Estelle nodded slowly, finally understanding Lord Chimi's hostility toward her.

*My defiance about the betrothal was a threat to his own plans. He hated me for it.*

"What was the second installment?" she asked.

"It was Lord Chimi who told Jacco exactly where and when to find Sir Hector the day he was killed. King Jacco rewarded him handsomely for his deed. And today, Lord Chimi paid my husband the rest of what was owed." She fell silent, watching the two men laugh together over some shared joke. "Lord Chimi will never return to Kyrenia fortress again, I assure you. He's King Jacco's man now."

Estelle took in Louise's words with something akin to horror.

The shifting loyalties in the kingdom of Cyprus were as twisted as grape vines. In the end, she realized, all of these people pledged fealty to one thing: power. And, judging from the crowd of nobles and burghers in this chamber, Jacco was the most powerful person in Cyprus.

"Come forward, mademoiselle." Jacco beckoned to her.

She moved toward the dais.

The veiled woman seated next to Jacco whispered something to him.

"Before you kiss my ring, you must bow to my mother. She desires it."

*Cropnose.*

Estelle curtsied low. "Your ladyship," she murmured.

"Your Grace," the woman corrected her. "I am Queen regent until my son weds."

"Yes, Your Grace."

Jacco extended his hand. "Kiss my ring."

She climbed the steps of the dais, bent over his hand, and kissed the heavy golden ring on his finger.

He studied her with a smirk. "Just as lovely as I remember."

"Thank you, Your Grace."

"I prefer the title 'Majesty,'" he corrected her.

"Thank you, Your Majesty."

The chamber was deathly quiet. No one wanted to miss a word of this interaction, Estelle was sure. She would do her best to stay upright and conscious, but her trembling knees and racing heart threatened to betray her.

A servant scurried forward with a velvet sack. He held it open for Jacco, who pulled out something shimmering and gold.

*God save me, there it is. The crown.*

Memories rushed back. The weight of it in her hands. That moment before the hearth in the abbot's house, unveiling it with Gabriel's help. The rubies aglow with reflected flames. The scent of pine needles and wet earth underfoot when she tried to hide it.

"Such a lovely crown. The rubies are as big as pigeon's eggs." Jacco held it up for all to see. "When I choose a wife, perhaps I'll give it to her."

His mother made a sharp noise in the back of her throat, her eyes on the crown. The covetous look in them was plain to see.

"Where is Étienne?" Estelle asked, no longer able to contain herself.

Jacco beamed. "Your brother is well, very well indeed. He's . . . resting."

He turned then, his gaze going to an ornate silver perch behind the throne. "I miss my falcon," he mused. "She's been poorly of late. But my new falconer has a book filled with all manner of remedies. I think she's pulling through the worst of it, thanks to him. Shall we see?" He raised his voice. "Call in the falconer."

Footsteps sounded behind her. A man dressed in a fine silk tunic and matching cap carried a hooded peregrine falcon to the dais, mounted the steps, and settled her on the perch.

He turned to face the king.

*Gabriel.*

A hundred questions pushed against her lips. She struggled for a breath.

Jacco grinned, clearly delighted at her shock, then made a dismissive gesture at the assembled courtiers. "Enough entertainment for one day. Off you all go."

The chamber slowly emptied as the courtiers reluctantly complied with his order. Estelle's eyes locked with Gabriel's.

She had never seen him look so sad.

Finally, the chamber was empty of courtiers save for Jacco, his mother, Gabriel, and Estelle. Several guards ringed the dais.

"Now to the matter of your brother."

Her attention snapped to him. "Yes," she said quickly. "How can I help arrange his release?"

He smirked again. "You thought your falconer friend would help free your brother." Jacco slipped forward to the edge of the throne. "But blood does tell. And no one knows as well as I do how much a son can love his father."

Jacco's mother balanced on the edge of her chair, rigid with anticipation.

"Who is *your* father, Gabriel?" Jacco coaxed.

Silence.

"Tell her!" he commanded.

Gabriel raised his chin, gazing beyond Estelle to the far end of the chamber. "Nicolau Baldaia," he said dully.

Estelle's knees nearly gave way.

"Unfortunately, Señor Baldaia is away." Jacco's cheerful tone grew pensive. "I would have loved to see you reunited with him, mademoiselle. He is well acquainted with your family, I understand."

*Do not faint. Stay upright.*

"Nicolau Baldaia is a liar." Her voice rang out, clear and strong.

"The information he gave you about that crown and how it came to be in his possession was untrue."

To her astonishment, Jacco nodded. "Such a shame, isn't it? In the morning, I'll send another letter to my sister informing her it was Baldaia who threatened you and made off with the treasure, just as you claimed." He fiddled with the crown in his lap. "I'll also tell her that Lord Chimi is my agent, and it was he who betrayed Sir Hector. She already mistrusted Lord Chimi, I assure you. Now her last shred of faith in him will vanish like a puff of smoke."

"Then what?" Estelle asked warily.

"Then . . ." He held up a small vial of Venetian glass. "You'll resume your duties for my sister. And when the perfect moment presents itself, you will poison her."

A roaring in her ears threatened to drown out every other sound in the chamber.

"Poison her? But she'll never let me close to her again. She no longer trusts me!"

"Her trust in you is frayed, but not destroyed." His eyes took on a distant, dreamy look. "There are so few left in her circle. She must be cautious severing those last ties. Who is useful? Who is not? I believe you're still quite useful to her. I see worry on your face, but let me reassure you, mademoiselle, you won't return to Kyrenia empty-handed. I'll send a gift for my sister along with you—a collection of gems from the homes of her staunchest supporters as an apology for causing her undue distress. Rubies, pearls, and the like. I've been saving them for her. Though I imagine she'll pawn them immediately. Such poverty in that fortress." He made a tsking noise with his tongue.

"What about my brother?" Estelle asked.

"If you succeed, your brother will have the choice of returning to fight for that incompetent oaf Louis or accept a well-paid position as a knight in my court. Of course, if you fail to do as I command, he'll lose his head."

She fought to stay upright. No matter how urgently she tried to draw in a breath, she could not.

The last thing she saw before losing consciousness was Gabriel launching himself at her, arms outstretched to catch her as she fell.

# CHAPTER 48

Winter 1461
Nicosia, Cyprus

GABRIEL HELD Estelle in his arms. Her skin was pale, her lashes dark against her cheeks. He cradled her gently, whispering her name until she regained consciousness.

"Gabriel?" Her eyes slowly adjusted to the light. "Why are you here?"

"You're hurt." He studied the bruise on her cheek, tightening his grip on her.

"What a sweet scene!" Jacco's booming laugh echoed through the chamber.

A look of pure terror seized Estelle's face at the sound. She began to tremble.

"My spies told me there was something between you. I imagined a dalliance of some kind, but I did not realize how much tenderness you share." Jacco rose from the throne and descended the dais, making a slow circle around them. He pinned Gabriel with an icy stare. "Why on earth did you pledge your loyalty to me when your love was trapped in Kyrenia's dungeons?" His gaze flicked to Estelle. "You would be wise to untangle yourself from this man, mademoiselle. Perhaps we should both be wary of him, in truth."

Estelle struggled to stand.

Gabriel helped her up. "I love you," he said softly. "I would never betray you."

"Why are you doing this, then?" Her voice was barely a whisper. "I don't understand."

She edged away from him, the confusion and pain in her expression tearing at his heart.

Jacco held up the vial. "Mademoiselle de Montavon, you have much to do. I dearly hope you succeed. I've a true fondness for you."

Gabriel ached to wrest the vial from Jacco's hands and smash it on the stone floor. But what good was that? Another would be quickly procured. No, the only thing to do was stand like a stone and reveal nothing of his emotions. It was a skill honed over many years during his childhood, when he'd had to witness the abuse of his mother by his father's wife too many times to count. He'd only lost control once, and he had the scars to show for it.

To his astonishment, Estelle spoke up. "How do I know my brother still lives?"

Jacco chuckled. "I've made provisions for you to visit your brother before you return to Kyrenia." He signaled to a guard at the door, who opened it to admit a bearded man dressed in immaculate silk robes. "Ah! Signor Derian."

By Estelle's expression, Gabriel knew she recognized the man.

"My old friend will be your guide, mademoiselle. When next I see you, I hope you'll pledge fealty to me."

Jacco gave the vial to a guard, who thrust it at Estelle. Without another glance at Gabriel, she straightened her shoulders and followed Signor Derian from the chamber with quick, confident strides.

One thing was certain: Estelle was as practiced as he at concealing her feelings. For he'd felt her shaking in his arms a moment ago; he'd seen the fear in her eyes. Would she ever allow him to touch her again? To explain himself? He swallowed hard against the lump forming in his throat.

Jacco studied him with a look of barely repressed glee.

"That was easier than I thought," he said. "I wish I could keep you at my side, tending to my falcons. But you'd be wasted in the role. No, your value lies elsewhere. In Kyrenia for now. And soon Famagusta."

Gabriel took that in, unsure what to make of it. Jacco had mounted a siege against Famagusta not long ago and was rumored to be preparing for another. So far, the Genoese—who had controlled the port city for many years now—had fought Jacco's forces off.

"Your father told me just how intimately acquainted you are with the city and its harbor," he continued. "When the time is right, you'll accompany Étienne de Montavon and the other Savoyard knights there, then see them aboard your father's galley."

"What?" Gabriel stared at him, incredulous. "Where will it take them?"

"Alexandria, of course. The sultan wants a gift of valuable Christian captives he can use in some future exchange—or keep for his own entertainment if he wishes. I care not what he does with them, in truth."

An outright refusal danced on Gabriel's tongue. So the tale Jacco had spun for Estelle about Étienne having the opportunity to return to Kyrenia was nothing more than a lie. It took all his self-control to stay quiet. Nothing good would come of turning Jacco against him at this moment. The only way he could help Étienne was to stay near him. Perhaps there would be a chance to free him before that galley sailed for Egypt.

He maintained his calm demeanor. "As you command, my king."

Jacco cocked his head, scrutinizing him with curiosity. "However do you keep such a mild expression? Your father has a reputation for a terrible temper. He has strung up and tortured monks in my name, ravished respectable noblewomen, put his sword through the hearts of Nicosia's most respected citizens. You'll do the same for me one day. For it's in your blood, even if you conceal it well."

An attendant crept to Jacco's side and whispered in his ear.

A broad grin split his face. "Ah! Another convert awaits an audience with me. One of the queen's most trusted advisors. That insufferable little circle of vultures is finally turning on her. In time, they'll all come to me."

# CHAPTER 49

Winter 1461
Nicosia, Cyprus

ESTELLE FOLLOWED Signor Derian and the guard through the palace. Torchlight sent shadows in every direction. They entered the corridor where Sir Hector's former chambers were located. Estelle widened her eyes at the sight of the hound curled before the door.

"What's he doing here?" she asked Signor Derian. "He was at Kyrenia, I thought."

"The hound followed Sir Hector out of Kyrenia, and found his way to the palace after his master died. Now he manages to turn up at this doorstep every evening."

The hound was thinner than she recalled, his eyes sunken in his skull.

"Poor boy," she said as they passed. "You miss your master."

His tail thumped the floor.

"Now up these stairs," her guide urged her. "That's it."

They climbed the winding steps of a tower. At the top lay a door with a tiny window in the shape of a half-moon.

She stood on tiptoe and peered inside. Signor Derian and the guard stayed close.

"Étienne!"

He reached through the cut-out moon and took her hand. "By all the saints, it's good to see you."

She squeezed his fingers, reassuring herself that they were warm, they were all there. He looked well, if a bit fatigued. Instead of his red-and-white Savoyard livery, he wore clothing of the Cypriot style.

"Are you hurt?" she asked him.

"No, but you are. Who did that to your face?"

She ignored the question, peering beyond him into the chamber. Fine furnishings and tapestries adorned the space. A neatly made bed occupied the far wall.

"I'm fed and well housed," he assured her. "Conditions are better than in Kyrenia, that's certain. It's not easy to find someone who speaks good French here, though."

"Signor Derian does." She glanced at the notary, comprehension dawning in her mind. "That's why they sent him with me, so we can't talk privately."

Signor Derian's chin dipped in a slight nod. The guard hovered just behind him—a hulking, menacing presence. She turned back to her brother, determined to ignore the men.

"I've been given a task. If I don't do it, they say you'll be killed." She dropped her voice. "If you see any chance of escape, you must flee. Promise me!"

"I promise. What is this task you speak of?"

"She's seen him," the guard said curtly. "That's enough talk."

Signor Derian's expression was apologetic. "That was my command from the king: to show the mademoiselle her brother lives, and is well. I've done so. We must leave."

"A few more minutes," she begged, clinging to Étienne's hand. "Please."

How could she tell Étienne the truth in front of the notary? Frantically, she spun through memories, searching for a clue only he would understand.

The guard pushed past Signor Derian and grabbed her arm.

"Easy, man!" Étienne's voice grew alarmed.

She twisted away from the guard with all her strength, but could not wrench free.

"Étienne, remember when we used to play chess—the move you always won with? Remember how much I hated it?"

"Yes." He searched her eyes, his voice firm and reassuring. "I remember."

"Away from there!" The guard gave her arm a vicious yank.

She cried out. He suddenly released her, roaring a string of curses.

"Devil take you, stupid mutt!"

Estelle whirled to see the hound tugging on the guard's tunic, a low growl rumbling in his chest.

She turned back to her brother. "I'm meant to use that move," she said urgently. "Only it's not a game this time."

The guard bellowed, kicking at the dog, and the animal retreated down the steps. Estelle followed, her vision blurred with tears.

"Don't do it, Estelle. I beg you—don't do it." Her brother's voice broke on the last words.

When they came to the bottom of the staircase, the hound trotted away, fearful of the guard. Signor Derian tucked Estelle's hand through the crook of his elbow.

"You had a chance to pledge your loyalty to the one true king early on," the notary said quietly. "Why didn't you do it? Your position is precarious now, your brother's more so."

Estelle barely heard him.

Despite her tears, she felt victorious. Étienne had understood. He knew the task before her.

And he would rather die than have her go through with it.

Not for the first time, the thought occurred to her that either way, one of them would die. If she poisoned the queen, she would be executed. If she did not poison the queen, her brother's head would go on a spike.

She remembered all the times he'd grinned at her after trapping her queen with a knight. The knight, with his odd, jumpy movements, sprang upon her queen in a silent ambush while she was busy worrying about bishops and castles. Whenever Étienne succeeded with the move, he'd made a great show of knocking the queen over and crying, "The queen is dead! The queen is dead!"

How would Estelle ambush the queen with her vial of poison? Her opportunities would be sorely limited even if she was granted proximity to Queen Charlotta again.

If she wanted her brother to live, she would have to find a way.

# CHAPTER 50

Winter 1461
Kyrenia Fortress, Cyprus

THE MULE CART rolled to the gates of the fortress. Shielded by the canvas window covering, Estelle heard muffled conversations outside, the shout of a guard, the creak and groan of the gates opening to admit them.

She grasped the velvet sack on her lap tighter. The vial of poison lay hidden in her bodice, nestled by her heart.

That she would even entertain the idea of murdering Queen Charlotta was terrifying. But the image of her brother's head on a spike was far worse.

She had no choice.

A motion caught her eye as she descended from the cart. Sir Hector's hound trotted panting to her side, his dark eyes shining.

"Did you follow us all the way from Nicosia?" She patted his head.

"The last thing we need is another mouth to feed," one of the guards grumbled. "We should put him outside the walls."

Estelle turned to him. "He was Sir Hector's shadow. A more loyal hound has never walked this earth." She gestured to a stable hand. "Take him into the stables and find him some water and a bit of food."

The boy hesitated.

"Gabriel would want you to do it," she added quietly.

He dipped his chin and whistled to the hound.

The guards' boots tramped out a dull rhythm across the courtyard and into the dark core of the fortress. Estelle followed them reluctantly to the queen's study.

Queen Charlotta sat at the table surrounded by advisors, a letter in front of her. All of them watched Estelle progress across the room, studying her with suspicion. Lord Chimi was conspicuously absent.

"Your Grace." She curtsied low.

"Rise." Queen Charlotta eyed the velvet sack. "Jacco said you've brought me jewels."

Estelle placed the sack on the table.

One of the barons snatched it and pulled out a handful of gems, holding them out for all to see.

"Astonishing—he kept his promise." The queen brandished the letter. "My brother claims that under pressure of torture, his agent Nicolau Baldaia confessed to stealing the crown and jewels from you on the roadside. That you were hiding in the woods, trying to conceal this treasure from Baldaia and his men."

"It's the truth, Your Grace."

"Nicolau Baldaia is responsible for much of the violence directed at my subjects. His gang of brutes has violated innocent women and girls; they've tortured monks and priests; they've murdered without mercy. And yet he simply let you ride away unscathed. I wonder why he would spare you?"

The others watched Estelle in silence, waiting for her reply.

Should she reveal the truth about Gabriel's intervention that day? Did the queen know Gabriel was the Catalan's son? That he now worked for Jacco?

Whatever Gabriel's role in Jacco's world, how or if he had conspired with his father, there was still much she did not understand about the reasons for his behavior. She did know that without him, she would not have survived those weeks of imprisonment. She would not betray him now.

"Perhaps for the same reason the Pretender has so far spared my brother Étienne, one of the king's best knights," she replied. "I don't presume to know the inner workings of the minds of violent men, Your Grace."

The queen contemplated Estelle for a moment. "Your face is bruised. Who did that to you?"

"Lord Chimi."

One of the barons scoffed. "How convenient to blame the man who has fallen into disfavor."

Queen Charlotta turned on him. "Disfavor? He betrayed Sir Hector. He's been spying on us for months, perhaps years, sharing our secrets with the Pretender. I should have known long ago what he truly is—a traitor!"

The man shrank back, averting his gaze. The queen drew in a long breath.

"Jacco promises me more jewels if I allow you to resume your duties for the court, mademoiselle. I am certain he has some hidden motive, but I need that wealth to secure men, food, ships. My council, on the other hand, wants you locked away."

Estelle's heart sank. The men likely assumed, correctly, she was now an agent of Jacco's.

The queen's gaze flicked from Estelle to her advisors, then to the guards at the door. "Because the Bastard has spies everywhere in this fortress, he will know if you're imprisoned. He has vowed to doom more of my trusted men to the same fate as Sir Hector if he hears such news. So for the moment, you will be lodged in the ladies' quarters and under close guard every time you are in my presence."

A sliver of hope radiated through Estelle's chest. Praise God and all the saints, she wouldn't be sent to the dungeons again.

Several days and nights passed with Estelle back in the chamber she had once shared with several other ladies in the queen's retinue. Now she was the only one. Whether they had escaped Cyprus altogether or gone to swear fealty to Jacco, she had no idea.

Whatever the case, she passed the time pacing the perimeter of the sparsely furnished space. There were no candles allotted to her, so once the light of day faded from the window that looked over the courtyard below, she retreated to the bed and climbed under the single woolen blanket, listening to the shifting waters. Sleep was elusive. The vial of poison pressed against her breastbone, its presence never far from her mind.

When Estelle was next escorted to the queen's chamber, she was surprised to see both monarchs seated at the table. A handful of advisors ranged around the room, talking amongst themselves.

At Estelle's appearance, the chatter ceased.

King Louis leaned back in his chair, his fleshy face breaking into a smile. "Ah! Étienne de Montavon's sister."

"Yes, my king. He's been imprisoned by the Pretender." She fell to her knees. "I beg Your Majesty for support in negotiating his release—"

One of the barons grabbed her upper arm. "Insolent girl!" he said. "It is not your place to make demands of your sovereign."

The king flapped a hand as if he were swatting a fly. "On your feet, mademoiselle."

Estelle shook off the baron. She rose, keeping her gaze on the king. All that mattered in this moment was Étienne.

"Mademoiselle, we have already attempted to negotiate your brother's release to no avail." The king shifted in his chair. "It's a damned shame. No one else in this accursed fortress holds a candle to Étienne de Montavon at the gaming table. What can we do to bring him back in one piece?"

The queen turned to her husband. "My dear, we've lost so many men already. The few remaining to us are too precious to lose in such a doomed endeavor."

"Nonsense." A petulant look returned to his face. "My father is sending more ships and more men. His latest letter said so. We can afford to spare a few. Étienne de Montavon isn't just an excellent card player. When I was ambushed at the Pass of St. Catherine, he covered for me so I could fall back. I might be dead if it weren't for him."

Estelle listened in astonishment. The idea that bumbling, ineffectual King Louis would become her brother's champion had never occurred to her.

Her thoughts darted to the vial in her bodice. The instant Étienne was released, she would throw it into the sea.

Two of the barons put their heads together, conferring in whispers. Then one spoke to the king. "Your Grace, it does not seem wise to undertake a rescue. The Pretender's palace is well fortified and heavily guarded."

King Louis glared at the man. "Your king desires to rescue his knight. It shall be done, and I will hear no more objections about the matter."

He returned his gaze to Estelle. "Soon, mademoiselle, you shall have your brother back. And I shall have a fine opponent at the gaming table once again."

The contrast between his satisfied grin and his wife's sober, hollow-eyed face was stark. To a man, the barons and other courtiers leveled hostile stares at Estelle.

It was all she could do to repress the shout of joy bubbling up in her chest.

Étienne was going to be rescued—and she would not have to become a murderess.

It was not until she had been locked in her chamber again that a terrible thought struck her.

What if the rescue failed?

# CHAPTER 51

Spring 1461
Kyrenia Fortress, Cyprus

MORE DAYS and nights passed with no word of Étienne, no word of the rescue attempt, no word of anything at all. Estelle considered herself fortunate that each evening a guard brought her a tray containing a few stale biscuits and a flagon of ale.

Her only diversion was standing at the window, observing ships entering and exiting the harbor. Estelle's spirits soared when she spotted a familiar galley gliding into the harbor one afternoon—the craft of Scottish privateer Drummond Fordun. She'd been amazed and pleased to learn during her visit to Rhodes that he had married her dear friend, the artist Anica Foscolo.

Watching his galley maneuver into the harbor, she couldn't help waving. To her surprise, one of the crew waved back. Had that been Master Fordun himself? The figure was too distant to make out. She smiled, savoring the feeling of human connection. Someone other than her captors knew she was in this chamber. The knowledge made her feel a bit less alone.

That evening, when the guard brought her tray, there was a note on it.

*The queen orders you to accompany her to Rhodes Town. You will sail at first light tomorrow.*

She sank down on the bed, the note slipping from her fingers.

Back to Rhodes Town? The news should have made her ecstatic, but instead, it gutted her. She'd returned to Kyrenia to protect her brother. So far, she'd failed miserably at the task. And now she would be forced to leave when he needed her most.

Estelle curled on her side, burying her face in her hands, and wept.

In truth, she was just a pawn in a game of cat and mouse between Queen Charlotta and Jacco. She was a woman without power, without influence.

*Why did I ever think I could make a difference in my brother's future?*

After a while, she forced herself to go back to the window, fortifying her courage with great gulps of sea air.

Twilight settled over the restless waves. The first visible stars glimmered in the north. The distant shriek of a gull drifted up from the harbor.

Slowly, a feeling of acceptance replaced the worries in her mind.

Yes, she had to leave Étienne, but what could she do for him here? She had no way to carry out her task for Jacco locked in this chamber day and night. She drew the vial from her bodice and held it in her palm.

What was in it? There were herbs, flowers, mushrooms that all contained deadly poisons. This brew could be composed of any number of them.

Estelle sighed, weighing the bottle in her hand.

She knew she would not sleep tonight.

Estelle was ready when the key turned in the lock at dawn. She followed the pair of guards out the doors into the harbor. The sun was just beginning to illuminate the highest reaches of the stone walls. Light reflected off the guards' helmets, making her eyes ache.

Passing the stables, she peered at the gloomy interior. She'd not seen Sir Hector's hound since the day she returned to the fortress.

*I pray the stable hands have kept him well.*

She'd barely had the thought when the hound padded out into the sunshine and drew up alongside her.

"Go back," she admonished him. "I'm leaving, boy."

But he kept apace with her, tongue lolling from his mouth. His brown coat stretched tightly over his jutting ribs, and his legs looked impossibly thin. He'd not last much longer here, she realized with dismay.

She spied the queen and her attendants on the deck of Master Fordun's ship and steeled herself for the journey. Now that she had been imprisoned in Kyrenia's dungeons, would several nights in a cramped galley cabin be as awful as she recalled?

*No. Nothing will be the same again.*

Climbing into the *grippo*, a rowboat that ferried passengers and cargo from the dock to vessels anchored in the harbor, she whistled softly. The hound scrambled into the craft, nuzzling her with such excitement that she nearly fell. One of the guards extended a steadying hand. It was lean and brown with long, graceful fingers.

Beautiful and familiar.

She fought back the words crowding her throat.

The helmet obscured most of Gabriel's face. Even his eyes were in shadow, lost in the depths of the eye slit.

"Careful, mademoiselle." He handed her down into the hull of the *grippo*. Before releasing her hand, he spoke again under his breath. "Your brother lives. Have faith."

She did not react, did not even look at him. There were eyes everywhere, and he was vulnerable. How Gabriel had gotten that guard's uniform, how he'd returned to Kyrenia when at least a hundred people had witnessed him in service to Jacco last week—none of those questions mattered. He lived, and so did Étienne.

A rolling swell set the *grippo* rocking and she sat down hard on the bench, the hound curled at her feet. The rowers took their positions.

A hollowness deepened in her chest with every stroke of the oars. There was so much she wanted to ask Gabriel, so much she did not understand. Would she ever get the opportunity to speak with him again?

He and the other guard strode along the dock and back to the fortress's interior doors without a backward glance.

*Please, God and all the saints, keep him safe.*

The silent prayer looped in her mind until they reached the Scotsman's galley. When she clambered aboard, Master Fordun came to greet her.

"Mademoiselle de Montavon, it's good to see you again." His eyes flicked to the hound at her side. "I see you've brought a friend."

Fearing this might be her only chance to speak with him, she responded to his welcome with a plea.

"Master Fordun, my brother Étienne is held prisoner by the Pretender in Nicosia. Please, if there's anything you can do to help free him, I beg of you—"

One of the queen's attendants stepped between her and Master Fordun. "Come along." She took Estelle's arm by the elbow. "The captain can't be bothered with your prattling."

"To the contrary." Master Fordun towered over the woman, his expression fierce. "I'm the captain of this vessel, and I give the orders here. Step aside so I may speak to the mademoiselle privately."

The woman bristled. "I'll tell the queen you said that. A queen trumps a captain."

"Not on my ship, she doesn't."

With a toss of her head, the woman stomped away.

Master Fordun bent closer to Estelle. "I'll do my best to help him, mademoiselle. You can be sure of that."

The kindness in his eyes made her want to cry.

"Are they treating you well?" he asked quietly.

"I'm a prisoner in this place," she admitted. "I have no idea why they put me on your ship. But nothing makes sense here."

"I think I know why. Your father told me before I left Rhodes harbor that the grand master wrote to the queen and asked her to bring you along."

"Truly?"

"I've never known your father to tell a falsehood." He grinned.

"Thank you." She could barely push the words past the lump in her throat.

He turned away, responding to a query by one of his crewmen.

Searching the deck for the queen and her entourage, she found them in the stern under a canopy of waxed canvas that served as a shade.

"Mademoiselle." The queen beckoned to her.

"Yes, Your Grace?"

"Why have you brought Sir Hector's hound aboard?"

"He'll soon starve in Kyrenia. My father will find him a place in the grand master's kennels. Sir Hector was your most loyal advisor, Your Grace. He would have wanted his hound to be treated with kindness."

Queen Charlotta's expression was inscrutable, her gaze on the hound. Estelle held her breath.

"I agree," the queen finally said. "Why did you seek the captain's counsel just now?"

Estelle exhaled. "Captain Fordun is a friend of my father's. My father has many friends of influence in Rhodes Town, Your Grace."

*See,* Estelle added silently, *I am not completely without power.*

Standing in the blazing sun, enduring the queen's scrutiny, her mind strayed to their weeks at St. Hilarion castle, to the friendship she'd imagined blossoming between them during those idyllic days. The queen had been lighthearted in the mountains, quick to smile, eager to study alongside Estelle. They had supped side by side, the queen showering Estelle with compliments. But now, weighed down by responsibility and disappointment and betrayal, her good spirits and kindness had vanished. And so had her trust in Estelle.

Queen Charlotta's expression grew troubled.

"Perhaps these friends will be of service to your brother, then. You will be disappointed to learn that the rescue effort for him failed." Her voice faltered. "Three of our men died; others are gravely injured. I have no idea if your brother is alive or dead, but I will pray for him and all the Savoyard prisoners under the Pretender's control." She signaled to her other ladies, turning away. "Let's go below."

Estelle bowed her head. The queen, to her credit, had not blamed her for the lives lost. But King Louis had sent those men to their deaths at Estelle's urging.

*Do I have their blood on my hands?*

She squeezed her eyes shut, pushing away the anguished thought, thankful Étienne had not perished in the rescue effort. Thankful Gabriel had risked his life to tell her so.

The crew hauled up the anchor. Trumpets blared. Oars dropped into the water in crisp precision. Estelle stayed above decks in the shelter of the covered stern, her eyes on Kyrenia fortress. The ships in the convoy passed through the sea walls one after the other, heading northwest to Rhodes. The fortress receded little by little until it grew so distant she could no longer make out the figures of men on the parapets nor the banners rippling from its highest towers.

"Thank you, Gabriel." The wind caught her whispered words and snatched them away. "Whatever happens, you'll always have my gratitude. And my love."

# CHAPTER 52

Spring 1461
Rhodes Town, Island of Rhodes

THE MORNING after they arrived at the grand master's palace in Rhodes Town, Estelle was introduced to an elderly Frenchman, a long-standing agent of the Order of St. John. From that day forward, he rarely left her side.

It did not take her long to realize he was there to ensure she conveyed a faithful version of the queen's words to the grand master. During each encounter with Lord de Milly, each meeting with an emissary of Pope Pius or the King of France, the old man sat in silence, nodding occasionally, his rheumy eyes on Estelle. He never corrected her, never held up a hand or stopped her mid-sentence. There was no need. Estelle was entirely true to the queen's utterances.

But his presence meant she never had a moment alone with the queen—and no way to deliver the contents of the glass vial unnoticed.

During a meeting with the grand master in the great reception hall one afternoon, Estelle translated the queen's plea for a supply of much-needed provisions to Kyrenia. Lord de Milly pointed out Rhodes itself was short of foodstuffs, but he agreed to her request.

Queen Charlotta leaned closer to Estelle. "Tell him about Jacco's attempts to lure recruits with the promise of high pay—using my king-dom's looted wealth to do so!"

Explaining the predicament, Estelle tried not to think about her own complicity in Jacco's scheme. But the thoughts rose up all the same.

*He recruited me, too. For a betrayal of a different kind.*

"The queen believes your own servants are now at risk, my lord," Estelle said. "If you could forbid the practice, it would help—"

She trailed off as a contingent of Savoyards who had arrived in Rhodes harbor the previous evening were admitted. While the queen made her greetings to the group, the grand master fielded questions from knights, moneylenders, lawyers, and other visitors eager for his attention.

One man, a Provencal ship captain, described some injustice done to him. His face darkened with anger as he urged the grand master to bring the matter to the full council of knights.

Lord de Milly's pet peregrine falcon, seated on its perch behind him, beat the air with her wings and screeched. After a few moments of this, the grand master looked around, bemused. His eyes fell on Estelle and he beckoned her over.

"You're a falconer's daughter—tell me, what ails my falcon? Is she hungry? She does not often fuss."

"My lord, these birds can sense our feelings." She glanced at the glowering man a few paces away. "His agitation makes her restless, I fear."

"But what of my predicament?" the man cried. "Take the bird away, if you would, my lord. I must be able to set forth the truth!"

"If you like, my lord, I can fetch a falconer to remove her to the mews," Estelle offered.

The bird quieted, cocking her head to one side as Estelle spoke.

"Speak again," the grand master said. "I think it calms her." He gave the ship captain a stern look. "Have your notary write down the predicament and your proposed solution, monsieur. Good day."

Estelle waited to speak until the ship captain retreated. "Captain Fordun said you asked the queen to bring me here. May I ask why?"

Lord de Milly tented his fingers and rested his chin on them. "When news came of conditions worsening at Kyrenia, Monsieur Pelestrine and your father asked for my assistance in bringing you back to Rhodes."

"Monsieur Pelestrine?" Estelle was taken aback. "I thought he'd returned to France."

"He did indeed, not long ago. From what I gather, he would not be alive today without your care and intervention on his behalf." Lord de Milly glanced at the falcon. "She came with you from Kyrenia this winter, and she's my favorite."

"I'm glad to hear it, my lord."

He dropped his voice. "If you return to Cyprus again, I can do nothing for you. There is no safe place for you on that island."

She flushed. "My brother is being held prisoner by the Pretender in Cyprus. Could the Order arrange a prisoner exchange so he can be freed, my lord? He's a favored knight of King Louis—"

"This is not news to me, mademoiselle," Lord de Milly broke in. "Captain Fordun and your father both have asked for my help with the matter. But the Pretender has ignored our attempts to negotiate on the knights' behalf."

Behind him, the falcon fluffed her feathers, retracted her neck into her shoulders, and fell into silence.

"She's settled again," the grand master observed. "I don't know why I should be surprised. After all, she's in your father's care. And you do have the look of him about you." A smile played around his mouth.

Estelle tried to keep her expression from crumbling. "There's something of Papa in me, that's sure. And in my brother."

"Your brother may yet find freedom again. The Pretender has been known to show great mercy and generosity at times. Take heart in that."

She bowed her head. "I will try."

The queen and the Savoyards approached. In Queen Charlotta's hand was a letter.

"Lord de Milly." The queen widened her eyes meaningfully at Estelle.

Estelle struggled to clear her mind and resume her role of interpreter.

"King Louis writes with news of Kyrenia," the queen continued. "There are abandonments almost daily amongst the ranks of soldiers and vassals. The food suppliers are disappearing. They are reduced to eating horsemeat, rats, mice. They've even eaten his pet falcons."

When Estelle translated that, she couldn't help but look at the falcon on her perch.

"My husband also sends word that Jacco plans to move several of our most valued men, knights taken captive during the battle at the Pass of St. Catherine, to Famagusta."

Estelle's voice weakened.

Queen Charlotta's gaze settled on her a moment. There was something complex and dark in her expression. Malevolence? Sorrow? It was impossible to say.

"They are to be sent to Egypt for the sultan to do with as he wishes. Our spies in Alexandria say they will likely be given to his favored courtiers as captives. There are many in the sultan's circle who still resent Christian knights for invading their city during my grandfather's reign and taking wealthy citizens as slaves. This is their retaliation."

The statement swept over Estelle like a blast of icy wind, silencing her. The elderly translator next to her cleared his throat and spoke in her place. As the grand master absorbed the news, his gaze rested on her for a moment. The sympathy in his eyes was unmistakable.

Perhaps there was still time to save her brother. Her mind jumped to the glass vial. Her hand fluttered up toward her bodice. With every scrap of willpower she possessed, she forced it down again.

*Somehow, some way, you must find an opportunity. You must strike.*

The next afternoon during their meeting with Lord de Milly, Estelle noticed something strange. It was not exceptionally hot. And yet the grand master's face was covered with a sheen of sweat.

Though he normally carried himself with grace and strength, he slumped to one side, leaning his weight against one carved arm of his high-backed oak chair. His eyes were glassy, fixed somewhere above the queen's head.

"Lord de Milly," the queen said in a gentle tone that Estelle had rarely heard since those joyous days at St. Hilarion. "Perhaps we should rest a while."

Hearing Estelle's translation, the grand master attempted to sit up straighter.

"I am quite well, Your Grace," he said a bit sheepishly. "Please continue."

But a moment later, Lord de Milly nodded off entirely. His chin lolled on his chest, his beard crushed under his jaw. Estelle trailed off mid-sentence, looking uncertainly at the queen. Lord de Milly's personal interpreter cleared his throat in obvious embarrassment.

"My lord," he said.

Silence.

The interpreter bowed to the queen. "Please retire to your chamber, Your Grace. We will resume your meeting once Lord de Milly is feeling better."

Two servants bustled forward, fussing over the grand master.

Estelle followed the queen and her attendants from the chamber.

At her doorway, Queen Charlotta paused.

"Something is gravely wrong with him," she worried aloud.

"Yes, Your Grace," Estelle agreed. "He looks terribly ill."

"The hospital is renowned for its physicians—will he be cared for there? Or does Lord de Milly have his own physicians in the palace?"

"He does, chief among them a man trained in Damascus and Egypt, known to be the best of his kind," Estelle said. "The grand master could not be in better hands."

The queen's expression relaxed. "Come into my chamber," she said. "I want you to write a reply to my husband for me in French." She dismissed the elderly translator and turned to a servant. "Send for fruit and wine. The mademoiselle and I will need sustenance this afternoon."

Estelle's jaw nearly fell open. Her opportunity was here. She stood frozen in the corridor, unable to take another step. The vial nestled against her breastbone, just above her thrashing heart.

Queen Charlotta swept into the chamber. Beyond her, on the table in the center of the room, stood a silver bowl filled with white roses. Their fragrance seeped into Estelle's lungs even from this distance. The queen reached for a rose and withdrew it from the bowl, then held it to her nose.

Turning back to Estelle, an expression of remorse unfurled on her face.

"You have proven yourself a worthy translator once again. Despite what the barons say, I've not found cause to mistrust you. I miss the companionship we once shared." She dropped the rose on the table, seeming to wrestle with her thoughts. "St. Hilarion lingers in my mind. Those memories are a happy respite from the difficulties of my days. It seems so long ago, does it not?"

Estelle slowly crossed the threshold, her heart thudding so fiercely she was sure the queen could hear it.

"Lord de Milly is my staunchest ally. Were he to die . . ." The queen's lips trembled.

"He'll need our prayers," Estelle said. "After we eat, perhaps we might go to the palace chapel and pray for him."

Queen Charlotta nodded, looking comforted. "An excellent idea."

Estelle closed the space between them.

# CHAPTER 53

Spring 1461
Rhodes Town, Island of Rhodes

FOLLOWING Queen Charlotta into the luxurious parlor with its view overlooking the sea, Estelle paused by the bowl of roses. Inhaling sharply, she filled her lungs with their sweet scent. With a quiet whoosh, she expelled the air from her body.

*Courage.*

Beyond the queen, the azure sea sparkled under the sun. Dark shapes slid across the water in the distance. Perhaps a fleet of merchant ships sailing from the Black Sea, carrying timber and furs.

*Étienne will be on the water soon, destined for Africa, if you do nothing.*

She barely heard Queen Charlotta's words from that moment on. The servants brought trays of fruits, cheeses, nuts. A pitcher of wine. They set it all out on the table and withdrew. The queen and her lady-in-waiting went into the bedchamber to remove her formal outer garments before the meal.

Estelle stood, staring at the table, the silver pitcher and matching goblets, the platters of food.

Dame Fortune had presented her with the perfect moment. All she had to do was empty the vial into the pitcher. She would feign sipping from her goblet; she would watch over the rim while the queen drank from hers.

And Étienne would be saved.

*How can I trust Jacco's promise? What other choice do I have?*

She squared her shoulders. Took a sip of air. With shaking hands, she pulled the vial from her pouch and broke its wax seal.

Crossing silently to the table, she thrust out the vial and poured.

By the time Queen Charlotta and her attendant returned, Estelle was back in her seat. The food was tasteless, though more ample and varied than any she'd had in recent memory. She waited for the queen to sip several times from her goblet.

And then, feigning a headache, she stood and excused herself.

As she turned to go, the queen gasped.

Estelle froze in place, head bowed.

"Those roses!" the queen exclaimed, pointing at the silver bowl in the center of the table. "What's happened to them?"

The lady-in-waiting made a humming noise in the back of her throat. "It must be the heat, Your Grace. I declare, they look as if someone wished them dead."

The roses had completely wilted. The petals' delicate edges were no longer creamy white; they had taken on a sickly greenish-gray tint.

"Good night, Your Grace," Estelle said to the queen over her shoulder. "Forgive me for leaving before we could go to the chapel."

"We'll do it tomorrow," the queen replied in a pleasant voice. "Providing you're well enough. Good night."

Thinking back on it now in the solitude of her own chamber, Estelle squeezed her eyes shut, hot tears sliding down her cheeks.

No blanket was required on such a warm night. She lay on the bed, staring out the window at the sky. A thousand stars glowed at her, implacable witnesses to her sorrow.

It had taken all of her resolve to break that wax seal. But when she'd made the final decision to pour, it had been easy.

Her sobs grew more violent as the memories spun through her mind. She buried her face in her folded arms, despising herself more thoroughly than she ever thought possible.

*It's Étienne's forgiveness I must ask for, not the queen's.*

For by deciding not to murder the queen, Estelle had sealed her brother's fate.

How much longer would Jacco wait for her to poison his sister? He was not a patient man by nature. He was restless, changeable, moody.

Estelle was not a murderess. She could walk the earth secure in that knowledge. But she'd had the chance to change her brother's fate —and she'd failed.

*I am nothing but a scribe and a translator, a person of no influence at all.*

Even as the words passed through her mind, she gritted her teeth and pushed them away.

*Do something,* she ordered herself fiercely. *As long as Étienne still breathes, there is a chance to save him.*

At dawn, she slipped from her chamber and made her way to the mews. When her father arrived for work, she told him what King Louis's letter had reported.

"Can you get word to Captain Fordun? Perhaps he can sail to Famagusta," she implored him. "With the help of Lord de Milly's agents, they can find Étienne and the others before the ships leave for Alexandria."

"Drummond Fordun has sailed away from Rhodes harbor, bound for Crete."

Estelle's resolve crumbled at her father's words. Tears welled in her eyes, and she made no effort to fight them off. Papa swept her into his arms.

"There's little else we can do for Étienne but pray," he said. "I wish it weren't so. I haven't told your mother anything of this. I can't bear to."

She had not told him of Jacco's most terrible threat—that he would behead Étienne if she failed to poison the queen. The words would destroy him.

Instead, she tightened her arms around her father. "Don't lose hope," she managed to push out. "We can be hopeful—must be hopeful—until we have a reason not to be."

Papa smoothed away a lock of hair that had worked its way loose from her headwrap, tucking it under the linen again.

"If only there were someone of influence we knew in Cyprus," he said.

"There is," she replied, "but he'll be of no help to us."

"Who?"

"Nicolau Baldaia. He's one of Jacco's agents. He travels the island with his men, looting and destroying, murdering Queen Charlotta's supporters."

Her father stared at her incredulously. "How do you know this?"

"I saw him. I was one of the lucky ones—he stole what was in my possession, but he did not harm me."

"Did he know who you were?"

She nodded. "I reminded him. Sometimes when I open my mouth in difficult moments, foolish words tumble out."

Papa drew in a quick breath, then let it out slowly. "How did you escape him?"

"The falconer who worked under Michel Pelestrine, Gabriel, came to my aid. With his help, Baldaia let me go."

"Did the falconer wield his sword?"

She shook her head. "He spoke with the Catalan, and whatever he said sent Baldaia on his way again."

"That seems unlikely."

"I agree." Estelle hesitated, unwilling to share all she knew about Gabriel's relationship to Nicolau Baldaia. "I did not understand it at the time, but now I believe I do. Gabriel works for Jacco, just as the Catalan does. He may have been in his service all along."

Her father was silent, his eyes never leaving hers. "Gabriel," he repeated softly after a moment. "You care for him."

It was a statement, not a question.

She looked back at him unblinking. "I do."

"Michel told me before he left for France that Gabriel was his only trusted friend in Cyprus."

"He's my only friend there, too," Estelle admitted. "Or he was. I'm not sure if I trust him, but he did more to help Michel—and me—than any other soul I met there. We'd both be dead without him."

"Perhaps he's got no choice but to work for Jacco now. Perhaps he was forced into it, like so many are."

"It's the only explanation that makes sense—except for one thing. Gabriel doesn't let anyone force him to do anything."

"The Pretender is a man of great power," Papa pointed out.

"That may be, but Gabriel could slip away from any man if he wants to. It's one of his gifts."

"If that's true, then he chooses to work for Jacco," her father said soberly. "And he's not who you thought he was."

# CHAPTER 54

Summer 1461
Famagusta, Cyprus

GABRIEL ROCKED BACK on his heels, surveying the equipment. Polished jesses, leashes, and hoods sat in neat piles on the table before him. Sweat rolled down his spine. What he wouldn't give for a splash in the sea, a cooling dip to wash off the sweat and dust of summer.

*"Geraki!"* a voice called. "The king wants a word with you."

He stood with reluctance and forced himself to turn. "Right away."

With a heavy tread, he headed to Jacco's study. A pair of guards accompanied him inside.

The Pretender stood over a table strewn with a map of Famagusta and various markers delineating weak points in the city walls. "Ah, the falconer appears. Or should I call you shadow? For how you slip between worlds undetected is a mystery I'll never solve."

Gabriel had managed to travel back and forth between Nicosia and Kyrenia for months, delivering elaborately concocted "spy reports" to Jacco on a regular basis. Nothing he reported to Jacco was particularly

illuminating. Mainly a running list of the ever-growing group of Charlotta's supporters who had abandoned her for Jacco or fled Cyprus
altogether out of sheer self-preservation. And he'd provided descriptions of the precarious conditions within the fortress. Even the king
was reduced to eating rats, he told Jacco. This elicited a kind of glee
Gabriel had previously only witnessed in small children.

"The time has come for you to accompany the Savoyards to
Alexandria. Your father has sent a vessel to Famagusta harbor. You'll
bring the knights aboard his galley and see them off on the voyage."
Jacco slid a jeweled dagger from a sheath at his waist and stabbed it
through Famagusta's city walls on the map before him. "I'd hoped our
siege of Famagusta would be finished by now, but we've had some
unfortunate delays. I'm sending some of my Sicilian cutthroats along
with you, for safety's sake."

"But the city is still controlled by the Genoese, my king," Gabriel
pointed out.

"You'll have to use your own wits to get your party inside the walls,"
Jacco said airily. "I've had a devil of a time gaining entry myself. Oh,
and I'd advise you to be discreet. My supporters are not particularly
welcome in Famagusta just now."

Gabriel lost track of the lies he told on the journey.

Rolling along the dusty road from Nicosia to Famagusta, he stayed
close to the mule cart while Jacco's Sicilian guards fanned out on their
horses, framing the contraption like a noose ready to tighten at the
first sign of trouble. Étienne had been the most difficult to deceive,
and Gabriel was sure the man didn't believe the nonsense spewing
from his mouth anyway. But the point was to keep the Savoyard men
calm and quiet until they were safely ensconced in his father's Famagusta home.

At that point, his plan would diverge from the order he'd been
given by Jacco. Instead of escorting the Savoyards aboard his father's
galley, he would spirit them away. Just how remained a mystery. They
might have to steal a *grippo* and glide by cover of night along the coast

to Kyrenia. The chances of that plan succeeding were slim at best. But he had no better idea. Not yet, anyway.

He knocked on the wooden wall of the cart. "I spy the city walls," he shouted. "Safe lodging and a meal await you."

He hoped this was true. He had plenty of coin, but the situation in Famagusta was reported to be so dire as a result of Jacco's siege that he doubted they'd find much, if anything, to eat. Many homes in the city had been abandoned, then looted by desperate souls in search of sustenance and valuables. His father's house could be one such dwelling, for all Gabriel knew.

"Looking forward to it," Étienne responded. "We're in your debt, falconer."

"Thank God," came another muffled response. "I'm famished."

Gabriel rolled his eyes. Savoyard knights did not know the meaning of the word *famished*. They missed one meal and thought they were dying. Gabriel was the son of a slave. He knew hunger, had been seized by its razor-sharp claws too many times to count. Mamá may have been Father's favorite, but she'd been under the thumb of his wife. A woman who despised her. A woman whose death he'd wished for every day of his life once he was old enough to understand the way things worked in his world.

He had even entertained the idea of killing her himself.

The city walls loomed before them. Great chunks of stone were missing from the towering ramparts that Jacco's troops had bombarded with cannon shot. The ground was littered with shards of rock, ruined wagons, abandoned pikes, and broken arrows. He tilted his head back again, sweeping his gaze to the parapets. A splintered ladder rested haphazardly against the wall, one of its rungs swinging in the breeze.

He'd heard the reason Jacco's men had failed to breach the walls was due to the diminutive size of their ladders. He saw now this was true. They weren't quite high enough to allow a man to reach the parapets. Jacco might fancy himself a superior king to Louis of Savoy, but military tactics were clearly not his strong suit.

Gabriel signaled to the Sicilians. He'd made them swear not to speak Italian in view of any Genoese at the city gates. It was common knowledge that Jacco employed Sicilians for most of his dirty work. The Genoese would imprison them in the blink of an eye, or worse, string them up, if they made their origins known. If questioned, they were to speak Catalan.

City guards stood four abreast at the gate, swords drawn. Overhead, several more aimed crossbows at their group. They all wore the distinctive red leather chest plates and white tunics of Genoa. Gabriel thanked God for his mother as he greeted them in Italian flavored with the accent of their home city. She had made time each evening to teach him languages he might need to survive his future. Thinking of her wisdom now, his eyes stung with tears.

He repeated the lie he'd told Étienne and the others yesterday when they'd left Nicosia, showing the captain a letter from the Knights Hospitaller complete with a signature he'd forged himself. Their group was headed to Rhodes, he said, sent by the Order of St. John as part of a prisoner exchange. Gabriel had chosen this tactic because the Genoese were long-time allies of the knights—the Order was the only powerful force left in Cyprus not considered an enemy of Genoa.

"How will you get to Rhodes?" the captain of the guards demanded. "There are few vessels in the harbor, for no sane captain has dared to approach our port since the Pretender launched his latest attack."

Gabriel had not been expecting this.

"A Catalan merchant galley awaits us." He injected his voice with as much confidence as he could muster. "Underwritten by a Genoese insurer." He summoned a name from memory, a Genoese associate of his father's who was one of Famagusta's aldermen.

The captain frowned, studying Gabriel through a narrow slit in his helmet. "The tolls are high these days. Not many can afford to pay."

Gabriel pulled out a purse. "The knights are generous. And there's more where this comes from. They're eager to see the matter through, and they're grateful for the sympathy of their Genoese brethren."

He tossed the purse to the captain, who weighed it in his palm, cocking his head as the rattle of coins rang out.

"*Bene.*" His men relaxed their stance, and the gates rumbled open. "I hope you've brought your own provisions," he added as the wagon rattled past. "There's nothing to eat save rats and pigeons in this accursed place."

A muffled groan of indignation rose up from within the mule cart. "God's teeth," one of the Savoyards shouted in French. "That had better be a lie."

Gabriel glanced at the captain, wondering if their easy entry had been too good to be true, if the fellow was about to let out a roar of indignation. But he had already turned his back on them. If he'd understood the man's words, he made no indication of it.

When they were settled in his father's home, the stark reality of the situation slammed into him. He had many mouths to feed and nothing to give them. But the first order of business was to head to the harbor and see what awaited them there.

Étienne and the other Savoyards retired to the upstairs bedchamber, eager for a rest. Leaving the Sicilians in charge, Gabriel slipped out, moving quickly through the streets he knew so well.

The city was filthy. Many of the fine homes he remembered from his youth were shuttered. Some doors had been hacked open, their yawning doorways revealing damaged walls, mounds of refuse and human waste. He tied a kerchief over his mouth and nose, repulsed by the stench, and thanked all the saints his father's home was unscathed.

When he reached the harbor, he saw a handful of vessels anchored there, but none with the distinctive red banners of his father's galleys. The docks were sparsely populated with merchants and traders, and a few sailors trundled goods from the docks to warehouses. A ship glided in from the sea, trailed by a second galley.

He crossed his arms over his chest, studying the approaching vessels. Apparently, word had got out that Jacco's latest siege had failed. The harbor was slowly filling up again. His father's galley would likely be here soon, ready to carry the Savoyards away to Alexandria.

Turning down the docks toward the seawalls that extended out from the harbor into the water, he cocked his ears toward every snippet of conversation that drifted by. Genoese, mostly. Some Arabic.

Then the distinctive sound of Catalan. He slowed his pace, melted into the shadow of a warehouse.

"Señor Baldaia's orders were to wait for the king's agent," a man said. "We can't sail until we have the cargo as promised."

"How much longer can we wait? There's nothing to eat in this city. The crew grows restless—and hungry. I don't want a mutiny on my hands. Already I've seen small acts of rebellion aboard. This morning, I awoke to discover the banners had gone missing from the masts."

These men were crew members of his father's galley, Gabriel realized with a jolt of worry. The vessel *was* out there. Just missing its banners.

He froze, his mind racing. Perhaps if he and the Savoyards simply failed to appear, the captain would sail away despite his father's orders. The fear of a mutiny had forced many a captain into such a decision. Yes, that was it. He'd stall. He'd tell the Sicilians they would have to wait for his father's galley to arrive. Make up some story . . .

From behind him, another voice spoke up in Catalan. "Captain!" the man called. "We've arrived with the cargo as promised."

Gabriel turned to see two of the Sicilians emerge from the shadows, their eyes boring into him. He cursed himself. They'd likely followed him the whole way.

*You have no choice. Stay a step ahead of them, man.*

He moved into the light and approached the Catalans with a smile. "Greetings, Captain. I'm Señor Baldaia's son Gabriel. At your service."

# CHAPTER 55

Summer 1461
Famagusta, Cyprus

ALL GABRIEL COULD SCAVENGE for their supper was a ceramic canister of barley and a cask of wine forgotten in a dusty corner of the cellars. For a moment, he'd entertained the idea of trapping a few of the rats scuttling in the dark down there, then decided against it. Rats were for starving men. The Savoyards were merely hungry. There was a difference between the two.

The Sicilians seemed as worried about losing sight of him as they were about their captives. He, too, was a captive, he realized now. Jacco had likely told the men he would try to bolt—or free the Savoyards before they could board the galley.

Which was true.

He could not find a moment alone with Étienne, had no way to discuss an escape attempt. And in truth, what were his options? The four Savoyard knights had no weapons. He had a sword and two daggers, but they faced eight Sicilian guards armed to the teeth, ready to slit their throats at the first sign of rebellion.

The night passed with excruciating slowness. His eyes did not close once. He was consumed by ideas, strategies, plans, all of which grew more fantastical and convoluted as the night wore on.

By dawn, he was pacing the courtyard as the men readied themselves to leave. His eyes burned. His jaw ached from clenching his teeth. And he had no plan whatsoever. For now, he was resigned to accompany the galley to Alexandria. Perhaps once he arrived there, he could contrive some method of escape.

Even as he had the idea he dismissed it. Though his mother had been born and raised in Alexandria, he knew no one in the city. He likely had relatives walking its streets at this very moment, but he would not even recognize them if he passed them in the marketplace, nor did he know their names.

His mother's Egyptian name was a mystery to him. The Greek name she'd gone by in Cyprus, Alethea, meant *truth*. An apt name, a fitting name, one he'd always loved. But she'd been born someone else entirely. A free girl, the daughter of a prosperous merchant. For the first ten years of her life, she'd known no worries.

And then a raid by Christian knights had changed everything.

"Falconer!" One of the Sicilians loomed before him. "Why do you tarry? The sun is nearly up. We're to report to the harbor at sunrise. Let's go."

Shaking the cobwebs from his brain, Gabriel reflexively patted the hilt of his sword and felt for the daggers strapped to his belt. He turned to the Savoyards, whose hands were bound in front of them.

"We're off to the harbor," he said. "It's a short walk." Holding Étienne's gaze, he added, "Careful. The streets are full of refuse. You'll have to watch your step, or you might fall."

Étienne nodded. "Noted."

The group passed through the courtyard doors and Gabriel locked it securely behind them. The Sicilians tightly flanked the Savoyards as they picked their way along the narrow streets. A tense silence descended.

Gabriel stationed himself at Étienne's left side, a few steps ahead of him. When they came to a bend in the lane where the remnants of a burned donkey cart lay atop a pile of rotted vegetables, the rattle of an approaching wagon echoed ahead of them.

"Make way!" Gabriel shouted.

The driver urged his mule onward, the wagon rolling closer. The men moved toward the wall to let it ease by. Stepping around the pile of refuse and burned wood, Étienne stumbled and fell, letting out a grunt of pain.

Gabriel bent to help him stand. The mule cart was passing them now, barely an arm's length away. Quickly, Gabriel slipped one of the sheaths off his belt and stuffed it into Étienne's boot. It was his small dagger, the blade within it not much longer than the length of his hand, but it was better than nothing.

Étienne brushed him off brusquely, standing. "Devil take this city—now I'm coated in muck."

"Move along!" One of the Sicilians prodded Gabriel in the back with a fist.

Gabriel repressed the urge to whirl and strike him. "As you wish," he said mildly.

It was a trick he'd learned over the years. When his father's wife bullied and harassed his mother, he'd fought an all-consuming desire to pummel her with his fists, learning to maintain a neutral expression, to be outwardly calm.

Even if, inside, he was boiling with rage.

The process of boarding the galley was an orderly one. Gabriel's heart sank when the Savoyards were led below decks to a locked cabin where his father's crew normally stored valuable items such as silks and cloth of gold. His dismay grew when he heard the low growl of a familiar voice.

"True to your word, just as I'd hoped." His father approached him with outstretched arms and he allowed himself to be embraced. "Finally, we're on the same side. As I always knew we would be."

Gabriel gathered his composure. "Once I saw what Louis of Savoy was made of, I realized the error of my ways."

His father let out a shout of laughter. "Well said." He clapped Gabriel on the shoulder. "Let's go to the stern deck and take some sea air. It's stifling down here."

They moved past the rowers on their benches, past sailors loading weapons into wooden boxes near the steps leading above decks. Back outside, Gabriel saw a second vessel following them. He examined the bow deck of his father's galley, his gaze running over the swivel gun and the crossbows mounted on the gunwales. The second galley was similarly armed.

When they were a short distance from shore, the wind picked up. He half listened to the crew shouting orders, watched sailors swarm over the decks unfurling the sails, heard the scrape of oars being pulled inside below.

*I can't face Estelle again if I don't do everything in my power to free Étienne.*

"Look there." His father pointed into the distance. "Two ships approaching from the north."

They were three-masted galleys like this one, Gabriel saw, their banners fluttering in the wind, their sails straining at the riggings.

When the galleys closed some distance between them, his heart began to thud faster. The lead vessel looked familiar. He'd seen those purple-and-green banners somewhere before. But where?

Then it struck him. This was Scotsman Drummond Fordun's galley.

Nervous energy swept up his spine at the realization.

*Thank you, Santa Maria.* Had he screamed the words aloud or merely thought them?

A mad plan took shape in his mind. He would fire cannon shot in the Scotsman's direction, not to deliberately harm the vessel, but to incite a skirmish. If he could get the man's crew to board his father's galley, they could help him free the Savoyards. Of course, that would require explaining the situation with a sword at his throat, not the best of times to convey important information.

*My father will recognize those banners in the next instant.*

"They could be pirates," he said quickly. "I'll prepare the swivel gun as a precaution."

His father nodded.

Gabriel headed for the bow deck and began readying the gun to fire, keeping one eye on the vessels. They were close enough now he could see figures standing on deck. The tallest among them would be the Scotsman, he knew.

"They're Hospitaller ships," his father bellowed. "Enemy craft. Prepare for battle."

"The gun's ready!" Gabriel primed the weapon's preloaded breech chamber. "On your command."

Lighting the linstock's match with the oil lamp that hung on the mast, he blocked the view of the weapon from the gunner, who had just emerged from below.

"What are you doing?" the man spluttered, trying to muscle past Gabriel.

In desperation, Gabriel turned and pushed the gunner with all his might, sending him tumbling to the deck.

"My father ordered me to man the gun," he snarled in his most commanding voice. "Stand down."

The Scotsman's ship was still out of range, or so Gabriel hoped. Praying he would not do any real damage to the vessel, he fired. The boom resonated across the water, the splash of the cannon shot sending foam high into the air. It sparkled against the azure sky, some of the spray reaching Captain Fordun's craft.

A roar went up from the Scotsman's crew. The ship began to turn in the water, figures racing over the deck to ready their own weapons.

"What have you done?" the gunner demanded, staggering to his feet. He rushed Gabriel, aiming a blow at his head.

As they grappled on the edge of the deck, the report of a cannon rang out, rolling across the water like a clap of thunder.

A colossal splash sent up a wave over the deck, soaking Gabriel and the gunner. Several other crew members rushed to the bow, readying the crossbows, while the ship's timbers creaked from the savage turning of the wheel by the ship's navigator.

In the melee, Gabriel made an impulsive decision. It would likely cost him his life, he knew.

But he did it anyway.

Springing to the gunwale, he tensed his muscles.

"Gabriel!" his father roared from the stern.

Ignoring him, Gabriel sucked in a deep breath and dove into the water. As his body knifed beneath the waves, he swam with all his might toward the Scotsman's galley.

# CHAPTER 56

Summer 1461
Mediterranean Sea, Cyprus

ANOTHER TREMENDOUS SPLASH sounded in the water somewhere to his left. Gabriel ignored it, his lungs burning with effort, his open eyes stinging from the salt water. He put every last bit of strength into swimming to the galley's port side, out of the line of fire.

A sailor caught sight of him as he burst gasping for air from the waves. "Captain!" the man shouted, pointing.

One of the crossbowmen trained his weapon on Gabriel.

"I'm a friend to the knights!" Gabriel's words were garbled by his ragged breath. "A friend to Captain Fordun!"

The Scotsman's figure appeared. He leaned over the gunwale, studying Gabriel with suspicion. "I've seen you before."

"I'm a falconer to Queen Charlotta. We met in Famagusta years ago. I'm a friend of Michel Pelestrine. And Estelle de Montavon." Gabriel could barely get the words out through gasping breaths. He choked on seawater and began to cough.

Captain Drummond turned to a crewman and gave an order. A moment later, a rope ladder was tossed overboard. Gabriel lunged for it and managed to haul himself up over the gunwale.

He collapsed on the deck, chest heaving. There was no use wasting time on long explanations. He sought the Scotsman's gaze.

"Étienne de Montavon and other Savoyard knights are locked in the aft cargo cabin of the main galley. They're being taken to Alexandria as captives for the sultan. Will you help me free them?"

"Their crossbows are in range, Captain!" someone bellowed.

"Damn those devils." The Scotsman extended a hand to Gabriel. "We're boarding those vessels, you can be sure. Whether we get the captives out alive is a question for Santa Maria."

"Thank you, Captain." Gabriel struggled to his feet.

Captain Fordun looked him over. "Have you caught your breath? Ready to fight?"

"I was trained by the knights at Kolossi. I've got two blades on me, and I'm—"

"Enough said." Captain Fordun signaled to several heavily armed crewmen. "On my orders. Ropes and hooks out. Weapons ready. Gunner, crossbowmen, cover us!"

"Ay, Captain," a chorus of voices rang out.

Seabirds shrieked overhead, circling the masts.

*Steady,* Gabriel told himself. *Clear your head.*

With dread in his heart and seawater churning in his gut, he followed Captain Fordun across the deck.

The crossbowmen and gunners launched cannon shot and iron-tipped arrows at the Catalan vessels. The crewmen tossed their ropes over the galleys' gunwales, embedding the sharp hooks into the wood. When they drew within jumping distance, Gabriel leapt aboard his father's ship, agile as a cat. Captain Fordun's men followed.

Once aboard, he faced sailors he had seen on this galley moments ago, rowers with calloused palms who were trained to fight. He sidestepped a man toppling over, a dagger jutting from his belly, and delivered a sword thrust to a crossbowman who was fumbling for an arrow.

"Below decks," he panted to Captain Fordun over his shoulder. "This is our chance!"

With a pair of swordsmen at their backs, they hacked their way down the steps into the dim hold. The rowers' benches were empty now, the oar slits revealing glimpses of the rich blue sea. Behind the door of the cargo cabin, the shouts of men rang out. A powerful thud shuddered the timbers around them. Then another. The door buckled once, twice.

In the next instant, the captives achieved their aim. The door burst open, split down the center plank.

The Savoyards tumbled out in a sprawling tangle of arms and legs. Étienne was the first to his feet. The dagger glinted in one outstretched arm, and his eyes were wild.

"Stand back, pigs!" he growled. Then his expression shifted. He glanced from Gabriel to Captain Fordun, brow furrowed in confusion. "You're no Catalan."

"Thank all the saints," the Scotsman said in perfect French. "Let's be off before we lose any more men."

One of his crewmen rummaged in a wooden box by the steps. Pulling out two short swords and a wickedly curving dagger, he handed the weapons to the Savoyards. Captain Fordun slipped a short sword from his belt and offered it to Étienne.

But the heavy thump of boots descending into the hold made them hesitate. At least half a dozen voices filled the air, shouting in Catalan. Gabriel's muscles tensed at the sound of his father's deep voice.

*We're trapped.*

"Rush them!" the Scotsman roared.

Everyone barreled forward, weapons brandished. The fight began in earnest. Gabriel stayed close to the Savoyards, his sense of responsibility for their survival overtaking his own self-preservation. They were excellent fighters, he soon saw with relief, capable of defending themselves. More and more Catalans streamed down the steps, pursued by members of the Scotsman's own crew.

Screams of pain and bellows of rage pounded in Gabriel's ears. The mingled aromas of blood and sweat filled the air. He fought doggedly, fending off the sword thrusts of his father's first officer.

"Traitor!" The man targeted Gabriel's shoulder with a savage thrust of his blade. "You filthy bastard. You miserable son of a—"

Gabriel feinted and drove his sword into the man's thigh, inciting a scream of pain.

The officer sank to the floor with a deep groan, hobbled, and Gabriel whirled in search of the Savoyards. To his horror, his father had Étienne in his grasp, a dagger to his throat.

"No!" Gabriel lunged desperately toward them.

*Estelle.*

Her name throbbed in his brain as he struggled forward.

"Don't kill him, Father!" The words exploded from Gabriel's throat, hurtling through the brawl.

"You betrayed me, Gabriel." His father's roar felt like a palpable blow.

Then the Scotsman leaped out from the shadows and plunged a sword into his father's back. The dagger clattered to the floor. Étienne made a desperate leap away, raising his own sword as he whirled on his assailant.

"No!" Gabriel grasped Étienne's sword arm. "I want the last strike."

Étienne backed away with a curt nod.

Gabriel knelt. His father's eyes were closed, his chest rising and falling in quick, shallow breaths. Blood oozed from his wound, pooling on the wooden floor. The chaos around him forgotten, Gabriel cradled his father's head on his lap.

Why, after a lifetime of fearing and hating this man, did he feel sorrow at this moment? A fierce sense of regret gripped his chest. He slumped over his father in a protective huddle, overwhelmed by grief. It rushed through his veins like a tidal wave, crushing him.

His father's eyelids fluttered open. "When the king told me you'd joined us, I felt more joy that day than I have in years." His voice was gravelly and weak, his eyes glazed with pain. "I wrote to your brothers in Barcelona, told them you'd voyage there to join them after this accursed war ends. I planned to formally recognize you as a Baldaia." He struggled for air, an ominous gurgling in his lungs. "But now I see you've never been loyal to me, despite our blood bond."

Tears slid down Gabriel's cheeks. He bowed his head. "Forgive me," he whispered. "But there are enough Baldaia men in the world. I'm proud of the name Mamá gave me. I would not be the man I am today without it, and I don't need another."

When he looked in his father's eyes again, they were blank and dull, empty of life.

The thing he had wished for countless times had happened.

Nicolau Baldaia was dead.

So why did he feel as if a savage hole had been torn in his heart?

# CHAPTER 57

Summer 1461
Rhodes Town, Island of Rhodes

THE TOLLING of the palace chapel's bells woke Estelle just past dawn. Queen Charlotta had been spending more and more time there, kneeling in prayer, appealing to God and all the saints to let Lord de Milly live. Estelle had come to know the pattern of the pealing bells each hour and during the call to prayer. And this pattern was different —an insistent, repetitive clanging that went on and on without cease.

She sat up, listening. The shutters were flung wide, as they had been every night since the roses died. When they were shut, her heart writhed like an eel in a basket and the walls closed in around her; it was all she could do to keep from screaming.

Estelle went to the window. A three-masted ship approached Rhodes Town from the east, followed by two smaller single-masted vessels, their sails stowed and lashed for the approach into the harbor. Their oars dipped and flashed in the morning sun. They looked like a child's toys from this distance, and she smiled to think of her younger siblings exulting in such lavish playthings.

Another set of church bells pealed somewhere far below her. A moment later, more chimes rang out. Soon bells clanged all over the city.

Estelle backed away from the window. She had heard such a phenomenon here before. Five years ago, the day a plague slithered into Rhodes Town, every church bell in the city had tolled an alarm. Could it be happening again?

She was fumbling into her clothes when a crier called up from the palace courtyard.

"The grand master is dead! Lord de Milly is dead!"

Estelle's knees buckled, and she sank down on the bed. Shock roiled through her. Yet no tears came. After all the weeping she'd done these past few months, she was curiously detached from her feelings, as if her well of emotions had run dry.

A single thought repeated in her mind: *God protect us all.*

The inhabitants and servants of the palace filed out the gates to St. John's Church, just steps from the grand master's residence, to pay their respects to their dead leader. The church was filled to capacity with knights and agents of the Order. Citizens gathered outside its doors, weeping and praying. Estelle threaded her way through the crowd, searching for her parents.

*"Ma chérie!"* Maman clutched Estelle by the arms, examining her with a worried expression. Then her brow smoothed. She hugged Estelle to her bosom and laughed aloud. "You dazzle me."

The pride in her mother's voice made Estelle's heart glow.

"Ah, there you are!" Papa hurried toward them, arms outstretched.

"I left the little ones with Christine and hurried up here as soon as I heard the bells," Maman told him. "We'll keep the sad news from them a bit longer."

They all stood entwined while the bells of St. John's pealed and the people of Rhodes Town continued to stream up the Street of the Knights.

"What's this? A happy reunion on a sad day." Paolo Foscolo, Anica's father and Papa's dearest friend, approached. He smiled at Estelle. "Anica hopes very much to see you. How does Étienne fare in Cyprus?"

A hard knot of remorse tightened in Estelle's stomach. Papa put a steadying hand on her shoulder.

"I wish I knew," her father replied. "Truth be told, he was taken prisoner by Jacco the Pretender."

Signor Foscolo shook his head in consternation. "I'll pray for him, my friends."

The crowd swelled further. People jostled for a view of the illustrious mourners filing into the church.

"Is the queen in there?" Maman asked.

Estelle nodded. "She was a great friend of Lord de Milly. He was kind to her, very generous."

"The Catalans are poised to take power in the Order," Signor Foscolo said. "And they've resisted many of Lord de Milly's requests for aid to Queen Charlotta."

Estelle's breath quickened. How would Étienne survive if the Order stopped sending supplies, soldiers—if men like Captain Fordun ceased to make the dangerous journey to Kyrenia?

She bit her lip, trying to stop her mouth from trembling.

And what of Gabriel? She'd never stopped caring for him, despite the knowledge that he was Nicolau Baldaia's son. He was in her thoughts day and night. If she could see him once more, ask him all the questions swirling in her mind—

"Estelle!"

She snapped her head around at the sound of the familiar voice.

Disbelief flooded her veins. She swayed, but the gentle pressure of Papa's arm around her shoulders kept her upright.

Étienne walked toward her, flanked by Captain Fordun and—no, it could not be . . .

She put a hand to her mouth, stifling a cry. Gabriel walked alongside her brother, his gray eyes shining at her.

Étienne broke away from the other men and flung his arms around her. Papa and Maman encircled them, tears streaming down their cheeks.

"You've come back to us, son." Papa's voice broke. "Thank God."

"Are you hurt?" Maman asked. "Are you well?"

Estelle could not speak. She just held her brother, afraid he might vanish like a puff of smoke if she released him.

"I'm well." Étienne turned in a circle as if to demonstrate his good health. "See? No harm was done to me. I'm like a cat. Nine lives." He grinned.

"A cat with powerful friends." Captain Fordun drew abreast of them. "And a sister who has more courage than most men."

Papa tightened his hold on Estelle. "She's always had the heart of a falcon, this one."

Her gaze slipped to Gabriel. His eyes were still fixed on hers. There was a soft light in them, a tenderness she'd rarely seen.

"It was you," she said, suddenly understanding. "You brought him back to me."

"Don't be modest, Baldaia," Captain Fordun said. "Accept credit where it's due."

Papa's genial expression dimmed. "Baldaia?" He studied Gabriel with a sober expression. "Any relation to Nicolau Baldaia?"

"Yes," Gabriel admitted. "I'm his son. But I don't share his name, Captain Fordun."

The Scot dipped his head. "My mistake."

Estelle slipped free from her father's grasp and went to Gabriel's side. Taking his hand, she turned to face the rest of the group.

"Gabriel has saved my life more than once. You have him to thank for both Étienne's good health and mine. Please trust me. There's a story behind this that explains everything—" she broke off and glanced sideways at Gabriel, hoping he would jump in. But he remained silent, a muscle working in his jaw.

"Clearly a good story, too." Captain Fordun's mouth quirked in a grin.

"I spoke out of turn," Estelle added when it became clear Gabriel would not break his silence. "We're mourning Lord de Milly today. The story can wait."

Gabriel's gaze was fixed on her father. "I'll be more than pleased to explain everything to you when the time is right, Monsieur de Montavon."

Papa's expression was hard for a moment longer. "I have just one question about Nicolau Baldaia," he said to Gabriel. "Does he still walk this earth?"

"No. My father is dead."

Papa said nothing, but the relief Estelle felt at Gabriel's words was reflected in his eyes.

"It's clear I owe you my gratitude, young man." Papa glanced at their linked hands. "And I suspect we won't be strangers to one another much longer."

Gabriel smiled, tightening his grip on Estelle's hand. The last vestiges of remorse, doubt, and worry haunting her thoughts vanished. She turned to him, drinking in the joy etched on his face.

In that moment, the world and all of its sorrows fell away.

# CHAPTER 58

Summer 1461
Rhodes Town, Island of Rhodes

ESTELLE ACCOMPANIED Queen Charlotta and her retinue from the reception hall through the torchlit corridors. The new grand master, a Catalan, had kept their meeting brief and formal. Unlike Lord de Milly, he seemed immune to the impassioned pleas of the queen. He'd shifted often in his seat, his eyes roaming restlessly over the crowd, and called the meeting to an end far sooner than Estelle had anticipated.

"How many times did he say the Order cannot provide more aid to the Kingdom of Cyprus?" Queen Charlotta glanced at Estelle sidelong. "Two or three?"

"Three times, Your Grace."

"Cannot or will not?" The queen sighed. "Lord de Milly was our staunchest ally. Without him, we've no champion in this place." She slowed her pace as they neared her chambers. "Can my only recourse be to return to Kyrenia and die with my king? I'll never swear fealty to my bastard brother, even if all my subjects fall under his command."

"You've kept fighting all this time, Your Grace." Estelle tried to keep her voice low and reassuring. "You do have other allies. What of them? The pope? The King of France? Your father-in-law in Savoy?"

"My letters make little impact, I'm afraid."

"Perhaps you could visit them yourself, then," Estelle suggested. "First Rome, then Savoy."

"It would force them to listen, if nothing else. I've thought on it often, but the idea is daunting. I believe it's the only way forward, though." She gave Estelle a searching look. "You must join me. Your Italian is quite good, and once in Savoy you'll be my trusted interpreter. And this way you can still act as my scribe. Your hand is always steady. As are you." She reached out and twined her fingers around Estelle's. "You've never failed me, never betrayed me, despite what the barons whispered in my ears all these years, despite my bastard brother's lies. At the time, I felt I had no choice but to send you to the dungeons, but I shall always regret the decision. Your loyalty is beyond question."

Estelle stared at their linked hands, her heart pumping faster.

The queen's voice took on a new resolve. "Your brother must accompany us as well. He's a fine knight. And brave. He'll be our guide to Savoy. Yes, with the two of you in my party, I'll have fewer worries about whom to trust."

Estelle opened her mouth and closed it again, searching in vain for the right words.

"You've not been compensated adequately for your devotion to the kingdom." Queen Charlotta leaned in. "I've supporters in Rome who will accommodate my party in fine style. You won't want for anything. You'll be paid in gold, I assure you."

Estelle had already spoken to Papa about returning to France with her family. Lord de Milly had bequeathed a sum of Rhodian florins to Papa in his will; it was more than enough to pay off their debts. The Count of Chambonac, his former employer, had offered lands and a title as recompense when he sent Papa to Rhodes all those years ago. In a month's time, Papa would return to France a viscount, and one day, with God's grace, the title would be Étienne's.

But until then, her brother would want to make his own way in the world. He would want to accompany the queen, she was sure. He'd be right to do it, too. Only a fool would return to Kyrenia.

"Your Grace," Estelle began. "It is a generous invitation, and I'm grateful. But I must think on it. My family's fortunes have improved, and they expect me to return to France with them."

The queen studied her intently. "Do you truly wish to be stuck in the countryside of Auvergne, with only cows and horses for companions? Here is another point of consideration for you. Marriage. You'll meet many wealthy men in search of wives on these travels. I will make it my business to find an appropriate attachment for you, a man who meets with your approval and can elevate your station in life. It will be a blessing for your family."

The lure of adventure, of visiting Rome and Savoy in the company of a queen, tugged at Estelle's imagination. But as for the promise of a husband, there was only one man she could imagine in her marriage bed.

And she would not find him in Rome.

# CHAPTER 59

Summer 1461
Rhodes Town, Island of Rhodes

THE MOON ROSE SLOWLY over the sea, turning the sky to silver. Estelle
let out a long sigh of admiration.

"The sky in Rhodes has a kind of beauty I never knew in France,"
she confessed to Gabriel. "There's a power to it that casts a spell
upon me."

"I'm spellbound, too." Gabriel drew her closer to him and kissed
her temple, her cheek, the line of her jaw. She leaned into him, languid
with desire.

They were seated on a stone bench under a fig tree in a garden just
outside the city walls, a piece of property gifted to Drummond Fordun
by the grand master in his will. Captain Fordun had made a point of
offering it as a quiet refuge for Gabriel and Estelle before their paths
diverged once again.

The summer air was redolent of roses and jasmine. In the glow of the moon, Estelle picked out the distant shape of a bird winging across the sky. Was it a falcon? A crow? Watching the bird's silent arc overhead, she was reminded of the many times she'd longed to fly away from Cyprus.

"That's freedom we'll never experience." Gabriel tilted his head back. "I wished for wings as a child. I wished I could give a pair to my mother, too."

"There's so much about you I still don't know," Estelle said quietly.

"Ask me anything, my love."

"How long were you working for Jacco, truly?"

"He asked many times. I only agreed after you were imprisoned. I saw no other way to get enough coin to keep bribing the guards. I knew Jacco would pay me well. On that count at least, he's reliable."

She took both his hands in hers. "You seemed certain we'd be attacked on the road between Kyrenia and Bellapais Abbey. I've often wondered if you knew your father was coming."

Gabriel shook his head. "I was as surprised to see him as you."

"What did you say to each other when you let him take the crown?" Her curiosity had never been sated on this question. Even though she knew the answer did not matter anymore.

"He promised not to harm you. His price was the crown." Gabriel's voice was flat now, his gaze fixed somewhere over her head.

"You change when you speak of him. The light in your eyes dims."

"He saw to my education, saw that I got work with the knights. I have him to thank for that." Gabriel's voice grew bitter. "But my mother—what he did to her was unforgivable. I can't think of him without remembering."

"What did he do?" Estelle whispered.

His eyes met hers. The pain she saw in them was awful.

"No, don't tell me what he did. Tell me about your mother. Please."

Gabriel nodded. "Each night, her voice was soft in my ear when she settled me in bed after the sun went down. I would lie in the crook of her arm and she would teach me languages: Arabic, the ancient Coptic language of her Christian ancestors, the French her own mother taught her. Her father had been a wealthy merchant in Alexandria who spoke many languages himself. But she had a special gift, a way of picking up new words and phrases with ease, for after coming to Cyprus she also spoke Greek, the Cypriot dialect, Italian, and Catalan."

He fell silent a moment, his skin glowing like polished silver in the moonlight. "In truth, Estelle, I can't tell you her story without telling his. If it weren't for my father, I would not be skilled with a blade. I'd lose my seat on a horse; I'd be able to do no more than scratch an X for my name. I would know nothing of ships, crossbows, or swivel guns. My mother was educated, too, but what slave has time to read or the means to possess books, paper, quills?"

Gabriel raised one of her hands to his lips, then settled it on his chest, over his heart.

"Mamá influenced my father in the right directions for my sake. She encouraged him to educate me as he did my half-siblings, the Latin-born boys whose mother was his legal wife. He was an intelligent man. He knew Cyprus was poised on a knife's edge. The Mamluks, the Ottoman Turks, the Genoese, and Venetians circled the island like sharks in their galleys, tearing bites from the Lusignan kingdom. Meanwhile my mother suffered, and I watched. When he came to her bed, I knew she would face a beating the next day from his wife. I got between them many times, but not enough."

"Your scars . . ." Estelle could barely breathe, remembering the raised, pale ridges on his skin.

"That snake picked up a pan of hot oil one night and flung it at my mother. I managed to intercept most of it."

Estelle's eyes pricked with tears.

"Finally, when his wife died, my father did something unexpected: he freed my mother and bought her a small house in Famagusta. Not long after that, Mamá got word that her own mother still lived and was in Alexandria with a cousin's family. I'd been working aboard my father's vessel since leaving service for the knights, and between voyages I'd stay with her in Famagusta. Seeing how joyous she was at the news, I arranged for her to sail to Alexandria on a Genoese merchant's vessel with me as her companion. The day we were to leave, my father sent guards to lock her in the house. As for me, they forced me onto one of his galleys. I sailed the seas for the next year, trapped on his ship. I nearly went mad with fury in the first weeks."

He studied the moon for a moment in silence. Then he spoke again, very softly.

"My mother's spirit suffered after that. She endured him, his bouts of violence, his episodes of generosity and kindness that always soured. She lived for me, for my visits to her, but longed for her people, got lost in her memories of Alexandria. A sweating sickness came to Famagusta a few years later, and she was too weak to fight it off. The Coptic monks cared for her in her last days, then buried her."

Estelle could think of no words of comfort that could possibly provide solace, so she threw her arms around his neck and burrowed against his shoulder.

"If I could have gotten her to Alexandria—how happy she would have been." His voice grew shaky. "I failed at the one thing I could have given her. After all she gave me."

"Your father took that journey from her, not you," Estelle protested. "You had no control over that. It's not your fault."

He shrugged. "I left Famagusta after she died because it pained me to be in her house; it still smelled of the lily water she bathed in. I joined a group of knights traveling to Nicosia, lost myself in drink and gambling, and the one thing I had left of her—the house—slipped through my fingers at the gaming table."

Estelle wept, overcome with sympathy for the grieving young man he'd been, alone in the world, full of sorrow and rage.

He drew in a long breath. "And that's when I met Michel Pelestrine."

"The saints were watching over you that night." She blinked back her tears, thinking of the Frenchman's kind smile and steady gaze. "He saved your life. And then you returned the favor."

His expression grew mystified. "Me? It was you who got him back to Rhodes."

"You nursed him back to health first."

"Fair enough." He leaned in to kiss her.

She returned the kiss with enthusiasm, sliding both her hands inside his shirt and running them over his chest, reveling in the flicker of taut muscles under her touch. Tenderly, she caressed the scars that spanned his flesh like a spiderweb.

"I love you," she whispered. "I want you in my bed."

He found the pulse point on her throat, his breath fanning her skin. "Likewise."

Longing seized her, a thirst crying out to be quenched.

"Every night, not just once." She climbed atop him, straddling him. "I want to share a bed with you till the end of our days."

Gabriel loosened her cotton under-blouse, studying the swell of her breasts with an appreciative grin. "Is this a proposal of marriage?"

She smiled. "Perhaps it is."

"I'd like nothing more." His voice was pitched very low. There was a throb of heat in it that made her pulse surge. "You've occupied my thoughts since the day we met."

Estelle leaned back, one eyebrow raised. "You didn't like me that day. It was obvious."

"No," he admitted. "You were infuriating at first."

"Infuriating? That's a strong word."

Even as she said it, she recalled thinking the same thing about him.

He chuckled. "It's the truth. But it wasn't enough to stop you haunting my dreams, interfering with my work."

"When did you know you loved me?"

His face grew serious. "When you arranged for Michel to leave Kyrenia. I saw the kindness in you—and the steel. I hoped there was a place for me in your heart, too."

"For a time, I was afraid to admit I loved you because I wasn't certain I could trust you," Estelle confessed. "But when you came to me in the dungeons, I knew my heart belonged to you—no matter the consequences."

He kissed her. "How will we chart a course together? You're still in service to the queen. I'm bound to go to Barcelona."

"What takes you there?"

"My father's will is to be read there. My half-brothers will get his wealth, as they're his legal sons. He told me he planned to bequeath me his name, but it's too late for that now. I still feel compelled to go, though part of me wonders if there's some trick he held back. Some way to punish me for betraying him in the end."

"Even he wouldn't be so cruel!"

"You'd be surprised." Gabriel gave her a troubled look. "What did he do to your family? You still haven't explained."

"I once told you someone tried to steal me away and sell me across the sea. Your father was behind the plan. But thanks to Papa, his scheme was thwarted."

She shuddered, thinking back on it, then shook off the memories. Lingering on thoughts of the past was useless. The future was what mattered now.

"I don't know if I'll stay in service to the queen," she confessed. "I'm in her favor again, but for how long? I'd be better off returning to France with my family." She tried to imagine a way forward. "You can meet me in Auvergne after you leave Barcelona."

He was quiet a moment. "I'll do everything I can to make that happen," he finally said. "And when I meet you in France, I'll ask your father for your hand in marriage."

Happiness rippled through Estelle as he spoke.

The moon slid higher in the sky. A breeze whispered over them, carrying traces of the sea.

Gabriel removed her headwrap with gentle hands. He unlaced her bodice slowly. The longing that gripped her every time she was in his presence rose up unbridled as his hands slipped between fabric and flesh.

"You touch me as if you know my body well." Her voice was rough, shaky with desire.

"I've mapped it in my mind more times than I should admit." His soft lips warmed hers with a long kiss, then traced a dizzying path downward from the hollow at the base of her throat.

The air must have cooled around them as the moments slipped by, the sky must have darkened, but Estelle knew nothing save the exquisite pleasure of Gabriel's touch. Her sighs of pleasure intertwined with the throaty calls of a pair of doves in an orange tree nearby. It was later, much later, when they reluctantly disentangled themselves and adjusted their clothing. Gabriel helped Estelle secure her headwrap and lace up her bodice. Her lips were swollen from kissing.

"I wish we could stay here all night." She pressed her body to his, unwilling to break the spell of their moonlit sanctuary.

"One day, we'll share a home and a bed. All I want is a life with you at my side." His words swept over her like a gently breaking wave, exhilarating and full of promise.

She smiled into the dark. "That day can't come soon enough."

# CHAPTER 60

Summer 1461
Rhodes Town, Island of Rhodes

ESTELLE AND GABRIEL walked down the Street of the Knights from the grand master's palace, careful to keep a respectable distance between them. In the days since Lord de Milly's death, Estelle had been surprised by the queen's willingness to grant her a measure of independence. But Gabriel had not.

"She wants something from you," he said now, glancing back over his shoulder at the palace gates. "I wouldn't be surprised if she gave you a sack of coin to grease the wheels of her plan. She'll find a way to bend you to her will with kindness. It's worked for her before."

Estelle pressed a hand to her breastbone, feeling the hard outline of a jewel under her high-necked blouse. Sometimes she could swear Gabriel was a mind reader. The queen had gifted her a necklace this morning. It was strung with a single large opal set in gold, and on the back was an inscription: *For the queen's scribe, with gratitude.*

As they ambled through the knights' quarter toward her parents' home, citizens trudged past them laden with baskets. Market day was coming to a close. Merchants led heavily burdened donkeys through the streets, weariness from the day's activities evident in their eyes.

Estelle caught sight of a familiar face, a Syrian spice trader whose market stall was always impeccably clean and smelled of anise and cinnamon. Her mother had favored the man, charmed him with her dimpled smile, and he'd been a reliable source of dragon's blood for Papa. Catching his eye as they passed, Estelle nodded at him. He grinned, returning the nod.

"Friend of yours?" Gabriel asked.

"An honest and generous spice trader," she replied. "He would not have sold you the dragon's blood he'd first promised me."

Gabriel laughed. "Will I ever hear the end of that?"

"At the time, I hoped never to see you again. I'm glad I didn't get my wish."

They cut through an overgrown garden bursting with oleander shrubs and jasmine. The arched form of a half-ruined structure at the garden's far end beckoned to her. Curling strands of jasmine hung down from the stone, forming a screen of sorts.

They slipped behind the fragrant vines. Estelle held up a hand, palm facing out, and Gabriel fitted his own against it.

"I don't want this moment to end," she whispered. "Let it be the first of many just like this."

Gabriel did not smile. Something in his serious gaze unsettled her.

"Under the moon last night, when we spoke of our dreams, a shared future felt possible to me, Estelle. But the truth is I've nothing to offer you. No wealth, no title. And until I sort out my father's will, I'll live by my sword with no place to call home." His expression hardened. "You deserve better than that. The best thing for you would be to go back to France with your family and marry a man who can give you a comfortable life."

The joy that had buoyed her since he appeared in Rhodes Town vanished at his words. She leaned against him, pressing her ear to his chest. The steady thrum of his heartbeat should have comforted her, but instead it filled her with an almost unbearable longing.

"I'll wait for you, my love. No matter how long it takes."

"Will your father agree to that?" He swiped at a tear on her cheek. "I won't make you—or him—a promise I cannot keep."

She had no answer. They walked the rest of the way to her family's home in silence. Estelle fought tears with every step, feeling hollowed out inside. Each time their sleeves touched, her heart leaped.

"Jean-Philippe! Those honey tarts are for later!"

Maman's voice floated over the wall of the back garden.

"Let's say nothing of this to my family." Estelle turned to face Gabriel. "It's an evening to celebrate, even if we feel no joy."

He nodded. The sorrow in his eyes made her tears well up all over again.

They entered the gate and went inside. The voices of her family mingled in the courtyard, raised in laughter and excitement. Gratitude surged in her like a rising tide, soothing her sadness. Her family was here, they were safe, and soon they would all sail back to France. She could ask for nothing more.

Except . . . Gabriel's measured footfalls behind her were a reminder of all she was about to lose. He was right, of course. The dreams they'd spun in the moonlight were nothing but fanciful imaginings that crumbled into dust under the harsh light of day.

The pain of that realization hurt almost more than she could bear.

Estelle whirled and flung herself against him, seeking his lips. He gathered her in his arms. She twined her fingers in his hair, melding her body to his. He trailed kisses down her neck, nuzzling the hollow between her collarbones, igniting a flare of desire that left her weak-kneed.

"I want you." She whispered the words, her eyes closed against the burn of tears. "Not some Frenchman. You, Gabriel."

She wished she could free herself from the constraints of cotton and silk, give herself to him with abandon.

"You're the love of my life." His voice was hoarse with longing. "I've always wanted you. And I always will."

He kissed her once more, reverently. Then he took her hand.

"Your family awaits." He led her to the courtyard.

The children swirled around her, eyes gleaming with excitement.

"My tiny giants!" Estelle teased. "How I've missed you."

She kissed them both, then swept Isabeau up in her arms. A dark shape behind Jean-Philippe startled her.

"Is that Sir Hector's hound?" she asked in astonishment.

The animal bounded to her side, tail wagging vigorously.

"He's *our* hound," Jean-Philippe corrected her. "His name is Bruno."

Papa approached, grinning. "I couldn't bring myself to leave him in the kennels. Besides, we've always wanted a guard dog." He nodded at Gabriel. "Welcome to our home. There's plenty of honey-sweetened wine on the table. And our guests promised to bring the best Cretan red on the island, along with some entertainment."

"Guests?" Estelle put her squirming sister down.

"I didn't want to mention it in case they weren't able to come, but Captain Fordun and his wife will be joining us."

At his words, there was a commotion in the entry hall. Estelle recognized the Scotsman's booming laugh.

When her old friend Anica appeared in the doorway, Estelle gasped. Anica had become a willowy, elegant woman in the years since they'd last met. Her face was a perfect blend of her Greek mother and her Venetian father. The impact of her brilliant smile rippled around the courtyard, silencing the group.

"Anica!" Estelle embraced her friend, laughing and crying all at once. When they separated, she spied a small girl clinging to Captain Fordun's hand, toddling unsteadily forward.

She looked from the girl to Anica. "Is this . . . ?"

Anica nodded. "Our daughter."

"Refuses to be carried. It's slow going these days." Captain Fordun exchanged a glance with his wife, a wry smile on his face.

Musicians plucked out folk tunes on their lutes in a corner as the wine flowed and the celebration began in earnest. When Étienne appeared wearing the colors of Savoy, a cry of welcome went up. Papa handed him a cup of wine and toasted his good health.

Maman pressed a handkerchief to her eyes. "All our children in one place! This is a sight I feared I'd never see again. Do you realize it's been four years since Estelle sailed off to Cyprus?" She turned to

Gabriel. "Perhaps today we might hear how you managed to keep both our daughter and son safe in that nest of vipers."

"It's true. We owe you our thanks for our son's life," Papa said soberly. A hush fell over the group. "And for our daughter's." He raised his cup. "We're in your debt."

Gabriel inclined his head as everyone drank in his honor.

"What will you do next?" Captain Fordun asked him. "So much change is in the air now that Lord de Milly has passed on."

"I have some family affairs to tend to in Barcelona," Gabriel said. "After that, I'm not sure."

Captain Fordun's gaze turned to Étienne. "What about you?" he asked. "For God's sake, please don't tell me you're returning to Kyrenia. I can't stomach another rescue attempt."

Étienne shook his head. "The queen has asked me to accompany her to Rome and Savoy. It's a challenge I'm glad to accept." He looked at Gabriel. "Queen Charlotta wants to bring falcons for the pope. We'll need a falconer to keep them alive on the journey. What say you? Accompany us to Rome. It's on the way to Barcelona. You can continue your journey from there. Your family's affairs will surely keep a while longer."

Estelle's hopes soared with his words. She held her breath, anticipating Gabriel's response, willing him to accept.

"That's a tempting proposition," he said after a long moment. "I'll think on it."

"What of you, my dear friend?" Anica asked Estelle. "Will you return to France with your family?"

"Of course she will," Maman put in. "She belongs in France, just as we do."

"I will return to France one day, but not just yet." Estelle squared her shoulders and swallowed hard. "The queen has asked me to accompany her to Rome and Savoy as well. Since Étienne will be in her retinue, I see no reason not to go."

"No reason?" Maman spluttered. "You have every reason. You barely survived the Cypriot court. Why on earth would you stay in Queen Charlotta's retinue?"

"Because I wish to make my own way in the world."

Papa regarded Estelle quietly, a slow smile spreading over his face.

Captain Fordun threw back his head and laughed. "Something tells me the queen's search for a falconer is over."

Gabriel's eyes were bright. "You're a very observant man, Captain."

Étienne clapped Gabriel on the shoulder. "A wise decision, my friend." He slung an arm around Estelle, and the three of them faced the rest of the group.

"Any messages for the pope?" Étienne asked, breaking the silence to much laughter.

The musicians struck up a familiar, beloved tune. Maman and Papa joined hands, swaying in time to the music. One by one, the others followed. The afternoon sun slanted into the courtyard, anointing the circle of dancers with gold.

Estelle took her place next to Gabriel. The joy in his expression made her spirits soar.

This was not the end for them. It was a new beginning. They would find their way in the world, side by side.

"A shared future is within our sights after all, my love." She twined her fingers around his, her heart swelling with happiness.

His voice was low and tender in her ear, his breath warm against her cheek. "And it begins now."

Thank you for reading *The Queen's Scribe*. Curious to learn more about Estelle and her world? Continue reading for a preview of *Island of Gold*.

# HISTORICAL NOTES

In 2020, I began researching medieval Rhodes for the *Sea and Stone Chronicles*, a new collection of novels that I imagined would be set entirely in Rhodes. But as I delved into books and articles about the Knights Hospitaller of the Order of St. John, headquartered in Rhodes at that time, I learned they had a long history in Cyprus, too. In fact, one of the historical figures I planned to write about, Grand Master Jacques de Milly, had spent part of his career there. Curious, I dug deeper.

I was astonished to learn a teenaged, widowed queen had ruled Cyprus for a moment in time during the exact era of my research. In 1458, fifteen-year-old Queen Charlotta took the throne alone, held off her power-hungry half-brother's massive siege and—when her second husband Louis of Savoy proved a weak leader—sailed around the Mediterranean entreating allies to help save her crown. Furthermore, she was in Rhodes visiting Jacques de Milly when he died in the summer of 1461.

When I unearthed the fact that, several years later, Queen Charlotta had her infant son interred in Jacques de Milly's tomb, I became even more intrigued. Though the histories don't reveal much about either of these leaders' personal lives, this detail sprang out at me. Whatever their relationship had been like, she chose to bury her only child alongside him. I imagine her husband, King Louis, had no say in the matter. He was not in Rhodes at the time.

Well, I was done for. I had to write about this woman and her world.

It was a different challenge than any of my previous books because there was so much history to pack in. So many mysterious deaths, outright murders, betrayals, alliances, seafaring intrigue, and a civil war between two half-siblings.

I've done my best to adhere to the major events as the chroniclers of the time recorded them, starting with Prince João's death in 1457 and ending with Jacques de Milly's death in 1461. It would have been easier for me to compress or conflate some of these dates and events to fit my storytelling purposes, but I didn't feel comfortable with that. I hope you've enjoyed this wild ride through a strange chapter in history alongside an unsung woman leader.

Also, before I get deep into the details about what is fact and what is fiction, please note that I go in-depth about Queen Charlotta and the Cypriot court, medieval seafaring, falconry, and more on my blog at www.amymaroney.com.

### The story behind *The Queen's Scribe*

Why did I choose a fictional heroine, Estelle, for the novel? Simple. Because I love seeing history through the eyes of fictional people living alongside historical figures. I can unleash my imagination and create worlds that way. It's how the magic happens for me.

Also, Estelle has inhabited my heart since I first wrote a story starring her in an anthology a few years ago. She's a minor character in *Island of Gold* (her parents take center stage), but she quietly waited her turn for a moment in the spotlight. I'm lucky she stuck around.

Back to Queen Charlotta. She was christened 'Charlotte' but raised in her Greek mother's apartments and knew very little French. She relied on interpreters and scribes for the rest of her life. A surviving letter she wrote in French in 1464 is described by historian George Hill as "extremely confused and ungrammatical."

As with all Lusignan monarchs, Queen Charlotta's true title was 'Queen of Cyprus, Armenia, and Jerusalem.' The latter two designations were titular only, and I choose not to identify Charlotta with that long-winded moniker in the book to keep things simpler.

Dorothy Dunnett, in her excellent novel *Race of Scorpions*, refers to Charlotte as 'Carlotta,' and the queen may have spelled her name that way. I chose to use 'Charlotta' because it felt less confusing to have a character first known as 'Charlotte' in my novel become 'Charlotta.'

I called Charlotta's mother 'Eleni' Palaiologina, using the Greek spelling of her name. She is usually called 'Helena' by Western European historians. Queen Eleni suffered from an unidentified illness in young adulthood that robbed her of the ability to walk. She vehemently opposed Charlotta's marriage to Louis of Savoy because Greek Orthodox custom decreed that people who married their first cousins would go to hell.

I chose to call Charlotta's first husband 'Prince João,' which is the Portuguese spelling of his name. Western historians refer to him as 'John.'

'Jacco' was used by Dorothy Dunnett as the name for King Jean's son by his Greek mistress (Marietta of Patras, referred to colloquially as 'Cropnose' because Queen Eleni was reputed to have either bitten off or cut off her nose when she discovered her in bed with her husband). Western historians refer to him as 'Jacques' or 'James.' The Greek-influenced variation of the name used by Dunnett worked well for my story, too.

Jacco was the apple of his father's eye. King Jean did bequeath him the Latin archbishopric of Nicosia, its palace, and its revenues when he was a young teen. Jacco is described by chroniclers and historians as a handsome, spoiled, charming, and easily angered man. His actions as described in the historical record show a man who was capable of great generosity and tremendous cruelty.

## More on names and people:

Signora Rosso was inspired by the long history of Venetians in Cyprus. There was a thriving Venetian merchant class in Nicosia.

Nicolau Baldaia is based on an actual Catalan pirate known to haunt Famagusta and surrounding waters during the era of my story. Piracy was a huge problem in the area during the fifteenth century. That's why merchant galleys traveled in fleets and were armed with mounted guns and crossbows.

Lord Podocataro is based on the Podocataro brothers, Cypriot nobles who displayed shifting loyalties when it came to the war between Jacco and Charlotta. Signor Derian is fictional, but notaries were important members of Cypriot society and there was a thriving Armenian community in Nicosia. Jacco did escape over the walls of the Armenian quarter at least once.

Gabriel is fictional, but his story as the son of a wealthy Latin man and a slave is imaginable because slavery was a big part of life in medieval Cyprus. Since Christian and Muslim forces were continually at war in the area, there were always captives that needed ransoming on both sides. Alexandria, a short boat ride from Cyprus, was a target of Christian raiders, and attacks such as the imagined abduction of Gabriel's mother from her wealthy neighborhood in that city did happen. I found instances of Latin men bequeathing money, homes, and goods to slave women or freeing them after years of captivity. Households included children from both legal wives and slaves.

**More on history:**

The French Lusignan kings, who took control of Cyprus and Jerusalem in the late twelfth century, had been bleeding money and power for a hundred years by the time Queen Charlotta ascended the throne in 1458. But during the dynasty's glory days in the thirteenth and fourteenth centuries, Cyprus was a magnet for travelers, especially pilgrims making the long sea voyage to Jerusalem. It was known for its luxury goods such as cloth-of-gold, silk, jewelry, and mechanical birds.

Famagusta became a wealthy port city and a haven for Christians from the Middle East and Africa (though it began a long period of decline when Genoa seized control of the city in the fourteenth century). There was a thriving community of Coptic Christians from Egypt and a Coptic monastery in the city. Famagusta and Nicosia were home to many other ethnic and religious communities, from Jewish to Armenian to Venetian to Maronite. Although Muslim and Christian forces were often at war, they also made allowances for matters of trade. Alexandria housed Western merchants of various European origins. Muslim merchants, diplomats, physicians, and other professionals worked or lived in Cyprus, too. The island was a true melting pot, and its common language reflected this.

The majority of the nobles in Cyprus throughout the Lusignan era were French. During the centuries of Lusignan rule, French was the language of high administration while Latin was used for writing trade contracts. As the years wore on, the nobility began speaking both French and Greek. The locals spoke a blend of Greek, French, Arabic, and Italian (all essential for trade). I refer to this language in the book as "the Cypriot dialect". Cypriots who claimed French roots used an oddly accented, archaic French of the middle ages. Travelers visiting the island in the fifteenth century from France could not understand them.

Hawking and hunting were extremely popular during this era in Cyprus. Visiting travelers reported the kings of Cyprus owned hundreds of falcons, hawks, and hounds. Elaborate hunting expeditions took place in the forests and mountains. In addition to donkeys, mules, and horses, the kings of Lusignan used camels to transport their supplies on such trips. They also used cheetahs (though they called them leopards at the time) to help track and kill prey. I referred to these cats as leopards in the book.

The fifteenth-century French knight Jean de Francières wrote a hunting/hawking manual that included plentiful advice from three famous falconers, two from Cyprus and one from Rhodes. I found the manual digitized online in the French National Library, and its descriptions of 'dragon's blood' as a curative for falcon ailments inspired the scene when Gabriel and Estelle meet at the Nicosia marketplace. Spices from Africa and Asia were readily available in Cyprus and much cheaper than in Western Europe.

Cyprus was historically known for its astonishing songbird populations. In addition to native birds like the blue-feathered bee-eater, Cyprus was also home to African and Asian birds brought to the island by merchants, such as parakeets and peacocks.

The Knights Hospitaller did own a sugar plantation and fortress called Kolossi in Cyprus. It was a major source of revenue for the organization and it was mostly powered by slave laborers.

**More on the Cypriot court:**

In the waning days of the Lusignan dynasty, Queen Eleni dominated her husband and filled the court with Greek supporters; she was a generous benefactor to the Greek Orthodox churches and monasteries of Cyprus. Since King Jean was a timid and ineffectual ruler, the men of the king's council countered the Greek influence by bringing Prince João to the court. He was a much more assertive man than his father-in-law and made an enemy of the queen. After Prince João's murder, the council lobbied for Louis of Savoy to replace him. The Duke of Savoy (Louis's father) insisted that his son be designated "the one true king" rather than Charlotta's king consort. After Queen Eleni died, King Jean appealed to his nobles to allow Jacco to rule after him, but the matter was not resolved by the time of the king's death. (Historians aren't certain if his end was due to natural causes or poison.)

The Cyprus Codex, a musical composition of the Lusignan court in the early 1400s, is the largest known surviving single source of medieval courtly music. It was likely created for Cyprus's first Queen Charlotte (grandmother of Queen Charlotta), an educated and cultured woman born in France.

Christine de Pizan's *The Book of Deeds of Arms and of Chivalry*, written around 1410, was a handbook on the art of war that explains the tactics, strategy, and technology of medieval warfare. In this era, European books were hand-copied by scribes, because printing presses had not yet been introduced in Europe. Charlotta's grandmother, Queen Charlotte, was one of the few women in the world who could have conceivably owned a copy of that book.

There are fragments of wall paintings that show a kneeling couple and a falcon in a chapel at Pyrga on Cyprus. Some researchers believe the chapel is part of a former royal hunting lodge and the couple are King Janus and Queen Charlotte. This is where I got the idea for the hidden treasure at Bellapais Abbey.

Bellapais Abbey was founded by the Canons Regular, who came to Cyprus soon after it was taken over by the Lusignans. In the thirteenth century it began attracting a steady stream of pilgrims, thanks to its possession of the 'Relics of the True Cross'. By the late fourteenth century, it began falling into disrepair and the monks abandoned their vows. I chose to use the archaic spelling of 'Bellapais'; however, the modern spelling is 'Bellapaix.'

St. Hilarion Castle was described in several sources as a retreat for Cyprus's royal family. The ruins of the place today only hint at its onetime magnificence, but Kyrenia fortress is still visible from its rugged mountaintop location.

Jacco did orchestrate Queen Eleni's chamberlain's death and then fled to Rhodes for several months, where he was welcomed by the knights. He was also responsible for killing the Viscount of Nicosia upon his return to Cyprus. He was credited with convincing his father to appoint Sir Hector de Chivides as the man's replacement.

Charlotta's coronation was indeed marred by her crown falling from her head as she rode away. This was widely seen as a bad omen for her reign.

Charlotta did urge her council to send diplomats to Egypt so she could build support there, but by the time they went, Jacco had already secured the Sultan's allegiance. A plague was blamed for killing several of the queen's emissaries in Alexandria.

When Louis of Savoy married Charlotta in October, 1459, it quickly became apparent he was not the leader the king's council had hoped for. According to historian George Hill, Cypriots found their new king to be 'unattractive, poor-spirited, sickly, and of cold and melancholy temper.' He did neglect to visit Pope Pius on his way to Cyprus, a critical diplomatic error.

After her husband proved a disinterested leader, Charlotta turned to Lord de Milly and her father-in-law, the Duke of Savoy, for aid. As I've already established, her French was weak. Unlike when she was a child in a Greek-dominated court, now she had to communicate with her husband and potential allies in French. The need for trusted interpreters only grew stronger as civil war loomed. While Estelle is fictitious, the royal court of Cyprus depended on skilled interpreters and scribes to carry out its diplomatic work, and there were undoubtedly people like Estelle working closely with the queen.

## More on the war between Jacco and Queen Charlotta/King Louis:

Word came in 1460 that Jacco had recruited an Egyptian army and would sail to Cyprus and attack. The court moved to Kyrenia fortress. Kyrenia was the most secure fortification on the island, with a protected harbor. Enemies of the Luisgnan kings typically faced imprisonment in its dungeons.

The Knights Hospitaller and the Duke of Savoy sent ships at various intervals to help during and after the siege of Kyrenia. At least one Savoyard ship stopped in Genoa before continuing on to Cyprus.

Charlotta did order all the monasteries and convents to turn over their wealth to her cause to finance her war with Jacco, and she did sell many of her own jewels. The journal by the first Queen Charlotte's courtier describing hidden treasure is a figment of my imagination. (It is true that the royal family and most of the kingdom's wealth were moved to Kyrenia during the Mamluk attack that resulted in King Janus's capture. The 200,000 ducat ransom payment was a financial blow from which the Lusignan dynasty never recovered.)

The siege of Kyrenia by Jacco and his army of Egyptian Mamluk soldiers took place as described.

Jacco generously rewarded turncoats and freed serfs in large numbers, turning many Cypriots to his cause. His henchmen did terrorize supporters of Queen Charlotta and confiscate their wealth. Many of Charlotta's allies were beheaded and their heads displayed on spikes in Nicosia. Jacco favored Sicilians for such work.

During the siege of Kyrenia, the biggest destructive event was a cannon attack that chroniclers said originated from a Greek church. It killed dozens of men. The siege did abruptly end when the Mamluk army returned to Egypt in anticipation of a transfer of power there.

Queen Charlotta did sail to Rhodes to seek aid from Lord de Milly. The knights did say if Louis came with her, they would not defend the throne for him. Lord de Milly helped her, and ships from Savoy did arrive during her stay in Rhodes. She had a victorious return, retaking the fortress of Paphos before sailing back to Kyrenia. The subsequent failed attempt to seize Nicosia from Jacco was the only significant military effort credited to King Louis by chroniclers.

King Louis was quoted by chroniclers as deploring the terrible conditions in Kyrenia and sending out supporters for his favorite milk-fed veal. He was an enthusiastic gamer who loved fine food and amusements.

Though many supporters of Charlotta and Louis deserted them for Jacco, a few remained loyal. According to chroniclers, Sir Hector de Chivides did meet his end by riding out in search of veal for King Louis. Jacco took credit for beheading Sir Hector and displaying his head on a spike in Nicosia. Carceran Chimi and Anthony Synglitico, members of the royal couple's inner circle, were blamed for telling Jacco when and where to find Sir Hector that day.

After Lord de Milly's death in the summer of 1461 in Rhodes, Queen Charlotta decided to seek help from Pope Pius and other potential supporters in Western Europe. She set off on her quest shortly thereafter, but eventually lost her throne to Jacco. The Lusignan dynasty ended with him.

**Key resources:**

*George Boustronios: A Narrative of the Chronicle of Cyprus*, 1456-1489. Translated from the Greek by Nicholas Coureas. SHC, Nicosia, 2005.

Dunnett, Dorothy. *Race of Scorpions*. Vintage Books, 1999.

Durrell, Lawrence. *Bitter Lemons of Cyprus*. Faber and Faber, 1957.

Hill, George. *A History of Cyprus, Volume 3: The Frankish Period, 1432-1571*. Cambridge University Press, 1948.

Shafak, Elif. *The Island of Missing Trees*. Bloomsbury Publishing, 2021.

Thubron, Colin. *Journey into Cyprus*. Penguin Random House, 1975.

Additionally, I relied on many academic papers. Several of the authors are listed on the acknowledgements page.

# ACKNOWLEDGMENTS

I am very grateful for my writing critique partners, Elizabeth St.John and Cryssa Bazos. This book was particularly challenging to complete, and their support, ideas, and insights made all the difference.

Jenny Quinlan, thank you for your excellent guidance both at the developmental and copyediting stages. Patrick Knowles, thank you for the beautiful cover. Thank you, Tracey Porter, for the lovely map. Thank you to all the members of the Coffee Pot Tweet Group for encouragement and inspiration, and to all the other authors who have supported me along the way. Jack and Sallyanne Wilson, your hunt for typos and inconsistencies was brilliant, as usual. Julie Cassin, I'm so lucky to have your eyes on my words before they go out into the world —thanks for being my first reader.

I am indebted to the academic researchers whose work is available on Academia.edu, and I've sourced critical documents through Interlibrary Loan and through communication with individuals. I am particularly grateful for the work of Nicholas Coureas, whose important research on the Cypriot court and many facets of medieval Cyprus inspired and informed my writing. Big thanks as well to David Jacoby, Benjamin Arbel, Cécile Khalifa, Philippe Trélat, and Marina Tymviou for their fascinating research about this lost world and the people who inhabited it. Thank you to all of the librarians who had a hand in getting documents to me, and who have answered my queries with patience and professionalism.

As ever, thank you to all the family members and friends who cheer me on. You lift me up when I need it most.

To Dahlia and Nora, thank you for inspiring me to write about strong women of the past.

Finally, *The Queen's Scribe*, like all my other novels, would not exist without my husband Jon's encouragement and love.

# ABOUT THE AUTHOR

Amy Maroney studied English Literature at Boston University and worked for many years as a writer and editor of nonfiction. She lives in Oregon, U.S.A., with her family. When she's not diving down research rabbit holes, she enjoys hiking, dancing, traveling, and reading. Amy is the author of *The Miramonde Series*, an award-winning trilogy about a Renaissance-era female artist and the modern-day scholar on her trail. Her new romantic suspense collection, *Sea and Stone Chronicles*, is set in 15th-century Rhodes and Cyprus.

Join Amy's community of readers and get monthly updates about her research and next books (plus great deals on historical fiction) at www.amymaroney.com.

If you enjoyed this book, please take a moment to leave a review online or spread the word to family and friends.

# ALSO BY AMY MARONEY

*Sea and Stone Chronicles*

Island of Gold

Sea of Shadows

*The Miramonde Series*

The Girl From Oto

Mira's Way

A Place in the World

Get *The Promise*, a free prequel novella to *The Miramonde Series*, when you join Amy's community of readers at www.amymaroney.com

# ISLAND OF GOLD (PREVIEW)

## PROLOGUE

Languedoc, France
1435

CÉDRIC OFFERED the falcon a strip of rabbit meat. Ignoring the tidbit, she retracted her neck low into her shoulders, plumped her feathers, and fixed him with a baleful glare.

"Still off your feed?" he asked softly. "What ails you, my girl?"

A low growl of thunder startled him. He glanced through the open door to the courtyard, where rain pummeled the cobblestones. The scent of rotting straw hung in the air. If only sunshine would break through the clouds and give the land a chance to dry out.

Then a familiar figure filled the doorway, jolting him out of his thoughts.

"Philippe," he said in surprise. "But you're early—"

"It's your father," his sword master replied, breathing hard. "He's wounded."

Cédric dropped the pouch of rabbit meat and pushed past Philippe. He broke into a run when he glimpsed a guard and a servant across the courtyard, carrying his father through the front doors of the main house.

Inside the great hall, he cleared the broad oak table near the hearth with one sweep of his arm. Pewter and crockery smashed against the tile floor. Quickly, the men settled Papa on the table and removed his leather cuirass and chain-mail shirt. A deep wound gaped at his lower abdomen, leaking blood. His moans reverberated to the rafters.

Cédric yanked an embroidered flax runner off a nearby chest. It was one of the few reminders of his mother left in the house since her death on his twelfth name-day, nearly four years ago. With trembling hands, he wrapped it around his father's waist. The mingled aromas of sweat and blood filled his nostrils.

"It was the *écorcheurs*," said the guard, removing his helmet and running a hand through his matted hair. "They surprised us on the road back from the seminary."

"They took my purse, my boots, my belt," Papa managed to croak. "The ring off my finger. And ran me through with my own sword."

"Those devils. I'll kill them!" The words exploded from Cédric's lips without warning. Philippe pressed a restraining hand on his shoulder. His heart thrummed crazily against his ribs all the same.

A servant hurried in with a jug of wine.

"Where is Yves?" Cédric demanded, tying the ends of the cloth together to bind his father's wound. The faint outlines of pink silk roses embroidered by his mother vanished under a relentless tide of scarlet blood. His eyes burned with tears at the sight.

"Your brother went to check on the mill this morning," Philippe said, accepting a cup of wine from the servant. "I've sent someone to fetch him. And the priest."

Cédric propped up his father's head and held the cup to his lips. He spluttered and coughed, then swallowed a bit of wine. A gust of wind and rain swept through the open doorway, the flames in the hearth dancing in response.

"These cursed rains," Papa muttered. "There will be no harvest this year."

Cédric stared at the fire, refusing to watch death tighten its grip on his father.

"And bandits circling like wolves." Philippe's voice was steady, but it held a trace of anger.

Papa sucked in a ragged breath. "My boy, look at me."

Cédric dragged his gaze from the hearth with reluctance.

"Yves will take my place as viscount. Stéphane is safe at seminary, his path to priesthood is secure. But you—" His father struggled for air, grimacing. "God forgive me, I've not prepared you, Cédric. You care more for falcons than swordplay. You're not ready to enter service for a *seigneur* . . ."

Philippe leaned closer. "I swear to you as a servant of the Knights Hospitaller that your son has the makings of a strong fighter. I'll be sure his training is complete before he enters any lord's household, my friend."

Papa sought Cédric's eyes again. "You can change your fate, but not if you spend your life bowing to the whims of other men, understand? One day you must make your own fortune."

The worry and pain in his expression made Cédric's heart twist.

"Vow it to me, son."

"I vow it." Cédric tried to swallow, but his throat felt dry as dust.

Papa's face relaxed. His breath grew faint, his skin pale. "You will make your own way in the world," he whispered. "But first you'll learn to live by your sword—and stay alive."

## Chapter 1

Summer, 1439
Auvergne, France

The thudding of dozens of hooves sounded on the road. Cédric put a hand in the air, motioning for silence. The men all exchanged somber glances. One of them crossed himself, then whispered to his horse in low tones. Cédric held his horse's bridle with one hand and clenched the hilt of his sword with the other. He glanced at the mule cart sitting in the shade of a hawthorn tree. It slowed their progress immeasurably.

But there was no other choice. His entire future was bound up in that cart's cargo.

The riders began to pass by, shouting amongst themselves. The creak of leather, the metallic clank of swords, the snorting of horses filled the air. Cédric tightened his grip on his sword. He thanked God the weather had been dry this past week. The road here was hard-packed and dusty. Their presence would not be easily read in muddy furrows and hoofprints.

The approaching horses slowed.

Had the bandits seen something? Heard something?

*God save us.*

Then he distinctly heard one of them shout, "To the ferry!"

The hoofbeats quickened, the group sweeping down the roadway to the north, toward the river. He had bribed the ferryman to stay quiet about their passage when they'd crossed that river at dawn, but could only hope the man would keep his promise.

"We're nearly to the commandery," he told the men after a few tense moments of silence, climbing into the saddle again. "We'll arrive tonight, God willing."

"If we aren't skinned alive first," one of his companions retorted, fear still plain on his face.

"We've made it this far," Cédric said. "All the way from Bruges. We'll get there with our skins attached, fear not. And then you'll get your portion."

"How do we know we'll be safe there?" the man challenged him. "That band of rogues may have laid siege to the place this morning."

Cédric shot him a hard look. "The knights will not be bested by a pack of bandits, of that you can be sure. No more talk. Let's move out!"

As they rode back into the sun and headed south toward the rolling hills of central Auvergne, he hoped his claim was true. The commandery, like all possessions of the Knights Hospitaller, was strongly fortified and protected by skilled soldiers. But the *écorcheurs* were trained fighters as well, many of them mercenaries who had worked for powerful lords in the past.

A crow's raucous call in the woods to his left startled him back to the journey at hand. The lump of dread in his gut hardened with each turn of the cart wheels. Neither he nor any of his companions could resist glancing over their shoulders constantly as the day progressed, and they spurred their tired mounts forward with muttered promises of grain and hay.

They arrived at the commandery before nightfall, just as he'd hoped. Their exhausted horses plodded through the great iron-studded doors into the courtyard, where torches burned at intervals along the walls. A cloaked figure approached across the cobblestones.

"Cédric?"

In the wavering light, Cédric made out the familiar face of his father's dearest friend.

"Philippe!" Somehow he found the energy to spring down from his mount and embrace the sword master.

Stablehands emerged from the shadows as the other men dismounted.

The doors clanged shut behind them. For the first time in many days, Cédric drew a deep breath.

"I can't tell you how relieved I am to be here," he said to Philippe.

"Your cargo is sound?" Philippe nodded at the cart.

The mules pulling it looked ready to collapse.

"Fortune was kind on our journey," Cédric allowed.

Philippe turned to the other men. "Go inside. There's hot stew awaiting you, and we'll have water heated for baths."

"First I must take the falcons to the mews," Cédric said, though a hot meal and a bath sounded immeasurably better. Still, what was the point of transporting the birds all that way only to lose sight of them at the last?

Philippe nodded. "I'll come with you."

The other men collected their panniers and followed a servant through the commandery's inner doors.

Slinging an arm over Philippe's shoulders, Cédric smiled a little. "Why we're not dead on the roadside is a mystery."

"A mystery?" Philippe pointed at the heavens as they walked toward the stables and mews, a stablehand leading the mule cart behind them. "God was watching over you."

Cédric cast a glance at his surroundings, taking in the stone chapel and the other buildings that faced the central courtyard. An atmosphere of hushed prosperity and organization emanated from the carefully tended property.

"The knights live well," he observed. "How do you like your lot here?"

"Square meals, hot baths, quiet evenings. It can get a bit dull, to be honest. Nothing like my years working for the knights in Rhodes. But that was a young man's game."

"Dull sounds appealing at the moment," Cédric confessed. "I've longed for a quiet night since we left Bruges."

In the mews, Cédric and Philippe unloaded the wooden traveling cages and settled them in a secure, dry corner.

"Are their eyes seeled?" Philippe asked as Cédric withdrew the canvas coverings from the cages.

Cédric nodded. The hooded gyrfalcons, secured to their perches with leather jesses, barely stirred. "It was done in Norway before we left for the open seas."

He'd helped the Norwegian do the job, carefully stitching the falcons' eyelids shut with needle and thread. The stitches wouldn't be removed until the birds reached their final destination.

"Is there an under-falconer on duty here tonight?" he asked.

Philippe nodded, pointing at the dim figure of a man at the far end of the mews, who raised his hand in greeting. "He's seasoned, knows how to tend to these creatures."

"Are my father's birds healthy?" It was far too dark in here to get a good look at them now, Cédric realized.

"Just as they should be," Philippe assured him.

"You saved us, you know. If you hadn't persuaded the Order to buy Papa's falcons—"

"I only did what an old friend does for those he loves," Philippe said gruffly.

Together they walked out of the mews.

The other men had already eaten their fill in the refectory and retreated to the bathhouse. Cédric and Philippe sat at the end of a long table illuminated by several candles and the flames of a small fire in the hearth.

Cédric guzzled his wine and fell upon his bowl of mutton-and-barley stew as if he'd not eaten in days. Philippe ate nothing, just sipped from his own cup. Finally, when Cédric put down his spoon, he felt Philippe's eyes on him and glanced up.

"You must have a hundred questions." He poured himself another cup of wine.

"Not quite that many." Philippe's grizzled face twisted in a smile. "But a few, yes. You were gone longer than I imagined. I feared the worst. It was reckless of you, making this journey." He leaned forward, his expression hardening. "An enormous gamble."

"I was ready for it. Thanks to you."

"I had nothing to do with your survival. As I already said, you have God to thank for that."

"Not true," Cédric protested. "I never would have found a place in a *seigneur*'s household after Papa died without the blade skills you taught me. Surely, you can admit that."

"Swordplay always came naturally to you, even as a boy. And you've got courage. A bit too much of it, if we're honest." Philippe chuckled.

"Courage, maybe. But not luck. I chose the wrong man to work for in the end."

Philippe shook his head. "The *seigneur* died because of his own pride. He should have stayed within the keep of his castle rather than ride out to meet the *écorcheurs*. It was a tactical mistake."

"They were burning and raiding the villages on his lands! Wouldn't you have done the same?"

The sword master regarded Cédric thoughtfully for a moment. "When you consider what you came home to, perhaps fortune wasn't so unkind after all. Your family needed you."

Cédric fell silent, reflecting on his friend's words. He had retreated to the family lands after his employer's death with only the clothes on his back, a horse, and a sword. He had discovered his brother in debt, the mill providing much of their income rendered useless because of too many years without decent harvests.

"Perhaps you're right," he admitted.

"Indeed. You got your father's falcons safely here and kept the debtors at bay." Philippe pinned him with a glare. "Why you had to go chasing dreams in the North Sea is beyond me. Though I knew you had more chance of surviving the journey than most. Your time with the *seigneur* was exactly what you needed. There's a difference between swordplay and fighting for your life."

"Let's not forget who came up with the idea of big rewards for fulfilling a rich man's wishes," Cédric pointed out. "No one forced you to tell me the Count of Chambonac desired gyrfalcons."

"Just because a nobleman says he wants rare birds doesn't mean you should travel all the way to Norway to get them," Philippe said drily.

"Fair enough." Cédric shifted his weight on the bench. "What news of the count, anyway?"

Philippe put down his cup. "He snaps up castles like a wolf seizes deer in its jaws. Another one fell to him in the spring. But he is more merciful than some noblemen. He allowed the lady of the castle to bury her husband instead of putting his head on a pike. His new residence was completed not long ago, and the gossips say it's built entirely of pink stone."

"Will he honor his bid to pay handsomely for these falcons, do you think?"

"Nobles are an unpredictable bunch," Philippe said, shrugging. "One thing is certain, though. They all covet the falcons of the north. When you call upon the Count of Chambonac, whatever the outcome, I shall be at your side."

"But you're needed here," Cédric objected. "Trust me, I've survived enough violence for several lifetimes in the past few years. No matter what I encounter on the roads of Auvergne, I can fend for myself."

Cédric studied his old sword master in the flickering candlelight. His weathered skin was scored with fine cracks and lines, but he was still a formidably strong man. And the stubborn set of his jaw was all too familiar.

"Agreed," Philippe said, meeting his gaze. "But until those gyrfalcons are handed off properly, you can count on my sword just the same."